The Hybrid STORIES

Edward Kendrick

Fireborn Publishing Copyright Statement

The Hybrid Stories

Cover Artist: Allison Cassatta

Includes:
Sui Generis
The Housemate
Editor: Jamie D. Rose

Print ISBN: 978-1-941984-80-2
First Print Publication: April 2015

This book is written in US English.

PUBLISHER

PO Box 5216
Haverhill, MA 01835

Sui GENERIS

Edward Kendrick

Blurbs

Captured and tortured, Brand becomes...unique. He escapes and with Mag's help, he sets out to exact revenge. Soon life becomes complicated when they meet others willing to help them. Will they find his captor, and if so, what then?

Captured, imprisoned and tortured, Brand becomes...unique. After escaping, he vows revenge on his captor, Fedor. With the help of his friend and housemate, Mag, the search begins. Then others who also have a vested interest in finding Fedor become involved.

These others, who call themselves Enforcers, are not run-of-the-mill by any means. Their leader, Antton, convinces Mag that Brand is more than he seems. When Fedor captures Mag to demoralize Brand to force him to come to him, Brand and the Enforcers, including Randulf, set out to rescue him.

With that mission successfully completed, Brand admits he cares for Mag as much as Mag does him--something he has been previously unwilling to reveal.

Then Brand is invited to join the Enforcers--and accepts. The Enforcers receive another assignment and Brand and Mag meet Lew, Randulf's ex-lover. There's no love lost between those two, but Mag suspects that deep down they care for each other. He vows to force them to admit it--to themselves and to each other--if they survive the coming battle.

Chapter One

Brandon 'Brand' Huxley whirled around when he heard footsteps behind him. A man stood at the top of the fire escape on the far end of the roof, silhouetted by the ambient city lights. Given that Brand was wearing tattered jeans and a well-worn, sleeveless black T-shirt, he had the feeling he knew what the man was and why he was there.

"Move it, kid. It's illegal to sleep or store personal possessions on public or private property without permission. I'd really hate to have to arrest you."

Hissing in a breath between his teeth, Brand nodded. "I know, officer. I was just enjoying the view." He pointed to the flare of a firework as it lit the night sky.

"Uh-huh. Well enjoy it somewhere else. Okay?"

The officer stood there, obviously waiting for Brand to get moving. So Brand did, hiking his battered backpack over his shoulder then walking quickly past the cop and climbing down to the alley.

"Psst."

Brand looked around, spotting a kid about fifteen, maybe sixteen, peering at him from between two dumpsters. Brand held up one finger, pointed to the cop who was on his way down the fire escape, and then touched his lips to warn the kid to be quiet.

Moments later, the officer walked by Brand, saying, "Find a shelter. It's your best bet. That or hike it out of the city."

Brand nodded, resisting the urge to tell him the shelters were always full. He was certain the officer knew that.

When the man was out of sight around the corner, the kid stepped into view. "I know a safe place," he said.

"Thanks, but so do I. I was just having a little R&R up there watching the fireworks." Brand pointed to the roof of the building.

The kid shrugged and wandered away, calling back over his shoulder. "Don't say I didn't offer."

Brand chuckled. "I won't," he muttered, while going down the alley in the opposite direction.

Five minutes later he was on another rooftop. From his vantage point, he had a clear view of the alley running off in either direction between Fourteenth and Twenty-second. A pair of bicycle cops came down it, checking darkened doorways and around dumpsters, shooing off any transients they found. That didn't sit well with Brand. Not because of why they were doing it, although he found the law repressive at best. Even the homeless had the right to find somewhere to sleep if they could, like the rooftop he was on at the moment. He pulled back as the cops got closer, not wanting to be rousted again.

When they had passed, he checked the alley one more time, cursing the cops under his breath for clearing it of its human denizens. "Go after the rats and the stray dogs," he muttered. "They're more dangerous than a street kid or a man who's lost his job and his home."

He chuckled softly. "Maybe I should get a job as a homeless advocate, handing out food and advice to those who need it. God only knows I'm out on the streets every night myself. Might as well do something useful while I'm looking for Fedor." He pondered that idea for all of a minute. *No, I need my freedom to move around when and where I have to. I'll never find him otherwise.*

Resting his hands on the low parapet at the back of the roof, he leaned over again, his gaze searching the length of the alley. The bright flash of another firework lit it up in eerie shades of green and blue. It was—as far as Brand could see—empty except for the ubiquitous mangy dog sniffing around a dumpster two blocks down.

Time to move on. Fedor's not going to come down here. Not when he'd be the only person in the alley thanks to the cops. I'd see him before he saw me. That is not his intention, I'm sure.

Slinging his backpack over his shoulders, Brand made short work of getting off the roof. From there he moved to the alley between Lawrence and Larimer. It was quickly apparent the police had been along it as well, so he kept going. Three blocks later he found an alley that had either been missed in the cops' sweep or the people who regularly used it as their 'home' had returned once the cops were well away from the area.

As he moved down the alley, looking for a likely rooftop, he heard someone call his name. Turning, he smiled slightly at the middle-aged man coming toward him. He and John had become friends of a sort when their paths had crossed at a now defunct local shelter. They'd spent a few early evenings panhandling on the Mall then bedded down at the shelter if there was room. When there wasn't, they'd find a safe place in some alley or down by the creek. John had considered himself Brand's protector, probably because he stood several inches taller than Brand's five-ten. Not that Brand needed a guardian, but he never said that to John. At that point in time, he'd been happy to have John's company.

"Hey, kid, I swear you don't look a day older than the last time I saw you," John said, giving Brand clap on the shoulder before stepping back.

"I could say the same about you," Brand retorted, eyeing him.

John snorted. "A nice lie, but I'll take it. So what you been up?"

Brand shrugged. "Not much. You?"

"Same old, same old, kid. Keeping it together best as I can since my brief stint in jail."

"I heard about that. Sorry, man."

John waved his hand in dismissal. "A bed, three squares a day… made it almost worth it. Still…" He looked up and down the alley. "Guess the cops haven't been down this one yet tonight."

"They have," a voice piped up from behind a dumpster. "Came, kicked us out, but we're back." A girl about sixteen, if that, came out to stand in front of John and Brand. "Should be safe enough now, if you're looking for a place to crash." She grinned, introducing herself as Doll. "Too few of them, too many of us. It's a losing battle for the cops once it gets dark."

"Still, be careful, Doll. They see you too many times, they're gonna stop giving warnings and jail your pretty little self," John said.

"Yeah, I know. But I'm…"

Brand had moved away as the two were talking, so he missed the last of what she was saying. He liked John, but had other things he needed to be doing and having the man hanging around with him would make it that much harder.

Scurrying farther away, Brand slipped into an unlit doorway, pulling back into the shadows. John walked by a minute later, still chatting with the girl. Brand wondered if he was even aware it was just the two of them now. *Probably not.*

Inching forward, he watched the pair turn the corner out of the alley onto Eighteenth. Then, spotting a dumpster next to a convenient fire escape, Brand leapt onto it and from there made his way to the roof of what he knew was a restaurant popular with the baseball fans. He sprawled on his stomach, looking over the edge, watching as a pair of street kids sidled in off the street. They were obviously keeping a weather-eye open for the cops or trouble from anyone who had already taken up residence for the night.

An hour passed. Things quieted down as the people who had come downtown for the Fourth of July fireworks made their way to the parking lots and from there, home. No cops visited the alley. Those stragglers looking for a place to spend the night moved on when they realized all the viable spots had been taken. One man came up to the roof, saw Brand and beat a hasty retreat when Brand scowled at him.

Best that you do. Brand smiled darkly as he continued his surveillance.

Forty minutes later he spotted his prey. A tall, blond man came into the dark alley. He was dressed in slacks, a dark blue shirt, and a battered leather jacket. *The build, the pale blond hair…* The man's head turned right and left as he surveyed the area, the streetlamp highlighting his features for a moment.

It's him.

Brand kept his gaze locked on Fedor while he reached for his backpack. When his knee came down hard on a sharp bit of debris, he hissed softly in momentary pain.

Fedor must have heard him because he looked up. His thin, aristocratic lips curved in a grisly smile as he started toward the fire escape.

Suddenly, the headlights of a police cruiser flooded the area when it pulled into the alley. For a moment Fedor froze, then, giving Brand a mocking salute, he turned, walked swiftly to the corner and vanished from sight.

Seconds later, backpack in hand, Brand was jumping from the bottom rung of the fire escape to the alley floor. Ignoring an officer's orders to stay where he was, he raced to the street but it was too late. Fedor was nowhere to be seen. Not that it surprised Brand all that much. The man was as slippery as an eel, as Brand's mother used to put it. Most predators were and Fedor was on the top of the food chain when it came to preying on the innocent and not so innocent.

With a sigh of disgust, Brand hoisted his pack over one shoulder and continued his search. It was close to dawn when he finally gave up and headed back home. *Tomorrow is another night, to paraphrase some movie line.*

* * * *

Magnus Larsson, nicknamed Mag, woke with a start when he heard the door open. He was sitting up on the sofa where he'd fallen asleep while studying much earlier in the evening. "Cutting it close, aren't you, Brand?" he asked, frowning.

"Not close enough," Brand muttered to his housemate. "I almost had him. Would have too, if I'd been more careful. Just after I spotted him I knelt on something sharp. I should have kept quiet but it hurt." He smiled ruefully.

"Did you cut yourself?" Mag, asked in concern. When Brand shook his head, Mag added tartly, "You're supposed to be better than that."

"You'd think, wouldn't you?" Brand dropped down on the sofa, running his hands through his too long, brown hair.

Mag studied him, seeing the self-disgust in his dark green eyes. "There'll be other times."

"Yeah, I know.

Mag's gaze moved down to Brand's slender but muscular torso and the sleeveless black T-shirt that covered it. He resisted, as always, the urge to lick his lips in appreciation. Not only was he so far out of Brand's league that it was ridiculous, he was also well aware that for Brand, sex was now a tool and nothing more. It hadn't been like that once, but after Fedor had gotten his hands on Brand, that had changed. Why? Mag didn't know, but it had and now Brand was searching for Fedor with a passion bordering on mania.

Brand caught Mag's look and smiled slightly. "If you need some…"

"Naw. Even if I did, I'm too damned tired and you should be too. Besides which, I have to be up and moving too soon to get to work. Time and tide wait for no one."

Brand stretched casually, casting a sideways glance at Mag. "Maybe I'll pass on school tonight."

"Nope, not happening. We made a pact. We get our diplomas and make something of our lives. Neither of us is going to end up back to the streets again."

"True. But damn it, Mag."

"Brand"—Mag leaned over to rest his hand on Brand's knee—"if you're supposed to find him, you will, one way or another. So you had a near miss tonight. Maybe it was meant to be."

"Going all fatalist on me," Brand grumbled, but he did smile at his friend. "Okay, point made. I'll get some sleep, go to class, and then I'll get back out there and keep looking." He sighed tiredly. "If nothing else, I know I was right about one thing, he's still here and still in the downtown area, if tonight was any indication."

"Just like…" Mag shook his head, snapping his book closed. "I'm going up to bed."

"You can say it. Just like when he got his hands on me."

"Yes," Mag replied softly. "You owe him for that."

"And I *will* repay him."

Chapter Two

After getting home so late and then studying before going to bed, Brand slept until five that evening. His dreams were filled with scattered but distorted visions of his time with Fedor. When he woke, he felt drained. A long, hot shower, followed by a cold one, helped to restore some of his energy.

When he got downstairs, he found Mag was home from work and had prepared supper, for which he was profoundly glad. He needed sustenance if he was going to make it through his classes. *And the rest of the night, once I figure out a way to home in on Fedor's hunting ground, so to speak.*

If last night was any indication—and he thought it might be—Fedor had shifted from the uptown area to lower downtown, farther away from the central business district. He didn't find that too much of a surprise. With the cops clearing the streets and even the alleys, of all the homeless people around the retail shops and restaurants, they would naturally migrate closer to the train tracks and the creek.

Where they go, so does Fedor.

Or at least he hoped that was the case.

"Did you study?" Mag asked, turning from the stove where he was putting the finishing touches on the chicken Marsala.

"Yep, though I almost fell asleep over the nutrition book."

Mag chuckled. "Not your strong point I know, but necessary. You should be doing this"—he tapped the skillet—"not me."

"Tomorrow night, I promise."

With a laugh, Mag replied, "Uh-huh. Which means you'll call our favorite Chinese restaurant and have them deliver."

Brand just shrugged, pouring coffee for Mag and getting one of the insulated containers that held his drinks from the fridge, before setting out plates and silverware on the small kitchen table. They ate quickly since they had to get to school, washed the dishes, and headed out.

****

Four hours later, when they were back at the house, Brand went upstairs to change clothes. He came back down dressed in a pair of old jeans and a black tank with a well-worn blue work shirt over it, his old backpack slung over his shoulder. He was surprised when, five minutes later, Mag joined him, dressed in comparable clothes, although he was wearing a T-shirt rather than a tank.

"You're not coming with me," Brand stated firmly.

"Then I'll just follow you," Mag retorted. "Now that you know where he is, more or less, having me along might give you an edge if you find him."

"You have no idea what you'd be going up against."

"Not because I haven't asked," Mag pointed out caustically. "All you've said, and it wasn't much, was that he grabs guys like us—well, like we used to be—off the street and puts them to work as part of his stable of whores."

Brand nodded. "That pretty much covers it," he agreed, adjusting his backpack so he didn't have to look at Mag. "If he got his hands on you, I don't think you'd survive."

"You did."

"I'm… stronger than you."

Mag stepped in front of him, looking up at him. "When are you going to tell me what really happened?"

"Never," Brand spat out angrily. "So drop it. I got out and that's all that matters."

"That's up for debate."

"That I managed to escape?" Brand asked, a tiny smile playing over his lips.

"No. Escaping was good, but he destroyed something in you before you did, Brand. He turned you into someone I wasn't sure I wanted to be around the first time I saw you after you came back. You're hard now and… and dangerous."

"Only when it comes to him," Brand protested.

Mag shook his head. "No. With everyone. Think about it. How many of the people you used to be friends with are still your friends? I'd be willing to bet I'm the only one. You pushed the rest away and you tried with me, but I wasn't about to let it happen."

Brand chuckled softly. "Given that we're sharing this house, and made a pact about school, I'd say that's true."

"It wouldn't be, if I'd listened to you."

"Why did you?" Brand cocked his head in question.

"Because we were friends before, and I thought… no, I *knew* you needed someone to help you stay focused on what's really important, above and beyond stopping Fedor."

"So you decided to take on that role, and have for the last two months. Although why…? He shook his head in bewilderment.

"Because I care," Mag replied softly. "Even though I barely know who you are anymore, I still care." He moved away, eyeing his friend. "I spent half a year wondering if I'd ever see you again. Got off the streets, worked two jobs to save enough money to be able to rent this place—as ratty as it is—so you'd have somewhere to come home to if you… Well, you know."

"You still *are* working one of them," Brand pointed out. He sighed then. "You're better than me. I should find a job to help out."

"You will, once you get over this obsession with finding Fedor." Mag held up one hand. "Before you get mad, I understand why but still it *is* an obsession. So, back to what started this whole conversation, I am coming with you tonight. Tomorrow is Saturday; I don't have to work."

Brand scrubbed one hand over his face. "All right," he said with a small smile. "If you insist."

"I do."

* * * *

Mag's eyes widened when Brand leapt onto the dumpster, as if it was only a couple of feet tall. When Brand knelt to give him a hand up, Mag said with a bit of awe, "You're a lot stronger than you look."

"Naw, just lots of practice," Brand replied off-handedly, as if it was nothing unusual. He grabbed the handrail of the fire escape, swung onto it, and started up, with Mag right behind him. "Stay low," he said, when they got to the rooftop, hunching down as he made his way to the corner where they'd have a view of both the alley and the street.

"Yeah I know. We don't want to be hassled by cops."

"Them or punks. But we also don't want Fedor to spot us if he's around. We'd lose the element of surprise."

Mag crept up beside him, trying not to let his fear of heights get to him as he asked, feeling foolish for not having done so before, "What does he look like?"

Brand chuckled wryly. "Yep, knowing would help. He's tall, has pale, blond hair, and an aquiline nose, sort of like Dante's."

"As if I know what Dante's nose looks like."

"Okay, good point." Brand took out his penknife and scratched a sketch of what he was talking about into a brick on the side of the roof's parapet. "Like that."

"Got it. That should make him stand out. At least somewhat. It sort of reminds me of Professor Caine, but he's short and dark-haired."

Brand thought for a moment then chuckled. "Yeah, I don't see him prowling the streets looking for victims."

Mag watched as Brand carefully leaned over to look up and down the alley. They'd chosen it because there were some people settling in for the night. From where he was kneeling, away from the edge of the roof, he could still see two boys at The End of the alley who looked to be in their late teens. They were leaning casually against the wall of one of the buildings, eyeing the male pedestrians who were walking by.

Mag asked softly, "Could they be working for Fedor?"

Brand shook his head. "Doubtful. He never let… He doesn't put anyone out on the street with someone else."

Mag wanted to ask why, but there was something in Brand's expression, a tightness that made him change his mind. *Sometime, though, I'm going to* make *him talk about it, for his own good.* He didn't know how he'd accomplish that, but he'd figure it out.

"Anything?" Mag asked when Brand sat back on his heels.

"No. But we have all night."

"We're going to spend it here?"

Brand shrugged. "It's a catch-twenty-two. If we do, he'll be somewhere else. If we move on, he'll show up here ten minutes after we're gone."

"Can I ask something?"

"Sure."

"Why don't we just stake out wherever it was he kept you?"

"Because"—Brand glanced away—"it's too dangerous."

"Now tell me the real reason," Mag said sharply.

"Okay," Brand replied with a dark look. "Because I don't know where that was."

"Hang on a second. How could you not know? I mean he sent you out to do… what those guys are doing." Mag pointed in the direction of the two teens they'd seen.

"I wish it was that easy," Brand murmured so softly Mag could barely hear him.

"Then explain it to me so I understand."

"I…" Brand stopped talking suddenly, leaning forward, his gaze locked on something below them in the alley.

Mag reluctantly inched forward, trying to see who had caught his attention. There was no one in sight as far as he could see except a raggedly dressed, white-haired homeless man who was shuffling away toward the entrance to the alley. "That's not him," he barely whispered, his lips brushing Brand's ear as he pointed to the man.

Brand sat back on his heels again, frowning. "No. Still, I was certain for a moment that he was down there."

"If so, he's either a ghost or invisible, because I didn't see anyone but that guy."

Brand's look was sour when he replied, "Trust me. Fedor's not a ghost. I guess… I suppose I thought I saw him because I want to so badly."

Mag smiled, giving him a fast hug. "Imagination plays tricks on us all at times. But unless he's an expert at disguises, that man wasn't him."

"I know that," Brand replied testily. "Maybe it's time to find another alley and try again."

Chuckling, Mag replied, "Catch-twenty-two, but maybe."

* * * *

They spent the rest of the night moving from alley to alley with no luck. If Fedor was out there, he didn't appear where they were.

Brand began to wonder if it *had* been his imagination when he though he saw Fedor. *Or, perhaps, he was there and saw I wasn't alone. Not that that would have fazed him in the least under normal circumstances. Still…* He smiled wryly. *These aren't normal circumstances. Not in the grand scheme of things.*

Saturday night they tried again, with no success, leaving Brand tense and jumpy. After getting some sleep, again filled with dreams bordering on nightmares, he appeared downstairs mid-afternoon to find the ground floor empty. He knew, because he'd checked, that Mag was up and moving.

"So where the hell are you?" he growled. Taking one of his drinks from the fridge, he tossed it back and washed out the container to be used again. Then he opened the back door, wondering if Mag was out in the small yard for some reason.

He was, and he didn't seem happy when he whirled around to look at Brand. "If I get my hands on whoever did this," he said, pointing to his tiny but productive garden.

Brand could see why he was upset. Someone had torn up every vegetable. Not the way a dog would, by digging them out, but they were literally torn out and scattered around the area.

"Well that sucks. If they wanted something to eat, why didn't they take it with them?"

"They didn't even try eating. It's vandalism, pure and simple," Mag replied in exasperation, picking up a carrot, waving it in front of Brand's face. "See?"

Brand grabbed his wrist, trying not to laugh, even though it wasn't a laughing matter. "I see. The question is who would do such a thing. We barely know our neighbors, and we don't play loud music when they're trying to sleep, so I'd say they're out."

"Anyone dumpster-diving would have taken the veggies with them." Mag smiled tightly. "The way we did a time or three."

"True." Brand paced to the fence, checking the lock. Not that it really would have kept anyone out. The fence was only a deterrent to dogs prowling the alley, low enough to climb over unless one was small kid. He suspected even a determined five-year-old could get over it—or through the gate.

As he turned back to look at Mag, he saw a frown, followed a panicked expression, cross his face.

"You don't suppose…" Mag said hesitantly.

Brand knew what he was asking and shook his head. "Why would Fedor do something so infantile?"

"To let you know that he knows where you're living?"

"I suppose that's a possibility, but it's hardly a terrifying way to go about it. Blood poured on the porch or a dead animal dropped in front of the door, would have sent a stronger message."

"He's toying with you. Maybe tomorrow it *will* be the animal."

"And maybe it's just vandalism, pure and simple, by punks with nothing better to do with their time."

"No." Mag pointed to the neighbor's yard where there was a much bigger, and untouched, garden. "If that were the case, they'd have done the same thing there, don't you think?"

Brand had to agree. "Probably."

Sighing, Mag started to pick up the vegetables that were salvageable. "Now what do we do?"

"You go to work tomorrow and we both go to school, as if nothing was wrong. Then I keep on hunting for him. Sooner or later, our paths will cross again, his and mine. Only this time I'm going to be much more careful."

"Meaning what?" Mag asked, as he started toward the house with an armload of vegetables.

"Meaning I'll do everything possible to stay off his radar so I can follow him without his knowing. As you pointed out a couple of nights ago, staking out his—his lair and catching him alone when he least expects it, would probably be a better option than trying to attack him in an alley with other people around."

"Would he be alone there?" Mag suddenly grumbled 'damn' under his breath when he couldn't get the back door open because his hands were too full.

Brand hurried over to help him and when they were inside, Mag dumped the vegetables into the sink, turning on the water to rinse off the dirt.

"I presume there are other people there," Brand said in reply to Mag's question of a moment ago. "I never saw them, though, other than… than the men…" He closed his eyes, taking a deep breath. "If he has cohorts, they paid no attention to me. He was the only one who did. He and…"

"You don't have to talk about it right now," Mag said quietly.

Brand managed to smile a bit. "But later on?"

"Sometime, Brand, you *have* to. You've been carrying around what happened to you deep inside. If you don't let it out…"

"Yes, Nurse Larsson," Brand said acerbically. "I think you're taking your studies too much to heart. I'm fine. I'm dealing. As soon as I catch him, it'll be over and I can move on." He knew he was overreacting and whirled around, striding out of the kitchen before he said something he shouldn't, or worse yet, took his anger out on Mag.

It's not his fault. He had nothing to do with it. And now, maybe, he's drawn Fedor's attention because I let him come with me the last two nights. So what do I do now? He grimaced, throwing himself down on the sofa. *If I knew the answer to that, this would be over.*

Seconds later, Mag was standing in front of him. "Talk."

"About what? How damned pissed I am that he seems to be eluding me? That's a given, I think. It's been two months. I should have found him by now. I almost did, last week, but I blew it. And why isn't he coming after me? That's what I can't figure out. He wants me back. He has to. I'm dangerous to him. If he did that…" Brand pointed to the sink full of vegetables. "*If* he did, then he knows where to find me for sure. I should leave before he comes after you as a way to… to punish me for running."

"Fuck no!" Mag said adamantly. "First off, where would you go? Secondly, even if you did disappear, that doesn't mean he wouldn't do something to me and then somehow let you know that he had. He kills me or… whatever, and it'll end up on the five o'clock news. You know he'd be sure that it did, just to get the message out to you that no one you know is safe."

"That still doesn't explain why he hasn't tried to catch me yet."

"Games, Brand. Games. Despite the fact you've been very close-mouthed about what happened, I get the feeling he might be the kind of man who would get a great deal of pleasure in tormenting you with 'what ifs' until you're wrapped tight as a spring. He lets you think you got away scot free and then does something like tear up the garden. Then he pounces. He allows you come after him, guns blazing, so to speak, and he swats you down like a lion would a baby gazelle. Once he has you, he puts you back in the fold but with no hope of ever escaping again, making his triumph over you even sweeter."

Despite Mag's rather picturesque descriptions, Brand had the feeling he'd hit the nail on the head. Fedor loved bloodshed and torture, both physical and mental. He lived to impose his will on others in the worst ways possible. It was why he'd chosen Brand in the first place. *Well, one of the reasons. I need to go on the offensive, more than I have. If I can. If… it's not all gone now.*

Brand shivered.

"What?" Mag asked, sitting beside him but not too close.

"Just… thinking. Wondering if getting to him is even possible."

"It is if you give him a real reason to come after *you*. He may want you back, and he may like the games, but he needs to be drawn out so you can repay him for what he did to you."

"Don't you think I've been doing that *already*? I'm out on the streets every night, damn it. I can't believe the only time our paths crossed was on the Fourth. He has to know I'm somewhere, looking for him."

Mag nodded slowly. "Perhaps it's a catch-twenty-two for him as well. He stays in one place and waits, so do you. You move, so does he in opposite directions."

Brand would have liked to believe that was the case, but he knew better. Not that he'd tell Mag. So he just nodded. "Perhaps."

It is *a game for him. The only question is, is he afraid I'll find him before he decides he's terrorized me enough that I'll be weak from fear when he finally tries to grab me? When does he think I'll reach that point? How will he know? I wish to hell I knew if the vandalism was by him or just random. There was nothing, no… message in it saying he did it. Besides, as I told Mag, he'd have done something more dramatic. A dead cat, a tortured dog, spilled blood, would be much more his style. But… maybe that's what he wants me to think.*

"Damn it," Brand growled, getting to his feet. He looked hard at Mag. "If I leave you here, and it was him, you're not safe. If I take you with me again, and that's what he wants me to do…" He shook his head.

"Hobson's choice," Mag agreed wryly. "Still…" He took out his phone.

"What are you doing?"

"I'm going to call work to say I'm sick. And"—he shot a defiant look at Brand—"I'll do it every day until we stop Fedor. That way I can sleep during the day and spend the nights on the street with you." He smiled slightly as he punched in the number. "The only thing we won't do is skip school. Got that?"

"Got it," Brand replied softly, amazed and yet not terribly surprised that Mag was willing to do this for him. He knew, although Mag had never come right out and said so, that Mag had feelings for him that went beyond friendship. Once, before Fedor, Brand might have—probably would have—reciprocated and acted on his own feelings for Mag. *Now, I'm not certain I have it in me anymore. I care for him, but is that enough to overcome how Fedor… changed me?*

Brand was brought out of his reverie when Mag said, "Done. Now all we need is a plan."

"More than just hanging around alleys and rooftops?" Brand commented with a small smile.

"Exactly. If it wasn't some asshole who vandalized my garden… if Fedor was responsible, I'd say he knows about me. I'm hardly your invisible housemate. If I had to hazard a guess, even though he didn't let us know he was around, he probably saw the two of us together sometime during the last two nights."

Brand nodded. "Unfortunately, I'm sure you're right."

"So we play into that but… yeah, that would work. We do it separately tonight and for as long as it takes."

"Uh-uh, no way. All he'd have to do is grab you and he's have the leverage he needs to force me to come to him on his terms."

"I'm not saying we stay ten blocks apart, but if you're at one end of an alley and I'm at the other, that should make him think he could get to me before you could do anything about it. I see him coming, I yell for help, hopefully he runs, and then you follow him. Done deal."

"Possible," Brand said thoughtfully. "But… we make it seem as if we really have split up. When we get downtown I take off in one direction, you go the other, then I double back and hit whatever alley we decide on, but carefully, so he doesn't know I'm there. You're more overt about getting up to one of the roofs."

"Like the last two nights?" Mag said, grinning. "That never was my thing, if you remember rightly. I was always one to find a spot behind a dumpster or in a doorway, because I hate heights. I'm surprised he didn't see us going up there. If I'd been alone, then for damned sure he would have."

Brand chuckled. "Got that right, and that's what we're going to play into." *And hope Fedor falls for it. That he* does *think we've split up and I'm somewhere else, because he knows I'm looking for him.*

"Then let's do it." Mag shivered, murmuring, "Now's when I wish I had some Dramamine."

"I thought that was for motion sickness," Brand said, giving him a fast hug. "You'll be fine. Just don't look down when you get up there."

"That sort of defeats the purpose of why I'm supposed to be on the roof, doesn't it?"

Brand grinned. "Then close your eyes when you do. He won't know the difference, if he sees you."

"That'll work."

* * * *

If he could have, Mag *would* have closed his eyes as he climbed up the fire escape. When he was with Brand, he knew he was safe because his friend was there to make sure he didn't fall. But now…

He made it to the roof in one piece then crawled down to the far end. When he got there, he huddled against the parapet, trying to regain his composure before chancing looking over it into the alley three stories below him.

Finally, gripping the edge of the parapet as if it was a life-line, he peered down. Despite Brand's suggestion, he wasn't willing to keep his eyes closed. If he was going to be any help at all, he needed to see who was in the alley.

Everyone and their brother. Guess they figure the cops aren't running a sweep this far down, or they've been through already and so it's safe.

Every doorway, every place behind and between dumpsters, seemed to have an inhabitant. He wondered if he'd even realize Fedor was among them if the man chose to disguise himself as a homeless man.

Not that he really did the one time Brand saw him out here, but still… He shook his head in dismay. *Blond. I'm looking for a blond.* Still gripping the edge of the parapet as tightly as possible, he leaned forward a bit more, then pulled back quickly, feeling dizzy. *I'm about as much help in finding him as a… a ditzy blonde.*

He was damned if he was going to give up however. Fedor wouldn't know he was there if he didn't show his face, so to speak.

An hour passed. Every few minutes Mag took another fast look at the alley below him. All its denizens were asleep, as far as he could tell, and none of them were Fedor…as far as he could tell.

Suddenly he was aware there was someone behind him.

Chapter Three

Brand was ready to move on to another spot. Fedor wasn't anywhere close by, unless he had disguised himself, which he hadn't the last time Brand had seen him. *Not that I'd know until it was too late.*

He glanced at Mag, who was on the roof of a building at the far end of the alley. He'd been splitting his attention between his friend and the alley for the last hour, undeniably proud that Mag seemed to be overcoming his fear of heights enough to actually watch what was happening, or not happening, in the alley.

Hefting his backpack over his shoulders, he moved rapidly from rooftop to rooftop, easily handling the different heights as he made his way across them to where Mag was kneeling with his attention locked on whatever was going on below him.

Without thinking he might frighten him, Brand walked up behind Mag.

Mag swung around, his hands tightly fisted, a look of terror on his face.

"Whoa, it's just me," Brand said, dropping down to kneel beside him.

Mag stared fearfully at him, his breath coming in fast pants. Slowly he relaxed, muttering, "You scared the hell out of me."

"So I see. I'm sorry. I didn't mean to." Brand hugged him quickly.

"I know." Mag sighed. "If you'd been him, I'd have been up shit creek."

"But you'd have done some serious damage to his knees in the process," Brand retorted, when he realized Mag held a penknife in one hand.

"Yeah, maybe." Mag managed a smile, then a weak laugh. "Not much of a weapon, but I felt safer having it."

"No doubt," Brand agreed, chuckling as he got to his feet again. "Ready to move on?" When Mag nodded, Brand held out his hand to help him up.

"I wish…"

"I *had* been him?" Brand asked.

"Yes. Then this would be over, or at least moving on to the next step."

"I'm with you on that, though I'd rather you see him before he gets as close as I was. I really do *not* want you in his clutches. You're supposed to be bait, not a victim."

"True enough. So where are we going next?"

They decided to move, block by block, closer to the creek, spending an hour or so in each of the alleys. It was close to morning when they finally gave up and headed home.

"If he was around, he's still playing games," Mag said, as they walked.

"I know but somehow I don't think he was. Or at least not where we were, when we were where we were." Brand chuckled. "If you get what I'm saying."

"At lot of 'weres', but I do. So we try again tomorrow night."

Brand nodded. "Or…"

"Or?"

"I was thinking. Alleys aren't the only place we'd go if we were still on the streets."

"The creek," Mag said, apparently getting what Brand was thinking.

"Yeah. It would be easier for him to find us, and"—Brand smiled, throwing one arm over Mag's shoulders—"you wouldn't have to be up high, having panic attacks every time you looked three or four stories down."

"I wasn't. Well, okay, yeah I was at first but I started to get better. A bit." Mag grinned. "I wasn't leaving fingernail marks on the parapets on the last couple of roofs."

"Still, the creek might work to our advantage. I should have figured that out a month ago, instead of playing hide-and-seek in the alleys."

"So tomorrow we try it and see."

* * * *

Right after class Monday evening, Brand and Mag headed home to change clothes. When they got close to the house, Brand said quietly, "Let me check it out first, just in case."

"To see if he's been there and left something? If he did, I can handle it as well as you can," Mag protested.

"Just… don't argue. Okay?"

Mag sighed in resignation. "Okay." He watched as Brand moved furtively to the front walk and then up it to the small porch, testing the door handle. After a moment, Brand disappeared around to the side of the house, so Mag thought it was probably safe to at least go closer. He was about to step onto the front porch when he heard the sound of swearing from behind the house.

Hurrying around to the back, he arrived just in time to see Brand jump down from the tall tree in the corner of the yard, landing lightly on the balls of his feet. He held something in his hand and when he saw Mag, he quickly put whatever it was behind his back.

"You might as well show me," Mag told him. As he said that, he looked up at the tree's branches. The lowest ones were a good eight feet or more off the ground. "How the hell did you get up there? You didn't have time to climb, get whatever he left, and…"

Brand shrugged. "I'm athletic?"

"I don't care how athletic you say you are, that's one hell of a distance to jump to. Just like when you get up on the dumpsters." He eyed Brand, shaking his head.

"This is what he left," Brand said instantly, obviously trying to deflect Mag's speculations. Bringing his hand from behind his back, he showed him a dead puppy with a piece of rope tied tightly around its broken neck.

"Fuck, fuck, fuck," Mag spat out in horror. "The puppy belongs to a kid a couple of doors down from us. Damn it. *Damn Fedor.*"

"Yeah, I know," Brand said dourly. "We should bury it. Better the kid thinks it ran away than… than this."

They did, in the dirt where Mag's garden had been just a couple of days ago. Then they went to the back door. Mag checked to be certain it was still locked and that the windows on either side of it were tightly closed. When Brand cocked an eyebrow, Mag told him, "I want to be sure he didn't get inside."

"He'd have locked up afterwards—or even if he's still in there," Brand pointed out.

"Yeah, well…" Mag inched the door open, peering around it into the kitchen.

"It's safe. He's not here," Brand told him.

"How do you know?"

Brand shrugged. "Instinct?"

For some reason he couldn't quite put his finger on, Mag thought it was more than that. *But what? How does he know?* Taking Brand's word for it, Mag pushed the door the rest of the way open and they went inside. Brand dropped his backpack on the kitchen table and opened the fridge, taking out one of his drinks and handing Mag a bottle of water.

Mag made quick work of the water, tossing the empty bottle in the trash. Smiling slightly, he said when Brand washed the container for his drink, "Someday you're going to tell me what sort of concoction's in those. More than just 'something I learned about in one of my nutrition classes'."

Brand grinned. "It's actually blood, mixed with protein powder and fresh fruits."

"Uh huh. The fruit and powder I'd believe from the frozen packages in the freezer and the can on the shelf. The blood? No way. And if it's so good for a person, why don't you let me have some."

"Hey, there's the blender, have at it."

Mag grimaced. "I'll pass. Veggies I can deal with but fruit, not so much so."

Brand waggled a finger at him. "You're supposed to have two cups of them a day."

"Do tomatoes count? They're a fruit."

Brand just rolled his eyes, picked up his backpack, and headed towards the stairs to the second floor. Mag followed slowly. He had questions he really wanted to ask Brand. Things that had been bothering him about how much Brand had changed since he'd gotten away from Fedor.

But now's not the time. This afternoon, though…

He vowed he'd make Brand sit down and talk to him. It was time. Past time, in fact, now that Fedor had stepped things up another notch.

* * * *

The moment Brand came down the stairs and saw Mag standing in the middle of the living room, he knew something was up. He wasn't certain he wanted to find out what.

"We have to talk," Mag told him. "Or more to the point, if you want to survive whatever Fedor has planned for you, *you* have to talk. To *me.* "

"Not happening," Brand replied tightly, as he headed toward the kitchen.

"Happening," Mag said, stepping in front of him. "Now."

"And if I don't?"

Mag sighed. "You had to say that, didn't you? Look, if you're going to make it out of whatever he's got planned, sane and alive, you have to… to tell me what's really going on so I can help you."

Brand started to protest but Mag overrode him.

"I want to help. I *need* to. Not just with stopping him, because that's a given. But with whatever it is that's made you so secretive you won't even tell me the least little bit about what he did that made you change so drastically."

"You really think my telling you will make a difference?"

Mag nodded. "Letting it out will, for you. You *cannot* keep it bottled up inside. It's not… healthy."

"Again the nurse in you comes to the fore," Brand responded with a half smile.

Shrugging, although he obviously didn't feel as casual about it as the shrug made it seem, Mag agreed. "It does. And for what it's worth, you know I'm right, even if you don't want to admit it."

Brand began to pace, his hands clenched at his sides. *He's put up with me since I've been back. He's stood by me, even when I tried to push him away, the way I did everyone else. But will he continue to once I tell him what really happened? I know what he thinks, that Fedor forced me into submission by any and all means possible and, that he turned me into some sort of sex slave.* He grimaced. *I wish that was true.* That *I could live with. That* he *could live with.*

"Brand," Mag said softly. "Please?"

Brand gave a slight nod. "Sit, and… and…"

"You'll tell me?" Mag did as he'd asked, perching on the edge of the sofa while he watched Brand continue to pace.

Without any preface, Brand asked, "Do you believe there are things that are, for a lack of a better description, beyond belief?"

"Isn't that an oxymoron? Believing the unbelievable?"

Brand nodded. "Perhaps, but the question still remains. Do you?"

"I don't know," Mag replied hesitantly.

"You know about werewolves and vampires and things of that nature. The myths about them?"

Mag snorted then. "Yeah. I've seen one too many movies with sexy vamps and snarling werewolves. Fun stories, but just that. As you said, myths."

Brand smiled sourly. "All myths have some basis in reality. One of those myths talks about dhampir, who are the product of a vampire mating with a human."

"That's a new one to me. No wait, wasn't that what Blade was supposed to be in those flicks?"

"Yes."

"Okay." Mag frowned deeply, staring at Brand. "So what does all this have to do with what happened when Fedor got his hands on you? And don't tell me he was some sort of vampire or werewolf and he turned you into one. That's fine in books and movies, but in real life"—he shook his head—"in real life, it's impossible."

"This *is* real life. I'm 'real life'. It is possible," Brand stated, his gaze locked on Mag's face. "Whether you believe or not, it is what it is. I am what I am."

Mag returned his gaze with an incredulous one of his own. "You're trying to say you're one of these dhampir things? You want me to… believe you're…"

Brand nodded sharply. "I was. I am, but…" He took a deep

breath. "Fedor did things to me. Things that made me change. Now I'm more than that."

"Bull*shit*!" Mag leapt to his feet, his hands fisting. "*This* is your explanation for why you're hunting for Fedor? And you expect me to believe it? Well you can go to hell, Brand. If he beat you, tortured you, forced you to become a sexual toy for clients—that I could accept. I know that happens. But this? Why the fairytales, Brand? *Why*?" Without another word, he spun around and raced out of the house.

"It's true," Brand shouted angrily before dropping down onto the sofa and burying his face in his hands. "It's not a fairytale, Mag," he whispered. "It's all true."

Chapter Four

Mag didn't stop running until a stitch in his side forced him to. He bent over, hands on his knees, trying to ease the pain and catch his breath.

He's crazy! Fedor did something to his head, his mind, twisted it, twisted him. But why? And why would Brand believe such insanity? Vampires, dhampir… they don't exist. It's impossible. But… but he believes *what he said. He thinks he is one.*

Mag straightened, looking around, and saw he was close to a small pocket park. There was a bench and he went over to it, sitting. Leaning back, he stared up at the slowly darkening sky.

What would make Fedor do that to him? What would it gain him? Does he run some Satanic cult that worships blood and… and vampires?

Mag vaguely remembered reading about a cult, in New Orleans he thought. The worshipers—if they could be called that—would kidnap children, kill them, and drain their blood. Then they'd drink it, thinking it gave them supernatural powers. Was that what Brand had gotten involved in?

No. He's too smart to even begin to believe such things. At least the man I knew before Fedor got his hands on him was. Yeah, sometimes Brand acted… strangely. We'd be somewhere, hanging out after dark, panhandling or just settling down in a safe place to sleep, and suddenly he'd jump to his feet and take off with no warning. But he always had an explanation when he came back. 'I thought I saw someone I used to know' or, 'Saw someone bothering so-and-so and I figured she needed help'. It was logical, even if I didn't see what he said he did. But that was just Brand. Never quite relaxed, even when he was sleeping.

"Mind if I join you?"

Mag turned quickly to see a tall, dark-haired, bearded man standing a few feet away, a smile on his face.

"Yeah, I do," Mag replied sharply. "I'm not looking for… company."

The man nodded. "Didn't figure you were but I think I might be able to help you with what's bothering you."

Mag snorted. "The only thing bothering me right now is you,

so go find someone else who might be interested in what you're offering."

Laughing, the man replied, "I'm not offering sex. It's not my thing. However, as I said, I might be able to help you"—he made finger quotes—"believe the unbelievable."

Mag was on his feet seconds later. "Who the hell are you and how did you know I… I said that to… to…?"

"To Brand? I was, I'll admit it, eavesdropping. He needs help if he's going to find and defeat Fedor. I'm offering it."

"By feeding into Brand's fantasies? And how do you know about them." Mag tensed suddenly, backing away. "You're part of it, aren't you? You're part of some cult Fedor runs. The one that messed with Brand's head." He kept walking backwards, looking for some way to get past the man and make a run to safety.

The man didn't move, although he kept his gaze locked on Mag. "It's not a cult. Trust me on that. Brand is someone special, as he tried to explain to you. Fedor knew that, which is why he captured him. Why he"—the man spread his hands—"why he experimented on him."

Uncertain, Mag stopped moving away. "Who are *you* then and how do you know about that, and Brand?"

"My name is Antton Ochoa. I am, to put it bluntly, a bitter enemy of Fedor's."

Mag shook his head, feeling almost amused for a brief moment. "So I'm supposed to think that the enemy of my enemy is my friend."

"What could it hurt?"

"Me, and more importantly Brand, if it turns out you're not what you say you are. For all I know, you could be working for Fedor and this is just another step in the game of terror he's playing."

"I could be, but I'm not," Antton replied quietly. "What Fedor did to Brand, and what he's done to others, has brought a death-sentence down on him. There is one problem however. He knows this and had gone to ground."

"Not hardly. Brand saw him, on the Fourth, and he's been to where we live at least twice since then."

"True, he is out there from time to time. He desperately wants Brand back, but I think he wants him so traumatized when that happens that Brand will do whatever Fedor tells him to. That's something that didn't happen the first time, obviously, since Brand managed to escape his clutches. We need to find out where he was being held when that happened."

"Brand doesn't know."

"Alas, I'm not surprised. I'm sure Fedor put some block on his mind so he wouldn't, just in case."

"Hypnotized him?"

"In a way." Antton sat down, asking, "Will you join me?"

Hesitantly, Mag did. "Are you… will you tell me what's going on?"

Antton smiled wryly. "If you're ready to believe the unbelievable."

"That Brand's a dhampir? I know he believes it. I'm not all that certain I do, even after what you've said."

"He is."

Mag studied him. "And you're what? A vampire? Is that what Fedor is, or what he thinks he is?"

"I'm the opposite end of the spectrum, a werewolf."

"Uh-huh."

"Would you like me to prove it?"

"If I said 'yes', you'd tell me you can't right now since there's no full moon."

"A myth, one of too many." Antton now studied Mag in return. "I think, perhaps, you need proof, if you're going to believe." He stood again, glancing around. "Come with me." He pointed to a small stand of trees at the back of the park.

"As if. One thing Brand and I did figure out. If Fedor gets his hands on me, he'll have a hold over Brand to make him return to the fold."

"And still, you haven't run away from me."

"Yet," Mag replied.

"Yet. All right, you sit here and watch, where it's safe." With that said, Antton moved swiftly to the trees. Standing between two of them, where the shadows were deep, he looked back at Mag.

At that moment, Mag realized how silvery-blue Antton's eyes were. They seemed to glimmer, even in the dark. *More so, in the dark, which is weird.* Almost instantly, it wasn't Antton standing there. Instead a sleek wolf with the same eyes looked back at Mag. "Not possible," he whispered unbelievingly.

"Possible," Antton said moments later, returning fully clothed to his human form. He walked back to where Mag sat, eyeing him warily as if he thought he would turn tail and run.

"If I hadn't seen it happen…"

"But you did. Now do you believe?"

"I'm… It could *still* be a trick. You could have hypnotized me somehow, the way you said Fedor did to Brand, to make him forget where Fedor had kept him prisoner."

"He didn't hypnotize him, he enthralled him. It should have been impossible, considering what Brand is, but Fedor is very old and very evil. Brand is still young." Antton chuckled. "Although not as young as he looks, I'm afraid."

Mag gulped. "How old?"

"Fedor? Well over three thousand. Brand? He's been around for, I believe, sixty years, give or take a couple."

Mag buried his face in his hands, trying to take in everything Antton had said… and done. Finally, he looked up at him. "I suppose you want to come home with me."

Antton chuckled. "You make it sound as if I was a stray dog."

"More like a stray wolf," Mag said, suddenly bursting into uncontrollable giggles. "I don't think… we have… a collar and a leash, but…"

"Not funny," Antton grumbled, but he was smiling. "Yes, I'd like to come home with you. I need to meet Brand and all three of us need to talk."

"My mantra with him," Mag said, sobering. "Maybe you'll have better luck than I have."

"We can only hope."

* * * *

Brand was in the kitchen when he heard the front door open. He set down his drink before going into the living room, trying to stay calm while praying it was Mag. *He has to come back. I need him. I can't do this without him. I can't.* Those words had run though his mind over and over since Mag had stormed out of the house.

"You came home," Brand said when he saw him. He didn't know whether to be elated or terrified Mag was going to be there just long enough to pack up and leave again.

"I did, and I brought a friend." Mag beckoned to someone still outside, stepping aside to let them enter. "This is Antton Ochoa," he told Brand, by way of introduction. "It seems," Mag smiled ruefully, "there *are* things beyond what most people really believe."

Antton stepped forward, holding out his hand to Brand. "It's a pleasure to meet you at last."

After warily shaking Antton's hand, Brand asked, "Who are you, exactly?"

"He's a werewolf," Mag said, before Antton could reply. "No, I'm not crazy. I saw him change." He hurried to Brand's side, hugging him tightly. "And if I'm not crazy, I guess you aren't either."

"Thanks for that," Brand said wryly, putting his arm around Mag's waist when he seemed about to step away again. "Would I be pushing things to ask why you brought him home with you? He could, after all, be working for Fedor."

"I could," Antton agreed. "If that was case, however, Mag would now be sitting in solitary confinement at Fedor's lair."

"You know where that is?" Brand asked, hoping against hope that he did.

"From what Mag told me, no more than you do. However, I suspect the knowledge is somewhere in your mind, but blocked by Fedor."

"That does us a lot of good," Brand muttered. He looked up at Mag and gave a small chuckle. "You're the nurse. How do we unlock it?"

"Unfortunately I'm not training to be a psychiatric nurse and even if I was, I doubt that's something I'd have been taught—not in my freshman year, anyway."

Brand nodded, returning his attention to Antton. "You still haven't proven, to me at least, that you're trustworthy."

"And how would I do that?" Antton asked a bit sarcastically. "Being what you are, you know I'm not a vampire. You know Fedor is. I could still, as has been pointed out by Mag, be working for him for reasons of my own."

Brand studied him, slowly nodding. "No, you're not a vampire, and Mag says he saw you change. It could have been a mind trick however."

"I can't control *your* mind, so if you want me to prove to you that I am a werewolf, I will."

"I might agree with you about the mind control, if I hadn't been in Fedor's clutches. He shouldn't have been able to do that to me, but he did." Brand finally released his hold on Mag so he could pace. He thought better when he was moving. "How did you know where to find Mag, and as a corollary to that, how did you know he and I are… together?"

"As I told Mag earlier this evening, I was eavesdropping and followed him when he stormed out of the house. I originally knew you lived here by following my nose. I can scent another werewolf a mile away or more, even if their scent is as strange as yours. I need your help, but I had to be certain I could convince you to give it to me, since it was obvious that until tonight, you were keeping things secret from Mag. Right now you may be the only link to finding Fedor."

"Now hang on a minute," Mag said in shocked surprise. "He…" Mag turned to look at Brand. "You said you were a dhampir. You never mentioned the werewolf part."

Brand's mouth tightened. "That was the reason why I didn't want to talk about what happened with Fedor. What he did to me."

"He turned you into a werewolf? Are you shitting me?"

Brand barely smiled. "I wish I was."

"Why?" Antton asked. "Wait, let me guess. He thought he could use you to find us. A werewolf, with the powers of a dhampir, but able to use those powers to find and eliminate those of my kind. You would be a fearful foe; just as you were to the vampires you hunted."

Mag frowned, again. "When did you hunt…? Oh, hell. That's why you'd up and disappear sometimes then come back with some lame excuse about seeing someone you thought you knew."

Brand shrugged. "I figured it was better than saying, 'I'll be right back after I take a vamp's head'."

"Well, yeah, but damn, Brand." Mag tapped one knuckle against his lips. "Antton says you're a bit older than you look."

"That was off the wall but yes, about forty years older," Brand agreed. "And… okay, don't shoot me."

"Would it do any good if I did? Even if I had a gun I don't think I'd have silver bullets to use on you."

Antton chuckled. "They don't need to be silver."

"Another myth?"

"Let's put it this way, if you hit his heart, he'd probably die, just like you would. The same holds true for vampires to some extent, although they are allergic to silver, so it takes them much longer to heal if you cut them with a silver blade." Antton glanced at Brand. "Which, I presume, you have."

Brand nodded. "Don't all dhampir?"

"Nice to know," Mag muttered. "Where the blazes did you…? Never mind, you can tell me later. So, back to what you were saying. Why would I be shooting you, Brand?"

"I'm not quite as poor as I've made it out I am. The homeless gig just gave me a reason to be hanging around on the streets."

"Ah ha. So while I've been busting my ass making enough money to pay the rent on this place, you could have afforded a much nicer one for us. And"—he shook his head disgustedly—"paid our tuition at a real college."

"We're *at* a real college… well, trade school. And why pay for it when we got in on need scholarships because we're smart and passed our GED tests with flying colors?"

"Because?"

"That's not an answer. And I don't have that kind of money. Even if I did, how would I have explained it to you when I was supposed to be down and out the same way you are? Were."

"Well…"

"Exactly."

"Gentlemen," Antton said, "all this is fine and dandy and interesting, but it's not getting us where we need to be at the moment, which is finding out just what Fedor did to you, Brand, and figuring out how to do something permanent about him."

"Do I have to tell you what he did?" Brand asked, shuddering. "Isn't it enough to know that he changed me? Can't we leave it at that?"

"Yes," Mag said, taking Brand's hand to stop his pacing.

"No," Antton replied at the same time. "In order to know what he thought he was creating, I need to know how he went about it."

"That's simple enough," Brand said bitterly. "He broke me. He tore me down, tore me apart, until I was nearly insane and close to death. Then he gave me blood. Not his blood, not vampire blood. That *would* have killed me since I'm already half vampire."

Antton shook his head. "If you're going to say what I think you are, our blood would have killed you just as quickly."

"So you'd think, but he was clever. He did it slowly, very slowly. First, he mixed in minute quantities with my food, once he allowed me to eat again. Then when I didn't get sick or die, he increased the dosages, as he explained to me at one point."

"I thought… I mean, the legends say that it's the *bite* of a werewolf that turns a human into one, not their blood," Mag commented.

"True enough," Antton agreed. He looked at Brand thoughtfully. "You're half human. I'm surprised he didn't try that first."

"He told me, in one of his bragging moments, that he did with another dhampir he had… had experimented on. The dhampir's blood killed the werewolf and did nothing to change Fedor's victim. Go figure."

"Possible I suppose, as vampires and werewolves are not compatible in more ways than you might think." Antton chuckled. "Still, there is a Serbian myth that when a werewolf dies, he becomes a vampire. I've never seen any proof of that."

"Well, when it comes down to it," Mag pointed out, "until today, I never saw any proof either species even existed outside of books and movies. Obviously, that's not true."

"Agreed." Antton smiled dryly. "We have to keep our existence hidden if we're going to survive. That's neither here nor there at the moment, however. What is, is what Fedor did to Brand. I would take it that he wasn't successful? That you can't find a werewolf the way you can a vampire."

"I'd say that's a given, since I didn't know what you were until Mag told me," Brand agreed. "Still, who knows if it would have been possible for me to tell in time, if I hadn't managed to escape before he finished his experimenting?"

"How did you do that?"

"Luck and determination." Brand sat, finally, staring down at his hands. "He kept me in a cell, chained up at first, except when… when he… he let his men use me." He glanced at Mag for a second. "You were half right, although he didn't sell me to customers. He just used that as a way to break me. That, starvation, taunts, threats… you name it. He's a master at torture, without leaving marks except"—he tapped his forehead—"in here."

When Mag took a step toward Brand, looking as if he wanted to hold or console him, Brand said, "Don't. I'm… I can't get this out if you try to make me feel… if *you* feel sorry for me and…"

"I understand," Mag replied softly, taking a seat in the chair opposite the sofa.

"Finally," Brand continued, his voice laced with pain, "he thought he'd broken me enough that the chains weren't needed. Of course, he didn't come right out and say that. Instead, he told me he 'regretted' having restrained me that way but it was for my own good, 'until I came to my senses and realized we had a mutual enemy that we needed to fight together'."

"Meaning werewolves," Antton said caustically.

"Of course. By then I was, I suppose, on the verge of starvation—and insanity. That's when he began to feed me again." Brand shook his head. "For a man who thought he was so clever, he didn't seem to realize what he was… creating. I didn't become the… well, dhampir wouldn't be the right word for what he wanted but that's what he was going for." He shrugged. "What he did create, slowly but surely, was what he seems to hate most: a werewolf. A very weak one at first, but a very"—Brand managed a small smile—"insane and pissed off… hybrid, I suppose you could say. Dhampir and werewolf in one body. Of course, I didn't let him know that. When I began to think for myself again, I realized my body tolerated the blood, even when he raised the dosages, and that I *was* changing."

Getting up then, Brand went into the kitchen, returning with one of his drink containers, sipping the contents slowly. When Mag looked at him aghast, obviously thinking he now knew what it contained, Brand chuckled. "It's not werewolf blood. I told you it was fruit and protein powder, and… blood. I wasn't lying, even though you thought I was kidding you—or hoped I was. Being that I'm part vampire, I do need human blood."

"Ugh," Mag muttered, shivering. "I'm glad I never snuck a drink."

"You wouldn't even have noticed it. Anyway, back to The End of my story. The more he fed me, the stronger I got, but I didn't let him know that. I bided my time, waiting for the right moment. He would lecture me on how—when the time came—I would help him rid the world of the cursed werewolves, leaving the vampires as the supreme species. I played along, pretending that had become my goal too. Eventually, he trusted me enough that he let me out of the cell. I needed exercise to improve my stamina, according to him. I wasn't allowed out on my own, of course. Not by a long shot. My hands were chained and I was collared, leashed, and led around by two of his minions—lesser vampires who did what he ordered them to." Brand scowled. "I knew them too well, and I owed them for what they'd done to me at his bidding."

"So now you know the layout of his lair," Antton said.

"A couple of rooms, yes. They never took me into any of the others, or outdoors, despite the block he apparently put on my mind so I wouldn't know where the place was. I wonder now if he'd ever have removed it, even if he'd managed to accomplish his goal. Either way, the closest I got to outside was walking past heavily curtained windows. I was never out of the cell without the collar and chains, but after a long while, my keepers grew lax. That was their undoing. Never"—Brand looked at Antton and grinned slightly—"underestimate the power of a pissed off hybrid. I might not have been as strong as you, being a pure werewolf, undoubtedly are, but I had one advantage. Hatred. It was usually early morning when they came to take me for my 'walk'. They had a lot of fun teasing me about how they were walking the 'dog', even though they just thought I was a weak dhampir with the ability to find werewolves as well as their kind."

Brand took another drink before continuing. "That morning, they were at their low ebb, so to speak, because it was almost dawn. I'd been sleeping so I was wide awake. Fedor had left, as he usually did, once he opened the cell and made certain I was restrained before they took over. I had my plan, and it worked. As we passed one of the windows, I grabbed the drapes, tore them off the poles, and threw them over the vampires then I dove through the window. I almost took the time to try to kill them. They deserved it for raping me when he ordered them to. But I decided escaping was more important. I ran like the hounds of hell were after me, as far and as fast as possible, then went to ground in an abandoned building." He glanced at Antton. "I can tell you where that was, but not how I got there.

"Anyway, to make a long story shorter, I spent two days there, scared he'd find me, but afraid to move on in case he and his people were close by looking for me. I didn't sense them, but then I hadn't sensed him when he captured me. I suppose he was too powerful, and I've only been a fully-fledged dhampir for forty years and a hybrid for much less time. Not that long in the grand scheme of things. I got out of the collar and was able to break the chains on my wrists, much to my surprise."

"The power of what you are now," Antton said, smiling proudly. "Once you come fully into it you'll be stronger than most vampires."

Mag eyed Brand warily when Antton told him that, before saying, "And then you came home."

"Yep. It took a while to track you down but at least you had sense enough to let some of the people we knew know where you were."

"Well, duh. I told you I got this place so that… well…" Mag looked away, chewing his lip.

"So I'd have a home, even though you didn't have a clue what had happened to me. For all you knew, I could have moved on to a new city or something."

"True, but I thought if you'd done that, you would have let me know and… hell, we've been over this before. I'm sure Antton doesn't want to hear us rehash it."

Antton chuckled. "Not really. I'm more than glad you did escape, Brand. I just wish you knew from where. Still we have one thing on our side; Fedor wants you back and seems to want you terrorized into submission when he finally decides to capture you again."

"Well, that's not working. He's just pissing me off big time."

"Good. Now I have a question for you—an important one," Antton said seriously. "How often have you shifted?"

"Once, when I finally realized what was happening. I waited until the middle of the day when I knew Fedor and the others were sleeping." He grimaced. "I'm not too certain I want to try it again. It ain't fun."

Antton came over, clapping him on the shoulder. "It gets better with practice, I promise. I think you need to try it a few times, with me. I can help ease the pain until you get the hang of it and teach you a couple of tricks, like coming back quickly and fully dressed."

"Do you *have* to teach him that?" Mag said, before turning a bright shade of red.

Brand actually laughed, and realized it was the first time since he began telling his story that he had. "Come on. You've seen me naked before."

"Yeah, well…"

Antton arched an eyebrow. "So the two of you are more than just friends?"

"No," they both replied, almost as one.

"We've messed around a bit but that's it," Mag added, sounding regretful that was all there was to it. "We're only human." He managed a bit of a smirk. "Well, I am. Brand seems to have other things going on I had no clue about."

After studying each of them, Antton nodded. "Not to be accused of giving romantic advice, but I'd say it's time the two of you explored your feelings, now that Brand has opened up. I suspect, if I'm not way off base, his emotions have been under tight wraps because he was afraid of what might happen if he let them out."

"Maybe," Brand said, almost under his breath. He smiled at Mag. "God only knows you tried to get me to talk and I fought that tooth and nail, which meant I had to keep everything else held tightly inside as well."

"That, plus what Fedor put you through, would be cause enough to be stoic and silent," Antton told him.

Brand just nodded, still smiling at Mag.

* * * *

Mag tried to return his smile, but he was afraid—afraid Brand would take it the wrong way, or the right way and not want what he was willing to give him.

That he'd had feelings for Brand almost from the first was a given, as far as he was concerned. That he'd tried to keep them to himself was also a given. He wasn't big on rejection. Sure, they'd played around some. As he'd told Antton, they were only human and had spent most of their time together before Brand had been kidnapped—and all of their time together after he'd come back.

At least all of it when we were both awake and I wasn't off at work. But we told each other we were just friends, nothing more. Even living together the way we are, we kept it to that, claiming it was friendship. Damned frustrating, as far as I'm concerned, but I wasn't about to push it and have him walk away. Still, he must have some idea of how I feel. Or not.

* * * *

Brand's smile fell away when Mag remained silent.

Do I care for him? I think so. Am I the man he needs? How can I answer that?

"You ask him." Antton's voice in his head had Brand turning in shock to look at him. *"Yes, I can mind-speak with you. It's part of what we can do. Before you get upset, I didn't read your mind, although I could have. I saw the worry you're feeling in your face and body language."* There was laughter in Antton's next words. *"I don't expect you to declare your feelings for him with me standing here. But you might want to try later."*

Brand nodded. "Maybe," he said softly.

"Maybe what?" Mag asked, tilting his head in puzzlement.

"Maybe we should come up with a plan to trap Fedor," Brand quickly improvised.

"That would be the next step," Antton agreed. "Do either of you have any bright ideas?"

Brand shook his head. "We've tried searching for him while being out where he could find me. I've seen him once and he saw me but was interrupted before he could do anything. Presuming, of course, he planned to and that it wasn't just the first move in his game."

"Hard to tell. What bothers me is why it took close to two months for him to start looking for you."

"Perhaps he had other problems to deal with?" Mag said.

"I can't think of anything that would be more important than finding me." Brand smiled slightly. "Not that I'm egotistical or anything, but still."

"Hold on. Mag might have a point there. After you got away, Fedor might have felt it would be a good idea to move somewhere else. He might not have trusted you couldn't break the block and remember where you ran from, once you were free. He knew he was changing you, although apparently he wasn't aware into what. The fact you managed to escape couldn't have made him happy on several levels."

Brand sighed. "So even if I did remember, it wouldn't do us any good."

"No, but"—Antton tapped his lips—"it would still give us a

starting place. Perhaps with help we could track him from there to wherever he's landed now."

"If he has moved on."

Antton grinned wickedly. "And if he hasn't, we're in luck."

"You're sure it was a house?" Mag asked Brand.

"From what parts of it they let me see, yes. I couldn't tell you how big it was. They only took me into a couple of rooms for my 'exercise', but I do know it wasn't a business, a warehouse, or what have you."

"Okay. You said you ended up in an abandoned building. What kind?"

"An old motel, half falling down. I don't think anyone's been there except squatters in forever, from the look of it." Brand grimaced. "And rats and stray dogs. It was off four-seventy I discovered, once I got up the nerve to leave. Seemed like I walked for miles until I got to a convenience store and found out where I was."

"Do you have a computer?" Antton asked.

Mag chuckled. "We're students. Of course we do." He went upstairs, returning with his laptop, handing it to Antton.

After bringing up a map program, Antton homed in on four-seventy in 'satellite' mode before asking Brand where the convenience store was. Brand studied the map as Antton scrolled it, then pointed. "That looks like it." Antton zoomed in, and Brand nodded. "That's it." A bit more scrolling and they found the motel.

Antton turned to look up at Brand. "You escaped in the early morning, you said. Where was the sun in relationship to how you were running?"

Brand snorted. "All over the place. I was zigging and zagging, going from one safe looking spot to another. I probably made more turns than I ran straight. So if you're trying to figure out which way to search from the motel, I have no clue."

"Did you cross the highway to get to it?"

"Well… no."

"So we have a semi-circle area to search, not a full one. Still a lot of space but not daunting."

"Says you," Mag muttered. "Especially since we're searching

for a house in an area full of them, from the look of it."

"A house that, unless I miss my guess, is somewhat off by itself. He wouldn't want to be close to other people who might either come knocking on the door asking to borrow a cup of sugar, or who would wonder why they never saw anyone around, coming and going to work or the store."

"Who borrows sugar these days?" Brand said, chuckling.

"You know what I mean," Antton grumbled. "How long did you run?"

"It seemed like forever but…" Brand closed his eyes momentarily. "It was still morning when I found the motel. I'd guess maybe nine or ten because the shadows were long, but not real long, if you get what I'm saying."

"I do." Antton glanced at the time on the laptop, bookmarked the map site and closed it down. "I suggest we all get some sleep and tomorrow morning, we'll go hunting."

Chapter Five

Antton showed up at what Brand considered the crack of dawn. He was driving an older model Ford SUV with tinted windows and Colorado plates. Once the two young men got in—Brand in the front seat, Mag in the back—they took off.

"I did some more searching when I got home," Antton told them, "narrowing down possible places to six."

"Based on their being away from other houses in their neighborhoods?" Mag asked.

"Exactly. It's a logical presumption. If we're wrong, then we're back to square one, which given the potential size of the area, will make this one hell of a long job."

"Oh great," Brand grumbled.

When they got to the area in question, Antton drove to the first house on his list. It took all of two minutes to decide it wasn't the one. As Mag put it, "I doubt he's running a day-care center," pointing to the fenced-in area visible from the street that held a large swing-set, a sandbox, and enough toys and tricycles to satisfy a small army of children.

The next house, while set well back from the road and surrounded by tall trees, was obviously occupied by a family with teens since two of them, carrying heavily-loaded backpacks, were leaving the house just as Antton drove by.

Antton had thought the third house was a possibility as it was surrounded by a tall, brick wall with an iron gate at the street end of the driveway. Brand disagreed. "When I ran, I didn't have to climb a wall or go over a fence."

"Okay, that eliminates the next house on the list," Antton replied, "leaving us two more before we have to start going door-to-door.

Mag's response to that was to cross his fingers.

When they slowly drove by the last house on Antton's list, Brand studied it as he had the others. Almost afraid to say anything out loud in case they were wrong about Fedor having moved on, he whispered, "Look at the back side window."

"Broken," Mag said gleefully. "This has to be the place."

"There's definitely no sign anyone's living there, if the state of the grass is any indication," Antton agreed. "It doesn't look like it's seen a lawnmower in a long time."

Brand frowned then nodded. "When I ran, I don't remember long grass. I wasn't really paying attention to things like that but…"

"We may have found the right house." Antton glanced at Brand. "Do you sense any vampires?"

"No. Of course, if Fedor is still in there I wouldn't feel him, but he did have his minions and as far as I can tell from here, they're not there."

"Let's go take a look," Antton said.

The house sat on a wide expanse of land, bracketed on three sides by trees, separating it from its neighbors. Antton drove to the next block, which was filled with suburban homes cheek-by-jowl to each other, and parked in front of one of them. Then the trio walked back to the house, stopping at the edge of the trees on one side.

"Still nothing?" Antton asked Brand.

After a brief pause, Brand shook his head.

"All right. You two wait here. I'm going to do a bit of recon before we chance going inside." With that said, Antton moved onto the lot, staying in the shade of the trees. Brand saw him pause, then seconds later a large, dark wolf crept through the grass to the side of the house and vanished around the back corner.

"That really freaks me out," Mag muttered.

Brand chuckled. "Me too, and I can do it. Not like he does, but then I've only shifted once."

"Why just once?"

"It hurt like hell, to put it mildly. He said it gets better but…" Brand shuddered. "I guess your body gets used to doing it."

"Not my body," Mag said adamantly. "I'll stick with being strictly human."

"And a very wonderful human at that," Brand told him softly.

Mag dropped his gaze, mumbling, "Thanks."

"It's true, and your body…" Brand stopped when he saw the

front door to the house open, tensing in anticipation of trouble, even though the sun was well up by now. He was more than relieved to see Antton standing there, beckoning for them to join him.

The first thing Antton asked when Brand stepped inside was, "Is this the place?"

Without replying, Brand headed from the entrance foyer down the hall toward the rear of the house. Pushing open the door at the far end, he found himself in the kitchen. A door to the left lead to an empty room he remembered well.

"It had furniture the last time I was here," he told the others. "I think it would have been used as a parlor if it was owned by a family. As it was, it only had a sofa and a couple of chairs, not in the best shape." He pointed to the side window. "My escape route." An obvious statement since the bottom pane was shattered.

Antton nodded. "He kept you in the basement, you said."

"Yes." Going back to the kitchen, Brand opened another door, revealing a pantry with the back door of the house facing them. To one side was a second door. "Through there are the stairs. I'm… I'm not sure I want to go down there."

"You should," Antton said firmly. "Facing your fears is better than avoiding them."

Mag took Brand's hand, gripping it tightly. "We'll be with you."

Swallowing hard, Brand nodded. The stairway was narrow, ending at a concrete-walled room with a furnace in one corner. "There." He pointed to a steel door in the opposite corner that stood slightly ajar.

"Nice of him to leave it unlocked," Antton said scathingly as he opened it the rest of the way.

There was a short hallway with four more steel doors, two on either side. Each one had a small barred window. Brand walked to the first one on the right. "My home away from home," he spat out, his anger coming to the forefront, overriding his fear.

"Also unlocked," Antton said after testing the lever that served as a handle then opening the door. "Love the accommodations."

There was a metal bed, bolted to the floor, with a thin mattress on it, restraints at each corner. Four chains were bolted to the wall opposite it with manacles at The End of each one. The only other item in the windowless room was a lidless toilet.

Mag's breath hissed in as he surveyed the cell. "How the hell did you manage to survive?"

"Half the time I was unconscious. The rest..." Brand shivered. "At first I had no way of knowing how many days were passing. I could have been here for a week or a year. Of course, he never bothered to tell me. He only said that in time I'd be free. 'When I was ready' was the way he put it. Freedom didn't include my daily exercise regime, once he began allowing that." He stepped back into the hallway. "Can we get out of here now? Please?"

"Mag, take him back upstairs," Antton said. "I want a few minutes more down here to see if I can pick up on anything that might help us find out where he's moved on to."

"Are you all right?" Mag asked once he and Brand had returned to the ground floor.

"Fuck no!" Brand regretted his angry reply when Mag flinched, saying more calmly, "Not really, but I will be." Then he smiled, barely. "Come on, let's explore a bit while Antton's doing whatever he's doing. I'd like to see the rest of the place. Okay, maybe 'like' isn't the right word but..."

"I understand. Upstairs first?"

"Yeah, sure." Brand actually managed a chuckle. "Maybe we'll find a casket or two."

"That myth is true?" Mag asked, following Brand out to the stairs going to the second floor.

"Not really. No caskets, no 'earth from the homeland'—usually just nice, comfortable beds behind well-secured doors and windows."

"Can I ask something?"

"Sure."

"If you hunt vampires, how do you kill them if they're sleeping in a really safe place?"

"Take their heads."

"That's not what I meant and you know it."

"Sorry. I hunt them down while they're out at night. It's surprising how many of them either don't know about dhampir or believe they're invulnerable because they can go invisible if they think I'm around. They should know I can sense them no matter what." They were upstairs by then. Brand tried the first door they came to, which opened under his touch. "See, fancy accommodations."

Mag snorted. "If you go in for minimalist décor."

The room was empty, as were the others they checked out, although from the marks in the carpets, it was apparent there had been furniture in each of them at one point in time.

"I wonder which moving company he used," Mag said after they exited the fourth room.

"United Vampire Lines," Brand replied with a smirk.

"I suspect," Antton said, startling them when he appeared at the top of the stairs, "he had his minions—as Brand calls them—hire a van to transport what he wanted to keep. The rest is probably in a dump somewhere."

"Did you find anything that'll help us locate his new lair?" Brand asked.

"I know his scent now. Unfortunately, unless I'm within a mile or two of him, that really doesn't do us much good."

"Still better than what I can do, as far as sensing him," Brand said.

"But you will be able to pick up on any of his followers when we find him. That will be an inestimable help. You can tell us how many others we'll be dealing with."

"There's still one problem," Mag pointed out. "How do we find him in the first place?"

"Use you as bait," Antton replied.

"Hell no!" Brand put a protective arm around Mag's shoulders.

"He'll be quite safe. I plan on bringing in a few people to help us, now that I've found you," Antton told him.

Mag cocked one blond eyebrow. "I hope the 'people' are like you."

"Two are. The other two are vampires. As I told you, there's a death sentence on Fedor's head. It was placed there by the ruling council, which consists of two vampires and two werewolves, all of them quite powerful in their own rights."

"Are you, for lack of a better word, this council's enforcer?" Brand asked when he realized he had no idea where Antton fit in the scheme of things.

"I am, and that's what we call ourselves. Enforcers."

"That's sort of... Mafia like." Brand smiled slightly. "But whatever you call yourself, it makes me feel a bit better about Mag's safety, especially if the others are as well."

"They are. The vampires are not as old as Fedor, but then very few are. However, between the five of us we should be able to take him down once we find him."

"*If* we find him," Brand said.

"We will. For now, however, I suggest we get back to my place and come up with a specific plan for doing that." Antton took out his phone as he led the way back to where they'd parked. From what Brand could tell, he was alerting the others to meet him there.

Chapter Six

"Nice digs," Mag said, when they were inside Antton's home. The house was large, set on an acre and a half of forested land in the foothills outside the city. The furnishings in the living room were modern but more of the comfortable sort rather than lots of steel-framed leather and glass. One big bay window overlooked the rambling front yard while a second one gave a marvelous view of the mountains behind the house.

"Do you run a lot out there?" Brand asked.

Antton nodded. "In both forms, actually. Speaking of which, I think it's time for you to have a real lesson on shifting. That you managed to do it the first time without any help is impressive but as you said, it was also painful." He turned to Mag. "Do you want to join us?"

"Umm, if it's going to hurt him then no. I'm not certain I could just stand by and watch."

"Very well. We'll be back in half an hour or so. Feel free to look around."

After they left, Mag took Antton at his word and explored the rest of the house. The ground floor consisted of the living room, a dining room with a long table that could easily seat ten people, a very well appointed kitchen and, much to his surprise, a large media room with a huge TV, two gaming systems, and a computer that would put most people's to shame.

Upstairs there were four large bedrooms, all with king-sized beds, dressers, walk-in closets, and en-suite bathrooms. It was obvious which one was Antton's because it had the best view of the mountains, with a small table and two comfortable chairs in front of the window.

As he walked back downstairs, feeling duly impressed with what he'd seen, he thought he heard a noise from the living room. He hurried the last few steps, wanting to find out how Brand's lesson had gone, and froze when he got to the arch leading from the hallway into the room. A very tall man with shoulder length blond hair was standing in front of the fieldstone fireplace, staring at the painting above it.

Mag backed away as quietly as he could, praying the man hadn't heard him approach.

There was a low chuckle then the man said, "I'm safe enough. You can come in. I'm Randulf, a friend of Antton's."

Mag remained where he was, studying the man. Finally he came closer. "You're not Fedor. The nose is wrong."

Randulf tilted his head. "Just what's wrong with my nose?"

"Nothing... nothing..." Mag stuttered, looking up at him. Randulf towered over him, a good five inches taller than Mag's six-one. "It's a very nice nose and it's not like Dante's."

Randulf roared with laughter. "Good gods, I hope not."

"Now what's wrong with my nose?" A second man appeared suddenly at the far end of the room. He wasn't nearly as tall as Randulf. His hair was deep auburn and so long that even tied back, it hit well below his shoulder blades.

Mag gulped. "Who... Who are you?"

The man bowed. "Dante, but not Alighieri. He's long dead. Of course, technically, so am I."

"You're a vampire? Well, duh. I guess that's a given," Mag said, beginning to relax slightly.

"I am, whereas Randulf there is a werewolf." Dante turned to Randulf. "Where are the others?"

"On their way still, I presume. Ulrik was in Germany last I heard. I have no clue about Vesper."

"Vesper is in the house."

The three men all swung toward the sound of the deep voice. A man stood in the darkened doorway between the living and media rooms. "Would someone mind closing the drapes? I'm not as old as Dante, so the sunlight is a bit bothersome."

Mag walked swiftly across the room to do as he asked, closing the drapes over both windows.

"Thank you, young man," Vesper said, finally coming into the room. He was probably six-foot with raven-black hair cut short and well styled. "I am, as you probably gathered, Vesper—and a vampire. You are?"

"Mag. Magnus Larsson."

"Scandinavian?"

"Way back when. Swedish actually, on my father's side."

"Then you and Ulrik should get along famously. He's Swedish too. Has been for"—Vesper glanced at Randulf—"two hundred years?"

"Give or take."

"Two hundred and eight, I believe," Antton said as he and Brand joined them.

Mag quickly crossed to Brand, looking him over carefully. His sweat-soaked hair hung lank around his face but there was pride in his expression.

"You seem to have survived in one piece," Mag said with a smile.

"Barely, but after three shifts, I have the hang of it now. On the last one I didn't feel it at all, well barely anyway." Brand grinned. "And I can come back fully clothed."

"Well, damn." Mag laughed, hugging him.

While they talked, the newcomers studied them. "It's true," Vesper said, "you are a… well, a hybrid I suppose, would be the best description. Truly *sui generis*."

Brand nodded. "Very unique, I agree. Dhampir, meaning half human, half vampire, plus I'm now a werewolf, as well, thanks to Fedor." He looked at the men inquisitively. "And you are vampires in two cases, and I presume a werewolf?"

Each one introduced himself, Dante adding, "I suppose we should be happy you consider Vesper and me friends, Brand."

Brand chuckled. "You still have your heads, so yes I do. Besides which, Antton warned me there would be two of you. I'd rather not breach his hospitality by killing you."

"Nice of you," Dante replied dryly.

"Now all we need is Ulrik and we can get started," Antton told the others. "Until then, I suggest we eat."

"Raw meat for everyone," Mag whispered softly to Brand.

The men all laughed, Dante pointing out that even a whisper could be heard by all of them as if he'd spoken out loud.

Mag grimaced and apologized.

"No harm done. We're used to humans thinking that's all we eat," Randulf told him. "Raw meat for werewolves, straight blood for vamps."

"In actuality"—Vesper grinned—"I like a good lasagna with lots of garlic."

"Another myth blown to smithereens," Mag muttered, much to the amusement of the others.

* * * *

When Antton and the other Enforcers headed to the kitchen to see what was available to make dinner, Brand stopped Mag by dint of taking his hand to lead him to media room.

"You want to play games?" Mag asked.

"Not those kind," Brand replied quietly as he closed the door. "I… we need to talk."

"I think that's my thing to say, not yours," Mag told him with a grin.

"I'm serious, damn it. I don't like their idea of using you as bait. What if something goes wrong?"

Mag sat down on the sofa in front of the TV before replying, looking up at him. "They said I'd be well protected."

"I know but we're talking about Fedor. He's older than sin. Hell, he's my definition *of* sin, with a capital 'S'." Brand knelt down in front of Mag, gripping his hands. "I don't want you hurt. You mean too much to me."

Mag's pulse quickened at his words. "I… I'll be all right. They promised."

Brand grimaced. "Is that all you can say? I tell you I care about you and you just say 'I'll be all right'?"

"More than that, now." He freed one hand so he could stroke Brand's cheek. "I care about you too. Probably… no, definitely more than care. I have since forever. If using me to catch him means you'll be able to live free of fear, then it's worth it."

"If anything happens to you, I'll die," Brand told him

fervently. "Now that I'm willing to admit how I feel to you, but even more to myself, I don't think I could stand losing you."

"Nothing is going to happen. Everything will go just as they plan. It has to!"

"I think," Brand said, getting up then sitting down beside Mag, still holding his hand, "you shouldn't say that. It borders on famous last words or something."

"No. It has to do with trust. I trust them because I have confidence in Antton. But more than that, I trust you to make sure Fedor's caught and destroyed." Mag winced when Brand's grip tightened painfully.

"Sorry," Brand whispered, releasing Mag's hand. "I just don't know if I'm worthy of your faith in that respect. No way am I in his class, or even in Antton's and his friends'."

Mag put an arm around him, pulling him against his chest. "I suspect you're close, and getting closer. No, you don't have their age or experience, but you're sort of a triple threat. You can find vampires, no matter where they are, and you're a werewolf with all that entails."

Brand turned his head to look at Mag. "That's two. What's the third?"

"We, I think I can safely say, love each other—or damned close to it. Not to be hokey or whatever, but love is a power in and of itself."

"But is it enough?" Brand replied, sounding doubtful.

Cupping his jaw, Mag kissed him. "I guess we're going to find out, aren't we?"

Brand nodded then slowly smiled. "I guess we are." Spearing his fingers through Mag's blond hair, he kissed him hungrily. "You know," he said, breaking the kiss long moments later, "the next time we go to bed, it's not just going to be to relieve tensions."

Mag kissed him lightly. "Has it ever really been that? I mean, yeah, that's what we told ourselves but still…"

"Does it matter, now we're admitting our feelings? Somehow I suspect it will show in our… our love-making too."

"If we ever get a chance to do it again," Mag grumbled when someone rapped on the door, telling them dinner was ready.

"Oh we will. Trust me on that. Once all this is over, I plan on showing you just how much I care for you, in all ways possible."

They kissed again, Brand pouring all his feelings into it, aware that Mag was as well. And then, quite reluctantly, they got up. When Mag opened the door, Dante stood there, a knowing smirk on his lips.

"Work now, fun later. Ulrik has finally arrived."

* * * *

"Good evening."

The man who spoke—Ulrik, Brand presumed—stood at the far side of the kitchen. There was something vaguely familiar about him, although Brand couldn't put his finger on what it was. He seemed older than the others, at least in appearance. Brand would have guessed around thirty-five. His hair was dark blond, cut short, and he had a mustache, but otherwise was clean shaven.

"Evening," Brand replied, eyeing him. "You're Ulrik?"

"I am." Ulrik bowed his head briefly in acknowledgment. He smiled a bit wickedly. "How quickly you forget… kid."

It took a moment to sink in then Brand muttered, "Shit."

"What's wrong?" Mag asked, stepping defensively in front of Brand.

"It's okay," Brand told him, moving beside him, resting one hand on his shoulder. "Ulrik here is an old… friend, I guess you could say. Although last time I saw him he looked older and dirtier and hairier, to put it mildly. And"—he shook his head—"he called himself John."

"No way! I met John a couple of times. No way are you him," Mag said determinedly. "He was an old man."

"Middle-aged, thank you very much," Ulrik replied, "and it was an act. Anyone can seem older than they look if they put their mind to it. It's all in the attitude."

"And the clothes, and the hair and…" Antton chuckled. "Ulrik is quite good at that, when necessary."

"But why?" Brand wanted to know.

"When I met you the first time, I was searching for a rogue—

not Fedor. We had no idea he was anywhere within a thousand miles of the city. You seemed like a good kid and having you hanging around sometimes made my cover more complete. I knew what you were, so I figured if nothing else, you might spot the vamp I was after and your actions would give me a heads-up."

Curious, Brand asked, "Did I?"

"Nope. Found him all on my lonesome, called in the troops, and now he's history. That was maybe a week after you vanished. If I'd paid more attention, I might have figured out sooner that there was more to you not being around than met the eye. By the time I did, it was too late. I reported it to the council, given what you are. They put us"—he thumbed toward the other Enforcers—"in charge of finding out if your disappearance was by choice or otherwise."

Mag snapped his fingers. "That's why you found me and asked that night."

"Yep. I figured if anyone would know, it would be you, as close as the two of you were. When you said Brand had taken off without telling you where or why, that pretty much cinched it, as far as we were concerned. After that, it was an all-out hunt for him."

"With no luck," Dante added, "until I ran into an old friend. He said there was a rumor that Fedor had surfaced long enough to grab someone new for his experiments."

"And that he'd been hiding somewhere in this area," Vesper said. "At first we figured the most logical place would be in the mountains." He smiled wryly. "Do you have any idea how many abandoned towns and mine sites, as well as caves, there are up there?"

"Too many," Randulf grumbled.

"And here he had me hidden right in the city," Brand muttered miserably.

Antton nodded. "We did have some of our sources keeping an ear and an eye open for anything that said that was possible but it's a big city, what with all the suburbs."

"A big city, lots of mountains… how the hell did you think it would be possible to find him, even if he was still here and not halfway across the world?" Mag asked angrily.

Ulrik shrugged. "Luck?"

"How did you know I'd escaped, and why didn't you show up as soon as you found out?" Brand looked between the men questioningly. "No, never mind. I think I know the answer. I started looking for Mag, and you figured Fedor would come looking for me. Right?"

Antton nodded. "Sorry, but yeah, you're right. Before you think we're total asses, catching Fedor is and always has been—what did some TV show call it?—our prime directive."

"*Star Trek*," Mag told him. He pulled out a chair and sat down hard, scowling at them. "So Brand be damned when it came right down to it. If he led you to Fedor, that was all that mattered. And now you want *me* to be the bait to bring the bastard out of hiding." He paused, frowning deeply. "If you were tracking Brand, why didn't you see Fedor that night in the alley when he did? And since you know where we live, why didn't you have someone watching the house. Fedor's been there at least twice."

"I did see him in the alley," Vesper said quietly. "Unfortunately, he spotted me at the same time and retreated. Possibly he was afraid I and the others were guarding you."

"I thought the cops showing up was why he ran," Brand said.

"Do you really think he'd be afraid of a couple of police officers?"

"Well… no. I guess not."

"Exactly," Vesper said.

"We have been watching your house, waiting for Antton to decide it was the right time to talk to you," Randulf told Mag. "However, Fedor is very old and very wily. He can be in and out of a place before you know it, if that's how he wants to play it. And in this case, it is."

"His reign of terror, as you two put it," Antton pointed out.

"Which isn't working," Brand stated with a confidence he wasn't certain he really felt. He pulled out the chair next to Mag's and sat, looking squarely at him. "Is it?"

Mag smiled ruefully. "It's beginning to. The more I hear, the more I wonder if we"—he glanced at the Enforcers—"if they can really stop him."

"We're going to try, but it will take all of us, and that includes the two of you," Antton replied. "You're…"

"The bait. Yeah, yeah, we know." Mag reached for Brand's hand, holding it tightly while looking at the other men. "So what do you want us to do?"

"Eat dinner," Antton told him, chuckling. "We're all hungry. Ulrik's here now, we have a good meal fixed, and I, for one, am not going to let it go to waste."

* * * *

"That was *good*," Mag said half an hour later.

Dante laughed. "You sound surprised. Didn't think vamps and werewolves could cook?"

Mag snorted. "Until a couple of days ago, I didn't know you existed, so what do you think?" He started gathering up the dishes, taking them from the dining room table into the kitchen with Brand's help. When they finished, they went into the living room to join the Enforcers.

"I now call this meeting to order," Antton said, smiling briefly once everyone was seated. "We need to come up with a way to keep our young friends here safe while at the same time putting Mag in a position to be captured by Fedor."

"Without Fedor knowing we're around," Randulf pointed out.

Vesper nodded, looking thoughtful. "As I said earlier, he does know I'm in the city. He might suspect I'm not the only one who is."

"I'd say that's a given at this point," Antton said in agreement. "It doesn't mean he's going to give up. He's just going to be twice as cautious, especially if he knows we found where he was holding Brand."

"How would he?" Mag asked.

"He'd be a fool not to have someone checking on the house occasionally. Probably a lesser vampire who could sense that we'd been there. We didn't do anything to cover our tracks."

"On purpose?" Brand wanted to know.

"No. There wasn't any real reason why we should have. As

Vesper said, he has to know at least some of us are around."

"Then setting up a plan for him to try to come after me or Brand is pointless," Mag said. "He wouldn't dare go up against the five of you."

"Don't count on it," Dante said. "He's old, bordering on ancient, very evil and thinks he's invulnerable. He'd love to show us how clever he is by grabbing you right from under our noses."

"Which we won't allow," Ulrik stated firmly.

Brand shot him a look of disbelief. "If he's that clever, how can you stop him? I've seen him, *once*, since I escaped, and you know he's been to our place. You said… well, Randulf said, you all have been watching our house and yet Fedor managed to tear up Mag's garden and the next day he left the dead puppy. Somehow that doesn't make me feel as safe as you'd like me to think I am."

"I told you…" Randulf started to say.

"I don't give a damn what you told us, I'm not letting you put Mag in danger." Angry now, with no way to release it without throwing a temper tantrum, Brand jumped to his feet, grabbing Mag's wrist, pulling him up beside him. "We're leaving. We've done fine on our own so far. If he shows his damned face, I'll take his head. I *am* capable of doing that. It's why I… Why I exist. Right?" He sighed suddenly, his anger abating when he realized it was driven by fear.

"Brand," Mag said quietly, "they're trying to help us."

"I know. I'm sorry. I'm just…"

"Scared out of your mind, just like me." Mag hugged him hard, urging him to sit again.

Brand resisted, saying, "I'm better standing, pacing, so I can work off some of my tension."

Vesper smirked, looking at the two young men. "Might I suggest you…?"

"Enough," Antton said firmly. "This is getting us nowhere. The question before us is how to put Mag in the right place so that Fedor thinks he has a chance of kidnapping him."

Mag took a deep breath. "Let him. Then follow him to wherever he's hiding. That way you can get him where he least expects it."

"And where he's most protected, so that's not an option," Ulrik told him.

"Besides which, following him would probably be impossible," Dante added. "He's not going to jump in his car and drive there."

Brand stopped his pacing when an idea occurred to him. "He knows Antton, Vesper, and possibly Ulrik are here. Vesper, because he saw him, Antton if he's been paying attention, since he came by the house and took us out to Fedor's old hideout. You"—he pointed to Ulrik—"because we ran into each other on the Fourth. The way he feels about werewolves, he has to have picked up on what you are."

"True," Ulrik agreed. "So?"

"The three of you play on that. Be more visible, more obvious about protecting Mag. Fedor's ego should demand that he draw you into following him back to… wherever so he can show the world, or at least our world, and how powerful he's become by capturing or killing you. Meanwhile, Randulf and Dante stay well in the background, just in case I'm wrong." He looked at the others questioningly. "Does that make sense?"

Most of the Enforcers nodded slowly, obviously thinking about it. Dante was a bit less circumspect. "Out of the mouths of babes, as they say."

"I'm not a babe," Brand grumbled.

"You're a lot younger than the rest of us," Ulrik replied, "so yeah, you are."

At the same time, Mag murmured softly under his breath, "I disagree. You're a real babe. Umm… whatever the masculine equivalent of that is." He turned red when everyone laughed and he obviously remembered they were all graced with extremely keen hearing. "Shoot me. He is."

Brand dropped down beside him, smiling. "Thanks for that. Saying it and"—he chuckled—"giving everyone a laugh. It helped me relax a bit."

"Then my job here is done. Can I leave now?"

"No, I need you beside me and… we'd better get back to what we were doing."

"Which was plotting how to covertly, overtly, watch the two of you," Antton said.

"What do you do on a daily basis?" Ulrik asked.

"Normally, up until a couple of days ago, I work," Mag replied. "Then in the evenings we go to college, and if things really were normal, we'd go back home, study, and get some sleep."

"You don't have a job, Brand?"

"No. I've been sleeping days so I could spend the nights searching for Fedor."

"Okay. It's a fair bet Fedor knows all this. If I were him, if I thought as deviously as he does, I'd grab Mag from his job."

"Definitely from his job, Ulrik, since Fedor would figure no vampires could be involved during the day. Of course, being ancient, he can tolerate sunlight to some degree." Dante said. "Where do you work, Mag?"

Mag smiled wryly. "Where else could an ex-street kid get a job? At a coffee shop that has food as well."

"Good. That gives Ulrik and Antton a reason to be hanging around."

Randulf shook his head. "Too obvious."

"But that's what we're going for," Dante protested.

"But if they're blatantly out there for him to see them, he's going to smell a setup."

"So what do you suggest?" Antton asked.

"That's what I trying to figure out." Randulf rapped his fingers on The End table beside his chair. "What's around the coffee shop, Mag?"

"It's on a corner. Next door on one side is a parking lot, then an apartment building. On the other side are small businesses. There's a convenience store across the street opposite the parking lot and more small businesses across the other street."

"When do you get there, and leave, and do you take breaks away from the place?"

"Eight, four-thirty, and breaks are usually around ten for fifteen minutes, and at two for half an hour for lunch." Mag added, before they could ask, "Most of the time I bring my lunch and sit outside in back where there's a picnic table."

"What do you think?" Randulf asked, looking at Ulrik and Antton. "Is it doable?"

"We should scout it out, but I suspect so. I've seen the place, so we can do that now." Antton stood, holding out his hand to Ulrik who took it. Instantly they were gone.

"Whoa up," Mag exclaimed. Then he grinned. "One myth that's for real."

Randulf chuckled. "Yep. Now I guess we should figure out how to put Brand out there and track him, just on the off chance we're wrong about who Fedor will go after."

"I'd appreciate that," Brand said sardonically.

Smiling slightly, Randulf continued. "Since I gather you've been out hunting him at night, you should keep that up. He's used to that pattern from you."

"You think it's possible he's just going to go straight for me, despite the idea he'd want Mag just to add another layer of torture to what he's been doing do far?" Brand asked.

Dante nodded. "As has already been pointed out, he might like to lure at least some of us into following him when he does make his move. And have no doubts, he *will* move."

"So," Mag said, "it sort of comes down to who he'd rather catch—Antton and Ulrik because he hates werewolves, or you and Vesper to show he's superior to any vampire who might try to catch him, especially if they're Enforcers."

"Precisely," Dante replied.

"What about Randulf?"

Randulf smiled wickedly. "I'm the secret weapon."

Brand looked up at him, all six foot six or more of solid muscle sheathed in a tight T-shirt and leather pants. "You're about as 'secret' as… as the Sphinx in the desert."

Laughter ensued before Randulf said, "I'm an alpha, as are Antton and Ulrik, but I've been around a lot longer than them and have some interesting abilities as a result. There is no way a vampire can sense me or control me, not even one as old as Fedor. I can also shift so that my human form is different from what you see now."

"And I thought Ulrik was good at undercover work," Brand

said.

Randulf nodded. "He's very good, but more the way a cop would be. Mine is purely physical."

"Humm. Could you be me?"

"No. I have several forms I can take, but they're all individual to me alone. I can't 'become' another person in the sense you're asking."

Brand nodded. "So you could be around and Fedor wouldn't know it."

"Exactly, and I will be—both with Mag and with you."

"Don't you have to sleep occasionally?" Mag asked.

Randulf chuckled. "Occasionally. I take, you should excuse the expression, catnaps."

"Bad one," Mag muttered, just as Antton and Ulrik reappeared.

"There's plenty of places we can use," Antton told them without preamble.

"Question," Mag said, holding up his hand before realizing what he'd done. "Okay, this isn't class," he muttered. "Anyway, won't he sense you're around?"

"That *is* the idea," Ulrik pointed out.

"Right. Sorry. Nerves talking, not common sense."

"Quite understandable," Antton said. "Now, if there are no more questions, we should get you home."

"And hope he hasn't left us another 'present' while we've been gone," Brand said.

Chapter Seven

It was decided that Randulf and Dante would accompany Mag and Brand home and stay until morning, after making it seem as if they'd left. Since neither of the Enforcers had come by car, they borrowed Antton's SUV. When they got to the house, Dante drove slowly by it and around to the alley where he parked and they all got out.

"Looks okay so far," Brand said after a quick visual check of the backyard and the tree. "No dead animals."

Dante went to porch. "Let me check inside." He misted, slipping under the back door.

"He'd make a good burglar," Mag said. "He doesn't have to worry about locks or alarms."

"Which we don't have," Brand pointed out. "Alarms, that is." He began pacing, opening his senses for any signs of vampires other than Dante. He knew he wouldn't feel Fedor but he wouldn't put it past him to send a couple of his lesser vampires to try to pull something as part of his reign of terror.

"Anything?" Randulf asked, apparently picking up on what he was doing.

"Nope. All clear unless *he's* in the neighborhood somewhere."

Mag looked around fearfully as if anticipating Fedor would show up any second. When Dante opened the back door, he scurried into the house, quickly followed by Brand and Randulf.

Dante stopped them as soon as they were inside. "I presume the two of you aren't into blood as a form of wall art."

"Shit," Brand growled. "Now what?"

"It looks like he paid another visit. Much earlier this evening, since the blood is dry, but it's there."

"I wish to hell he'd just show his face, grab one of us, and get this over with," Brand said angrily.

Mag walked into the living room and swore, not too quietly. "The landlord is not going to be a happy camper."

Brand followed and had to agree. Two walls were liberally

spattered with blood, heavily at the top with long streams coming down from there almost to the floor. Fedor, presuming it had been him, had also left a message in blood on the third wall. It said, "It ends soon."

"What's his definition of soon?" Brand spat out.

"I suspect it depends on how much longer he wants you looking fearfully over your shoulder," Randulf replied. "Still…" He took out his phone and called Antton to let him know the latest developments.

"We should probably take you back to Antton's so you can get some sleep," Dante said. "I doubt you'll be able to here, after this."

"Hell no. We're not running scared," Brand said adamantly. "Right?" he added, looking at Mag.

"Right," Mag agreed, although he looked as if he wasn't quite as certain as Brand.

Randulf grinned. "Didn't think you'd take us up on the offer. You two have guts. So Dante and I will make an obvious exit then return less openly. If Fedor is around somewhere, he'll sense Dante's back. I don't *think* he'll do anything tonight but we're not taking chances."

"Thanks," Brand said. He glanced at the walls again, trying to repress a shudder. "Come on, Mag, let's see them out and then go upstairs." Turning back to Dante, he said hopefully, "He didn't get up there did he?"

"No sign of it. Or at least if he did, he didn't do anything."

"Good." He headed through the kitchen into the backyard, followed by the others. Then he and Mag watched as Dante and Randulf drove away before going back inside.

"We probably have five minutes before they're back," Mag said, as soon as he closed and locked the door.

"Not enough time to do anything…exciting," Brand replied with a bit of a grin.

"No, but…" Mag wrapped Brand in a tight embrace. "We can make out a little." He didn't give Brand any chance to object, kissing him quite heartily—a kiss Brand returned very enthusiastically, exploring the taste and feel of Mag's mouth when Mag opened to his questing tongue.

"Told you," Dante said from behind them a few moments later.

"Like I doubted you?" Randulf replied with a laugh. "Sorry to break up your fun, guys," he said when Brand and Mag spun around to look sheepishly at them, "but it really is necessary for the two of you to get some sleep. Preferably in your own beds. Emphasis on 'beds'. Plural."

Brand nodded. As much as he'd have liked to continue what he and Mag had been doing, he knew Randulf was right. Now was not the time. *Later though, when all of this is over.* He smiled softly at Mag. "Guess we'd better do as ordered."

"Yeah," Mag agreed with a sigh. "Not that I'll actually sleep, but… yeah."

* * * *

Brand struggled against whoever was holding him down with their hand covering his mouth.

"Hold still and be quiet, damn it," someone spoke in his mind. *"We have company."*

Freezing, Brand looked up into Randulf's deep amber eyes. "Who?" he mouthed once Randulf removed his hand.

"A friendly vampire," Randulf told him sarcastically. *"Who do you think?"*

"Mag!" Brand shot straight up and would have taken off for Mag's room if Randulf hadn't grabbed him.

"Fedor has him. They're leaving now."

"Damn it, we have to stop him!"

"Will you *shush*? Dante's following and I've notified the others. Things are finally falling into place."

"What if he loses him?" Brand reached for his jeans, lying on the chair beside the bed.

"He won't." Randulf tilted his head as if listening to something. "Fedor's moving fast, but not as fast as he could by a long shot, according to Dante."

While pulling on his jeans, then slipping his feet into his shoes, Brand said, "So we were right, but why did you want me to be quiet?"

"Because Fedor was still here when I woke you. I sort of figured you'd want to tag along with us. Antton will be pissed, but..." Randulf shrugged. "You might want a shirt too."

"Antton can just suck it up. If you'd left me behind, you'd have had one pissed off me on your hands."

Randulf chuckled, even though his expression was fearsome. "Ready?"

"Not quite." Brand hurried to the closet, returning with a sheathed sword strapped to his back. With a thought, he made it invisible. "Now I'm ready."

Randulf gripped Brand's hand. Seconds later they were at Antton's. "Where are they?" he asked the moment they landed.

"According to Vesper, who joined Dante, they're about two miles outside of Golden and moving fast toward the mountains."

"You have a visual?" Randulf asked the others.

"Yes." Antton—and Ulrik, who was standing by the fireplace—locked their gazes with Randulf for a second.

"Okay, let's head out," Antton ordered.

It took two stops in order to get more visuals from Vesper, before the quartet was deep in the mountains.

"Where the hell are we?" Brand asked.

"In the middle of the forest," Ulrik said, with a trace of asperity.

"No duh." Brand looked around, seeing nothing except trees and more trees. "How close are we to him?"

Antton closed his eyes momentarily. "Vesper says they're at a small lake east of where we're standing. Time to shift."

"What about..." Brand tapped his sword then realized the others couldn't see it. "My weapon?"

"It will come back when you regain your human form, just as your clothes do," Antton replied tersely, his concentration obviously somewhere else.

The three werewolves and Brand shifted. Brand knew what

Antton's wolf form looked like from his lessons: lean, muscular, and covered with dark fur. Ulrik's fur was a deep blond, bordering on brown, like his hair. Randulf's was much paler, a yellowish-white, and he was massive. Brand felt insignificant next to him, and very plain as his fur was a muted shade of brown blended with gray.

"Follow me," Antton mind-spoke.

The werewolves raced through the forest, Antton in the lead, Randulf bringing up the rear. Antton stopped suddenly at the edge of the trees where they met a wide band of rocky earth.

Swinging his head left and right for a moment, Antton told them, *"Now we'll be stealthy. Vesper says there's a small structure on the far side of the lake from where we're standing. He doesn't dare to go any closer than where he is now, but Dante has, although he hasn't entered it so far."*

Foot by foot, the werewolves moved slowly along the tree-line that followed the edge of the lake. Suddenly Vesper appeared in front of them, his hand held up to stop them.

Antton tilted his head then relayed Vesper's non-verbalized words to the others. *"Dante thinks the cabin, which is all it is, is a ruse. He senses natural caverns beneath it but hasn't gone inside yet to confirm it. Fedor entered and hasn't left. So far, Mag is fine, if unconscious. Dante couldn't determine if he's enthralled as well."*

"What are we going to do?" Brand asked, wondering if they could hear him.

"We can," Randulf reassured him.

"Why can't Fedor hear us?" Brand asked.

"Because I'm shielding our mind-speaking," Randulf replied.

"We'll split up," Antton said. *"Randulf, you stay with Brand and go to the back of the cabin. Wait until I give you the order to enter. Dante says there are shuttered windows on all four sides, and only one door, in front. Ulrik, you take the left side, I'll take the right, Vesper and Dante will go in first since as far as Fedor knows, they're the only ones who followed him. Of course, Fedor probably suspects we're not too far behind."* He turned his attention directly on Brand. *"Something I should have asked long before this. Can you sense vampires in your werewolf form?"*

Brand nodded. *"I know where Dante is, about five hundred feet from us. There aren't any in the cabin but that's as far as my senses reach at the moment. If there are some in the cavern, I probably won't know where or how many until we enter it."*

"That's good enough for now. All right, gentlemen, shall we?"

The werewolves fanned out, moving stealthily to their assigned locations. When Brand and Randulf reached the rear of the cabin, they waited for Antton's order to enter.

"According to Dante, the entrance to the lower level and the cavern is a trapdoor. There's a chair attached to it to hide its location. He and Vesper have already gone down to the cavern's entrance. It's in a small cave. I have the visual."

Brand saw the picture and wondered how he was going to teleport there, to say the least of into the cabin. *Should have known* was his instant answer when Randulf gripped his shoulder gently with his jaws. Seconds later they were standing with the others, surrounded by what appeared to be impenetrable rock walls.

"Randulf, Brand, shift please," Antton said.

They did. Then at Antton's request, Brand opened his senses, searching for the presence of vampires. He understood why he was supposed to do that when he realized the ones he felt were all to his left. "The..." What he was going to say was interrupted by Antton telling him to think it instead of speaking. *"There are four vampires behind here."* He walked over to touch the cave wall.

"Guarding the entrance, one would presume," Ulrik said. *"Now, how to open it."*

Antton paced over, sniffing the wall. Then he nodded, placing one paw just below one of several rocky protrusions. *"If I'm not mistaken, when I push on this, the wall will swing open, so be ready."*

Antton did as he had said and they burst through the widening space when a section of the wall moved. They were in a second, larger cave with a wooden door set into a paneled wall at the far end. Between them and it, just as Brand had predicted, there stood four vampires. Whether the vampires had expected them or were there just as a precaution didn't matter. They attacked with a vengeance, using clawed fingernails, fangs, and weapons in an attempt to repel the invaders.

Dante and Vesper closed in on the largest of their foes, while Antton bit, snapped, and clawed the second of the four, managing to bring him to the ground.

"Brand, your weapon would come in handy right now."

Brand skittered past Ulrik, who was holding his own against the third vampire. Closing in on Antton's prey, he lifted his now unsheathed sword and brought it down on the vampire's neck, decapitating him. Then Brand swung around, looking for who needed his help next.

Randulf was obviously toying with his chosen vampire, feinting blows while dancing lightly out of his reach seconds later. The frustrated vampire angrily took to the air. With a gleeful laugh, Randulf grabbed his feet, whirling him around to slam him into the stone wall. "Ouch, I bet that hurt," he commented when the vampire's head split open like a cracked egg. "Still, better safe than sorry." With a quick twist, he tore the vampire's head from his body.

Brand heard Dante mutter, "The bigger they are, the harder they fall," and saw him and Vesper double-team their vampire, tumbling him to the floor. He was beside them seconds later, his sword hissing as it cut through the air and into the vampire's neck. Dante thanked him, while wiping away blood from the deep scratches in one of his arms. Vesper had fared a bit worse. The right side of his face was lacerated, as was his shoulder under his tattered shirt. "The bastard needed a good manicure," Vesper muttered, tearing off what remained of his shirt to sop up the blood. That was hardy necessary because, even as Brand watched, his wounds began to heal.

Then Brand remembered Ulrik. The werewolf seemed to be having more trouble now than the others had in closing in on his prey. The vampire was swift and wily, raising up to the ceiling then swooping down to rake his nails across whatever part of Ulrik's body was closest before rising up again. Ulrik leapt, trying to catch an arm or leg in his jaws. Brand heard him say, *"I'm getting too old for this."*

"Allow me," Randulf said, striding over to stand beside Ulrik. When the vampire swooped, veering when he realized it was now two on one, Brand grinned slightly. Between them, Ulrik and Randulf had herded the vampire to him. With a wide sweep of his sword, he beheaded him.

"Now I know why Antton wanted you in human form,"

Brand said, staring up at Randulf. "Your reach does exceed your grasp, so to speak."

Randulf snorted. "I'm not sure that applies in this situation, but the basic idea is right on."

"Upstairs," Antton ordered, heading out of the cave. Everyone followed and when they were in the cabin, Antton and Ulrik shifted to their human forms. But only for the moment, according to Antton, who said it was easier for all of them to talk that way.

"He knows by now Vesper is here, and possibly some of the rest of us, if he's aware his guards have been destroyed," Antton said. "The question is, what are we going to run into on the other side of the closed door?"

"I can mist and go find out," Dante suggested.

"And fall right into a trap, since he'd expect that," Vesper said tartly.

"I sensed two vampires close to the entrance," Brand put in. "They seemed alert but not worried, if that makes sense."

"Too bad you can't feel Fedor," Randulf said, pacing restlessly.

"If I was able to, none of this would be happening in the first place," Brand grumbled in reply. "At this point, I'm about ready to just walk in there and tell him to go to hell."

"Not happening," Randulf told him sharply. "It wouldn't solve the problem. We'd just have to rescue you as well as Mag."

"Hold on a minute," Ulrik said. "That could be just the element of surprise we need. But he can't go in alone. As Antton said, he already knows Vesper was following him. He probably senses Dante as well. So the three of them go in together. Randulf can continue to hide our presence."

"Only mentally," Randulf cautioned.

"That should be enough, as long as we stay back until it's time to attack. All we need is a visual and one of us can pick that out of Brand's mind without Fedor being aware."

Antton nodded thoughtfully. "It could work, and there's the advantage that Fedor doesn't know Brand is a werewolf. Add our strength and speed to what Brand already has as a dhampir, and he's a force to be reckoned with."

"I am?" Brand said in surprise.

"Yeah, kid." Ulrik chuckled. "Given time and more training, and you'll make the rest of us look like newbies beside you."

Brand grinned, relaxing momentarily. "Then you'll have to start calling me something other than kid."

"We'll see; you're still younger than me."

Antton sighed, even though he was smiling a bit. "Okay, can we get back on topic? Brand, you can make your sword invisible but will Fedor feel that you have it anyway?"

"No clue. When he kidnapped me, I didn't have it with me. It was daytime and I rarely carried it then. I mean, why bother? There's no way I can sense a vampire old enough to be out in direct sunlight—like Fedor—I haven't been around long enough." He thought a moment before saying, "On the other hand, even if he does know I have it, he can't take it away from me. It's pure silver."

"True, although if he has any humans with him, they could," Antton said. "And he does have one that we know of—Mag."

"Mag would never do that."

Randulf shook his head. "He would if he was compelled to, and that would be quite easy for Fedor to do. Or, contrary to that, you'd hand it over if he threatened to harm Mag."

Brand chewed his lip, nodding. "Yeah, maybe."

"Maybe?" Randulf stared at him in surprise.

"I'm a dhampir. My sole reason for existing is to rid the world of vampires like Fedor. I'm not certain, when it comes down to it, that I can override that."

"Then you keep it hidden until the right time comes and we'll pray Fedor doesn't figure out you have it."

Vesper, who had been pensively silent up until then, said, "He knows. Even though they were fighting us, I can't believe that one of his guards wasn't in communication with him. So he'll know Brand has the sword and exactly how many of us are here. The only thing he won't know, as Antton pointed out, is that Brand's a werewolf."

"In that case," Antton said, "we might as well go in together and let the chips fall where they may. Our number one priority is destroying Fedor, preferably without his killing Mag in the process."

* * * *

They approached the door to Fedor's lair silently, each man—be he in human or werewolf form—tense in anticipation of what they would find on the other side.

Dante reached for the knob, only to have the door swing open before he could touch it, as if of its own volition.

They faced a large cavern hewn out of the subterranean rock below the cabin. If it weren't for the stone walls, it could have been the living room of a very wealthy suburbanite. Plush Oriental rugs lay the floor. Two long, heavily upholstered sofas faced an ornate coffee table in the center of the room. Off to one side there was a mahogany table with eight high-backed chairs surrounding it. Long drapes covered the walls of the other side and the far end, giving the impression there should be windows behind them.

Three men sat on the sofas. One—tall and blond with an aquiline nose—stood, saying with a sneer, "Welcome to my humble abode." As Antton and the others started toward him, he held up his hand. "I would suggest you stay exactly where you are if you want to survive this encounter. Except for you, Brand." He smiled wickedly, beckoning Brand forward.

Brand turned to his companions, saying quietly, "There are at least a dozen vampires surrounding us."

"Fifteen to be exact," Fedor told them, "plus my two friends here. As if that wasn't enough incentive for you to do as you're told"—he walked to the drapes at the back of the cavern—"I have an added motivator for you." He pulled back the drapes.

His action revealed a circular, barred cage, reaching from floor to ceiling. Mag stood inside, his hands lashed by long, leather thongs to the bars on each side of the cage, his fingers close to but not touching them. His head hung down, but when the light hit him, he looked up, revealing deep bruises on his face that matched the ones on his bare chest.

"What have you done to him?" Brand asked angrily.

"Nothing life-threatening… yet. He resisted when I attempted to confine him, so I had to teach him the error of his ways."

"You bastard!" Brand strode toward the cage, searching for the entrance. Fedor did nothing to stop him, only watching with amusement.

When Brand reached out to touch what appeared to be a lever on one bar, Mag shouted, "No. It's electrified." He twisted one hand, showing Brand the burn mark on the palm.

Fedor turned his attention to the others, especially the werewolves. "If you attempt to free him… well, you know what happens when a shock of electricity runs through your bodies. Instant, multiple shiftings back and forth from human to wolf. Not, I'm told, a pleasant experience. And that presupposes you make it past my vampires *to* the cage." Gripping Brand's arm, he forced him to walk to one of the sofas. "Sit, and we shall all discuss rationally what will happen next."

Brand hesitated, not sitting, but jerking his arm free. Surprisingly, Fedor allowed him to do that, smirking in amusement while pointing to the sofa. Rolling his shoulders as if to loosen the tension he was feeling, Brand then reached back, gripping the hilt of his sword.

"Naughty, naughty," Fedor scowled viciously, advancing to stop him. He spat out an oath when Brand moved like lightening to avoid him, his sword appearing in his hand.

Then all hell broke loose.

* * * *

Mag watched in horror when Fedor's vampire minions began appearing as if from nowhere. Logically, he understood they'd been invisible, but…

The werewolves did what they did best, attacking the vampires with fangs and claws. Dante and Vesper held their own against two of their kind, before Dante, with a wicked grin, warned the others to move back. Apparently Vesper and the werewolves knew what was coming because they did. Flames erupted, instantly turning four of the enemy vampires to ash, doing major damage to one of the rugs in the process.

The two vampires who had been visible at the beginning of the fray now soared upward. Then, as one, they flew down toward Dante. Randulf got to him before they did, knocking him aside with a huge paw. His jaws snapped closed on one of the vampire's arms and with a swing of his head, he sent him hurling against the stone wall of the cavern. The vampire's forehead hit first, spattering blood and brains down the rock surface.

* * * *

Brand did not stand by idly while all this was going on. Instead he stalked Fedor, his sword held at the ready.

Fedor vanished. But apparently could not resist calling out in derision, "Now what, Brand? You can't kill what you can't see or sense."

Brand followed the sound of Fedor's voice. "You might be surprised what I can do," he replied mockingly.

"I doubt it." The disdain in Fedor's words was obvious.

Brand felt Fedor trying to enter his mind and fought it with all his might. Suddenly he had an ally and knew Randulf was adding his shielding powers to combat Fedor. Knowing Randulf had his back, so to speak, Brand laughed. "You may be old, Fedor, but in the grand scheme of things, you are less than nothing."

"And you? You are *my* creation now and I *will* have you back." The rage in Fedor's voice told Brand he was losing control.

"You couldn't keep me then. What makes you think you'd be any better at it now?" Brand taunted, praying Fedor would reply. One more word from the ancient vampire was all he needed.

He got more than he'd bargained for. He felt sharp nails pierce his bicep and he cried out in pain. Still, the core of what he was and what he had become responded. Rather than dropping his sword, which he knew was what Fedor intended, he took it in his other hand. Steeling himself, he used Fedor's grip on him as a fulcrum and swung around, lashing the blade of his sword where he was certain Fedor stood. An agonized scream tore through the cavern. Brand didn't know what part of Fedor's body he'd hit, but he did know now where his head was, as the screaming continued. Tearing free of Fedor's grip, he swung the sword one last time, feeling it bite into flesh and bone. Then Fedor reappeared, his head rolling to stop against the sofa. His body fell to the ground and it—and his head—disintegrated.

Thought he was above the rest of us. More powerful… and therefore, he didn't need to fight or protect himself. Brand shook his head disbelievingly; thankful, however, it had been the truth of the matter. He had the feeling, had Fedor gone on the defensive sooner… *I don't* even *want to think about what might have happened.*

Still, the battle wasn't over. Brand ignored the pain in his arm and turned to see where he could be of some help.

Ulrik was down, fighting for his life against two fanatical vampires, blood streaming from various wounds. Brand was beside them almost instantly, lopping off the head of one. He started to swing again but Randulf, now in his human form, took over, gripping the second vampire's head in his large hands, tearing it from his body.

"Remind me not to get on your bad side," Brand muttered before moving on.

"Never happen," Randulf replied.

Soon enough, the fighting waned. With their leader now dead and gone, the other vampires—the ones who were still alive—seemed to lose their urge to continue the fight. Two simply vanished. The remaining three capitulated rather than take the chance Brand would give them their ultimate death. Those three were herded toward the cage containing Mag.

Antton asked one of them how to turn off the electricity to the cage. Reluctantly, the vampire pointed to shelves on the cavern wall above a work table. Brand hurried over, trying to ignore the items on the table. Some of them he remembered, not at all fondly, from when he'd been in Fedor's clutches. At the back of one shelf was a lever. He pushed it down and returned to the others.

Vesper grabbed the arm of his vampire prisoner, pressing his hand to the cage. When nothing happened, Brand immediately opened the cage and went inside to free Mag. Wrapping his arms around him,

Brand led him out. Moments later, the captive vampires had been thrust inside and the cage was closed. Vesper went to the shelves and raised the lever, turning the electricity back on. "That should hold them, unless they decide to vanish."

"If they do, they will be hunted down, just like their companions," Antton said firmly.

"Why not kill them now?" Brand asked, even as he took Mag to the less bloodstained of the sofas.

"The council will want to have a few words with them. If they were willing to kill for Fedor, who knows what other rogues they might have worked for," Antton replied. "Their information might help us find them."

Brand nodded, his attention, now firmly on Mag as he gently touched the bruises on his face. "Are you all right?" he asked softly.

* * * *

Mag tried to smile. "I've been better." Then his glance lit on Brand's arm. "Holy shit." He called out, "Someone come help him."

Dante, who at the moment wasn't involved with caring for the injuries of the others, came over. "Looks bad," he said, eying the deep punctures in Brand's bicep. "But he'll live to fight another day." With that, he hurried away, going to check on Ulrik, whose wounds were worse than those of any of the others.

"Now that's what I call compassion," Brand muttered. "He's right though. I'm already healing."

Mag studied the punctures and had to agree. They were starting to close and the bleeding had slowed to a trickle. He wished his battered body would heal even half as fast. Fedor had seemed to take great delight in pounding on him as he forced him into the cage, tethering his hands so he couldn't fight back.

He jumped, coming back to the present, when Brand said, "We need to get you home or better yet, to a hospital. Who knows what damage he did to you that's not showing."

Mag took a deep breath, felt his ribs protest and nodded. "I don't think he broke anything but..."

"Come," Randulf said, joining them. He turned to the others, announcing he was taking Mag and Brand back to their house.

"The hospital," Brand protested when Randulf took their hands.

"How will you explain what happened to him?" Randulf asked, releasing his hold on them to expertly run his hands over Mag's torso. "He's right, Brand, nothing broken, and no internal injuries. Fedor was punishing him, not trying to kill him. That would have been counterproductive." With that said, he took their hands again.

Almost instantly, they were in Mag's bedroom.

"Now into bed with you," Randulf ordered Mag.

"Who made you my father?" Mag grumbled in response. Still, he did sit on the edge of the bed, wincing in pain when he bent over to take off his shoes.

Brand immediately knelt in front of him, telling him to lie back, even as he unlaced Mag's shoes and pulled them off of him.

Mag looked down at Brand, grinning weakly. "If I felt better…"

"I'd be doing more than just helping you undress," Brand replied with a chuckle. "You're already halfway there as it is."

"And quite capable of finishing on my own," Mag told him when Brand reached for the closure on his jeans.

Randulf shook his head. "That would be my cue to leave, I suspect."

"Not before I thank you for all you've done." Brand stood, holding out his hand. "So… thank you."

"You're more than welcome. It was actually fun in a strange way. I haven't been in a battle royal in a long time." He smiled wryly. "I suppose I should be happy about that."

"If I'm never in another one, it'll be too soon," Brand replied with a shudder.

Randulf nodded. "I suspect you won't be. On the other hand," he said thoughtfully, "you might make a good Enforcer with a bit more training."

Brands eyes widened with surprise. "Are you serious?"

"Quite. I'll talk with Antton and see what he thinks about it.

Anyway, for now, I bid you both good evening." With that said, Randulf vanished.

Brand turned to look at Mag and smiled softly. His friend and lover was sound asleep, his legs still hanging off the edge of the mattress. Gently, he moved him so he was he was properly on the bed then pulled the covers over him, deciding he could sleep in his jeans with no harm done. "Not like you haven't before, many times," he whispered. Bending over him, he brushed a kiss over Mag's forehead. Then he left, heading to his own bedroom and some well-earned rest.

Chapter Eight

Mag woke the next morning wondering if there was any part of his body that didn't hurt. *Well, any part above my waist.* Thankfully, his legs were fine as he needed to go to the bathroom in the worst way. Inching off the bed, he made what, at the moment, seemed like a mile-long walk down the hall to the bathroom. After taking care of the most pressing business, he looked at himself in the mirror over the sink.

Blue, yellow, and puce are so not my favorite skin colors. But it could be worse. At least I'm alive.

He stripped off his jeans, went to the shower, and turned the water on as hot as he could stand it. Stepping under it, he let it beat on his aching body.

"Want some company?" Brand asked from the other side of the shower curtain.

Mag gulped when his cock responded positively to Brand's question. "I… sure… I guess."

Brand chuckled, pulling aside the curtain just enough to join Mag without letting the water spatter out. "Damn," he growled, raking his gaze over Mag. "You look like you lost a fight with Mayweather."

"Who?"

"A boxer." Brand gently touched Mag's chest, pulling his hand back when Mag hissed. "Sorry. I was going to help you get washed and maybe"—he glanced down at Mag's cock—"with other things, but I don't think that's happening."

"I'm not fragile," Mag replied with both asperity and the need for what Brand was offering. "Maybe I'm only a human but…" He didn't get to finish his thought because Brand was kissing him then—very carefully, but definitely thoroughly. Any aches and pains he'd been feeling seemed to vanish in that instant and he returned the kiss wholeheartedly.

"You know," Brand said, breaking the kiss but keeping one hand at the nape of Mag's neck, "there is nothing wrong with being human. You have no problem letting your emotions out."

"With the right person." Mag traced his finger along Brand's jaw, smiling at him. "Now that all this is over, I suspect you'll have an easier time of it yourself."

"Maybe, but right now I have other things to worry about."

Mag tried to step away but Brand wouldn't let him. So he asked fearfully, "What?"

"How I'm going to make love to you without hurting you," Brand replied, quite seriously.

"Oh. Well. I… umm."

Brand grinned. "That left you almost speechless."

Mag ducked his head, feeling embarrassed. "It shouldn't have. It's not like we haven't before."

"Ah," Brand replied, "but before we were just screwing. This time I want to make love to you."

Looking at Brand, Mag whispered, "So do I. Want to make love, that is. I mean… to you."

"Are you sure you're… well, I won't say up for it because that's obvious from one standpoint." He stroked the palm of his hand up Mag's hard cock. "I meant it when I said I don't want to hurt you any more than you are."

"I wish I was like you."

Brand smiled. "That was sort of out of the blue but I think I get what you mean, at least when it comes to healing." He shivered, reaching behind him to turn off the water that had become decidedly cool now. Pushing back the shower curtain, he stepped out, waiting for Mag to join him. Snagging a towel from the rack, he used it to dry Mag, being extra cautious around the bruises on his torso and face. When he was done, he quickly dried himself then took Mag's hand, leading him to his bedroom.

"You should be all right on your back, if I'm…"

"So help me if you say careful…" Mag muttered. He stepped close to Brand, wrapping his arms around him tightly, ignoring the sharp twinges where his chest met Brand's, but not the erotic flames that spread through him when their cocks rubbed together. "Kiss me, then fuck… no, make love to me."

Brand did both, quite expertly, with Mag's willing

participation.

* * * *

"What comes next?" Mag asked, turning to look at Brand.

Brand grinned. "I don't think we've got the energy for anything more right now."

Lifting his head off Brand's shoulder, Mag moved to lean on one elbow, shaking his head. "That's not what I meant, although give it an hour, and I'm sure we will."

"Ever the optimist, even in your condition." Brand traced a finger lightly over the bruise on Mag's cheek. "Lovely shade of yuck yellow/purple."

"You're avoiding the question," Mag replied a bit querulously.

"Probably because I don't know the answer. We go on the way we have been—school, you working, me getting a job finally. That's one option."

"With you still spending at least some time out at night, hunting?"

Brand nodded. "It *is* what I do."

"I know. I suppose it won't be much different than searching for Fedor."

"Oh it will, because it won't be personal."

"Do you"—Mag tilted his head questioningly—"kill every vampire you run into?"

"No. If they're behaving then it's live and let live. If they're attacking someone rather than feeding carefully and wiping away the memory, then they're fair game."

"Are there a lot like that?"

Brand smiled slightly. "The city isn't overrun with them. On the other hand, they are out there. Unfortunately it's usually either young ones who haven't learned self-control or older ones who've gone rogue."

"I thought Antton and the Enforcers took care of the rogues."

"Apparently they do, when they're truly vicious and a threat to our existence. You can only put so many deaths down to feral dogs before people start to panic."

"Do you have to kill the young ones? Can't you, I don't know, talk to them or something?"

"I try, sometimes. It's not in my job description so to speak but still, yeah, sometimes I do."

Mag sat up, looking down at Brand. "You should join Antton and his friends."

Brand chuckled. "Funny you should say that. That was the second option. As Randulf mentioned, I might make a good Enforcer, with some training. But"—he took Mag's hands in his—"it's a decision we both have to make."

"Do you want to?"

Brand frowned. "Maybe. With the new abilities I have, I could be useful. Antton said that I'm a force to be reckoned with now."

Mag nodded. "It makes sense, I think. Especially when you learn all there is to know about what a werewolf can do."

Sitting up now, Brand said, "Okay, I'm puzzled. Why are you agreeing with this? Because I think you are. I figured you'd be dead set against it."

"In case you've forgotten, I saw what Fedor and his minions were capable of. It's frightening to think what they could, and probably would, have done given the chance to… to normal people, I guess you could say. Hell, maybe some of the others who were helping him had already. I suspect even Fedor did before he got fixated about finding a dhampir he could turn into a creature that could hunt and kill werewolves the way they can vampires."

"All right, I guess I understand. Still…" Brand studied him thoughtfully. "You really would be okay with my becoming an Enforcer?"

"Honest truth, I'm scared shitless about the idea because it's the kind of job that could get you killed. Still, I suppose it's sort of like being a cop or in the military. You take calculated risks based on what you know and how you've been trained and in The End, you stop someone who needs to be stopped."

Brand embraced Mag, holding him against his chest, whispering, "Exactly. I knew you'd understand."

"So you're going to do it?" Mag asked quietly.

"I guess I am. I wasn't certain at first. It had to be all right with you because… well, it just did." He kissed Mag's temple. "We've been through so much together, in such a short time. At first it was"—he paused—"it was just us being partners and friends I guess. Then, in the last few days, I realized you mean more to me than that. I told you, but…"

"You weren't certain I believed it."

"Yes. I knew how you felt about me. It took me a while to realize I feel the same. If you'd… if it wasn't okay with you then I wouldn't do it—join the Enforcers, if I'm asked."

"It's what you *have* to do, for your sake. For the sake of the people you'll save. And doesn't that sound all high and mighty." Mag laughed softly. "Still, it's the truth. Just don't leave me out of it. I may not be, well, Enforcer material, but when you need my help…" He turned to look at Brand. "If you do…"

"When I do, even if it's just you telling me I made the right choice, I know you'll be there for me."

"Always."

* * * *

Later that morning, once Brand and Mag were dressed and had eaten, Brand called Antton, asking if he and Mag could come over. Antton agreed, saying that since they didn't have a car, he'd pick them up. However, when the SUV showed up at their front door, it was Randulf, not Antton, in the driver's seat.

Brand cocked an eyebrow as he slid into the passenger seat. "I figured you'd be long gone, back to wherever you live."

Randulf smiled ruefully. "Most of the time I 'live' wherever I'm needed at the moment."

"You don't have a home?" Mag asked in surprise, after he got into the back seat.

"Define 'home'. I have a place where I keep most of my junk, but that's about all it is." He chuckled. "A storage bin that looks like a house."

Mag frowned. "Is it like that for all the Enforcers?"

"You've seen Antton's place, so what do you think?"

"Honestly, that you're even more homeless than I used to be, and that's saying something."

"Not homeless. Just a… a nomad. And how the hell did we get on this line of conversation?" Randulf turned his attention to driving while asking Brand, "Have you come to a decision?"

"Since I haven't been asked yet…"

"Okay. If Antton or the council asks, will you say yes?"

"Yes. I have a question though. Is Antton the right-hand man for the council, so to speak?"

"There are several high-ranking Enforcers, one for each geographical area. He's one of them and supervises the western half of the country."

"So I'd be working for him?"

"To start with. Then when he's sure you can handle it, you'd be available for anyone who needs you."

"Just like you and the others are," Mag put in.

"Yes. Ulrik's based out of Sweden. Dante's Italian—big surprise—and Vesper's a Londoner born and bred, so to speak."

"I thought he was British from his accent, as slight as it is."

Randulf grinned. "Don't tell him he has one. He thinks of himself as a man of the world and thus… is 'accentless' a word?"

"Works for me," Brand said.

"So anyway, back to the original question—yes, you'd be working under Antton."

Brand and Mag instantly broke into gales of laughter, causing Randulf to look at them in bewilderment. Then, apparently, he realized what he'd said and shook his head.

"That is not what I meant and you know it. Believe me, he's as straight as they come."

Brand asked, once he'd stopped laughing, "Are most Enforcers straight?"

Randulf nodded. "Most, but not all. But then that's true in any organization. If you're asking will you be ostracized by some of them the answer is, probably not. Still, when it comes down to it, we're all human, well human in our reactions to things, so who knows what you could run into? So far, I haven't had any problems and I suspect you won't either."

"Whoa. You?"

"Yes, me." Randulf chuckled. "As they say, don't judge a book by its cover. I wouldn't have figured either of you were just by looking at you. Ulrik sort of guessed because he'd seen you together often enough on the streets. But as he said, homeless kids tend to find someone else they feel safe with as a way of keeping from becoming targets of punks looking to cause trouble."

"Not always," Mag replied. "There are loners out there who don't trust anyone, and with good reason. But I guess that's neither here nor there at the moment."

"Nope," Randulf agreed, as he made a right-turn onto Antton's street. "In a minute we'll have… well, not more important things perhaps, but other things to talk about."

* * * *

"Are you certain?" Antton asked a few minutes later. "Because it will impact not just you, Brand, but Mag as well."

Brand looked at Mag and they both nodded. "We talked about it, in case you really did want me to become an Enforcer. He knows it's important, and that it's dangerous." Brand took Mag's hand, smiling softly. "As he put it—well, implied at least—for him it would be like being the partner of a cop or someone in the military. He'd be waiting at home, praying I came back alive and in one piece."

"Then what you two have is now a permanent arrangement?"

Again Brand smiled at Mag before replying. "Yes, it is as far as I'm concerned."

"It is," Mag said adamantly.

Antton tapped his lip. "All right then, I'll let the council know. Pending their approval, and I'm sure that won't be a problem, I'm putting you in Randulf's capable hands for training." He paused, glancing at Randulf. "Take Mag with you when you work with Brand. Under the circumstances, it won't hurt for him to know what's what and how to take care of himself."

"Why?" Brand asked before he understood. "He could become a target, the way he was with Fedor."

"Exactly. Although the situation would be different because it wouldn't be part of a plan."

"I'm not sure I like that idea." Brand looked worriedly at Mag.

"Then back out now," Antton replied with some asperity.

"He's not backing out," Mag pronounced, sending an irate glance Brand's way. "I might be just a human, but if I know what to expect, I think I can take care of myself if I have to. Hell, Brand, I lived on the streets and survived just fine. It's not like I'm some preppy rich kid."

Brand nodded, adding, "Now, but…"

"You were?" Randulf asked, seeming surprised.

"Way back when I guess you would have called me that. Then things went bad between me and my family and I got out of there fast. I decided"—Mag glared angrily down at his hands—"a conversion camp was not going to be in my future. And that"—he looked at the men—"is all I'm going to say about that. It's in the past and it's staying locked up there."

"Understood," Antton said. "We all have histories we do that with." He stood, telling them, "Now, as I said, I have to tell the council we have a new member. I suggest, Randulf, you start working with Brand as soon as possible. There are rumors that Alanna Jans is heading this way."

"Only rumors?" Randulf asked, frowning deeply.

"So far, yes. Obviously, we're trying to determine if there's any truth behind them."

"If she is, this could become very interesting, to put it mildly."

"Who is Alanna Jans?" Brand asked.

"I'll let Randulf explain," Antton said before leaving the room.

Randulf paced as he began talking. "Alanna is a very vicious, rogue werewolf. Once, many years ago, she was one of the sweetest, most docile female werewolves I've ever known. Then she made the mistake of falling head-over-heels in love with a human. No insult intended, Mag."

Mag nodded. "None taken."

"Unfortunately, this man was a bastard, to put it mildly. He used her, abused her, and then when he was finished, he turned her over to a friend of his as if she was just a piece of chattel."

"If she was a werewolf, why didn't she rebel and... and do something to him?" Brand asked. "Surely she was strong enough to have stopped what he did to her, at least on a physical level."

"That would have given away what she is and at that point, she wasn't willing to—for everyone's sake. Besides, as I said, she loved him and never quite came to grips with the fact he was only using her to satisfy his own insane needs. Needless to say, when he tried to dispose of her by giving her to his friend, she finally got the message. By then, she was broken mentally and emotionally. Something snapped and in The End she killed both of them, quite horribly. Since then, she has gone on a rampage, seducing and then killing human males indiscriminately. Before you ask why she hasn't been caught, she learned a trick or two along the way on how to stay beneath our radar until it was too late."

"The female of the species," Mag muttered.

"In this case, that quotation holds very true," Randulf agreed.

Brand asked, "If she's so good at hiding, how are we going to catch her?"

"Presuming she does end up in this territory, I'm sure Antton will come up with something. He's very good at that. If he wasn't, he wouldn't be in charge."

"Couldn't the same be said for any of the top Enforcers?"

Randulf nodded. "It could, but he's exceptional." He stopped pacing, leaning his elbow on the fireplace mantle. "Enough of that for now, Brand. I have to teach you how to use your werewolf abilities beyond shifting and returning fully clothed, which I know you've already mastered. Are you free for the rest of the day?"

"Until class, yes. Mag should go to work, though, before his boss thinks he's taken a permanent leave of absence."

Mag chuckled. "He probably already thinks that, so if you don't mind, Randulf, can you drop me off there? It's not far from our place."

"You could quit, you know," Brand said. "I wasn't kidding

when I told you I've got some money and now that you know why..."

"I think we still have to work. Otherwise, it would be hard to explain how we survive."

"Once the council gives their approval, Brand will go onto the payroll as a member of 'Ochoa Protection Services'," Randulf told them. He chuckled. "It pays very well."

"You're serious? There's a company for what we do?"

"Of course," Antton said, coming back into the room. "Mine. We need a front and what better one than a security company?"

"Makes sense to me." Brand grinned. "Do I get a badge and a gun?"

"Please say 'no' on the gun. He's dangerous enough as he is," Mag grumbled.

Antton chuckled. "The badge, yes. As for a weapon, Brand, you already have one that's much more effective against the sort of people you'll be going after."

Brand sighed. "True, but a gun..."

"Would be fairly useless unless you caught a werewolf in their human form. And before you ask, the council welcomes you to the Enforcers."

"Woot!" Brand gave a fist pump, grinning when Mag hugged him tightly and said, "Congratulations... I think."

"Yes, they are in order," Randulf said before turning to Antton. "We should set them up in a new house. One that's well protected, for both their sakes."

"Consider it done. I'll call you when I know where but for now. I think you should take them off somewhere safe and start Brand's lessons."

"I have to get to work," Mag pointed out.

"Sorry to have pulled rank on you, which I did, Mag. You are now officially employed by my firm as well, just as Brand is, and I'm giving you a couple of days before you need to report for duty."

"Now just a damned minute here! Don't I get a say in this?" Mag asked tightly. "I liked what I did, as menial as it was."

"You can say thank you," Antton replied, looking at Mag with a bit of amusement. "It's a good job, it pays well, and gives you a reason to be with Brand when necessary."

"Yeah, like I can fight vampires and werewolves." Mag touched his bruised cheek. "You can see how well I do that."

"You did exactly what you were supposed to, young man, and when you've been trained in self-defense, you'll be prepared to do more."

"I thought this was going to be Brand's training, not mine. I'm not one of you."

"You're part of Brand's life. A very important part, if I'm not mistaken. So as I told you earlier, it behooves both of you if you're able to defend yourself, Mag. I'll set it up with one of my people to work with you."

Mag nodded. "I see your point, but I still don't like that you went behind my back about my job."

Antton shrugged. "Get used to it. I run this area with a tight hand. I expect all of my people to do as they're told and that includes you."

Brand put one hand on Mag's shoulder. "I'll quit if this makes you so unhappy," he told him softly.

Mag looked at him for a long moment then shook his head. "They need you. I'll get over it. I mean his highhanded treatment of me. But so help me"—he glared at Antton—"if we don't like the house you get us, you'll keep looking until you find one that we do."

Antton laughed. "Deal. Now out of here, all of you. I have work to do."

Chapter Nine

"Where are we going?" Brand asked, watching the mountains get closer as they drove northwest of the city.

"To a piece of land the council owns where we're safe to be what we are," Randulf replied, turning off the highway at that point onto a two-lane road that began to climb sharply into the foothills.

Fifteen minutes later he made another turn onto a dirt road. Ahead of them, Brand could see a wooden gate with a 'No Trespassing' sign on it. Leading off from it in both directions was a low, rusty-looking wire fence. "Does that really keep hunters and what-have-you out?" he asked.

"More like it lets any of us who are here know if someone decides to come exploring. Antton's security company isn't just for show. This area is well monitored."

"Okay. Do alarms go off if someone tries to climb the fence?"

"Let me show you," Randulf said, parking the car by the gate. He got out and went over to the fence, pressing down on the top wire.

"Holy hell," Brand exclaimed, covering his ears.

Looking puzzled, because he obviously hadn't heard anything, Mag stared at Brand. "What?"

A moment later Brand uncovered his ears, just as Randulf returned to the car after opening the gate. "That's something like a dog whistle?" Brand asked him.

"Yep. An ultra-high frequency alarm. A human"—Randulf glanced at Mag—"won't hear it, but we can and then take the necessary steps not to be seen."

Mag frowned. "But Brand's in his human form."

"He still has the hearing sensitivity of a werewolf, just as he has the strength and speed of one, although it's less as a human than when he's shifted."

Grinning at Brand, Mag said, "So I can pick up a dog whistle and train you to do my bidding."

Brand snorted. "I think you already have."

"As if."

While they bantered, Randulf drove the car past the gate and deep in to the forested area beyond it, following a trail so narrow Brand wondered at times if the SUV would be able to navigate it. Eventually they came to a small clearing. Randulf parked at The End of the trail, announcing—to neither of the younger men's surprise—that they had arrived.

"We'll start by shifting," Randulf told Brand. "Mag, I'll let you listen in once we have."

"You can do that?"

"No I just said it to tease you," Randulf replied with a laugh. "Yes. I can do it, and perhaps when we've finished. Brand will be able to as well."

Mag grinned momentarily, getting a wicked smirk in return from Randulf, who told him, "When his mouth is busy with other things, it does come in handy."

Brand just shook his head, saying, "You have a one-track mind sometimes, Mag."

Mag winked at him before asking Randulf, "If you can let me listen in does that mean you're reading my mind? I'm not certain I like that idea."

"No. I'm using mind-speak, which is different. I *could* pick up on what you're thinking but that would be an invasion of privacy, unless you gave me permission."

"If you can, then any werewolf could and they might not be so polite as to ask first."

"Like me, they would have to be an old and powerful alpha to do that. Of all of us that you've met so far, Antton's the only other one who can and he's honorable enough not to unless it's an emergency."

* * * *

"That's a relief." Feeling better now about that at least, Mag leaned back against the SUV, watching when Brand and Randulf shifted. "You're very handsome," he said softly, studying Brand. Brand dipped his head in response as if saying 'Thank you'.

"First," Mag heard Randulf say, *"we'll test your senses."* He lifted

his massive head, scenting the air. *"There's a squirrel close by. Tell me where."* Mag didn't hear Brand's response but he must have found it because Randulf nodded. *"Now, find the fox."* There was a brief pause. *"You're not going to if you don't hunt for it. It's not standing around watching us,"* Randulf said somewhat dryly.

As Mag watched, Brand moved across the clearing into the trees after lifting his head to sniff, his ears cocked forward. A few minutes later, Randulf said, *"Very good. Now follow the deer and try not to let it know you're there."*

"He's not going to kill it is he?" Mag asked, suddenly understanding that in his wolf form Brand was a real predator who, if left on his own, might do just that and dine on the carcass.

There was a chuckle then Randulf said, *"Mag would prefer you not have the deer for supper."* A second later he told Mag, *"He went 'yuck', so I suspect the deer is safe enough."*

That part of the training continued for a while longer as Randulf determined just how strong Brand's senses were as a wolf. Then he had Brand return and they both shifted.

"You did well," Randulf complimented Brand. "Most newly created werewolves don't have nearly the sense of smell and hearing you already do. Now, in your human form, can you point out where the family of chipmunks is hiding?"

Brand tilted his head and actually sniffed the air the way he had in his wolf form. "Off to the right, about two hundred yards from here, I think. I'm not certain about the distance."

"Close enough—and impressive."

"Maybe my dhampir half is enhancing the werewolf in me?"

"That would be my guess," Randulf agreed. "Brand, wait here a minute, please. Mag, come with me." Randulf led Mag over to the SUV, telling him, "I'm shielding my words from him. I want you to tell him something you did while he was missing. Something you haven't told him. But, lie about one part of it."

"I… okay." Mag thought for a moment and nodded. When they got back to where Brand was waiting, Randulf told them to stand with their backs to each other. They did, although Brand seemed reluctant to a first, until Randulf told him it was another test. Mag began telling Brand about the night he had had to fend off a man who was quite certain, because Mag was in an alley well after midnight, that he was either selling drugs or himself to make some money.

Brand listened, obviously not happy with the story at first. At The End, he shook his head. "None of what you said happened after the man approached you is true. I don't know what he did want, but it wasn't what you're saying."

"It was so," Mag protested vehemently.

"You're lying again, I can tell." He turned to look at Randulf. "How?"

"It's one of the things most of us can do—with humans. When you've been a werewolf for a while, you'll also be able to do it with us if the lie is blatant enough."

"Oh boy," Mag muttered, "there goes any chance of my surprising you on your birthday, Brand."

Brand laughed, then sobered. "It also means I know you're telling the truth when you say you care about me."

"You doubted it?" Mag replied a bit petulantly.

"Not at all, but still, now I know for damned sure it's the truth, if that makes sense."

"I guess it does," Mag said, but he didn't feel too happy about the fact that he couldn't say the same about Brand. *Not that I doubt him, but….*

"He cares very deeply for you," Randulf told Mag. *"Trust me on that. Oh, don't worry, I wasn't reading your mind. I told you I wouldn't. You have a very expressive face."*

Mag nodded then, impulsively, he moved to Brand and kissed him. Brand looked surprised but seemed to have no problems returning the kiss.

"Now that that's settled, can we continue?" Randulf asked.

For the next hour, Randulf tested Brand's strength, speed, and agility in both his human and werewolf forms. At times he told him how he could improve one or the other when he was a wolf and taught him some tricks for moving more stealthily. Finally, he deemed it time to stop and head back to the city.

"Did I pass?" Brand asked, obviously worried.

"With flying colors, but then I was certain you would."

"You're very impressive, as far as I'm concerned," Mag added. "Scary in what you can do, but impressive."

"Scary is good," Randulf told them both. "However, Brand, you are to keep your abilities hidden unless you have to use them. Never tip off the enemy what you're capable of. That means no showing off in your human form either."

"I understand, and I won't. Well, maybe other than mind-speaking to Mag while I'm doing other things." He grinned and winked.

"When you learn how," Mag pointed out.

"Like now?"

"Oh hell."

Brand and Randulf laughed at Mag's consternation.

"Will I be able to mind-speak to him?" Mag asked. "It's not fair if it's not a two-way street."

"Doubtful, but who knows. Stranger things have happened when a human and a werewolf care deeply for each other. Time will tell, I guess."

* * * *

It was late when they returned to the city, so Randulf dropped Brand and Mag off at home. They changed clothes, gathered up their books, and headed to class. As they walked, Mag asked, "What's it like, being able to run free the way you did this afternoon?"

"Exhilarating, wild, humbling."

"Humbling?"

Brand nodded. "It made me realize how much we humans could learn from those we consider less than ourselves about living free and untrammeled by"—he flung his arm out to encompass the buildings, the street, the people—"all this. Look at them. So many frowns or worried expressions. So much 'Am I good enough?' written on their faces. Where's the joy that they're alive?"

"I suppose," Mag replied pensively, "it gets beaten out of people when they try to be what others expect of them instead of being who they really are—who they wanted to be when they were young enough they didn't know the expectations of others would force them into molds they didn't want." He smiled a bit. "Aren't we waxing philosophical all of a sudden?"

"I suppose we are." Brand stopped, looking at Mag. "Are *you* happy?"

Mag nodded slowly. "Overall… I think so. Things have changed, radically, you most of all. But yes, I'm happy. I have a life I like, even though it's a strange one now. I have… you. With all that you've become, I still wouldn't give up you or our life together." Putting his arm around Brand's shoulders, he asked the same question. "Are *you* happy?"

"Yes. Unequivocally, yes." He grinned at Mag. "Why, you ask? Because I have someone who accepts me for what I am." Whispering, he added, "Fur and all."

Mag laughed. "That was definitely unexpected. I thought, when I first fell for you, that I'd met someone with the same… aspirations. To keep it together and survive the best we could, and maybe someday make something of ourselves if we got the chance."

"I think we both still have that desire. If we didn't, we wouldn't be here." Brand pointed to the entrance to the school a few yards away. "We did survive the streets and a lot more. And now"—he chuckled—"we have to survive tonight's classes."

"Had to say that, didn't you?" Mag grumbled. "Okay, I'll see you when we're through or…?"

"No hunting tonight," Brand said quietly. "Just you, me, and a nice warm bed."

"After we've studied."

"Killjoy," Brand muttered. Then he kissed Mag quickly and they both headed into the building.

Chapter Ten

"Not bad," Brand said a couple of days later after Antton had shown him and Mag around their new home. "But it's a bit far from school. Is there a bus line close by?"

"Better than that," Antton replied. He dug into his pocket then tossed Brand a set of keys. "For the house and the car in the garage."

"You're kidding. A car?"

"Comes as part of the job. Your new jobs. It belongs to the company, but you two can use it until you can afford your own."

Brand glanced at Mag, who looked as surprised as he felt. "Do you know how to drive?"

"Of course. I even have a license. Don't you?"

Brand waggled his hands. "Sort of, but it's been forever since I've driven and I *don't* have a license. So I guess you're the designated chauffeur." Returning his attention to Antton, he thanked him, as did Mag. "Now all we have to do is move our stuff over here."

Mag laughed ruefully. "That'll take three boxes at most."

"Whatever it takes, do it now," Antton practically ordered. "I expect you at my place at noon. We have plans to make to catch Alanna Jans."

"Then she *is* headed here," Brand said.

Antton nodded. "She's here already."

"Then we'd better get moving."

With a wry smile, Antton told him, "Isn't that what I just said?"

* * * *

The move was accomplished quickly. As Mag had pointed out, they didn't have much. Clothes and a few personal items were about the extent of it.

"This is sort of sad," Mag said as they put the last of what turned out to be four boxes plus their backpacks into the car.

"It'll get better now," Brand told him with a hug. "Besides, when it comes right down to it, how much stuff do we need?"

"True enough," Mag agreed.

The pair unpacked at their new home in record time. They hung their clothes in the closet or stashed them in the dresser in the larger of the two bedrooms. Everything they used for school they put into the room on the ground floor that held a desk, several bookshelves, and two comfortable armchairs. The living room was furnished with a sofa, a matching recliner, and a fairly large television set, as well as bookcases.

"I guess he expects us to do a lot of reading," Brand commented.

Mag chuckled. "In all our spare time, that at the moment we don't have since he wants us at his place in twenty minutes."

They arrived at Antton's just after noon. He greeted them at the door, ushering them into his living room. Randulf was there, seated on the sofa, as was Ulrik, who stood looking out the window facing the mountains.

"I feel like the witches in Macbeth," Mag muttered. "All 'when shall we three meet againish'."

"Except there's five of us," Brand pointed out.

"Six actually," Antton said.

Brand smirked. "You're using ghosts now?"

"It should be so easy," Randulf grumbled. "You haven't met Llewellyn yet or you'd know why I said that."

"Another werewolf?" Mag asked.

Randulf just nodded, looking none too happy.

"A very late werewolf," Ulrik said sourly, turning to look at the clock on the desk.

Mag frowned. "If none of you like him, which apparently you don't, why is he going to be involved?"

"Because," Antton replied, "he has a very unique ability. He can pass as a pure human to anyone who can sense werewolves. That includes Alanna."

"Ah. So he's going to be the bait in the trap."

"Precisely. Presuming I don't kill him first. That man is never on time." Antton drummed his fingers impatiently on his thigh.

"Oh my, don't tell me I'm late again." A tall, extremely handsome man with long flowing red hair appeared suddenly in the middle of the living room. "My apologies my friends." His red-flaked amber eyes glittered with amusement.

Randulf snorted exasperatedly. "You'd be late to your own funeral."

Ignoring him, the man looked at Mag and Brand. "Newcomers, and one's a human. I am, as you may have surmised, Llewellyn, although most people call me Lew."

"Is there anything wrong with being human?" Mag asked with some sharpness.

"Of course not. Some of my best friends are." Lew looked Mag over with interest. "And I think you and I could be *quite* good friends."

"Sorry, but I'm taken," Mag replied.

"And?"

"And *he* doesn't play around," Randulf said, scowling.

"Oh my, Randy, do you mean you finally found someone?" The smirk on Lew's lips was decidedly mischievous.

"Don't call me Randy," Randulf snarled. "Not that it's any of your business, but Mag is not mine, he's Brand's."

"Which has to be you," Lew said, looking at Brand as if he was some sort of strange creature he'd never run into before. "Werewolf and…?"

"Human *and* vampire," Brand told him.

"Meaning a dhampir. I don't remember ever meeting one before. How on earth did you manage to be a werewolf too? Just mixing the two bloods should have killed you."

Brand grinned impishly. "I was lucky?"

Lew glowered for a moment then laughed. "I think I'm going to like you."

Mag saw the scowl that had been on Randulf's face since Lew had arrived deepen. *There must have been something between them once. Something that ended badly.* Not that he'd ask, since it was none of his concern.

"Gentlemen," Antton said firmly, "shall we get down to business?"

Everyone nodded, finding places to settle. Brand and Mag ended up on the sofa with Randulf, Ulrik sat on the bench of the bay window, and Lew claimed one of the armchairs.

"Alanna has made her presence here known," Antton told them. "As you may have heard on the news, a man's body was found by a dumpster behind a nightclub on the north side of the city. Since the club is across the street from a large open space area, the police are theorizing a pack of feral dogs may have been responsible for his death."

Mag shuddered, envisioning what the corpse must have looked like.

"And so it begins," Ulrik growled.

"That means I get to start haunting clubs and bars," Lew said. "The question is, which ones?"

"Not the kind you *usually* go to," Mag heard Randulf mutter.

Obviously overhearing him, Lew just grinned momentarily before asking, "What sort of club was it? That might help narrow the field."

"One of the more popular ones, with a live band for dancing. It's the type she usually uses," Antton replied.

"Get me a list."

"You'll have it by the time we're finished here," Ulrik replied tightly.

Oh boy, this is going to be an interesting… case, for lack of a better word. Mag glanced at Brand and from the dubious expression on his face, he seemed to feel the same way.

"You'll need backup," Antton said.

Lew smirked. "Not really, but if you're going to insist on it I'll take Mag. He's human, so I suspect that's why he's in on this."

"He's here because I am," Brand told him.

"You two are joined at the hip? And as far as that goes, why the hell are any of you here? Antton and I could have come up with a plan without the rest of you."

"Do you have any idea what you're going up against?" Randulf asked coldly.

"A female werewolf with a hard-on for human males. She should be easy enough to stop."

"Oh really?" Randulf sneered. "So you would have caught her when she was in New York, or London, or any of the other places she's struck."

"If I'd been assigned to do that, yes."

Randulf leaned back with obviously feigned casualness. "Then why weren't you?"

"The other head Enforcers weren't as smart as Antton. He asked for me. They didn't."

"With good reason. You're a show-off, a grandstander. You put anyone you're teamed with in danger—or worse."

"You survived," Lew spat out.

"No thanks to you."

"Enough," Antton roared, glaring at them. "Lew, you'll work with whoever I decide and it will *not* be Mag. He's not trained yet."

"I can take care of myself," Mag muttered. "I did on the streets."

"That's entirely different, I think," Brand told him.

"Yeah, I guess, but still…"

"Good Lord, you all are worse than a room full of kindergarteners." Antton waited until he had their attention again. "I'm putting both Ulrik and Randulf with you, Lew. Alanna is a force to be reckoned with. If you'd have done your homework, you'd know that. She's a female alpha and insane."

"Aren't 'female' and 'insane' synonyms?" Lew asked with a straight face.

At the same time, Mag leaned in to ask Brand, "In that case, why *are* we here?"

Ignoring Lew's comment, Antton turned his attention on Mag. "You two need to see how we do things. Even if"—he glanced sourly at Lew and the others—"they don't always run as smoothly as they did when we were planning Fedor's demise."

Brand nodded. "If I can help in any way…"

"We'll see. First we have to come up with something more

than just Lew hitting up clubs night after night and hoping he connects with Alanna before she kills again."

"With three of us—four if we use Brand—we could cover the ground much faster. If one of us spots her, we let Lew know," Ulrik suggested.

"And if she spots you, she'll flip you the bird and move on. Don't forget, she's powerful in her own right."

"What does she look like?" Brand asked.

"Average height. Five-six or so. We have a few pictures of her we've managed to get since she went rogue, all from security cameras at clubs. Randulf has seen them and he says her face hasn't changed since he knew her."

"Except to get harder," Randulf said. "Physically, she's much thinner and sexier. The last time I saw her in person, she was cute but decidedly not svelte and not voluptuously sexy either. She was"—he spread his hands—"as un-PC as it is to say, pleasingly plump and she radiated child-like innocence."

"Hair, eyes?" Brand asked.

"Blonde hair, usually straight and shoulder length," Antton replied. "Blue eyes, bordering on lavender. Her nose is… Hell, why am I describing her?" He went over to his desk, taking out a file. Extracting several pictures of Alanna he passed them around.

Lew whistled in appreciation. "Even as bad as these are, she still comes off as a real looker. Yep, she can try to seduce me anytime."

Maybe I was wrong. Maybe there wasn't anything between him and Randulf except a job gone bad. Mag glanced at Randulf. *Nope. If he looked any angrier at Lew's words, he'd be off the sofa attacking him. Or walking out, telling us he wasn't going to be involved as long a Lew is.*

"He's bi, and as Vesper would put it, a right bastard." Randulf's words echoed tightly in Mag's mind. *"So get that questioning look off your face, and the compassion as well. I don't need it or want it."* All the time he was mind-speaking to Mag, Randulf was glowering down at his tightly fisted hands.

"That *is* the idea behind what we're planning," Antton said in reply to Lew's comment. "Let her come on to you, or you to her, then get her somewhere safe so we can deal with her without endangering anyone else."

"No problem." Lew smirked. "I'm more than capable of getting her attention and taking it from there."

"Conceited ass," Brand muttered under his breath.

"It's not conceit," Lew responded, "if you're aware of your abilities and can carry through on them, which I do. Ask Randulf. He knows."

"What I know is that you're going to go down in a ball of flames if you come on to her flashing that kind of attitude," Randulf replied caustically. "She is not stupid. She'll pick up on the fact it's a trap before you can get past the 'Your eyes are like the sunset… beautiful, inspiring…'"

Lew glared at him. "I'd never use a cheesy line like that and you know it."

Randulf just cocked an eyebrow contemptuously before going back to studying his clenched hands.

Brand shook his head. "If those two are going to spend all their time fighting, why are you teaming them up together?" he asked Antton. When Antton gave him a scathing look, Brand seemed to shrink down into the sofa, whispering, "Sorry."

Ulrik, who had been fairly quiet up until then, said, "It's a legitimate question."

"And you know the answer," Antton snapped out. "Randulf's one of the best back-up men we have."

"You and I are almost as good and *we* don't really want to kill Lew if we can help it," Ulrik replied.

Randulf looked up. "I don't want to kill him. If I did, he'd be dead. I'm quite capable of watching his back in order to stop Alanna once he makes contact with her."

From the sour look on his face, it seemed as if Lew was going to say something before thinking better of it. Instead, he just nodded. "He *is* good at that."

"As much as you hate to admit it," Randulf retorted.

"Not at all. When it comes down to doing the job, you're fantastic. Despite what Ulrik said—and he's right, he and Antton are good—I'd rather have you as my backup."

Mag turned to Randulf. "If she knows you, how can you be there too? Besides which, you're a werewolf so she'd sense you."

"Remember I told you I can physically change my appearance? Obviously I'd do that if necessary. As for the other, true she would sense what I am, so I won't be 'with' Lew—except mentally—until the time is right. Despite what he may think"—Randulf sent a scathing look at Lew—"it will probably take both of us to control her and get her away from whatever club he finds her in."

Lew frowned. "You really think she's strong enough that I couldn't overpower her on my own?"

"Not without possible collateral damage to anyone in the vicinity," Antton said. "She truly has no morals now. She's an alpha so, as you're well aware, even in her human form she has all the alpha attributes. She was almost captured in New York by Theodule. He felt the same way you do, that he could handle her on his own. Not only did she kill him, she took out three humans as well before setting fire to the house he'd lured her to. At least," Antton added wryly, "she had sense enough to do that to cover her tracks. But it happened two years ago. Who knows if she cares anymore that people might learn of our existence?"

"So that's what happened to him." Lew shook his head. "He was a good man. I thought he'd retired, since I haven't heard anything about him recently."

Mag was surprised that Lew actually looked upset. *Not that I should be, I suppose. He has to have more going on than just an inflated sense of his own self-worth or he wouldn't be an Enforcer in the first place.*

"How often does she strike?" Brand asked.

"There doesn't seem to be a pattern," Antton told him. "In Rio, it was almost nightly for two weeks before she moved on. In Exeter, she killed twice in the space of a month. But"—he paused for emphasis—"she always shows up not too long after there's been a natural disaster. One could presume her thinking is that dogs who lose their homes because of that form into feral packs, thus giving her a cover for her own activities."

Brand nodded. "Here, it was the rainstorms just north of us that caused such devastation."

"Yes. As I said earlier, the club where the body was found is on the north side of the city."

"At least that should narrow our search," Randulf stated.

"Hopefully. Ulrik, see if the list of clubs has arrived."

Ulrik went to the computer, opening his email to check. "It has." He printed it out then handed it to Antton.

"This city has too damned many clubs, but at least there are only fifteen in the northern suburbs. It could be worse, I suppose," Antton muttered after reading through the list.

"Can you narrow it down to those close to open space?" Brand asked. "The way we did when we were looking for Fedor's house?"

"Excellent idea." Antton sat down at the computer, logging into a map site. "Two are relatively close to the Standley Lake, and three are within walking distance of open space tracts."

"Five clubs, five of us, how fortuitous. We'll start with them," Lew said, all business now. "I suggest we each take one and stick with it. That way we'll know the clientele and it will be easier to spot her when she shows up… if she does. We give it"—he glanced at Antton—"a week? And then widen the field if none of us finds her?"

Antton nodded. "That should work. With the exception of you, Lew, *we'll* have to keep very low profiles so she doesn't sense we're there."

Mag frowned in thought. "Why go into the clubs where she could be aware you're there? Just stake them out then let Lew know if she shows up."

"He has a point," Randulf said. "For Lew it's no problem to go in, but… yes, that would work better." He smiled at Mag. "I have a feeling you're a good strategist and since you're new to this, you can see things we don't because you're not set in your ways the way we are."

Mag beamed at his praise, murmuring, "Maybe."

"Definitely," Brand told him, giving him a hug.

"All right, we'll go with that," Antton said. He read through the list, assigning a club to each of the werewolves, including Brand. "We'll start this evening."

* * * *

Randulf barely waited for the meeting to be over before stalking out of Antton's house. He was almost to his truck when he heard Lew say, "Wait up a minute." He debated ignoring him.

"Don't," Lew said, moving swiftly to stand in front of Randulf. "Don't brush me off."

Staring at him with displeasure, Randulf muttered, "That's *your* trick, if I remember correctly."

Lew sighed. "Still galls you that I walked out."

"Walked? No, Lew, you ran for your life."

"Not even. I just saw the writing on the wall long before you did. It wasn't working, it never had and never would have, no matter how hard we tried. We're opposites, Randy." He grinned when Randulf scowled at him. "All right—Randulf. See, that's part of the bigger problem we had." He leaned against the fender of Randulf's Dodge Ram, stroking it. "Still hanging on to this old girl, I see."

"It runs… does what I need it to do."

"Which is what you want out of everything in your life. To conform to your specifications and damn them if they don't."

"Not true," Randulf spat out. "But I do think I rate at least a little respect when I'm in a relationship. Stepping out on me with… Fuck it, this is old history. Move it. I'm out of here."

"Not until you admit we could have made it work if you'd just been less rigid. And for your information, I wasn't stepping out on you. I told you that a hundred times. I just needed to be with someone who saw me as… as interesting in my own right."

"Someone who looked at the packaging and ignored the conceited bastard inside."

"What's wrong with having a good package? Okay, perhaps I should rephrase that, although you never seemed to mind my 'package'. Yeah, I'm good-looking, and yeah, I know it and play on it. But while we were together, which wasn't all that long in the grand scheme of things, I never bedded anyone else—male or female—unless it was…"

"The fuck you didn't!" Randulf said derisively before Lew could finish. Walking around the truck, he got in, turned it on and revved the motor. When Lew jumped back, Randulf chuckled. Not that he was happy. Far from it. But at least he figured he'd thrown a small scare into Lew. Putting the truck in gear, he made a U-turn, pulling up beside his ex-lover. "Remember, tonight you're looking for Alanna, not the first woman who's willing to spread her legs for you." With that said, he roared off down the drive to the street.

* * * *

"And fuck you too," Lew spat out angrily. He felt someone's hand on his shoulder and spun around, in the mood to deck whoever it was. Instead, he smiled slightly when he realized it was Mag.

"I'd ask if there was trouble in paradise but from what I'm getting, there never was a real paradise between the two of you," Mag said.

Lew shrugged. "For a couple of weeks, maybe a month. We're both alphas and want our own ways. Trouble is, he's more alpha than me and felt he had to be in control of every situation. And why the hell am I telling you this?"

"Maybe because I'm human and new to this whole world so, to some extent, I'm unbiased. I don't really get the total alpha thing when it comes to relationships. In other ways, sure. Antton's the head man in this area because he's got the power and the know-how. From what everyone was saying earlier, Randulf's the perfect Enforcer—warrior, I guess. He's big, he's smart, and he knows what to do to deal with whoever you all are after."

"You think I don't?"

"No clue, since I've never seen you in action. But you wouldn't be with the Enforcers if you weren't good at something."

Lew snorted out a laugh. "True. I'm not in Randulf's class as a fighter, or even Antton's or Ulrik's when it comes down to it. My skills lie elsewhere, but I can and do hold my own when I have to."

"A lover, not a fighter," Mag said, smirking.

Lew chuckled. "When needs be."

"And you played that card when you had to, while you and Randulf were together?"

"Yeah," Lew admitted. "But it was never personal, despite what he thinks. He should *know* that, damn it."

"It sounded…" Mag paused. "Maybe I shouldn't say this, but it sounded like something happened that might have gotten him killed because of you."

Lew ran a hand through his hair, staring off into the distance. "We were after a rogue. I'd convinced him I was on the same page he was—that it was time to show the world who the real top species was—and that I knew someone else who felt the same way. The idea was I would draw him to a place outside the city so the three of us could make plans. He was… interested. Both in the idea and in me personally. When we got to the house, Randulf wasn't there yet so I…" He smiled ruefully. "I kept the rogue busy."

"In your own incomparable way."

"Yeah. Randulf walked through the door at just the wrong time. Instead of taking things the way he should have, he attacked. The rogue shifted and launched an attack of his own. We're no slouches in our human form, but against an enraged werewolf who thought, quite rightly, that he'd been drawn into a trap… Well, he managed to do some real damage before Randulf could shift. We ended up killing the rogue but Randulf's wounds were serious enough to warrant his ending up in our clinic."

"Werewolves have a clinic?" Mag asked in surprise.

"Well, we can't quite go to a normal hospital, now can we?"

"True, I guess."

"Anyway, Randulf blamed me for what happened. It wasn't my fault, I was just doing what I had to until he got there, but he didn't see it that way. We were already on the verge of separating. That was the final straw as far as he was concerned. He's hated me ever since."

Mag shook his head. "I don't think he hates you. He doesn't trust you. That's obvious. But hate? No."

Lew crossed his arms, staring at Mag. "On what do you base your opinion?"

"I was watching him during the meeting. He's full of anger, but… I don't know how to put this. I think he's angry because he still cares and he doesn't want to, so he won't admit it, even to himself. If he really hated you, he'd have walked the second he found out you were going to be part of the plan. And he's willing to go along and be your backup when the time comes."

"That's part of his job."

"Nope. It's part of *someone's* job. He could have told Antton or Ulrik to do it. Or, as I said, he could have backed out in the first place and someone else would have been brought in. He doesn't want you to get hurt and it sounds as if Alanna could do a lot of damage to you once she realizes what's going on."

"Or, when the time comes, he'll stand there, watch, and let her do her worst."

"No. He's too honorable."

Lew nodded. "He is that. I'm still not buying that he doesn't hate me, but…"

"You'd like to."

"Yeah, Mag, I would."

"Then the two of you had better work on repairing what got broken."

"It won't happen because he'll never let it."

Mag snorted. "I figured you for a lot of things, based on what little I saw today, but a coward wasn't one of them. So think about it." He turned away then, saying, "Brand and I have to go home so he can get ready for tonight and I can study."

"All right." Lew smiled slightly. "Thanks for the pep talk. It won't do any good, I suspect, but thanks anyway."

* * * *

On the drive home, Mag told Brand about his conversation with Lew. When he finished, Brand smiled, patting his thigh.

"Trying to play matchmaker?"

"More like peacemaker, I think. That means I have to talk to Randulf too."

"Leave it alone. It won't do any good. Even if you tell him what you think, Randulf's not going to buy into it."

"Even if he knew how Lew feels?"

"Mag, *you* don't know how Lew feels. Not really. Sure he might have… implied he wants to try to work things out, but you saw them together this afternoon. They're like oil and water; Lew the playboy and Randulf the rigid, authoritarian figure."

"He's not, you know. Or at least he hasn't been with you. He did everything he could to teach you how to handle your new abilities and never once got angry or upset when he had to show you more than once."

Brand smiled slightly. "Or twice or four times."

"That too. The same holds true during the battle with Fedor and company. He did what needed to be done but he never ordered anyone around in the process."

"Okay, but still…" Brand shook his head. "I don't think you stand an ice cube's chance in hell of getting him to see that he really does care for Lew. He doesn't trust him—not on a personal level. And if Lew was telling the truth, Randulf went all 'alpha' on him in their relationship, which made things even worse. That won't change because it's what Randulf is, by dint of age and what he can do."

"But if I could get them to let go of their anger long enough to just talk…"

"Lots of luck. Still, maybe, when all this is over…"

"I should try."

"Yes, my peacemaker, you should try, because it will drive you crazy if you don't."

Chapter Eleven

Two nights passed with no sightings of Alanna. By night three, the tension was beginning to tell on the Enforcers. It ramped up even more when Antton received a report that the mangled body of a young male had been found in an alley several blocks from one of the clubs they were focusing on.

As they had each of the previous nights, the group met briefly once the clubs had closed to compare information. Or as Ulrik wryly put it, lack of information. They were about to disperse when Antton got the call from one of his police contacts. He was swearing when he hung up.

"She's struck again," Antton said tersely, telling them about the dead body.

"She didn't pick him up at the club I was watching," Ulrik stated adamantly.

"Or at mine," Antton said, as his was the closest one to Ulrik's.

"I thought, when she killed, she left the bodies *behind* the clubs," Brand said.

"Usually, but not always," Antton told him.

"Do they know if the victim had even been to one?" Randulf asked.

"It's too soon to tell. The body was only found an hour ago. My man will keep me updated. However, if it *was* her and not feral dogs who killed him…" He sighed angrily.

"Either way, the word will get out and people will start to panic," Lew pointed out. "Two kills in a week will be hard to keep quiet."

"Antton?" When Antton looked at him, Brand said hesitantly, "You told me when we first met that you can pick up the scent of a werewolf if they're within a mile or so of you. Couldn't you, or one of the others, visit the site of the kill and see if you can track where she went?"

Antton glanced at the others, muttering, "Is 'stupid' tattooed on my forehead? Because it should be."

Lew chuckled. "It isn't. He's right though, one of us should do that and since you're the leader."

"No," Randulf put in. "It should be you, Lew, since you can hide the fact you're a werewolf, even from us. If she did kill that man and if she can be tracked from where she left the body, there's no sense in alerting her to the fact there's another werewolf close by. She's not stupid. She has to know there are Enforcers out looking for her."

"Oh she does, and she loves being able to evade us," Antton said.

"Then I guess it's up to me," Lew said, standing. He started to say something more then paused.

Probably was going to be one of his smartass comments about how he's the best man for the job. Brand was surprised, and so was everyone else from the looks on their faces, at what Lew did say.

"I think it would be a good idea if I had some back-up. Not too close, for the very reason that you're using me to track her if I can." His glance fell on Randulf. "If you're willing, because of all of us, you have the best mind shielding abilities." Lew smiled slightly. "Sorry, Antton, but in that respect, he's even better than you."

"No argument there," Antton replied.

Randulf hesitated then nodded, saying tersely, "Let's do it."

* * * *

"This is her kill," Lew mind-spoke to Randulf.

"Is her scent strong enough that you can follow it?"

"Here, it is. Presuming she didn't do something to hide it farther away, we should be good."

"I don't recall seeing any streams in the area, although if she headed toward Standley Lake there are some there," Randulf said.

"Then let's hope she didn't." Lew glanced at him. *"Give me a good half-mile head start."*

Randulf scowled. *"I know what I'm doing."*

Lew merely nodded in reply then started walking, swiveling his head as he sniffed the air, and occasionally kneeling to get closer to the ground, where Alanna's scent was stronger.

At one point, much to Lew's surprise, Randulf chuckled. *"If anyone was watching you, they'd think you need new shoelaces that would stay tied."*

Lew knew it was just Randulf's way of trying to release some of their tension, so he laughed softly and didn't bother to reply. But somehow it made him feel better.

For the next few miles, Alanna had kept to alleys or side-streets. She seemed to be heading north, despite several turns to the right or left, as if trying to throw off anyone who may have been following her.

Lew had a sudden thought and voiced it. *"Why is she on foot instead of driving?"*

"Can you tell which form she used?"

"Yeah, her human one, since her scent isn't as strong as it would be as a wolf."

"So either she doesn't have a car or prefers the freedom of movement she has on foot."

"Or…" Lew didn't like what he'd just thought. *"She expected an Enforcer would be smart enough to do what we're doing and is leading us to who knows where. It could be to throw us off about where she really goes to ground or to lead us into a trap."*

"Both are possibilities. That means I should probably pull even farther back."

"Good idea." Lew felt the distance between them widen.

After going another mile, Lew realized something. *"She's moved into an open space area, with streams, and she's not using them to cover her tracks."*

"Of course not! If she's leading us somewhere," Randulf replied scathingly, *"she wouldn't."*

Lew sighed. The truce, if that's what it was, and he'd thought they might have been establishing one, seemed to have vanished.

* * * *

Randulf sensed when Lew's mood soured and knew it was his

fault. *I shouldn't have sounded so… critical. He's doing what he's supposed to and was only pointing out what I can't see from where I am at the moment.*

"Give me a visual, please." Seconds later, he saw what Lew was seeing and nodded. *"Do you have a feel for where she could be going?"*

"There are houses up ahead, well-spaced from what I can see. Possibly one of those."

"Shades of Fedor," Randulf grumbled. Then when Lew asked, he gave him a brief rundown about where Fedor had held Brand prisoner.

They remained silent after that while Lew continued following Alanna's trail. Randulf stayed well behind him, as he had since they'd started.

"I was wrong."

"Meaning?" Randulf asked when Lew didn't elaborate. Lew gave him a visual of where he was at the moment.

What Lew showed him was a small strip mall. Randulf presumed that during the day it probably teemed with people but now, being close to four in the morning, it was dark except for scattered streetlamps and lights over the doorways. Then Lew gave him another visual, this time from in back of a building at The End of the mall. From the sign painted on the wall beside the door, it was supposed to be a large self-storage outfit. There were cars in the lot and people coming and going through the rear door. Randulf's first thought was the place had to be housing a rave.

"She's in there?" Randulf asked.

"Her trail leads here."

"So she's going for two kills in one night. Strange."

"My thought too," Lew agreed, *"unless…"*

"Unless?"

"If she's as insane as Antton said, she could be planning to take out another human just to thumb her nose at the council and the Enforcers—leave a trail for us to follow, thinking we'd be too late to stop her. I doubt she knows Antton has a police contact who let him know the moment the last body was found."

Randulf thought about what he was saying. *"If you're right, and I think you might be, we have to stop her before she latches on to some unsuspecting male."*

"No kidding," Lew replied tightly. *"Stay where you are until I get inside and see what's what."*

"Lew," Randulf cautioned, *"be damned careful and don't try to play, you should excuse the expression, the lone wolf."*

Lew chuckled low. *"Wasn't planning on it. Believe it or not, I do know my limits."*

"I know you do. I just… Never mind. Are you going in now?"

"Yes."

* * * *

Lew was stopped at the entrance by two doormen who wouldn't allow him inside until they'd seen his ID and patted him down. With nothing to hide—no drugs, no alcohol—he allowed it and paid the cover charge.

Once inside, he saw that there were several stages scattered around the huge room, DJs on each one. As if that wasn't enough, the place was packed with young men and women dancing while talking at the top of their voices to be heard above the electronic music spewing from each of the venues.

If you can call that music. The flashing lights, the noise, assaulted his sensitive eyes and nose. *How the hell am I going to find her in this… mess? Nightclubs are a snap compared to this.*

Deftly avoiding the dancers, he moved through the crowd searching for Alanna. For all that the doormen had patted him down, he figured they must have missed a lot on some of the kids because he could smell weed and alcohol, and from the glazed looks on some of the kids' faces there were other club drugs being passed around.

"Hey, handsome."

Lew looked down at the beringed hand on his arm and then at the scantily dressed young woman it belonged to and arched an eyebrow.

"Wanna dance?" she asked.

"Sorry, I'm with someone," he replied, lifting her hand off his arm.

"Bummer." She moved away, homing in on another male who seemed to be on his own.

"Any luck?" Randulf asked.

"Not yet. This is like hunting for a needle in a damned haystack."

Lew finally made it to the relative safety of one side of the room. Looking up, he saw a narrow balcony then located the stairs to get to it. He managed to make it up there with only two more young women coming on to him in the process. One of them called him 'Daddy', which he found vaguely amusing. He might not look twenty but for sure he wasn't in the over-thirty range either. At least not visually.

Leaning on the balcony railing, Lew studied the crowd on the dance floor. He knew for a fact that Alanna wouldn't pass for a kid. Twenty-five maybe, but definitely no younger. Unfortunately, interspersed in and among all the youngsters there were a small percentage of slightly older women and men. *Reliving their college days.* He chuckled in amusement.

"Depressing, isn't it?" a dulcet-toned voice said from beside him.

"Being one of the older ones here, relatively speaking?" he replied as he turned to see who was talking to him.

Blue-lavender eyes met his amber ones, glinting with amusement. "Yep. We're close to being old codgers." Even if he hadn't seen photos of her, he would have known it was Alanna just from the eye color. She used her hip to nudge him over enough so she could join him at the railing.

"Not even close, at least in your case." He raked his gaze over her and smiled.

"You're hardly in your dotage yourself," she replied, doing the same. "The question is, why are you here if you feel out of place?"

"A dare?" He chuckled, improvising quickly. "My younger brother was telling me about a rave he went to in LA and when I let him know I'd never been to one—well, as I said, he dared me to check them out. So here I am. I must say I'm not terribly impressed."

"I only come because I find them amusing," Alanna said. "All the kids—and they are just kids—trying to act so world-wise. For instance, look at that group." She pointed and for the next few minutes, they compared notes on what they thought of the rave attendees.

Finally, apparently tired of the game, she asked, "Do you smoke?" When Lew looked at her a bit askance she laughed. "Cigarettes, not anything else, although I'm sure we could get a joint or a blunt if we had a mind to."

"I don't, but if you're having a nicotine fix, we can go outside so you can indulge yourself."

"Exactly why I asked. I'd rather not stand out there on my own. You never know what sort of creeps are hanging around."

Like you.

"Too true, I'm afraid." He nodded toward the stairs and followed her down them, admiring the sensual sway of her hips. *Too bad she's what she is. Or maybe… Maybe it's a good thing?* His thoughts instantly went to Randulf and sadness overwhelmed him. *If only things were different perhaps I could make amends. But*—he sighed deeply—*he hates me too much. He'd never believe I meant it, so it won't happen, Mag's wishes to the contrary.* He smiled morosely and continued down the stairs behind Alanna.

* * * *

Randulf didn't mean to tap into Lew's thoughts. He was just going to ask if he'd found Alanna. But before he could, he felt sadness emanating from his ex-lover. Curious, considering the situation, he delved into the reason and got the surprise of his life.

At first he was angry. *Make amends my ass. After what he did?* Still, he couldn't help the flare of hope. *It would never work though,* he told himself. *This is Lew, the perpetual playboy who thinks, and acts, as if he's the gods' gift to anyone, male or female, who crosses his path. The man who can't settle on one person for fear he'll miss out on someone else. I should know. But still…*

His thoughts were interrupted when Lew sent him a visual. It showed a woman Randulf instantly knew had to be Alanna. She appeared to be talking animatedly while she looked up at Lew. They were walking toward the trees at the far side of the lot from the building housing the rave.

"Wait it out," Lew said. *"Don't move too soon."*

Randulf was tempted to reply, "I'm not an amateur," but thought better of it. Lew had to keep his attention focused entirely on Alanna as they waited for her to make her move.

* * * *

Lew managed to send Randulf one more visual of where they were before everything went south.

Alanna spun to face him, her hands gripping his arms with inhuman strength. "You're clever. You almost had me fooled, but then I remembered you."

"Me?" Lew looked innocently at her. "Believe me, we haven't met. I'd never forget such a beautiful woman."

As he spoke, Lew started to shift, but Alanna was faster. Before he could complete the shift, she was on him, her jaws clamped on his arm as it became his foreleg.

"Met? No. But I saw you several years ago with another Enforcer that I once knew." Her lips turned up in a vicious smile, revealing her long fangs imbedded in his leg. *"Did you really think you could capture me, you fool? All by your lonesome?"* She shook her head, throwing him to the ground and he howled in pain as flesh tore away. *"Playing the lone wolf? I suppose that suits you—Llewellyn. But"*—her ears lifted and she sniffed the air—*"no, not a lone wolf. Your accomplice will be too late to save you, I'm afraid."*

"Really, Alanna?" Randulf appeared at her side, his lip pulled back in a snarl.

"I will *kill him, Randulf."* She released Lew only to attack again, her jaws clamping down on the back of his neck before he could gather the strength move or retaliate.

"No, Alanna, your terrorism is over. You may be—you are *powerful, but..."*

Randulf's wide jaws closed over her shoulder, biting down to bone. She howled, releasing her grip on Lew to rake her claws down

Randulf's side. They tore through his fur, leaving deep gashes in their wake.

The fight progressed from there as the two werewolves fought for dominance. Lew staggered to his feet, waiting, watching, feeling himself weaken as blood flowed freely from his wounds. Then his chance came. Randulf forced Alanna to the ground, his huge paws holding her prone. As she fought to get out from beneath him, her throat was bared. Lew attacked, ripping it open.

The last thing Lew heard before he collapsed was Randulf's mournful, *"It shouldn't have ended like this for you, Alanna. You were good—once. I pray your soul finally finds the peace it deserves."*

Chapter Twelve

Antton and Ulrik were pacing the small waiting room of the local Enforcer clinic when Brand and Mag arrived. From what they had been told when Ulrik called, Randulf had managed to contact Antton for help after killing Alanna. Ulrik and Antton had arrived to find both Randulf and Lew in dire straits and had immediately transported them to the clinic.

"How are they?" Mag asked, once he'd gotten Antton's attention.

"They'll live," was Antton's terse reply.

Ulrik joined them to say, "She did a lot of damage to both of them. Her strength, born of her rage and insanity, was incredible. However, since they *are* werewolves," he pointed out, obviously sensing the depth of Mag's worry, "they'll heal. The doctors did what they could to close their wounds. Now they just have to sleep until their healing is complete."

"How long?"

"It could be only hours or a day or two, especially for Lew. He lost a terrific amount of blood and some flesh on his foreleg as well."

Mag shuddered, glancing fearfully at Brand.

"Stop worrying," Brand said, wrapping his arm around Mag's waist. "They'll be fine."

"It's not them I'm worried about. Okay, yeah, it is, but..." Mag shuddered again. "What if it had been you?"

Brand replied reassuringly, "I've got a double whammy going. I can already heal quickly because I'm a dhampir. Now with the werewolf added to the mix... Hell, I'd probably be up and about already, looking for more trouble."

"It takes a lot to kill one of us," Antton said. Then he shot a caustic look at Brand. "Do *not* think you can take on the rogues with impunity quite yet. You have a lot more to learn and you're still too young, as a werewolf, to have the kind of healing powers the rest of us do."

"All right. I understand." Brand looked well and truly

chastised.

"Just remember that when the time comes," Mag told him fiercely.

"I will. I will. I promise."

"Can we see them?" Mag asked.

"There's not much to see, other than two sleeping werewolves," Ulrik told him. He chuckled. "They're not even being forced to wear a cone."

Mag smiled slightly, imagining either Randulf or Lew in one of those. "They'd tear them off almost before a doctor put it on."

"Undoubtedly. And then force-feed them to him."

"So I guess we just wait." Mag walked over to one of the chairs and sat, staring at the door leading to the rest of the clinic.

Antton held a hurried consultation with Ulrik then told Mag and Brand, "Sitting around doing nothing will only make the waiting harder. Ulrik's going to take Brand on a training mission and you're going with him, Mag."

Mag shook his head. "I'm waiting," he said stubbornly.

"Go!" Antton pointed dictatorially at the exit where Ulrik and Brand stood waiting.

"You can't make me," Mag protested.

Antton took a step toward him only to pause when Brand hurried back to where Mag sat.

"I could use your moral support," Brand said quietly. "I have the feeling Ulrik's not going to show me how to"—he grinned—"pick the right wine to go with fish as compared to red meat."

Snorting out a laugh, Mag nodded and got to his feet. "Probably not. Okay, I'll come with but"—he looked squarely at Antton—"you let us know the moment there's any change with them."

Antton's lips curled up. With a mocking salute he replied, "Yes, sir."

* * * *

The training mission, which involved tracking and hunting with Ulrik as the 'bait', ended successfully. At least according to Ulrik it did, although Brand seemed to think he hadn't done as well as he could have.

"I should be better, faster," he grumbled, exhaustion showing in every line of his body. "I can find a vampire and follow him like that." He snapped his fingers.

"Of course you can. It's what dhampirs do," Ulrik consoled him. "However you're learning a whole new skill set now that's foreign to you for the most part. Practice and you'll get better. You'll have to if you're going to be hunting rogue werewolves as well as vampires."

"Can we do this again tomorrow?" Brand asked hopefully.

"Probably. Now, home with you and get some sleep. Both of you. Mag looks like he's about to fall on his face and all he did was watch."

"Which meant I had to stick with Brand and he wasn't exactly taking a stroll through the woods," Mag muttered. "If I keep doing this, I'll need running shoes."

Brand laughed, hugging him. "I think that can be arranged. Right now though, I wish I knew how to do the whole transporting thing."

"If you did, we'd only have to come back for the car later," Mag pointed out.

"True enough, and we need it to get to school."

"Aw hell." Mag sighed. "Okay, let's get back, pick up our stuff and hope we don't fall asleep during classes."

Ulrik chucked. "If you want, I can call the school and let them know you're not going to make it tonight."

"Nope," Mag said firmly just before he yawned prodigiously. "Once we start doing that, it could become a habit and we'd never graduate."

"It would just be one time," Brand said.

"No." Taking his hand, Mag pulled him toward the car. "We made a vow and damn it, we're keeping it."

"Yes, sir," Brand replied, mimicking Antton's salute from a few hours ago.

* * * *

"Why haven't we heard from Antton?" Mag asked early the next morning, as he got dressed.

"Maybe because he has nothing to report?" Brand replied. "He did say it could take them a couple of days until they're fully healed."

"I know, but…"

"Mag, relax. When he knows anything positive, he'll let *us* know. He promised."

"What if it's negative? Then he wouldn't."

Brand sighed. "Let's eat and then, if it'll ease your mind, you can call him or we can stop by the clinic."

"The clinic," Mag said without a second's thought.

They arrived there less than an hour later. Just in time to hear Randulf shouting, "What the hell do you mean he's gone?"

"Damn, now what?" Brand muttered as he and Mag hurried through the waiting room and into the clinic proper. They had no problem finding Randulf's room, since Ulrik and one of the doctors were standing at the open door.

Mag had the feeling Antton was in there with Randulf. His suspicions were confirmed when he wriggled his way past Ulrik, closely followed by Brand. Antton was standing beside a vacant bed. Across from him, Randulf was pulling on a shirt that was just about as worn as the jeans he was wearing.

"Find him," Randulf ordered, glaring at Antton.

"Easier said than done," Antton retorted tightly.

"How can you not know where he is?" Mag asked hesitantly.

Randulf turned to him, spitting out, "He took the easy way. He teleported. Who the hell knows where he ended up?"

"But I thought…"

"That he was too injured?" Antton sighed. "He was, but apparently it didn't stop him."

Mag looked at him in dismay. "He could be dying somewhere."

"Or having a good laugh at our expense," Randulf said angrily. "At my expense," he muttered under his breath.

"He wouldn't do that!" Mag protested.

"You don't know him." Randulf dropped down on the bed with a shake of his head. "Wherever he is, I'm sure he's fine. He's a survivor. We all are."

* * * *

At the same time that the others were talking about him, Lew woke, uncertain where he was. The last thing he remembered was a desperate need to leave the clinic before Randulf was healed enough to shift into his human form. He had no desire to face him and see the return of the hatred in his eyes now that the assignment was over.

Although partially recovered from the battle with Alanna, Lew knew he was still too weak to have gone very far. Easing himself up, he stood on three legs, keeping any weight off the fourth, and moved his head gingerly. His neck hurt but it was bearable.

Still, a few more hours of sleep are called for. The thing is, am I somewhere safe enough to do so?

Limping, favoring his foreleg, he began to explore his surroundings. There was a desk, bookshelves, and two armchairs—none of which looked familiar.

And yet it has to be somewhere I've at least picked out of someone's mind or I couldn't have come here.

He sniffed and discovered scents he recognized.

How the hell*? Maybe…? Yeah, when Mag said he and Brand has to go home after our—talk. He said he'd spend the evening studying, probably so he wouldn't worry too much while we were out looking for Alanna. Guess this is where he was going to do it.*

Relieved that he hadn't ended up somewhere where he'd be found by Antton—or worse yet, Randulf—he went back to where he'd awakened, in the shadows behind one of the armchairs. Curling up, his head resting on his three good legs and his injured foreleg stretched out to keep any pressure off of it, he fell asleep again.

* * * *

"Can't you, I don't know, track where he went somehow?" Mag asked Antton.

"Not when he teleported. If he'd left on two feet, or four, it might have been possible, but he didn't. Believe me, we checked."

"Why are *you* so worried about him?" Randulf asked Mag.

Mag looked at him as if he couldn't believe he'd even ask. "Because he's a friend and he's hurt."

"A *friend* wouldn't leave without letting one of us know where he was going."

Mag marched over to stand in front of Randulf, glowering at him. "He would if he thought someone he cared about hated him."

Randulf snorted. "He doesn't care about me, if that's what you're implying. There's only one person Lew thinks is worth his time. Himself. And for your information, I don't hate him."

"Yeah, you do." Mag spun around to look at the others. "You all do. Or at least"—he tempered his words—"you dislike him."

Ulrik gave a small nod. "He's not easy to like."

"Because you never gave yourselves the chance to get to know him! You're glad he's gone now, so you can move on to… to the next problem."

"Not true," Randulf said quietly. "I gave him a chance. I gave him several chances and he blew them."

"So now he's past history and you're fine with that."

"Yes, Mag, I am. I hope he's all right. In fact, I'm sure he is. He's gone to ground somewhere. He'll heal and go on with his life the way he always has. Selfishly."

Mag watched Randulf as he spoke and thought he saw something in his expression that said the man didn't really want it to be that way. There was a look of loss and yearning in his eyes.

He's lying. To me, and more importantly to himself. But I'm not calling him on it.

"Then I guess that's it," Mag said tightly. "I'm glad you're all right. I'm sure I… we'll be seeing you again. Brand, let's go home."

Antton held up a hand to stop them. "Ulrik's taking Brand out for more training."

"Of course he is," Mag replied sourly. Stopping just long

enough to hug Brand, he said, "Have fun. I'll see you when you get home," and walked out of the room.

* * * *

"Hang on!" Brand said, catching up with Mag in the waiting room. "What's going on with you?" He put his hands on Mag's shoulders, staring at him. "Why are you so concerned about Lew? Why is he so important to you? Are you…?" Suddenly he didn't want to voice the thought that had come to him.

Mag however seemed to know what his unfinished question meant because he shook his head. "No, I'm not… what? Infatuated with him or whatever you might be thinking? Damn, in case you don't know it by now, you're the only man I want in my life and have been forever, it seems."

Brand sighed in relief. "I know I shouldn't have doubted it, but…"

Mag wrapped his arms around Brand, kissing him very thoroughly. "There, feel better?"

"Much," Brand admitted. "I was… okay, jealous."

"Don't be. I just feel so damned sorry for Lew." Smiling, he stroked Brand's jaw. "I know what it's like to care about someone and think they don't return my feelings."

"Meaning me."

"Yes. I was wrong, but for the longest time I didn't know that. Anyway, I guess I'm seeing some of me in Lew and I wish there was something I could do help him—and Randulf."

"Unfortunately, it's probably too late. Lew's gone, and somehow I don't see Randulf doing anything to find him. Or"—Brand chuckled softly—"sitting still while you lecture him on why he should."

"Yeah, that's not going to happen and I know it." Mag kissed him again, quickly, before saying, "Right now though, you should go back so Ulrik can continue your training, and I'll go home and sulk because I can't play matchmaker."

Brand nodded. "I think you called it 'peacemaker' but either way, unfortunately, I doubt it's going to happen. Okay, I'll go learn more about what being a werewolf entails."

"And I'll"—Mag wrinkled his nose—"try to study for the exam one of my professors is giving and pray I pass."

"You will, with flying colors." Brand grinned. "Just think, when you get your degree, you can be my own personal nurse if I ever get wounded the way Randulf and Lew did."

"Gee, that's a nice thought. Not."

"You don't want to be my personal nurse?" Brand said, pretending to be hurt.

"That is not what I meant and you know it. So go learn what you have to do so that won't happen—getting wounded, I mean." He smiled, giving Brand one more kiss. "I'll always be your personal nurse and personal"—he waggled his eyebrows—"everything."

Brand groaned. "I wonder if I can sneak away and go home with you right now."

"No, you can't," Ulrik said from the doorway. He grinned at Brand. "Right now, kid, you're coming with me. So move it."

"I'm not a kid," Brand muttered as he ignored Mag's laughter and followed Ulrik out of the clinic.

Chapter Thirteen

On the drive home from the clinic, Mag could only think of two things. One was what he would do with and to Brand as soon as he got home, which made his cock perk up and take notice. Then he began trying to figure out if he really could make Randulf sit down and talk to him about Lew. That immediately tamped down on his libido.

Probably not happening but maybe, if I push it. Lew needs him and I really think Randulf needs Lew. He just has come to grips with that fact and admit it to himself. He chuckled. *Yeah, Brand's right, I do want to play matchmaker, for whatever good it will do.*

After parking the car in the driveway, Mag hurried into the house, dashing upstairs to change into something comfortable for studying. A few minutes later, dressed in an old pair of sweats, he came back down, grabbed a drink from the fridge, and went into what he and Brand had dubbed 'the study'.

The second he walked in, he froze. A sleek, red-furred wolf stood defensively in the center of the room, one foreleg lifted slightly off the floor.

"That better be you, Lew," Mag muttered. "If not, I could be in deep shit."

Moments later Lew stood there in a pair of jeans and T-shirt. He smiled slightly, replying, "You're safe." Then he chuckled. "What would you have done if it wasn't me?"

"Run like hell? Not that it probably would have done much good." Mag pointed to one of the armchairs. "You'd better sit before you fall on your face. Then let me take a look at your arm."

"Yes… doctor."

"Nurse actually, or I will be in a few more years. Now sit."

Lew did, being careful of his arm.

Mag went over, gently checking it. "Considering what they said happened to you, it looks remarkably good."

"We heal fast, generally. This"—he touched his arm—"is taking a bit longer, since she took a lot of flesh when she bit me. Too bad it didn't poison her."

"Well, if she'd been a vampire…" Mag settled down in the other armchair.

"True enough." Lew sighed, leaning his head back then turning to look at Mag. "Are you going to let them know I'm here?"

"Not if you don't want me to."

"Thanks."

"But you should let Randulf know you're safe."

Lew sighed morosely. "Like he'd care. He's probably glad to see the last of me."

"I don't think so. Okay, let me rephrase that. I think that's what he thinks, but I don't think he really is."

"A lot of 'thinks' there, and I'll add one more. I think you're crazy to believe that."

"Don't you at least want to find out? Damn, Lew, at least *try* to talk to him."

"No! We're not meant to be together. We're total opposites. We found that out the hard way. He's all about helping people, even beyond his job as an Enforcer. Me"—Lew smiled wryly—"I'm preoccupied with… well, with living my life free and easy with no commitments. Commitments only cause problems and pain."

Mag shook his head. "You don't believe that. Not really. If you did, you wouldn't be an Enforcer."

"Oh?" Lew arched one red eyebrow. "Like Brand said, I'm conceited. I like the looks of admiration when I pull off a capture, especially when I manage it on my own. Ego, Mag. Ego is what rules my life."

"Bullshit! If all you wanted was adulation, you'd be on stage or in the movies. No"—Mag looked thoughtfully at Lew—"that's all a front. Underneath, you're afraid no one will like you, which is stupid. You're a good man. You just have to quit hiding it."

"You sure you're not studying psychology? Not that you're right about me but damn, it sure sounded good. I'm not what you think, Mag. Everything I do, I do for me."

"Then why did you agree to go after Alanna?"

"Like I said…"

Mag snorted. "You weren't doing it alone. You were part of a team. Any one of them could have been the one to find her and take her out."

"Not the way we had it planned. I was the one…"

"Plans can go wrong," Mag broke in, looking pointedly at Lew's arm. "Plans *did* go wrong. Besides, from what Brand told me, you *asked* for backup. Specifically Randulf. So this wasn't a glory mission for you and I seriously doubt any of them are, no matter what you say. You're just like the others; you want to help keep us—humans—safe from rogues. That's what good, decent people do and that includes you."

"Are you finished?" Lew asked tightly.

"No. I won't be finished until I make you see you have to talk to Randulf and tell him how you really feel about him. Not the line of BS I'm sure you've given him but the truth."

"Which would be?"

"You care about him, a lot, on a very personal level."

Lew dropped his gaze, staring down at the floor. "He won't believe it. Not after all we went through the first time around."

"Convince him. Hell, that shouldn't be too hard actually since werewolves can tell when someone lying, if they want to."

Looking at Mag again, Lew almost smiled. "There is that."

"So you're going to talk to him?"

There was a long pause then Lew said, "Maybe."

"Definitely," Mag replied, taking out his phone.

"What are you doing, as if I didn't know? You promised me you wouldn't."

"That was then; this is now." Mag turned his back on Lew then punched in the number he needed. After a brief conversation, he hung up and put in a second number. When his call was answered all he said was, "I need your… help, if you're up for it." A moment later he said "Here, at my house. I'll show you." Then he closed his phone.

"I swear," Lew growled.

Mag just shrugged, got up, and when he got to the door of the study he said, "You had better not try to run."

"As if I have a chance to," Lew muttered when Randulf appeared in the middle of the room.

Grinning, Mag left, closing the door behind him.

* * * *

"I should have known this was a set-up," Randulf said angrily, glaring at Lew.

"Not my doing," Lew protested.

"I could have figured that out for myself, since you ran the second you were even halfway strong enough to."

"Why should I stick around? I did my job and I'm real sure everyone was glad to see the back of me."

"Let's just say that while they were worried you'd left too soon, they weren't heartbroken," Randulf replied sardonically.

"No surprise there and I'm sure you led the pack in feeling that way."

Randulf shrugged, leaning back against the desk, his arms crossed while he studied Lew. "You look like your trip didn't do you much harm overall."

"Trip? That makes it sound like a vacation, not an escape."

"I hardly think you'd vacation here."

"Or anywhere, right now."

"Why not? You could take a cruise, meet a bevy of lovely women or handsome men"—Randulf sneered—"and keep busy until the council needs your help again."

"I don't want that," Lew replied quietly.

"More into taking a… a skiing vacation? I can see it now… a cold night, a blazing fireplace, hot toddies, someone on either side of you competing for who'll end up warming your bed."

"Stop it! Damn it, stop. Yeah, I was like that once, I'll admit it. You've got every right to think I still am." Lew bowed his head, sighing deeply. "But I'm not. All that does is—well, as you put it—give me someone to warm my bed. That's not what I want."

"Right, and if I believe that…" Randulf shook his head. "I probably would have once. Hell, I did. Once. I learned better. You're no more able to be faithful than… than Henry the Eighth."

Lew almost laughed. He might have if he'd had it in him at the moment. Instead he said, "I told Mag his plan was stupid." He looked up at Randulf. "He thinks you still care for me."

Randulf nodded. "I kind of figured that."

"He's wrong, although I guess I have to give him kudos for trying to bring us back together. He's a dreamer, a romantic, and not terribly practical."

"He's a nice man who wants everyone to be as happy as he is."

"Well, he's shit out of luck, isn't he? He had the crazy idea that you'd try to tell if I was lying to you when we… when he set this up. Guess it really doesn't matter to you one way or the other whether I am or not. You'd rather go on believing I'm a bastard than take the chance I might really give a damn about you."

"I've heard that before, Lew. It wasn't the truth back then and you know it."

Lew looked up at him. "So it can't be now?" he said softly. "People don't change? I can't change? It's written in stone that I'm an unfaithful son-of-a-bitch as far as you're concerned—out for what I can get and then move on."

Randulf nodded. "That fairly well describes…" He hesitated. "Described you. Hell, why *should* I believe you're still not like that?"

Getting up, Lew said, "You probably shouldn't. Or can't, which is the same difference. So unless you think there's more we have to say to each other, I'm leaving." He headed to the door without a backward glance.

"Lew…" Randulf sighed. "Look at me and tell me…"

"That I'm sorry I fucked everything up? I am. Not that you care now."

"I asked you to look at me. Is that so hard?"

Not turning around, Lew said, "Damned straight it is because I'll see the disbelief, the contempt you feel for me, written on your face and right now I don't think I can handle either. So goodbye, have a good life, and maybe if you're lucky, you'll find the right man who'll make you happy."

Taking a deep breath, Randulf replied, "I think… that could be you."

Lew spun around angrily. "Don't! Don't toy with me to get your… your revenge."

"I'm well past wanting that. I don't think I ever did. Maybe, once, I wanted you to hurt as badly as I did. But no more."

"How can I believe that?"

Randulf smiled a bit. "Do what Mag suggested. Open your mind and read the truth. I… I miss you. I'm probably asking to be hurt again, but still… I miss you."

Lew studied him, opening his mind, and his heart to what Randulf was saying. Very quietly he replied, "I miss you too."

Randulf nodded. "I know you do."

"Reading me?"

"Yes, but not the way you're thinking. I don't have to. It's in your voice, in your expression, in every line of your body." Randulf held out his hand.

Tentatively, Lew walked toward him, stopping just close enough so that he could reach out and take it. "Am I that easy to read?"

Randulf smiled. "Sometimes. Not often, but yes—sometimes."

"I guess I'll have to work on that."

"Which way? To hide your feelings or let them show?"

"With you," Lew replied, "let them show. Then perhaps we can make this work."

"I'll have to do that too."

Lew nodded. "It might help. You're pretty good at bottling things up and then exploding when they get too much for you."

"Bad habit," Randulf admitted.

"Very."

"I'll try to do better." Randulf tugged gently on Lew's hand.

Lew allowed himself to be pulled closer. "Do you think we stand a chance?"

"Yeah, I do. Besides which"—Randulf grinned—"we don't want Mag pissed at us so, we'd better give it a try. Right?"

"Right. Pissed off humans are a pain in the ass."

"Definitely."

Lew hesitated, his gaze searching Randulf's face. "May I?"

"I'll be upset if you don't."

"And I don't want that, so..." Sliding his hand behind Randulf's neck, Lew kissed him.

* * * *

Mag was grinning ear to ear when Brand finally got home from his training.

"Glad to see me?" Brand asked, a bit puzzled since Mag had been less than happy when they'd parted earlier.

"Always." Mag proved it by giving him a very enthusiastic welcome home kiss.

"Okay. That was nice but..." He quirked an eyebrow in question.

"I got my studying done, so we have the rest of the night to ourselves."

"After class," Brand pointed out.

"Well, yeah." Mag was still grinning.

"All right, do you want to fill me in on what's got you looking like a loon?"

"It worked."

"Mag..." Brand sighed, flopping down on the sofa. "What worked?"

"I guess I *will* have to fill you in."

Brand chuckled. "That would be nice."

"When I got home, guess who was here?"

It took Brand a second before he replied, "Lew? This is where he came to hide out?"

Mag nodded, sitting down beside him. "It is, though I forgot to ask why, but he was here and I had a long talk with him and then I got sneaky. Well, not sneaky, because he knew what I was doing but I sort of tricked Randulf into showing up, which he did and"—Mag took a deep breath—"they worked things out."

"Sweet, but... Don't tell me you were eavesdropping."

"Nope. I was good and went upstairs but before they left Lew made me come down so they could thank me. Trust me, the way they were looking at each other, their next stop was the nearest bed."

Brand laughed happily. "So your mission was successful. I bet there will be a few surprised Enforcers when the others find out."

"And maybe," Mag said seriously, "they'll stop disliking Lew so much. Of course, that's up to him and whether he can tamp down on his ego. But I bet Randulf will see that he does. Or more, because they're together again, Lew won't feel like he has to be cock-of-the-walk just to impress them."

"And he really didn't impress them all that much. They used him because he's good at what he does, not because they liked him."

"As I said, maybe that'll change now."

"I hope so, for both their sakes." Brand hugged Mag. "You done good."

Crossing his fingers, Mag said, "I hope it works. I think it will."

Brand chuckled. "And if it looks like it's not, you'll have another long talk with them and make them see that it has to."

"Well, it does. They're meant for each other."

"Yes, Mr Matchmaker, it does, and I suspect it will. But right now, I should go change. We do have school and…"

"Then you patrol for a while, and then…"

"We spend the rest of the night proving we belong together too."

"Which we do," Mag said softly.

"Now and forever," Brand agreed, kissing him gently.

* * * *

Mag returned the kiss with feeling. *Maybe not forever, but for as long as I'm alive. And I guess that's all either of us can hope for.*

The End

The HOUSEMATE

Edward Kendrick

Blurbs

What do you do when you find out the man of your dreams may just be a creature out of a nightmare? That's what Ryan must decide when he invites Adrian to be his housemate.

Author Ryan Turner, accompanied by his cat, Constable, has just moved into the house he inherited from his aunt. Unfortunately the original owner, Adrian Devoe, also lives there. However, Ryan is unaware of this since Adrian is a vampire. Deciding there is nothing he can do to oust Ryan, Adrian, pretending to be a human with an allergy to sunlight, manages to wrangle an invitation from Ryan to become his housemate.

The two men become friends and slowly realize they are drawn to each other. Then Adrian's great-uncle, the vampire who turned him, appears to warn Adrian that Darnell--a vampire who almost killed Adrian during the Civil War--has reappeared, intending to finish the job.

The question then becomes, will Adrian be able to keep Ryan and himself safe when Darnell shows up? And if he can, will Ryan be able to accept that the man he has fallen in love with is a vampire and his great-grandfather--although not by blood?

Dedication

To G.A. Hauser, who inspired me and had faith in me.

Trademarks/ Copyright Acknowledgement

The author acknowledges the Trademarked or copyright status and IP owners of the following items mentioned in this work of fiction:

Wuthering Heights: Emily Brontë
Anna Karenina: Leo Tolstoy
Jane Eyre: Charlotte Brontë
David Copperfield: Charles Dickens
The Picture of Dorian Gray: Oscar Wilde
Death in Venice: Thomas Mann
Oliver Twist: Charles Dickens
Taurus: Ford Motor Company
Boy Scout: Boy Scouts of America Corporation
Movie Channel: Showtime Networks Inc.
Mr. America: Robert Bonham, Individual USA
ESPN: ESPN, Inc.
WD-40: WD-40 Manufacturing Company

Chapter One

He heard it again. An agonized scream coming from somewhere down the hall.

The first time it happened Ryan was certain it was part of some horrible nightmare whose details he couldn't remember. Still, feeling stupid but not wanting to take a chance that might have been real, he called the police. They came, searched the house from cellar to attic then told him in no uncertain terms that he was the only one in the house besides his cat, Constable.

"And no sign of forced entry," the lead officer said. Then he'd grinned knowingly. "Of course it could have been a ghost. Old houses are supposed to have them you know."

"And secret rooms and graves in the basement. Yeah, yeah. Trust me there's nothing like that here, including ghosts," Ryan had replied sarcastically. Not the best way to make friends with the cops he'd realized seconds later when the office scowled at him before turning on his heel and leaving with his partner right behind him.

So the next time Ryan had heard the scream—two days later—he went on his own search, starting with the other bedrooms along the hallway. There was no sign that anyone had gone into any of them since the cops had been there. He could tell because a fine layer of dust covered the furniture. *Meaning I'd better get out the dust mop. Or not. I don't use these rooms, or half the others in the house, so why bother for a bit of dust?*

The house was large. Much too large for one person. But he'd inherited it when his aunt had died at the ripe old age of ninety-five. Since he'd been about to be kicked out of his apartment for non-payment of rent, he'd figured he could do worse than move into a place that wouldn't cost him a dime. Especially since along with the house he'd also gotten a fair amount of money. It was being held in trust—doled out sparingly by her lawyer—but it was enough to keep him in food and pay the utilities if he was frugal.

The third time he'd heard the scream he searched again with the same results. Whoever or whatever was causing it hadn't shown their face. He was beginning to wonder if it *was* his imagination. Or—best case scenario—there was air in one of the ancient water pipes and the sound of it escaping just seemed like a scream.

That had been two days ago. Now it was happening again. With a sigh, and a grumbled, "Can it, would you?" he rolled over and tried to go back to sleep.

* * * *

Adrian pounded his fist into his open hand in frustration. *What the hell will it take to make him move out? Do this every damned night?*

He paced back and forth, tempted to scream again out of pure frustration. He wanted the guy gone. This was *his* house, not some ne'er-do-well punk's who thought he'd fallen into the gravy. *Nope, wrong way to put it. Was riding the gravy train? Yeah. Whatever.* It was still his home and the fact the man had inherited it wasn't fair. Not at all.

He knew he could enter the man's mind and order him to leave. But that would be tantamount to treating him like a slave. *That* he was unwilling to do under any circumstances. Ever.

"If only Ms Abigail had other family," he grumbled. "Some nice old-maid sister or niece who would take care of the place. But no-o-o she didn't, and so she willed it to what's his face. The out-of-work… punk. Ryan whatever."

Twenty-to-one he doesn't know which end of a broom to use, if he even knows what one is. And a vacuum or a dust rag... Of course I could do some cleaning I guess, but then he'd know I was here. Not good. Not at all.

Adrian glared at Ryan's closed bedroom door, tempted to open it and shout "Boo". He resisted only because he really didn't want the guy knowing he had a housemate. Instead he went back to the windowless room hidden behind the wall at The End of the hallway.

He'd helped built the house, and secretly put in the wall—which shortened the length of the second floor by eight feet—just before the Civil War. It was his wedding home, and as a stationmaster for the Underground Railroad he needed a place to house the escaped slaves who made it to the town of Kennett Square until they could safely continue their journey north to Canada and freedom. He'd done such a good job with it—and with the stairs that led from the room down to two secret entrances in the basement of the house—that to this day no one had found them. Now he resided in the room—as he had since his 'death'. At night he took advantage of the rest of 'his' house, either visibly or cloaking his presence as the situation warranted.

The house had remained in the family to this day. Fifty years ago Ms Abigail inherited it when her parents had died. She was the stepdaughter of Adrian's son Michael, who had had no children until his second marriage. And those children were only his because he'd adopted them after marrying the widowed Mrs Bella Connors. Adrian had died before Michael was two and the ownership of the house had passed on to Adrian's wife, and then to Michael when he was of age, thus remaining in the possession of the Devoe family until Ms Abigail willed it to Ryan, who was her nephew by way of her sister, Michael's other, younger, stepdaughter.

I suppose he's family too, damn it. Even so, he has to go.

* * * *

Contrary to what Adrian thought, Ryan wasn't an out-of-work punk. He was an author. Not famous, barely known except by a small circle of fans, but still an author.

"An underpaid one," he grumbled when he looked at his latest report from the bank. It showed a wire transfer from his publisher that might have kept a cat in food for a month, if the cat wasn't too hungry. *Speaking of which…*

He looked around and finally saw Constable's tail hanging out from behind the curtains on the window. That meant he was probably watching the birds in the backyard. Ryan was tempted to join him but he had a deadline to meet for his latest book.

Turning back to his computer that sat on the large oak desk occupying most of one wall of the study, he set to work. A few minutes later he felt something nudge his leg and looked down to see Constable about ready to leap into his lap.

"Uh-uh, cat, you know better," he admonished.

Obviously Constable wasn't in the mood to listen because seconds later he was curling up in Ryan's lap as if it was the best seat in the house. Ryan knew that as far as the cat was concerned, it was. It still didn't make it easy to type or even to concentrate, especially when a paw appeared over the edge of the desk, aiming for the keyboard. Ryan swatted it away and kept on writing. It became a game of wills, but in The End, much to Ryan's surprise, Constable finally got the message and went back to his spot on the windowsill.

Ryan continued writing well past lunchtime, feeling a sense of accomplishment when the part of the story that had been giving him fits finally fell into place. A small victory but one that made him think he might yet get the book to his publisher on time. He read over what he'd written, made a couple of minor edits and then closed out of the file and shut down the computer.

Food was in order he decided when his stomach started grumbling. Going to the kitchen, he threw together a large sandwich, put some cookies on the plate as well, and with it in one hand, a fresh cup of coffee in the other, he managed to open the backdoor and went out to the table on the patio to eat. He wasn't in the least surprised when Constable jumped up on the chair beside him, looking longingly at the sandwich.

"Mine," Ryan said, picking it up to take a bite.

"*Rrrow*," Constable replied, giving the sandwich an intense stare.

After a couple more 'rrrows' Ryan ceded the point, broke off a corner, making certain it contained meat and cheese, and dropped it on the ground. Constable pounced seconds later, devouring the offering then staring up at Ryan hopefully.

"Why didn't I just make a second one for you?" Ryan grumbled. He gave Constable another bit then ignored him while he ate the rest then the cookies. Finished, he leaned back, sipping his coffee while surveying his domain, as he liked to think of it.

The yard behind the fieldstone outer walls of the house sloped down to a small, meandering creek. At the bottom of the lawn a huge oak tree towered over a small, one-roomed structure that Ryan figured had probably been used as a servant's cottage back when the house had been built in the mid eighteen-hundreds. Now it held a few gardening tools and miscellaneous bits and pieces of cast-off furniture that someone probably hadn't wanted to lug to the attic.

Getting up, he wandered around to the front of the house with Constable at his heels. It was fairly imposing, with a wide porch running across the length of the main structure. The front door was made of dark oak, flanked on each side by long windows framed in the same oak. A flight of stone steps on one side of the house led to the entrance to the kitchen that projected out from the rest of the house. Above the porch was a peaked roof and set back from it a second matching peak that designated the rest of the second story of the house. Above that was a shallower peak over the attic. There were two chimneys, one for the massive fireplace in the living room, the other for a smaller one in the dining room. He had yet to use either one since it was still late summer, but he had the feeling come winter he'd be glad to have them. Kennett Square might be in southern Pennsylvania, but that didn't mean it didn't get its fair share of snow and cold temperatures.

He chuckled at that thought. *It's still a northern state. Hell, I'm halfway between New York City and Washington and they both get bad snowstorms at times.*

"So what do you think, cat? Are you ready to experience winter beside a warm fire, instead of huddled on my bed in a tiny apartment?"

Constable seemed to like the idea because he purred happily. Then a bird landed on one of the trees at the side of the house and he was off to stare up at it longingly, giving a cat-grumble when Ryan told him to leave it alone. With a roll of his eyes, Ryan went over, picked him up, and they went back inside. Constable headed of to who knew where and Ryan went back to the study to continue work on his book.

* * * *

It was just after dark, two days after his latest attempt to scare Ryan from the house, when Adrian awoke. He dressed in jeans and a T-shirt, casual clothing he'd become quite fond of in the past few years, and then made his way from his room to the main part of the house, misting through a minute gap between the juncture of the back and side walls of the upstairs hallway that he had created for just that purpose. *My house, not the punk's.* He wasn't certain why he still thought of Ryan as a punk. He knew he really wasn't. *But he's living in my home, without my permission, so that makes him a punk.*

As he entered the hallway, cloaking his presence first, he heard a low "*Meowww… meowww.*" After reaching out with his senses to locate Ryan—who he discovered was down in the living room—Adrian became visible again.

Constable was a few yards down the hall, staring at him, purring softly. Adrian knelt and held out his hand. As he had since the second time they'd met, Constable quickly came close enough to let Adrian pet him.

Their first meeting had been… interesting.

Adrian had come into the hallway the same way he had tonight. Cloaked from anyone's view. It was dark, with only the light coming from downstairs, dimly illuminating the top of the staircase. He'd first been aware of the cat when he heard a low-pitched rumbling growl. Then claws dug into his leg and he barely suppressed a shout of pain. Looking down he'd seen the cat. And, much to his surprise, the cat obviously saw him. *Or at least senses my presence and where I'm standing.*

Cautiously reaching down, he'd carefully disengaged the claws from his leg and stepped backwards. The cat followed, still growling menacingly. As he knew Ryan was downstairs since he could hear the sound of the TV, Adrian became completely visible. That didn't seem to appease the cat in the least as it stalked toward him again; obviously willing to do extreme damage to any part of Adrian it could reach. So, Adrian had taken control of its mind, sending calming thoughts that he was no danger to the animal.

The cat had responded by sitting back on its haunches and rumble-purring. Slowly, Adrian had knelt, reaching out to pet the cat. Meanwhile he carefully probed Ryan's mind to find out the cat's name.

"Well hello, Constable," he said softly when he learned it. "Aren't you a handsome creature?"

From that moment on, he and Constable had been friends. The cat was, in Adrian's opinion, the only saving grace to Ryan's having moved in.

Now, after giving the cat the attention he deserved, Adrian stood and moved silently down the hall to the top of the staircase. He could see the entry hall and the arches opening onto the living and dining rooms. From the sound of it, Ryan was watching some cop show. So, cloaking his presence again, Adrian went down to join him, leaning against the wall at the side of the room where he had a good view of both the TV and Ryan. He had to admit he much preferred Ryan's choices of shows to the reality ones Ms Abigail used to watch.

Constable had followed him down and now stood in the archway looking between Adrian and Ryan as if trying to decide which man deserved his full attention. Thankfully, as far as Adrian was concerned, the cat decided a lap was more important and jumped into Ryan's.

Adrian studied the young man as he had several times before. In his estimation, Ryan was good-looking in a disheveled way. His almost shoulder-length, wavy brown hair was in serious need of cutting. *Unlike mine, although once I wore it that long. Years ago.*

Ryan had on sweats that totally hid his fairly slender figure. His expression at the moment was locked in a frown while he watched a shoot-out that was happening in the show. He had none of the Devoe family's autocratic features. His lips were full, his nose slightly broad and his eyes... *Such a wonderful color. As blue as a midnight sky.*

Adrian shook his head, wondering why he'd even noticed

that. *He's human. He's a thorn in my side. And he has to go before… Before what? Before I change my mind and foolishly reveal myself to him because I find him attractive and it's been too long since…? Before someone shows up looking for me?*

The last was a remote possibility but it could happen. Lemuel, Adrian's great-uncle and the reason Adrian was what he was, rarely had any contact with his creation. But when he did, he brooked no interference. The same could be said for Darnell, but for different reasons. Reasons Adrian didn't even want to think about at the moment. Not when he had such an interesting man sitting barely four feet away.

Put that thought aside. To start with, he's probably not the sort of man who would be interested in another male. And more to the point, if he was I'm not at all certain I'd fall into the category, being what I am. Male, yes, but…

* * * *

The TV show ended, a commercial came on and Ryan's attention wandered. First it went to the story he was writing, as he pondered which way to go with The Ending. He'd originally planned on having the heroes walk off into the sunset hand-in-hand, so to speak. Now he wondered if they should end up in bed—again—engaged in mind-blowing sex as the curtain fell. He knew that's what his fans would prefer but he wasn't certain it was right for the story.

He scratched Constable's head, his thoughts moving on to the next problem—as it were—his total, and long-term, lack of anyone in his life. For a while he'd been in an on again off again relationship with a younger man who had lived in the same apartment building he had. It was an involvement of convenience more than anything else. A way to relieve stress when one or the other of them needed to. It had ended six months ago when the guy had moved in with a man he worked with. Since then Ryan had been celibate, concentrating on his writing and sublimating any sexual feelings by throwing his characters into steamy situations in whatever story he was telling.

Not the most satisfying way to live my life. Perhaps it's time to explore the town for more than food and a good movie.

He glanced down at Constable and noticed he seemed to be staring at the wall with great intensity. "See a bug, cat?" he asked with a laugh. The animal ignored him, keeping his gaze glued on the same spot.

Ryan frowned then shivered slightly. For some reason he couldn't explain he felt as if someone was watching him. *Maybe my screaming ghost?* He shook his head at that thought. *There's no ghost. It's nothing but bad water pipes. I really should call in a plumber to check them out.* He made a mental note to do that first thing in the morning and returned his attention to the TV.

Chapter Two

The next night, as soon as it was dark, Adrian left the house. He needed sustenance and feeding on Ryan was not an option, any more than it had been with Ms Abigail. Besides which, he was bored.

A person can only watch so much television before it starts warping their brain.

Not that Ryan had the TV on often enough to make that possible. He spent most of his time in the evenings on his computer, playing a game or hitting up social networking sites.

Adrian had wondered, soon after Ryan had moved in, if he did that all day as well. So one night he'd asked Constable. They didn't literally talk, the cat being, well, a cat. But Adrian had gotten images from Constable's mind of Ryan at the computer during the day. He seemed to be writing something rather than wasting time. Intrigued, Adrian had gotten on the computer late one night. From what he could tell after opening a couple of files, Ryan was an author. He didn't delve into the stories, afraid that somehow Ryan might know someone else had been looking at them. He did however open a folder titled 'Published Stories' and was surprised to find out it contained several books, all with Ryan's name on the covers.

Now, as he started the long walk into town, Adrian's thoughts went to some of the covers he'd seen in the folder. It reminded him of those on the romance novels Ms Abigail had been so fond of. Except there were two men instead of a man and a woman, and they weren't embracing.

He chuckled to himself, murmuring, "It's hard to make a bodice-ripper cover when neither man is wearing one I suppose. Still, is that the sort of stories he writes? Who on earth would buy such a thing? Apparently someone must, since he's been published."

Maybe there's more to him than I thought, in more ways than one. If he is writing stories involving two men... Of course the men could be... What? A team of spies? A pair of detectives? Lovers? He rather liked that last idea and decided to delve into one of the books the next night. *If they are lovers, then wouldn't Ryan have to have had firsthand experience to write about them? Or not. After all, you don't have to kill someone to be able to write a murder mystery. Or be a vampire or a werewolf to write about them if you have a fertile imagination.*

His thoughts were broken into when he saw the first lights from the houses at the edge of Kennett Square ahead of him. Soon he was entering the small downtown area. Much of it had changed of course, since his death, but the flavor of the past still permeated the buildings. He paused briefly in front of a church, remembering the day he'd been married in that very building. His sexual proclivities to the contrary, he'd loved his wife and adored the son she'd given him. And then Darnell had come into his life...

* * * *

"Good evening, sir."

Adrian looked up from what he'd been doing, in his office at the Devoe Bank, to see a handsome blond man, bearded and mustachioed, standing there. "May I help you?"

"Are you the bank manager?"

"I suppose I am, since I own the bank. I'm Adrian Devoe and you are?"

"Darnell Kimball. It's a pleasure to meet you." He held out his hand and they shook.

"How can I help you, Mr Kimball?"

"I need a loan to start my business."

"I see. What sort of business and do you have any

collateral to offer."

Rather than answering immediately, Darnell sat, looking intently at Adrian. Very softly he said, "I wish to open a small way station for tired travelers. I understand you're well versed in what it would take to do that."

Startled, and wary now, but hiding it behind a smile, Adrian replied, "Then you've been misinformed. I'm a banker. I know money. I know nothing about the ins and outs of the hotel business, if that's what you mean by a way station."

"I think you know exactly what I mean," Darnell replied, his voice taking on a menacing tone. "You have heard of the Fugitive Slave Law?"

"Indeed. An abomination but what does that have to do with me?"

"If you were caught hiding a slave on the run you could lose all of this." Darnell waved his hand around.

Adrian shrugged. "True, if I was doing so, but I'm not and I don't like being threatened. Please leave my office immediately."

"We'll meet again, Mr Devoe. That I promise you. And I will stop your illegal activities one way or another." With that, Darnell strode out of the room, closing the door sharply behind him.

Adrian took a deep breath. "Not if I have anything to say about it," he whispered. Then, after informing his people he was leaving, as it was close to closing time, he exited the bank.

Being very careful that Darnell wasn't following him, he made his way to his great-uncle Lemuel's home on the outskirts of the city. He arrived there shortly after dark to find Lemuel busy in his study, going over the books for the grist mill he owned.

Lemuel greeted him, closed the ledger, and they went into the living room. After asking if Adrian would like something to drink, which he didn't, Lemuel said, "You seem worried. Is there a problem at the bank?"

"No." Since Lemuel knew about Adrian's involvement with the Underground Railroad, being a station master himself, Adrian told him about Darnell Kimball's visit.

"Do you think he's an officer of the law?" Lemuel asked when Adrian finished talking.

"That or an agent for a southern slave owner, looking for an escapee."

"What do you plan on doing about him?"

Adrian smiled dryly. "Keep an eye open for him. I have two 'passengers' who will be moving on tomorrow evening. When they're gone, I'll shut down my 'station' until I know Mr Kimball has given up."

"Can the passengers be moved tonight?"

"Unfortunately, no. The conductor taking them to the next stop won't be able to be at my home until tomorrow afternoon at the earliest."

Lemuel tapped his fingers together. "We'll bring them here."

"What if Mr Kimball is watching my house?"

"I'll come by with one of my wagons and park it in the drive behind the house, close to the secret entrance. Tell them they'll have to move quickly and hide under the tarpaulin. I'll make certain this Kimball is not around when I arrive."

Adrian didn't have to ask how he'd accomplish that. He knew what his great-uncle was. He had known since he was a child and had discovered Lemuel in the process of feeding on a young man who worked for him. At the time, once he got over the shock, he found he liked the idea of having a relative who was a vampire, although he never told anyone else about it. "It would be more than my life is worth," Lemuel had said at the time, "and I'm harming no one. The people I use for sustenance have no memory of it when I'm finished and I only take a few sips. Enough to keep me alive."

"Good enough," Adrian replied to Lemuel's suggestion. "I'll have them ready when you get there."

Four hours later, Adrian and two very fearful runaway slaves were waiting for Lemuel to arrive. What he didn't know was that Darnell was waiting as well. Lemuel didn't sense until it was too late that Darnell was also a vampire. An old one. One who could be out in the early evening before the sun went down. Well after the fact they found out that he preyed on the passengers on the Underground Railroad. He saw them as insignificant beings that would not be missed after he drained them of their blood and left their desiccated corpses in some out-of-the-way spot in the forests that surrounded many of the towns he visited.

Adrian heard the wagon pull up behind the house. After cautioning the two men to remain where they were, he stepped outside to greet Lemuel, his hand on the butt of his pistol. It wasn't that he didn't think Lemuel would know if Darnell was around. It was just habit. Whenever he delivered any of his charges to the next person who would be responsible for them, he was prepared in case of trouble. It rarely happened but he believed in the adage 'Better safe than sorry'.

This time trouble came. Swiftly and deadly. One moment Adrian was nodding to acknowledge Lemuel's presence. The next he was fighting for his life against a foe so strong it took everything in him just to keep deadly fangs from tearing out his throat. He felt Lemuel trying to pull Darnell away, and saw the older vampire—for he knew the instant he'd been attacked that's what Darnell was—easily fling Lemuel against the wagon. Lemuel came back, clawed hands and fangs tearing at Darnell, but to no avail. If Darnell was surprised to find another vampire there he didn't show it. With another thrust, Lemuel was once more thrown away.

Adrian felt Darnell's claws ripping at him. Felt himself weaken as his blood darkened the ground around him. Horror suffused him—not because he was dying but because, as his vision faded, he saw Darnell speed to the door, grab the terrified slaves and then vanish as if he, and they, had never been there.

Later—he had no idea if it was hours or weeks—Adrian awoke to wracking pain. It felt as if his entire body was being torn asunder. When he tried to move he dimly realized his arms and legs were chained.

"Hush, hush," Lemuel said, stroking Adrian's sweat-soaked forehead. "It will be over soon." Then he bit deeply into his wrist and offered it to Adrian. "Drink—again. Drink deeply."

The moment Adrian did, his hunger overriding his revulsion, he felt the pain lessen until it became tolerable. "Am I…?" he asked hesitantly, his voice barely a rasping whisper.

"I'm afraid so," Lemuel replied, obviously understanding the question. "It was the only way to save your life."

"My wife? My son?"

Lemuel sat on the edge of the iron bedstead, his gaze filled with sorrow. "They believe whoever kidnapped the slaves took you with them. Your wife and your friends instigated a search but neither the slaves nor you have been found. The feeling is that the kidnappers killed you and buried your body somewhere. It is for the best that people believe that."

Adrian merely nodded, too exhausted from even the small amount of talking to respond.

For the next month Lemuel kept Adrian at his house, well hidden from anyone—and anything. Then he began to teach his nephew what he called 'the fine art of being a vampire'.

* * * *

And a fine art it is. Adrian sighed, pulling his thoughts back from the past. He was here for one purpose only, to feed. He continued on through town to the far side and the home of the local doctor. The woman had been born in Kennett Square, as had her father, her grandparents, and several ancestors before them. In each generation, one of the family members had become a doctor. Each doctor, from the time of Adrian's great-uncle on down to the present, had known about the existence of vampires and had done their best to help them when needed. Now it was Emily Beals, the wife of a Quaker pastor, that Adrian came to when he needed blood. She kept a special supply for him, garnered from the local blood bank. How she explained to them why she needed it he'd never asked, and she'd never told him.

"Welcome, Adrian," Emily said when she opened the side door of her house. He stepped into what was her very modern and well-equipped office. "Hungry?" she asked with a bit of a smirk.

"Close to starving and you look very tasty," he replied. It was their usual banter before they got down to business.

She went to a refrigerator at one side of the room, coming back with two bags of blood that he quickly drained.

"So," she said after depositing the bags in a biohazard container, "how do you like your new housemate? Have you introduced yourself to him yet?"

"No, nor will I. I'm trying to get him to move out, although not successfully." When she asked, he explained how he was doing that.

"Good Lord, Adrian, ghosts are so passé. Everyone believes in them, and no one is the least bit afraid of one. At least not unless they meet it face to face. And before you get any ideas, do not try covering yourself with a sheet to pretend to be one. Even a two-year-old knows that old trick."

Adrian sighed. "I know it's not the best idea I've ever had but damn it, Emily." He shook his head. "It's *my* house."

"You managed quite well when Ms Abigail lived there."

"I was used to her. Besides, she was a female and a good housekeeper."

Emily laughed. "How chauvinistic. I take it this young man is a bit of a slob? And why should it matter as long as he doesn't leave dirty dishes around and puts his clothes in the hamper when he'd done wearing them?"

"It's the principle of the thing. It's not his house."

"Ah but it *is*, Adrian. From what you told me, Ms Abigail willed it to him fair and square. Besides which he is family, in a remote sort of way." She knew all about Adrian, including his history, so he knew that she said that without fear of contradiction.

Adrian snorted. "Very remote. The son of Michael's younger adopted daughter so there are no blood ties."

"I know." Emily leaned back against the exam table, looking at him. "Is he cute?"

"What the hell does that have to do with anything?"

"It could explain the real reason you want him gone. So you won't be tempted."

"Ah, well, about that…" he mumbled.

"Aha. I hit the nail on the head, didn't I?"

"Perhaps, although I never really looked at him until a few days ago. Before that he was just some man sleeping in what was once my bedroom."

"Adrian, Adrian, what am I going to do with you?"

"Tell me to forget it? That there's not a chance in hell, even if I was more than just… looking?"

"I was going for more along the lines of revealing yourself to him. Not by telling him it's your house and all of that, but"—she shrugged—"does he ever leave in the evenings?"

"Once that I can think of. He told Constable he was getting cabin fever and needed to get out of the house before he went stir crazy so he was going to take in a movie."

"Who the heck is Constable?"

Adrian chuckled. "His cat. He talks to him a lot."

"The sign of a lonely person." She waggled a finger at him. "The next time Ryan goes out in the evening, follow him and then… Maybe bump into him? Not literally of course, although that could work too. Just find some way to catch his attention and then talk to him. That should get the ball rolling."

"Emily, that's all well and good as a plan, but I don't even know if he's interested in men. Although…" He tapped his chin thoughtfully.

"Yes?"

"He's a writer and from what I can tell, his books involve men with men. That's only from the covers, since I haven't read any of them but still."

"There you go. You even have the perfect reason to start talking to him."

"Hell no! I'm not going to admit I read trashy romances, even gay ones."

"Now that's being presumptive. Maybe he's a good writer and maybe the romance, if there is any, is well done."

"I… suppose that's possible."

"You won't know until you read one, now will you?"

"No ma'am." He gave her a hug, thanked her for always being there when he needed her—whether for blood or advice or just friendship—and left.

* * * *

Adrian did read one of Ryan's books when he got home, all the while keeping an ear cocked for any sign the young man might wake up and realize he was there, and on the computer. When he finished he found he was quite impressed. Not only with the quality of Ryan's writing but also the sensitivity of the story.

Perhaps I've been rash, trying to force him to leave. Living here will give him the peace and quiet to be creative. A lot of that for damned sure

"So how do I approach him, if I'm going to?" he asked under his breath while he shut off the computer. "Presuming I let him stay here. The alternative could be a lot worse if I chase him away and he sells the house to… God only knows who."

He felt something nudge his leg and just about jumped out of the chair until he realized it was Constable.

"Aren't you supposed to be upstairs with Ryan?"

The cat seemed to cock one eyebrow, although Adrian knew he was anthropomorphizing his reaction. He patted Adrian's leg again then sprang into his lap.

"I'd also lose you as a friend if Ryan left," Adrian murmured.

Constable seemed to understand because he rubbed his head under Adrian's chin.

"So… perhaps… if I can arrange to meet him…" He chuckled softly. "Then what? He asks me to move in here?"

That gave him an idea. *If I figure out a logical way to make his acquaintance, and pretend I'm new in town, and hint I'm looking for somewhere to stay… But how would I explain sleeping during the day and being up all night?* Then he remembered a book he'd read a while back about a guy who was allergic to the sun. At the time he thought the author had made that up. After doing some research on Ms Abigail's ancient computer he found out there really was something called polymorphous light eruption or PMLE. *I wonder if he'd buy that.*

"Only one way to find out." He lifted Constable off his lap, much to the cat's disgust, and made his way to his room, going invisible before passing Ryan's door just in case.

Chapter Three

Early the next evening, after an intense push to finish his story that kept him off-line so he could concentrate, Ryan suddenly realized it was Friday. *Boy, am I out of touch with the world.* He chuckled ruefully. *Meaning it's time I got out of the house. Dinner out and then see what the town has to offer besides the movie theater? Sounds like a plan to me.*

He went upstairs to shower and dress, taking the time to choose a nice pair of jeans and a decent shirt. When he checked himself out in the mirror he groaned, snagged a comb off the dresser and did his best to tame his unruly hair. Then he stuffed his wallet in his pocket, grabbed his keys and, after locking up, went to the garage to get his car. It was a faded black, ten-year-old Taurus that had seen better days but it got him where he had to go and back with no real problems.

When he arrived in town, he found a parking place in a small lot, and then walked along the main street, looking for a restaurant that appeared interesting. *Interesting and affordable* he reminded himself before opting for one that had a nice atmosphere and sandwiches and burgers, as well as more expensive entrées. After being seated at a table by the front windows, he ordered the house burger and then watched the passing scene.

A man wandered by, looking a bit bemused, and few minutes later came back from the opposite direction, still looking as if he was trying to find… Ryan had no clue what. He was tall, with short, black hair, a narrow face and heavy, dark eyebrows. *If he'd smile, he might even be handsome.* The arrival of his dinner drew Ryan's attention away from the man and moments later he'd forgotten about him.

* * * *

Adrian, being what he was, had no problem following Ryan into town even without a car. After stopping at the bus station to put his small travel bag in a locker—a part of his alibi for how he got to the town, he went back to where Ryan had parked. He saw him just entering a restaurant and had made a point of walking past it twice before crossing the street to the patio of a small coffee shop. He ordered a cup of tea and sipped it while he waited for Ryan to finish his meal and move on. He hoped the young man would go somewhere interesting—like a bar or a club—where he could casually make contact with him. *If he chooses a movie I'd come off like a molester or some such.*

Luck was on Adrian's side. Ryan left the restaurant half an hour later and stood for a moment, looking up and down the street. Then he made a beeline for a building a block away. It turned out to house another restaurant but this one had a long, mahogany bar along one wall. By the time Adrian entered, because he didn't want it seem as if he was following Ryan, the young man had found a vacant stool. He was chatting with the bartender who nodded then set a bottle of beer and a glass down in front of him. Ignoring the glass, Ryan took a deep drink from the bottle then turned, leaning back against the bar as he surveyed the room.

Adrian strolled over, took the stool next to Ryan's and, paying no attention to him, asked the bartender if he had any red wine. The man said he did, told Adrian what was available then poured him a glass.

"I've seen you before," Ryan said, sounding tentative. "You were wandering up the street earlier, looking sort of lost."

Realizing Ryan was speaking to him, Adrian replied, "I was. I'm new in town. I've been here a total of twenty hours, more or less." He smiled as he said that, taking a sip of wine.

"Oh?" Ryan cocked his head questioningly.

"I'm a Civil War history buff and part-time writer for a small online site," he said, winging it. "I know that Kennett Square was the home to several stations on the Underground Railroad and decided to use my vacation to spend time here doing research. Unfortunately, and I was stupid for not checking first, the only motel within walking distance is booked up for the next two weeks."

"No car?" Ryan asked.

"No car. I bussed in from Philadelphia, spent the day at the station and…" Adrian spread his hands.

"That must have been boring," Ryan said, chuckling. "Why didn't you at least explore the town? Maybe there's a B&B here with an available room."

"You don't know of one do you?"

"Sorry, no. I'm pretty new here too but I have a house so I've never needed to look. Oh, by the way, I'm Ryan. Ryan Turner.

"Adrian"—*I can't say Devoe, he'd smell a rat*—"Devereux."

"Nice to meet you, Adrian. So, you never said why you spent the day at the bus station."

"I didn't," Adrian admitted.

"And?"

"Okay, this probably sounds strange but I'm allergic to sunlight."

"You're right, it does, but I have heard there are people who are. I think they're called vampires." Ryan grinned. "Sorry, it was there."

"Yeah, I get that a bit too often."

"That must suck, no pun intended." Ryan frowned. "How can you ride a bus?"

"I make sure I'm well covered." Adrian touched his long-sleeved shirt. "I have a hat too, but I left it in the locker at the bus station along with my bag."

"That makes sense." Ryan finished his beer and ordered another. "You know, your last name sounds a bit like the name of my house."

"Your house has a name?" Adrian asked, pretending surprise.

"Yeah, Devoe House. It's been in my family since forever and apparently got tagged with that by the locals."

"Are you *serious*? If that's the Devoes I think it might be, they were part of the Underground Railroad."

"I suppose it's possible. I really don't know much about my ancestors I'm afraid."

"Did you grow up here?"

"Nope. My family traveled around a lot because my dad kept getting transferred as part of his job. When I graduated college I took off on my own and ended up in Chicago. Then my aunt died and she willed the house to me."

"Lucky man. I wouldn't mind that happening to me." Adrian took another drink of wine then asked with seeming hesitation, "I don't suppose you'd let me visit your house sometime? I'd really like to see one of the original Underground Railroad stations."

"I suppose that would be okay with me. I… If you want we could go there now?"

"Oh no. I don't want to spoil your evening out. Tomorrow night would be fine. Honestly."

Ryan smiled. "I'm not certain this is an evening out. Not the way you made it sound. I just had to get out of the house for a while. It seems like the only time I do is to go grocery shopping. Well, except for going to a movie."

"If you're sure…"

"I am. Finish your drink and let's go." Ryan drained the rest of his beer, waited for Adrian to do the same with his wine.

Then he stood, heading for the door with Adrian right behind him. "I parked in the lot down there."

* * * *

As they drove back to the house, Ryan kept taking surreptitious glances at Adrian. *I was right, he's not bad looking at all when he smiles. He seems nice enough too. Of course so did Bundy and look what he did.* He chuckled.

"Something tickle your funny bone?" Adrian asked.

"I was just thinking I'm taking a chance bringing a stranger home with me."

"If you'd rather not…"

"No, no. It's okay. Somehow you don't strike me as a mass murderer."

Adrian grinned. "Not recently anyway."

"This sounds cliché, but you should smile more often. It makes you look less like a scholar and more… human."

"I'm hardly a scholar. More like an interested layman with a flair for research and a reasonable ability to write about what I've discovered."

"That makes two of us. Well, for me it's more of a job, and not research so much. I write books."

"Seriously? What kind? Spy novels or adventures or what have you?"

"Umm, sort of, sometimes. But mostly mysteries." Ryan was reluctant to tell him what kind, figuring he'd think he was crazy.

"Really? I wonder if I've read any of them. I like a good mystery, especially if it's spiced with a bit of romance. You know the kind, where the intrepid detective falls for one of his clients and then has to rescue them from the killer at The End of the story."

Ryan cocked an eyebrow. "You like romances?"

Adrian shrugged. "If they're well done and it fits with the story. After all when you think about it, most good novels are love stories too, aren't they? *Wuthering Heights*, *Anna Karenina*, *Jane Eyre*, *David Copperfield*, *Dorian Gray*, *Death in Venice*. And then there's Dorothy Sayers, Ngaio Marsh, Raymond Chandler, Dashiell Hammett, as far as authors of mysteries go."

"Strange mix," Ryan commented as he drove up the drive to the house. "You do realize a couple of those involve gay characters."

"And your point is?" Adrian asked as they pulled into the garage and got out. "Romance is romance."

"That's very open-minded of you." Ryan was surprised, and he realized happily so for some reason, that Adrian felt that way. *Not that is means anything other than that he is… well not prejudiced I guess.*

Ryan led the way into the house and then the living room. "It's pretty much the way it was when my great-grandfather built it," he said. "At least from what my aunt told me one time when I came to visit." The room had a wide-plank hardwood floor—much of it covered by a large woven rug—exposed beams in the ceiling, a huge fireplace, and stone walls visible behind the bookcases and cabinets. He wondered what Adrian thought about the fact that no one had attempted to modernize the room. *Well the physical structure anyway. The sofa and chairs aren't a hundred and fifty years old, and for sure the TV isn't.*

* * * *

"I love it," Adrian murmured, sounding awestruck. *Of course I do. It's my home. My wedding house that I helped build.* "Is the rest of the house like this?"

"Yep. Come on, I'll show you," Ryan replied just as Constable appeared.

The cat meowed piteously while swiveling his head to look at both men. Then he started toward Adrian.

"Nice cat. Is he friendly?" Adrian asked, hoping Constable wouldn't act as if he already knew him. He was relieved when the cat paused, and then made a beeline for Ryan, rubbing against his legs.

"Very friendly," Ryan replied, picking up the cat. "Constable, this is Adrian. I'm giving him a tour of the house."

Constable seemed unimpressed. After allowing Ryan to pet him a bit, he wriggled out of his arms and stalked to the door to the kitchen, throwing an indignant look at Ryan.

"He's hungry. Again," Ryan told Adrian. "Do you mind if I feed him now?"

"Not at all. That way I can see the kitchen."

Ryan chuckled. "If you're expecting a cast-iron stove and a… I think it was called a dry sink, you're out of luck. It's fairly modern with all the requisite conveniences."

Adrian knew that, but said, teasingly, "You mean you don't cook over coals in the fireplace?"

"Not quite. I never did like being a Boy Scout for that very reason. Besides which there isn't a fireplace although I think the one is in the dining room might have been two-sided and the side to the kitchen was blocked off when the kitchen was updated."

Adrian nodded. "Things like that happen with old houses." It had been blocked off, much to his disgust, but there was nothing he could do about it at the time.

When they got to the kitchen, Ryan took an open can of cat food from the refrigerator, dished what was left into Constable's bowl then rinsed out the can and tossed it in the trash under the double sink. "I have beer, if you'd like one," he told Adrian. "Or coffee." He pointed to the coffeemaker on the butcher-block counter.

"Thanks, but no thanks. I'm more of a wine and tea drinker."

"Sorry, I don't have either. Okay, next stop on the grand tour is the dining room, and then the back parlor and the study, down here."

A few minutes later Adrian commented, "It's a big house but it's missing one thing."

"What?"

"A ballroom?" Adrian grinned.

"Oh good lord. If it had one I don't know what I'd use it for. I tend to stick to three rooms down here, the living room, the study because that's where I write, and the kitchen. You can probably tell that," he added with a chagrined smile, "since the other rooms are a bit dusty. I keep meaning to do something about that but…" He shrugged.

"It is a lot for one person to deal with."

"Yeah. Come on, I'll show you the upstairs."

They walked up the long bare-wood stairs to the second floor, Constable leading the way at this point as he'd finished eating.

"This is my room," Ryan said, opening the door to it. "From what I understand it was the original owner's master bedroom. There are three smaller ones and a decent sized bathroom. It's been modernized, thank goodness."

"That's probably a good thing." Adrian remembered well when the bathroom had been a large dressing room with a washbasin, stand, pitcher, and mirror. Baths were taken in the kitchen and the toilet was in an outhouse. Then, when Michael inherited the house from his mother in the early twentieth century, he'd turned the dressing room into a real bathroom, and Ms Abigail had brought in plumbers to bring it up to what is was now. Both modernizations had given Adrian fits-and-starts for fear the plumbers would somehow discover that there was an extra, unknown room and the stairs leading to the secret exit for the Railroad passengers. Thankfully that hadn't happened, any more than it had when the kitchen was upgraded.

"Well, that's about it," Ryan said, breaking into Adrian's memories, "other than the attic and the basement. The attic is full of castoff furniture and the basement is just"—he shrugged—"a basement with a heater, and a few rooms, one for doing laundry. And no"—he grinned—"I don't wash my clothes in a scrub basin. There's actually a washer and dryer."

As they walked back downstairs Adrian said, "You're lucky to have inherited this place, with all its history."

"I know. It's a hell of a change from my tiny, studio apartment, though I sort of rattle around here."

"I'm sure, with just the cat for company." Adrian paused before saying, "I suppose I should get going. Thank you very much for the tour. Maybe, if you don't mind, I could visit again sometime. I'd love to try to figure out where the secret hiding place was that your great-grandfather used to conceal the escaped slaves."

"You know," Ryan replied thoughtfully, "that's a good question. I mean where it could have been. I suppose somewhere in the basement makes the most sense but *if* it's there, for damned sure I haven't found it. All the rooms down there are just, well, empty rooms now, with shelves for whatever."

"It was often the case that a basement or an attic or a barn was used. Usually a barn actually, or a spring house."

"If this place had either of those, they're long gone. There is what I think was probably a servants' cottage down by the creek."

"Another possibility I suppose," Adrian replied, playing his role as an interested amateur historian. "Anyway, as I was saying, I'd like to come back again if it's all right with you, but right now I should leave so you can get to bed."

"You're planning on walking back?" Ryan asked. "It's a good four or five miles. I'll drive you to town and… what? Drop you off at the bus station?"

Adrian smiled wryly. "It is where my things are, and where I seem to be staying during the day unless I can find a place. That, as I told you, doesn't seem likely for another two weeks."

Ryan hesitated before replying. "Look, I know I'm taking a chance, and maybe you would be too since you don't know me any more than I know you. But you seem nice enough I think. And this is a big house. If you want… God only knows I have enough bedrooms and, well…"

"You're offering to let me stay in one?" Adrian did his best to hide the elation he was feeling. "I can't pay you much, but it you're willing to rent one to me…"

"Sure. Why not? Like I said, it's not as if I was using them. Can you afford, say, thirty dollars a week?"

Adrian chuckled. "You're renting the room cheap but I'm not going to turn down the price." He took out his wallet. He had fair amount of cash on him, and a great deal more stashed in his room. *After all, other than paying Emily for the blood, and buying clothes occasionally, what do I have to spend it on?* He also had an account with what had once been Devoe Bank before being bought out by a national chain when Michael had retired. Thankfully, as far as he was concerned, it had evening hours on Fridays so he could make withdrawals when necessary. *Oh the joys of my life. My several lives so to speak, since as far as they know I am supposedly the 'great-grandson' of the man who started the bank.*

"So you're willing?" Ryan took the money Adrian handed him, seeming quite surprised the man had actually taken him up on his offer.

"Definitely and"—Adrian grinned—"I'll even volunteer

to do some of the housekeeping chores, like dusting."

Ryan snorted out a laugh. "As I said, that is so not my strong point. Do you want to go get your bag now?"

"If you don't mind."

"Not in the least."

* * * *

Later that night, Adrian looked around the bedroom he'd chosen, once he and Ryan returned to the house. *That went much better than I hoped. I really expected I'd have to end up using my mental powers to influence him to invite me to move in. He must truly be lonely, just as Emily said. When it comes down to it, so am I and that may be why I'm willing to do this. For… companionship.* Not that he was certain that was the truth, or at least the whole truth.

Since the bag he'd picked up from the bus station held only a few bits of clothing, and the hat he'd told Ryan he used when traveling, he went back to his room behind the wall to get more jeans and shirts. He used the hidden stairway to carry them back into the house—since he couldn't mist and take them with him the way he normally entered the upstairs hallway—and put them away in the closet and the dresser.

Finally, in keeping with his promise to help with chores, he went in search of a dust mop, or at least some rags he could use. He knew they had to be somewhere since Ms Abigail had done a lot of the cleaning between weekly visits from the charwoman. He eventually found her supply in a cupboard in the kitchen while fending off Constable's attempts to explore what else was there.

"I swear, cat," he muttered, "if you had opposable thumbs I'd set you to work too."

Constable just gave him a cat grin and followed him back upstairs to the bedroom. While Adrian dusted, the cat sat on the bed, watching with interest.

"Never seen anyone do this before?" Adrian asked.

The cat actually nodded, which amused Adrian no end. It was the same in the other bedrooms, the worker and the watcher. Then, feeling a sense of accomplishment, Adrian decided to tackle the rooms downstairs. He might have finished them too, if he hadn't walked past the open study door and seen the computer. His curiosity about the other books in the one file had him turning it on and opening one of them.

He was almost finished with it when a tense voice asked, "What the hell do you think you're doing?"

Adrian swung around guiltily to look at a bathrobe-clad, scowling Ryan. "I… Well you said you were a writer and I'll admit I was interested and wondered if you had any of them on here and you're a damned good writer and… Yeah, I shouldn't have snooped. I'm sorry."

"No you shouldn't have." Ryan crossed the room to stand behind him, peering at the screen. "You liked that one?"

"Very much."

"All of it?"

Adrian's lips tilted up in a knowing smile. "*All* of it. You have a way of describing their sexual encounters that's erotic without being pornographic."

Ryan sighed with relief, or so it seemed to Adrian. "I always wonder if I'm overdoing them."

"Well I can't say anything about your other books, but in this one you hit it to perfection. Quite an accomplishment I'd say for a straight author."

"Now why would it matter if I'm straight or gay?"

"Experience," Adrian replied. "It seems to me that you must have quite a fertile imagination to know what the men are feeling if you've never experienced it yourself."

Moving to actually face Adrian, resting one hip on the

edge of the desk, Ryan replied, "Isn't that the essence of writing? Imagination? For instance, to use an example from our earlier discussion, Tolstoy was a man and yet he was able to write one of the most memorable heroines in literature."

Adrian nodded. "True enough. So you used your very active imagination to create those scenes?"

Ryan chuckled. "Now I didn't say that."

"I… see."

"I'd presume, since apparently you liked those parts of the stories, the fact I just might be gay doesn't bother you."

Adrian shrugged. "Not at all. After all, I might be too."

"Are you?"

"Yes. And that's contrary to the fact I was married once and even managed to produce a son. Are you?"

Ryan appeared surprised at Adrian's revelation but made no comment about it, instead replying, "Quite definitely. However"—he grinned—"that doesn't mean I'm going to fall in bed with you. After all, we barely know each other."

"Our sentiments are mutual. I'm not a man who would even consider doing that until I decided if I actually liked the man who might be… involved."

"Exactly. Anyway, now that I know you're not a thief, which is the reason I came downstairs in the first place, I'm going back to bed. I need sleep if I'm going to finish the book I'm working on and make my publisher's deadline."

"I quite understand. *Buonanotte*, as an old friend of mine used to say. I'll see you tomorrow evening."

* * * *

Ryan threw himself down on the bed as soon as he got upstairs, pulling the covers back over him. But sleep wouldn't come. All he could think about was the man who was now, for better or worse, sharing his house.

He has the most soulful eyes. And those cheekbones, those lips…

Ryan shivered, imagining Adrian's sensual lips pressed against his in a heated kiss or sucking his cock. He reached for the lube…

His hand slid down to his hardening member, stroking it, and his imagination took hold. It was Adrian's mouth, not his own well-oiled hand that was moving slowly down his shaft then up again. Adrian's tongue, not his own fingertip teasing the sensitive spot at the base of his cock's pulsing head. Adrian's fingers circling his hole when he arched up, then penetrating, touching, stroking his sweet spot. Soon, too soon, his balls tightened, his orgasm flooding over him. He bit down hard on his lip to keep from shouting out his release. After all, he didn't want Adrian to come running to be certain he wasn't being attacked. *Or… something.*

Crawling out of bed, he grabbed his robe from The End of the bed and made a hurried, tip-toed trip from his room to the bathroom. After cleaning cum off his chest, and the lube from his hands, he stared at his reflection in the mirror.

I look like a ragamuffin out of Oliver Twist. He combed his fingers through his hair, which did little to tame it. Not that it mattered since he was going straight back to bed. *Compared to him… He's the aristocrat. I'm, yeah, the street urchin. At least to look at us. Okay, enough with the literary associations.* He laughed softly. *The curse of being a writer? Maybe.*

Returning to his room, he dropped the robe and slid into bed again. His last thought as he finally fell back to sleep was, *I wonder if I'll ever find out how his lips really feel.*

Chapter Four

A week passed and the two men fell into a companionable routine. An odd one perhaps, since Ryan was up and moving while Adrian slept and vice versa, but it seemed to work. They would spend the evening more or less together, with Adrian appearing soon after Ryan finished supper.

"Do you want something to eat?" Ryan asked the first time that happened.

Adrian shook his head. "No thanks. I'll fix something later. I'm not much of a breakfast person and"—he chuckled—"for me it would be breakfast." He could eat, if he wanted to, but food held no real attraction for him and hadn't for the past fifty years or more.

Usually they settled in the living room to watch TV or read, or more often than not just to talk. Ryan told Adrian about his childhood and why he'd decided to become a writer. "Not that it as much a decision as a compulsion. I was always telling stories or writing them down. So when the time came I went off to college to learn the finer points of my art." When Adrian asked, he admitted he probably would never be a best-selling author and that, until he'd inherited the house, he'd been a shoe clerk and a waiter in Chicago to supplement his meager writing income.

Adrian in turn had given a purely fictitious account of his own childhood as the only son of a farming family in the Midwest. "I decided that wasn't the way I wanted to live my life as an adult so, like you, I went to night school. I majored"—he gave a mock shudder—"in business with a minor in history. After graduation I got a job"—he thought quickly about what kind of job would be done at night—"managing a nightclub. That gave me enough money to pursue my real passion, history."

Ryan frowned. "How could you…? Oh, right, a *night*club. No need to be out in the sun."

"Nope. Lots of neon, no sun."

One evening, at Adrian's suggestion, they explored the property surrounding the house. When they got to the cottage down by the creek, Adrian studied it as if he really was the historian he purported to be. "It could have been used as a hiding place. May I look inside?"

"Of course, although there's nothing there but more furniture, like in the attic."

When they were inside the cottage Adrian felt a swell of nostalgia. In one corner, half-hidden behind a broken-down chest of drawers, was a small cradle. The one he'd built for Michael just before his birth. Lovingly he ran his hands over it, wondering why it had ended up here. The last time he remembered seeing it, it had been in the parlor after Ms Abigail had first taken over ownership of the house. She'd used it, unbelievably, as a planter. He didn't recall her moving it but then he supposed that wasn't surprising. She would have brought it to the cottage, or had the charwoman do that, while he was sleeping.

"Are you all right?" Ryan's question brought Adrian back to the present.

"What? Yes. I was just admiring the cradle. If I were to guess, I'd say it was made well over a hundred years ago. But then"—he looked at the rest of the furniture—"so were some of the other pieces here. This is quite a collection of antiques, just like what's in the attic." He chuckled. "You could have one hell of a yard sale and make a small fortune."

"I don't think so. They belong here, not in someone else's house as a 'look what I found, Alice. And it was such a bargain' show piece." Ryan tapped his lip. "Maybe, sometime, I should return some of the things that are still in halfway good shape to the house."

Perhaps he's beginning to appreciate what he's inherited as more than a roof over his head. Adrian liked that idea.

"It could be fun to turn the house back into what it was when it was first built," Adrian said in agreement. "By the way, I'd be willing to bet the cottage was used for food storage, not for a maid or handyman. There would be cold storage down there." He pointed to a barely visible, square outline under the dust and a pair of distressed chairs at one side of the room. He knew it was there of course. And that it had also been used as a hiding place when he'd needed more space than the room in the house had allowed, if a conductor had come to him with a large cargo.

"Would the escaped slaves have been hidden down there until they could move on?" Ryan asked.

"It's very possible. As I said, Devoe House was a station for the Underground Railroad. This is the only place I've seen so far that would work. I should check out the rooms you mentioned in the basement. One of them could hold another hiding place. Or there might have been a set of shelves that hid the door to a room from prying eyes."

Ryan said, as they left the cottage, "I don't know that I'd have had the courage to run a station as you call it."

"It required Dedication," Adrian replied seriously. "And the belief that slavery was an anathema and no slave who managed to escape should be forced to return to his master."

"I guess I could get my head around that, but still..."

Adrian patted his shoulder. "I suspect, if it came down to it, you would have handled it. Maybe as an agent, one of the men who helped slaves find the Railroad, rather than a station manager, but The End would have been the same. Another slave would have been moved to safety."

Ryan nodded, looking at him, and then smiled. "I can see you—if you'd lived back then—using your home and your influence to make damned certain that happened."

"For sure I would have tried." Spontaneously, Adrian hugged Ryan. "We both would have." Immediately he pulled away, muttering, "Sorry."

"Why?"

"Because I shouldn't have."

"Hugged me? I didn't mind. I like hugs. Especially from a good-looking man who..." Ryan stopped talking, looking embarrassed. "Now I should be apologizing."

Adrian chuckled, putting one arm around Ryan's shoulders. "Not quite a hug, but... So enough with the apologies on both our parts. Now show me the rest of your massive estate."

Laughing, Ryan replied, "Hardly massive. And next on the tour, the apple orchard, or I think that's what it was."

Adrian smiled, keeping his arm where it was as they continued walking. *I should release him, as it were, but I like him this close. And I think... he likes it too.*

Chapter Five

Two days after their impromptu tour of the grounds around the house, Ryan was in the kitchen, humming to himself as he prepared his supper. He was happy because he'd finally finished the book. Now all he had to do was go through it, looking for any grievous errors before sending it off to his beta reader. He was also happy, he realized, because in another few minutes Adrian would join him.

So when there was a loud knock on the front door of the house, followed by an insistent ringing of the doorbell, it startled him so much he almost dropped the knife he was holding. Putting it down, he went to see who was there.

Opening the door, he was faced by a man of medium height with piercing dark eyes. "May I help you?" Ryan asked.

"I'm looking for… Ah, there you are." The man smiled and moved forward.

Turning, Ryan saw Adrian just stepping off the staircase into the entryway. He seemed briefly dismayed before hurrying forward. "Uncle Lemuel! Ryan, this is as you might have surmised"—he chuckled softly—"my uncle. Lemuel Devereux."

Ryan was looking at Lemuel at that moment and saw a slight widening of his eyes before he held out his hand. "A pleasure to meet you, Ryan."

"You as well, Mr Devereux."

"How did you find me here, Uncle," Adrian asked a shade too sharply.

There was a momentary pause as the two men looked at each other. Then Lemuel said, "I inquired around the town and someone said they thought they saw you about a week ago in a car with the man who owns this house. So I took the chance that, if you weren't here, he might know where to find you."

"I do," Ryan said with a light laugh. "Why don't you come in so that the two of you can... catch up? I'm fixing supper if you'd like something to eat, Mr Devereux."

"No thank you. I ate before I came out here. And please, Ryan, call me Lemuel. I wouldn't turn down a glass of wine though, if you happen to have some."

"Of course. Red or white? I know Adrian prefers red."

"That would be excellent." Lemuel looked quizzically at Adrian as they went into the living room. "How does he know that?"

"Because I'm renting a room from him while I do research on the house."

Again there was a pause before Lemuel said, "I see. I knew that's why you came to Kennett Square. I didn't realize you planned on settling in here."

Ryan watched, and listened to the two men with a feeling there was something going on between them he wasn't privy to. *Not that it's any of my business.* He went to the cabinet at one side of the living room that he'd turned into a small bar, taking a bottle of wine from one of the shelves, and glasses from another. Filling two glasses, he handed them to Adrian and his uncle and then returned to the kitchen to finish fixing his supper.

* * * *

"Why are you here?" Adrian asked quietly as soon as he knew Ryan was out of earshot.

"Darnell has been making inquiries in certain circles as to your whereabouts. Apparently he came out here approximately a year ago looking for you. From what I can ascertain it was around the time you were visiting me so, obviously, your paths didn't cross."

Adrian hissed in a startled breath. "Why now?"

"I wish I knew," Lemuel replied. "Finishing up old business?"

"That happened almost two centuries ago and as far as he knew, he killed me."

"It would seem he's found out differently despite my best efforts to the contrary."

"Damn it all to hell!" Adrian glanced toward the kitchen. "I should get away from here. I don't want the bastard coming after me and taking his wrath out on Ryan."

"A noble sentiment, but there's a saying, 'defend on the ground you know'."

"Nice words, but there's no way I could convince Ryan to leave. I mean, what possible reason could I give him?"

Lemuel shook his head. "Control him. He's just a human. Take over his mind and order him to leave. Something you should have done when he first appeared here."

"This is his *home*, Lemuel."

"Only because Ms Abigail had no one else to will it to."

"That still doesn't negate the fact…" Adrian broke off when he heard Ryan's footsteps.

"You two look like you're trying to solve the problems of the world," Ryan said, coming into the room. He took a seat in one of the armchairs, set his plate on his knees and began to eat. "Why so serious?" he asked after a couple of bites.

"He was just telling me about an ex-acquaintance of mine who is looking for me," Adrian said.

"If he's ex, why the concern? Ah got it. You owe him money." Ryan grimaced. "That'll bring any ex out of the woodwork."

Adrian chuckled. "No, I don't owe him money." He neglected to add that Darnell actually owed *him* something. His head on a platter for bringing Adrian so close to death that Lemuel had to turn him. *Of course if that hadn't happened, I never would have met Ryan.* He smiled to himself. *At least there's a reward at The End of the long, dark tunnel—as it were. Perhaps. We haven't gotten close to finding out if that's where we might be headed.*

"Adrian," Lemuel said, "you might consider going somewhere else before he finds you."

"And leave Ryan to become another of his victims if he shows up here? That will not happen." Adrian stated adamantly using his ability to mind-speak with his great-uncle, *"You said it yourself, take my stand where I know the territory."*

"Is this guy someone you work with at the nightclub?" Ryan asked, setting his plate on the side-table next to his chair. "Some big bruiser bouncer you fired and he hates you now?" He frowned. "How would he find you here anyway if you're on vacation?"

"Go with that idea," Lemuel suggested.

Adrian nodded—barely. "He wasn't a bouncer, but I did fire him, about a year ago, and he wasn't happy about that. He let everyone know he'd pay me back. I suppose he could have followed me here if he's still in contact with someone at the club. I didn't exactly keep it a secret what my plans were."

"Well there's two of us so if this guy does show up we can deal with him." Ryan grinned a bit. "It will give me fodder for a story. I've never actually been in a fight so I always wing it when that happens with one of my characters."

"Only you would look at it that way," Adrian replied with a laugh. "Hopefully he won't show. If he does I'll do my damnedest to solve the problem without it's coming down to a physical fight."

"If this was one of my stories, he'd be too cowardly to actually come after you face to face. He'd try something sneaky like"—Ryan paused thoughtfully—"taking a shot at you when you went out back or coming up behind you and pushing you into the creek to drown you so it looked like an accident. Only I'd see him and come to the rescue."

Lemuel said, smiling a bit, "You have a fertile imagination."

"Thanks, I think."

"It *was* a compliment. However"—Lemuel returned his attention to Adrian—"we can hope this man doesn't find you for both your sakes."

Again Ryan looked puzzled. "How did you find out about him anyway?"

"I own the nightclub that Adrian manages, along with several others."

"Good catch," Adrian said, chuckling in Lemuel's mind.

"I may be old, but I do still have a working brain," Lemuel replied tartly.

"Okay." Ryan apparently realized he hadn't finished his supper because he grumbled, "Cold burger and hot salad. Not exactly appetizing."

"So stick the burger in the microwave," Adrian suggested.

"Naw. Then I'd miss you two planning on how to deal with your nemesis."

"Nemesis?" Adrian chuckled. "Wasn't she a Greek goddess?"

"Well I'm tired of saying 'the guy who's after you'. If he really is. A year seems like a long time to hold a grudge."

"True, but still, maybe I should leave before he shows up, if he does," Adrian replied.

"No way! I told you, with two of us here he's toast if he does."

"Three of us because I intend to find a nice motel in town until this is over," Lemuel put in. "If you even *think* he's anywhere in the neighborhood you're to call me." Silently he told

Adrian, *"I'll stay in the secret room since I presume you're not using it at the moment."*

"You presume correctly."

"Are you sharing his bedroom and his bed?"

"Good lord, Lemuel, I hardly know him well enough to do that yet. It may never happen."

"It would make your life much more complicated if it did."

"I'm well aware of that," Adrian replied with some asperity.

"We'll need… Never mind, I'm sure Adrian knows your phone number," Ryan said in response to Lemuel's verbalized words.

"All too well, and he knows mine," Adrian replied. "The joys of working for a relative. He thinks he has the right to call me every time he perceives there might be a problem at the club."

"I would do that even if you were just a normal employee. I can't run a successful business if I don't keep my finger to its pulse."

"And boy does he do *that,*" Adrian said, continuing the fiction they had started about the nightclub and Lemuel's involvement with it.

Ryan chuckled. "I think I'm glad I'm self-employed. Well sort of. I do have to deal with my editors and my publisher and… Yeah, I guess I'm in the same boat as you, Adrian."

Lemuel stood at that point, telling the others, "I should get moving if I'm actually going to find a motel room before they're all booked up. Ryan, thank you for the wine and your hospitality. I shall see you again tomorrow although probably not until late in the afternoon. I do have a business to run, even if it's by email and phone calls for the time being."

"It was a pleasure meeting you, Lemuel, despite the reason behind it," Ryan replied.

"At least it gives me time with my nephew that's not

business related." Lemuel smiled at Adrian. The smile turned to a grin when he added, for Adrian's ears only, *"Behave yourself, if that's possible."* With that he strode out of the room, and moments later out of the house.

* * * *

"He's an interesting man," Ryan commented once Lemuel had left. "Though he hardly looks old enough to be your uncle. More like your brother."

"According to my father, Lemuel was a surprise. He was born when their parents were forty. I was born when my father was eighteen. So I'm actually just a couple of years younger than him."

The age difference was the truth, although not the reason why. Lemuel had died in sixteen sixty-four in what had just become the Province of New York. He was turned by the woman who he was courting, unaware of what she really was until she revealed her true nature. That hadn't sat well with him and as soon as he was able to he left the city and returned to his home in Boston. He was related to Adrian—through Lemuel's brother, Adrian's grandfather—but as his great-uncle.

"That must feel strange."

Adrian laughed. "It has its moments. Especially when I'm working and he tries to pull rank on me. Of course he can, since he owns the club, but sometimes it makes me feel like a recalcitrant younger brother."

"Ouch." Gathering up his unfinished meal and the empty wine glasses, Ryan headed to the kitchen. He held up Adrian's glass asking as he did, "Do you want more?"

Since Adrian was watching Ryan's ass at the moment with a great deal of admiration it took a second for him to get that the question was about wine and not… *Well I can't have more of him, now can I? I haven't had any of him so far unless you count the bug a couple of days ago.* "Sure, one more glass can't hurt."

"It could if you drink it on an empty stomach," Ryan called back before disappearing from sight into the kitchen.

I suppose, for the sake of not having him really wondering why I don't eat, I should. Adrian followed him into the kitchen, saying, "I could use a sandwich if you have the makings."

"Of course I do. Look in the fridge and take what you." He got a loaf of bread from the cupboard, setting it on the table along with a plate and a knife.

Soon Adrian had the plate with a cheese sandwich in one hand, a glass of wine in the other, and they returned to the living room. He settled on one end of the sofa, while Ryan took the other end and sipped his beer.

"Do you really think this guy is coming after you?" Ryan asked. "Oh, and what's his name and what does he look like, just in case he is."

"He always struck me as the sort who didn't let things go," Adrian replied. "That's one reason I fired him. He got into altercations with customers once too often because he didn't like something they'd said to him a day or a week before. His name is Darnell Kimball. He's blond with a very square jaw and about five-nine. The last time I saw him his hair was average length and he had a mustache and a small beard."

"Let's hope he didn't shave them off. It'll make it easier to recognize him if he hasn't."

Adrian smiled wryly. "True. He also has a perpetual sneer as if he's better than anyone else."

"Why the hell did you hire him?"

"He was good at his job." That wasn't quite a lie. Darnell *was* good at what he did, feeding on and then killing escaped slaves. Adrian just hadn't hired him to do that. Darnell was also good at hiding his presence if he didn't want other vampires to know he was in the area. Adrian hoped that Lemuel—being almost two hundred years older than when they'd last run into Darnell—might be able to sense Darnell now no matter what.

Ryan took a long pull on his beer. "So we sit and wait for the proverbial knock on the door, or random shot from the woods surrounding the house."

"That's about it I'm afraid. I suspect if he doesn't appear in the next couple of days he probably won't. After all, I've been here for a week already with no sign of him."

"You know what? If he does show up you can always hide in the cold cellar at the cottage. I'll tell him I have no idea who he's talking about and he won't be able to prove differently even if I let him search the place, which for damned sure I wouldn't."

"I suppose that might work," Adrian said thoughtfully. *As a place to put you if things go bad.*

"Good. So that's settled." Ryan popped up, going to get the remote from beside the TV. "Now, what should we watch to take our minds off of Mr Kimball?"

"Anything but a crime drama," Adrian said dryly.

They settled on a comedy on the Movie Channel and Ryan managed to stay awake until The End, although it took Constable kneading his leg every so often to accomplish that.

Then, yawning prodigiously, he went up to bed.

Adrian watched his exit with both amusement and a strong tinge of lust. He quickly tapped down on the latter. As Lemuel had pointed out, getting involved with Ryan would be… complicated at best.

Chapter Six

Ryan spent the following day, well into the afternoon, doing a first read-through of his book looking for continuity problems. Normally it wouldn't have taken that long but he found that he was listening with one ear for any unexplained noises. Finally, around midafternoon he was finished. Or more to the point, he'd done the best he could for the time being. He promised himself he'd go through it again much more carefully tomorrow. *And hopefully concentrate better.*

After shutting down the computer, he went into the kitchen, dumped out what was left of his cold coffee and made a new cup. Then he went out to the backyard patio with Constable right at his heels. As soon as he sat down the cat was in his lap and he realized it was the first time today he'd done that. As a matter of fact, he didn't remember seeing him after he'd fed him that morning.

"Were you playing watch-cat?" he asked him in amusement. He could just visualize Constable patrolling the downstairs in case Darnell Kimball was stalking around the outside of the house. Either that or sleeping with Adrian.

Now that's something I wouldn't mind doing in the least. Although I doubt we'd be sleeping if we were sharing a bed. At least I hope we wouldn't be. He licked his lips, trying to imagine what Adrian looked like under the clothes he wore. *All well-toned muscle and sexy as hell. A six-pack to die for, unlike me.* He patted his stomach, knowing that it could have been flatter. Not that he was anywhere close to carrying too much weight but sitting all day did nothing to help make him look like a one of the heroes in his books.

I should walk more and maybe pick up one of those exercise machines I've seen online. I'm not getting any younger and pretty soon it'll be too late to be svelte and appealing to—he chuckled—*well not the opposite sex, all things considered. But maybe to Adrian?*

"Telling yourself jokes?"

Ryan jumped, turning his head so quickly he could feel his neck snap. "Damn, you scared the living hell out of me."

"Sorry." Adrian dropped down into the chair beside Ryan, patting his shoulder. "Should I have announced my presence first?" he asked with a grin.

"Naw. I'm just jumpy. I have been all day."

"Even with big, fierce Constable hanging around to protect you?"

Ryan snorted. "Cat here was a nonentity a far as I could tell. I was beginning to wonder if he'd spent the day at the foot of your bed."

"Not that I'm aware of. But then I sleep hard so I guess it's possible."

"Speaking of which, you're up early for you."

"It's cloudy; you're out here, so I figured I'd join you. As long as I stay under the patio roof I should be fine."

Ryan studied Adrian's pale skin and grinned. "You need to get some of that spray-on tanning stuff."

Adrian snorted. "And turn bright orange?"

"I think they've improved it in the past few years."

"Well I'll pass. Although," he said almost wistfully, "it would be nice to have your tanned and healthy look."

"Hey, you look healthy and you have that lean and hungry thing going which is sexy."

"Or, according to Shakespeare, it means I think too much, making me dangerous."

"Nothing wrong with being a thinker. That can be pretty damned…" Suddenly flustered at the way the conversation was going or, more to the point, the way he seemed to be turning it, Ryan muttered, "Never mind."

Adrian cocked an eyebrow. "No, no, go on. I want to know where you were going with that."

Swallowing hard, Ryan said, "Someone who's intelligent and shows it without showing it off? That's sexier than some bodybuilder type who's all muscle and no brain."

"Then," Adrian said quietly, staring intently at Ryan, "that would make you very sexy."

Ryan tried to hide the sudden rush of hope he felt at Adrian's words by joking. "Meaning I'm far from being Mr. America? Should I be insulted?"

"Not in the least." Adrian smiled. "You're a nice blend of both—bright, witty, and handsome in a sort of casual way." He flicked Ryan's shoulder-length hair. "I suspect there's muscle not flab under the sweatshirts you seem to favor.

Is he coming on to me? Ryan could feel the heat rising in his face. "I… umm…."

"I didn't mean to embarrass you."

"You didn't. Well… you did but… Damn, I'm a writer. Why am I at a loss for words?"

"Because this is real." Adrian leaned closer, saying softly, "I woke up thinking about you. They were nice thoughts. Very nice ones. But I wasn't going to go beyond that until I came out here and saw you. And then you started talking about what makes a man sexy. I realized I find you very sexy… and interesting. All right, not quite true. I knew that a few days ago but I wasn't about to act on it. It wouldn't be fair to you, presuming you have any feelings for me." He chuckled wryly. "Now I'm starting to get tongue-tied because I don't know what to say next."

"I'm interesting?" Ryan said, latching on to that word rather that the fact Adrian found him sexy. "And why wouldn't it be fair to me?" he added, that being then next most important thing in what Adrian had said.

"Very interesting, now that I'm getting to know you." He ran one finger lightly down Ryan's arm, causing Ryan to shiver at the touch. "If I was less of a gentleman we wouldn't be having this discussion. I'd have come down here, grabbed your hand, and dragged your hopefully willing self upstairs to my bed."

"Very willing." Ryan barely got the words out before Adrian was kissing him. As he returned the kiss the only thing that ran through his mind was *This isn't really happening. I dozed off and I'm dreaming. But what a dream!*

"Boys, am I interrupting something important?"

Ryan and Adrian broke apart as if someone had thrown cold water on them. Lemuel stood there, looking less than happy.

"Fairly important," Adrian told him dryly. "We were exploring our mutual feelings."

"It looked more like you were exploring each other's mouths. Not an unpleasant diversion but…"

"None of your business," Adrian retorted.

"True enough I suppose." Lemuel shot Adrian a look that, to Ryan's way of thinking was both amused and on some level condemning as well.

Frowning, Ryan asked Lemuel, "How did you get in?"

"I walked around the house of course."

"Oh. Yeah."

"Have you… heard anything?" Adrian inquired.

Once again the interaction between Adrian and his uncle puzzled Ryan. It was as if there was something going on under the surface.

"Nothing," Lemuel replied. "I came by as I promised I would last night. I also thought, if the two of you are interested, that we might go out for supper. I found a very nice restaurant just outside of town."

* * * *

"What are you doing?" Adrian asked his uncle.

"Getting him away from here so a friend of mine can search the house and grounds for any sign Darnell has been here recently."

"You can't do that?"

"I have and I'm finding nothing but Darnell is much older than I and adept at hiding his presence as you well know."

"True. Who is this friend?"

Lemuel broke their connection, saying, *"I'll tell you later. At the moment Ryan looks as if he's going to ask if we've suddenly gone mute."*

Actually, all Ryan asked was, "Which restaurant?"

"Alvano's Bistro."

"Great. But..."

"But?" Lemuel cocked his head questioningly.

"It's very expensive," Ryan replied, looking uncomfortable.

"Since I'm treating both of you that shouldn't be a problem. So, if the two of you would change into something a bit less casual..."

Adrian and Ryan hurried upstairs to do just that, but while he put on slacks and a good shirt, Adrian continued his interrupted conversation with his uncle, saying, *"Now tell me who this friend is. Please."*

"Talbot Randel."

Adrian hissed in a breath. *"You cannot be serious! You know him? And more to the point you willingly associate with him?"*

"Considering what he is, he's actually a good... man. As long as you don't do anything to get on his bad side."

"How can a dhampir/werewolf hybrid be considered 'good'? One part of him wants to hunt us and the other part"—Adrian actually chuckled—*"is a mortal enemy so it would want to hunt and kill us as*

well."

"Talbot is the exception to the rule. Perhaps because *he* is *a hybrid. His vampire side has come to terms with his werewolf half, with the human part of him mediating. At least that's the way he describes it."*

Adrian finished buttoning his shirt and checked himself in the mirror while replying, *"I'll do my best to trust your instincts about him."*

"More than instinct. As I said, he is my friend, and he is waiting outside until we leave so we should be on our way."

Adrian stepped into the hallway at the same time Ryan did. Looking him over appreciatively, he commented, "Very nice."

Ryan rolled his eyes. "Slacks and my best shirt, which has seen better days, hardly constitute 'very nice'."

"On you they do." Adrian came up to him, brushing his fingers through Ryan's combed hair. "There, that's better."

"I spent hours…"

Adrian snorted. "Minutes, maybe, but I like the sort of untamed look it usually has. Now we'd better get moving before Lemuel changes his mind.

* * * *

Dinner was good, and relaxing. Adrian and Lemuel both chose the seared New York strip steak, very rare. So rare in fact that at one point Ryan said, "Anyone watching you might think you were vampires. Are you sure the chef even got those close to a flame?"

"Maybe within an inch of it," Adrian replied with a grin. "I just hate shoe leather."

"Uh-huh. I think it's still breathing."

"How is your fish?" Lemuel asked.

"Wonderful. I don't think I've had better since… well

ever."

When dinner was over, Lemuel drove them the rest of the way into town. They wandered the main street, commenting on the older buildings, one of which Adrian told them had been a station on the Underground Railroad.

"It was actually in a stable behind what was then an inn. Unfortunately the actual hiding place was demolished after the war as no one realized it would have historical value sometime in the future."

"That happens too often," Ryan said scathingly. He might have gone on to enumerate when, where, and how but he couldn't think of anything off the top of his head.

At that point, Lemuel suggested they head back home.

* * * *

When they parked in the driveway in front of the house the first thing they saw was a tall, raven-haired man leaning casually against a front porch pillar. Lemuel got out immediately, striding over to greet him.

"A friend of his I take it," Ryan commented.

"Yes," Adrian replied shortly.

"Not one of yours though."

"I've never met him." Adrian was out of the car by then. He walked slowly toward his great-uncle. Ryan followed a couple of feet behind him, looking unsure about what was going on.

"Adrian, Ryan, this is Talbot Randel," Lemuel said by way of introduction. "He's agreed to help us."

Talbot smiled slightly. "I'm not certain 'agreed' is the right word. Lemuel twisted my arm until I listened to his reasons for wanting this Darnell stopped. I must admit his logic is sound." He turned at Adrian. "I've done a little research. You have a formidable enemy, if that's what he's chosen to be."

"What are you?" Ryan asked. "A cop or a private eye?"

"I'm a private detective," Talbot replied. "My specialization is security."

"Security my ass," Adrian muttered to Lemuel.

"It's the reason Lemuel and I set up for my being here," Talbot said before Lemuel could reply. *"And before you get pissed, you were broadcasting loud and clear to anyone within mental earshot. You ought to know better than to do that. What if Darnell had been in the area?"*

Adrian winced. *"Sorry. I should have remembered."*

"No problem—this time."

While Adrian and Talbot were talking, Lemuel told Ryan, "He's in charge of setting up security at my clubs so when this problem with Darnell came up I asked for his help to secure your house."

"Okay." Ryan seemed a bit nonplused. "Look, why don't we go inside and discuss this. I'm not sure I want security if it means punching in codes and being afraid to open a window too far because I might set the damned thing off." He unlocked the front door as he was speaking and let the others inside.

The moment Talbot stepped into the living room there was an angry hiss. Constable stood in the middle of the sofa, his back arched, every hair on his body on end.

"Hey, cat, what the hell is wrong with you?" Ryan asked, moving cautiously toward him, one hand outstretched. "We're all friends. Or did you forget that?"

Constable snarled, his gaze locked on Talbot.

"I suspect it's because of me," Talbot said. "I was working with guard dogs earlier today and didn't change clothes before I came here."

Adrian took control of Constable's mind, the same way he had the first time he and the cat had met. He sent calming thoughts and let him know Talbot wasn't an enemy. Very slowly Constable relaxed his posture before jumping down from the sofa. Shooting Talbot a distrustful look, he stalked from the room.

Ryan let out a long breath. "I've never seen him act that way before."

"Has he ever been around dogs?" Talbot asked.

"Now that I think about it, no. Or at least not since I got him from the shelter."

"Well if he was a street cat before he got there, that could explain his reaction."

Ryan nodded and then asked if anyone wanted coffee or something stronger. No one did so they all found seats, Ryan and Adrian on the sofa, Talbot and Lemuel in the armchairs.

"First off, just to allay your apparent dislike of security systems," Talbot said, looking at Ryan, "I can set one up that uses your fingerprint. That negates anyone who knows what they're doing from being able to break a code. The system I have in mind will take up to four different prints. Unfortunately you're correct about the windows. When the system is armed you'll only be able to open them a few inches, but I can put stops on them in case you forget and try to open them wider. All you have to do at that point is disarm the system to open them more."

"And with my luck I'll forget to close them again and scare the shit out of myself when it goes off."

Talbot chuckled. "If you're that forgetful I can put in a panel, sort of like the ones in cars that show when a door isn't closed all the way. Just check it and if one of the lights is lit, go close the window it belongs to."

"Damn. Security for idiots," Ryan said with a grin.

Talbot nodded. "It's needed more often than you might think for businesses."

"That's all fine and dandy," Adrian said, directing his words to Talbot, *"but even if you really were setting up security, it wouldn't stop*

Darnell if he decides to mist in here."

"That's why I'll be around and about. I'm part dhampir—which I'm sure you know—and an older one to boot. Even as old as he is, I can find him if he tries that."

"When are you going to install the system?" Ryan asked.

"In the morning," Talbot told him. "Everything I need is in my camper. I'd do it tonight but it's late and I don't want to keep you up. Is seven too early to wake you?"

Ryan grimaced but shook his head. "It won't kill me to see a sunrise at least once in my life. What about Adrian though? He's usually going to bed about the time I get up."

"No worries," Adrian said with a straight face. "I sleep like the dead."

Lemuel and Talbot chuckled when Ryan muttered, "I told you I think you're half vampire."

"Are you planning on staying here, in your camper, Talbot? Or at a motel?" Lemuel asked at that point.

"Here. It's parked by the side of the house. I hope that's okay with you, Ryan."

"Yeah, sure. If you want you can even use one of the bedrooms."

"Thanks but I'm used to the camper."

"All right." Ryan obviously tried to repress a yawn, even though it wasn't *that* late.

"Lemuel," Adrian said, *"Are you doing something to Ryan?"*

"We all need to talk and we can't while he's in the room. Better that he goes to bed now."

* * * *

Apparently Ryan was all for that. He stood, apologized for being so tired and told them—with a bit of a grin—to be sure to lock up when they left.

To kill the time until Ryan had showered and was in bed, Adrian got wine for himself and Lemuel, and a beer for Talbot when the man indicated that's what he wanted. Then he turned on the TV, scrolling through the channels until he found a sports program on ESPN. He figured it would be something that wouldn't be of interest to any of them but would cover their talking if necessary.

"Now," Lemuel said a brief time later, "what exactly are your plans, Talbot?"

"Simple enough. Put in the system as I said I would and then leave. Or rather make it seem as if I was going to but I'll realize I'm missing an important component and leave to get it. Adrian, this was your house, according to Lemuel. Is there somewhere I can hide out so Ryan doesn't know I'm still around?"

"Two places actually. In the cold cellar in the cottage, or here in the house."

"The house would be better, but coming and going might be a problem without his seeing me."

"You forget, or perhaps you don't know, but it was a station for the Underground Railroad. There's a secret entrance I'll show you that you can use to get inside. Lemuel is using the room but I'm sure he'd be willing to share."

"Indeed," Lemuel agreed. "It's large, and Adrian has made it quite comfortable over the years since his turning."

"That would work. Is there a way to get from it into the rest of the house?"

"Well I just mist," Adrian told him. "But from what I understand that's not a dhampir ability."

"Nope. Teleporting is me, because of my werewolf side, but I have to see my destination first."

"That's okay. There's a well-hidden door in the basement, behind a set of shelves. It was for emergencies only and I think I used it just once, so the hinges are undoubtedly well-rusted by now."

"WD-40," Talbot replied. "I have some in the camper. I suggest we deal with it now, while he's sleeping."

"No kidding," Adrian muttered.

Talbot went to get the WD-40 and a few minutes later the three men were down in a small room in the basement that had served as a storage pantry.

"The shelves"—Adrian pointed to the ones he meant—"slide to the side just enough to reveal the door. That is if they're still movable after all this time."

They were, although it took all of his vampire strength to get them started. Then with a loud creak they slid two feet until The End hit the abutting wall. Behind them was a narrow door.

"Key?" Talbot asked while he liberally oiled the hinges.

"Yeah, that might help." Adrian misted under the door, returning a few moments later to hand it to Talbot.

The dhampir oiled the lock as well and then inserted the key. At first it didn't want to turn but with a bit of effort it finally did and Talbot opened the door. Behind it was the small entrance way to the station area and the stairs going up to the second floor.

"This will work just fine," Talbot said, stepping back into the basement. He locked the door, putting the key on his key ring. "I'd prefer to leave the shelves where they are for now. It won't do me much good if I can't get through the door from the other side because they're covering it."

"What if Ryan…"

"I'll put a block on his mind," Lemuel interrupted, "so he doesn't try to explore this particular room."

"I guess that's necessary. Still, I don't like that you keep messing with him that way," Adrian said tightly.

"Sometimes it's necessary and you know it," Lemuel

replied acidly.

"You could send him away," Talbot pointed out.

"My uncle and I have already had that discussion. It is not happening because he wouldn't leave willingly and I won't enthrall him to make him leave and"—he shot a hard look at Lemuel—"neither will you." He paused, realizing something, and added, "And you'd better not try it either, Talbot."

"All right. It was just a suggestion." Talbot scrutinized Adrian for a long moment and then smiled knowingly. "If I'm right he means more to you than just a friend. So you don't want to send him away for the simple reason that if he's gone and Darnell does find him, *you* can't protect him. *You*, Adrian, not Lemuel or me but you."

"Do you think I'm that egotistical?"

"If the shoe fits…" Talbot replied with a smirk.

"I'm not, damn it. I want him safe and I know that he might not be if he's here. But I won't use underhanded measures to make him leave."

"Then tell him the truth and let *him* make the choice. Because if he does stay he needs to know what he might be facing. And Adrian, it ain't no pissed off ex-employee."

Adrian sighed deeply. "If I do, then any one of us forcing him to leave by enthralling him might become a moot point. He'll run as fast and as far as he can just to get away from me and what I am."

"Adrian," Talbot asked quietly, "does he care for you?"

"I… think so. I hope he does."

"Then trust that his feelings for you will override the fear he may feel when he finds out you're not quite human."

Adrian almost smiled. "That's putting it nicely."

"Better than describing you as a ravening, blood-thirsty beast—which by the way from what I can tell, you aren't."

"He's not," Lemuel stated firmly. "None of us are."

"Darnell excluded I'd say," Talbot said.

"I meant any of the three of us in this room. But that aside, he has a point, Adrian. The best, the wisest thing right now would be to talk to Ryan honestly about us, and Darnell, and what might happen if the bastard shows his face here."

"I know. I know." Adrian rubbed his temples between his fingers, trying to will away the fear that idea spawned. "And I suppose…"

"There's no time like the present," Lemuel's tone of voice saying he understood what Adrian was going through, and that he commiserated with him.

Chapter Seven

Ryan awoke with a fearful start when he felt someone touching him. Groggily, he opened his eyes, trying to turn to see who was in his room. He couldn't move, and when he opened his mouth to speak no words came out. Then a face loomed over him. A square-jawed face with a blond beard and mustache. *Darnell!* Fear engulfed him.

"Sorry to drop in like this," Darnell said so softly that Ryan could barely hear him. "But we have much to discuss, you and I, about Adrian Devoe, or as he calls himself now, Adrian Devereux. Come with me."

Against his will, Ryan stood. In some part of his mind he was glad he wasn't naked. The last thing he wanted was…

"Me seeing you nude?" Darnell chuckled, beckoning for Ryan to follow him.

They didn't go far. Merely down the hall to a vacant bedroom. There, Darnell ordered Ryan to sit on the bed. Unable to resist, Ryan did. *What has he done to me? Drugged me somehow?* He shivered, a combination of rage and dread rolling over him.

"You're not drugged. I'm controlling you. Being what I am—I can. I can also read your thoughts, so ask your questions. Unfortunately I don't think it would be wise for me to let you speak aloud. You might decide to scream for help." Darnell smiled nastily. "I don't think that would be wise, even though I am hiding our whereabouts."

I don't believe you! You must have drugged me, or hypnotized me or… or something.

"No. You see, like your great-grandfather Adrian—and yes that's who he is to you—I am a vampire."

You're out of your mind!

"But very much in yours. Think, Ryan. How could I

know what's going through your thoughts if I couldn't read them? Do you know of any human who has that power?"

Ryan barely shook his head in reply.

"I thought not. Now, as I was saying, Adrian, his great-uncle Lemuel, and I, are all vampires." His voice was soft and compelling as he continued speaking. "I've only met Adrian twice and that was almost two hundred years ago. The second time I was certain I'd killed him. Obviously"—he hissed, literally hissed in anger—"I was wrong. Thanks in part to Lemuel's interference."

I don't believe you. I don't believe any of this. Whatever game you're playing… Good gods, how can you do this just because he fired you from the nightclub? Is it worth spending the rest of your life in prison just for losing your job?

"Is that what he told you? It's a lie. I'm certain everything he's told you is a lie. This is his house. From what I've learned he has lived here ever since his turning. Unbeknownst to his family down through the years. His wife, his son, his granddaughters, and now you."

Vampires are myths, fairytales, nothing more. You've obviously watched too many bad movies and taken them to heart. Ryan said that, but he wasn't certain it was the truth. Not anymore. Darnell *was* reading his mind. Darnell *had* made him come with him. Not by force but because Ryan couldn't resist his command.

"I see you're beginning to believe me. Perhaps one more bit of proof and you'll finally know I'm not lying to you. Not that it will do you any good in the long run."

As Ryan watched, Darnell opened his mouth and fangs appeared where his eyeteeth had been seconds before. Long, dangerous-looking fangs. Then Darnell held up one hand and his nails elongated into claws. Slowly, he dragged one claw down Ryan's forearm, leaving a thin bloody slice behind.

Ryan looked at the cut in disbelief. *He… those… that claw*

really did cut me.

Darnell smiled knowingly. "Now do you believe me?"

Mutely, Ryan nodded.

* * * *

"We have a visitor," Talbot said seconds before Adrian started up the stairs to the second floor. "Unfortunately, I didn't pick up on it until just this moment. He is good at shielding, but he relaxed it a bit for some reason. Perhaps"—he frowned, concentrating—"because he has Ryan."

"No, Adrian," Lemuel said adamantly before his nephew could react by dashing upstairs. *"If you do, Darnell will kill him just to show you that he's in command."*

"He's right," Talbot agreed.

Adrian sank down on the stairs, his expression a rictus of fear. *"Can you pinpoint where they are?"*

"To an extent. Wait here." Talbot moved with lightning speed to the hallway of the second floor. A few moments later he rejoined Adrian and Lemuel. *"They're in room at The End of the hall. The one by the blank wall, not the windowed end."*

Cold anger replaced Adrian's fear. *"Do you know—could you tell if Ryan is with him willingly?"*

"Do you think he would be?" Lemuel asked with surprise.

"No. That came out wrong. Is Ryan able to move and talk, Talbot?"

"Not from what I could tell. I heard one of his thoughts though. 'He… those… that claw really did cut me'. And Darnell's reply. 'Now do you believe me?'"

"I guess my telling Ryan about… about me in any way that he could accept is a moot point now," Adrian said in despair.

"Worry about that later," Lemuel replied sharply. *"For the moment we have to get him away from Darnell and then deal with the*

bastard once and for all."

"I can get him out of the room," Talbot said. *"Darnell won't know I'm there until it's too late, unlike with either of you."*

"You can break the compulsion he has on Ryan?" Adrian asked.

"Possibly, but whether I can or not doesn't matter right now. I can physically remove him from the room. After all, I am half werewolf with teleporting abilities."

"And do what with him? Darnell will be able to track him, if not you."

"The minute I give the word that I have him you two appear, Adrian first so that Darnell thinks Lemuel is the one who took Ryan. That should give Darnell more to worry about than a mere human. I'll dump Ryan in my camper. It's well protected in more ways than one. Then I'll join you." Talbot smiled gleefully as a long, silver sword suddenly appeared in his hands. *"With this."*

"And if you can't free him from Darnell."

"Oh ye of little faith. I'm within a few years of being as old as the bastard. I'll be in and out before he knows I'm around. Now give me a picture of the room, Adrian."

* * * *

True to his word, Talbot made it into the room where Darnell was holding Ryan. He sped to the bed, scooped Ryan up and they vanished.

Darnell let out a howl of rage that cut off short when Adrian stepped into the room.

"If you want me, you come after *me*. Not some innocent human," Adrian snarled.

"And now I have you. And Lemuel when he returns from wherever he took your minion."

As planned, Adrian didn't correct him about who had taken Ryan, only saying, "He's not my minion."

"Oh I know that and so does he, now that I've pointed out to him that you're his great-grandfather."

As Darnell talked, Adrian could feel him trying to enter his mind to control him. He fought back against that as best he could but it was a losing battle—or would have been if Lemuel hadn't joined him, both physically and mentally. Together they put an end to Darnell's mental attack.

"Ah well, if one thing doesn't work, another will." Darnell smiled rabidly as fangs and claws appeared. With unbelievable speed he wrapped one arm around Adrian's throat, claws digging into Adrian's shoulder while he pulled him against his body.

Adrian wasn't without his own weapons of the same sort. But when he raked one clawed hand across Darnell's arm the vampire merely laughed, the resulting wound healing in a matter of seconds.

"Don't," Darnell spat out when Lemuel launched his own attack. "I will kill him and this time he'll stay dead." With his free hand he gripped Adrian's chin, twisting his head sideways. "Step back or I tear it off," he ordered Lemuel. "And then it will be your turn."

"Can you fight against this?" Lemuel asked, raising his hands. Darnell howled as blood flowed from a wound in his side, staining his shirt red. "I can't kill you outright. My gift isn't that strong yet. But I can wound you more than once."

"Mere child's play." Darnell rose into the air, still holding Adrian. Baring his fangs, he sank them into Adrian's neck, withdrawing them only long enough to say, "Can you get to me before I drain him?" Then he bit again—deeply.

"Maybe he can't, but I can," a disembodied voice replied.

A blade flashed, lighted by the dim moonlight coming through the window and Darnell screamed in agony even as his claws dug further into Adrian's shoulder, keeping him pinned against his chest.

"Release him. Now!" When Darnell—hovering above the bed now—attempted to move toward the doorway, the blade flashed again. It sliced through Darnell's elbow, narrowly missing slashing Adrian in the process.

Adrian fell onto the bed, bleeding profusely from the damage Darnell had done to his throat. That was nothing however compared to the blood flowing from Darnell's severed elbow. Then, with one last flash of the blade, Talbot separated Darnell's head from his body. Within seconds, all that was left of the vampire was a fine shower of ash that flittered down to cover Adrian and the bedspread.

"Damn," Adrian managed to whisper. "Now I'll have to dust in here again."

Talbot became visible at that point, shaking his head in disbelief. "He almost kills you and that's all you can think about?" He sheathed his sword then watched as Lemuel attended to Adrian's wounds.

Despite their gravity the bites were already healing and the claw marks on Adrian's shoulder were almost gone. Lemuel still insisted that Adrian take a bit of his blood to speed up the process, which Adrian did with some reluctance.

Finally, deeming Adrian recovered enough to move, Lemuel suggested he go down to the camper and speak with Ryan. "He must be one very confused young man at the moment."

"He won't listen. Not after the way I betrayed his trust."

"You don't know that," Lemuel replied.

Adrian shot him a grim look as he got to his feet. "I do. He's not going to want me in his life now, so I'm going to honor that. The sooner I'm gone, the sooner he can move on."

"Just like that?"

"Yes, Lemuel, just like that." Adrian pushed his way past

his uncle, stopped at the door and turned back. "Thank you, both of you, for your help. And Talbot, thank you for saving… for keeping Ryan safe." With that said, he moved quickly out of their sight, misted, and entered the room he'd made his own since soon after his turning.

Chapter Eight

Ryan came back to his senses—as he thought of it—moments after the stranger set him down on the long bench inside the van. By then the man was gone.

He remembered the man dashing into the bedroom, picking him up and then… *Then what? I was there, now I'm here. But how?*

He almost expected to hear Darnell say, "You *wish* you were free," with a sneer and find that he was still in the bedroom.

Easing his legs off the bench, he sat up and looked around. *This is definitely a van, not the bedroom.* By the moonlight coming through the windows he could see a tiny kitchenette, the driver's seat, the steering wheel, and a miniscule table next to and beneath banks of cabinets. *Cozy, in a sort of cramped way.*

"But I don't belong here. I belong with…" he murmured. Then he remembered everything Darnell had told him. "It's a lie. It has to be!"

Still… He looked at the thin cut on his arm and remembered Darnell's clawed hand.

Maybe he's one, but not Adrian. And yet it explains why Adrian would never go out during the day. And why he suddenly showed up here. It suddenly dawned on him. *He… he was living here somewhere. He was the one who screamed—trying to scare me out of the house. The lying, mother-fucking son-of-a-bitch!*

Beyond furious, and not giving a damn whether Darnell was still around, Ryan left the camper. The front door to the house was locked and his hand was shaking so hard it took him a minute to get it unlocked once he found the spare key he'd hidden under a rock. Slamming it behind him when he was inside, he strode across the entryway to the staircase. He heard the low sounds of talking and took the stairs two at a time, arriving at the top just as Lemuel and Talbot came into the hallway.

"Where is he?"

"Dead," Lemuel replied.

For a second Ryan felt a wave of anguish flood him. "Darnell won?"

"No. Darnell is dead." Lemuel must have realized his mistake because he said, "I thought that's who you meant."

Ryan shook his head, his anger rising again. "Where is the… your bastard nephew. If that's what he really is to you."

"He is my grandnephew," Lemuel replied. "And he's gone."

"Damned coward. He couldn't stick around to face me."

"That 'damned coward' almost died to save you," Lemuel spat out.

"*Talbot* saved me," Ryan retorted.

"Only because Adrian showed up at the same time I spirited you away," Talbot said tightly. "Without that distraction Darnell would have followed us and brought your sorry ass back again."

"Oh," Ryan said weakly. Then he stiffened his resolve. "Then he took off like… like a thief in the night so he wouldn't have to face me. Well that's just fine because I don't want to see the lying bastard ever again. I don't want to see any of you again. Get out of *my* house."

"With pleasure, you ungrateful… ingrate," Lemuel growled.

"Ingrates are always ungrateful," Talbot said wryly as Lemuel moved quickly to the stairs and vanished down them.

"That means you too," Ryan said, glaring at the dhampir.

"Not yet. Not until we've talked."

"Go. To. Hell!" Turning on his heel, Ryan went into his

bedroom. He tried to close the door only to find Talbot holding the edge to keep that from happening.

"I don't leave until we've talked and"—Talbot's smile held a bit of amusement—"there's actually no way you can force me to. So you might as well sit"—he pointed to the bed—"and listen."

Childishly he knew, Ryan retorted, "Make me." The next thing he knew Talbot had grabbed his arms, walked him backwards to the bed and shoved him down.

"Now as I was saying, we talk. Or right now you listen while I talk. I know you're upset…"

Ryan snorted. "That's an understatement."

"I said *I* talk. You listen. To start with, yes this is your house because you inherited it. However it's also Adrian's. He built it—I'd say with his own two hands but I suspect he had help. Do you know the history behind the house?" When Ryan gave a brief nod, Talbot continued. "Then you get that it's been here since before the Civil War. If it wasn't for Darnell, Adrian would probably have died of old age, his son would have inherited it, and so forth down to you. But Darnell changed that."

"How?"

"As you know—now—Darnell was a vampire. Back then—and to this day—he fed off the living, draining then killing them. His particular favorites were escaped slaves who wouldn't be missed. He's old. Much older even than Lemuel, who was no spring chicken even back then. Yes, Lemuel was a vampire when all this happened and Adrian knew and accepted it." Talbot smiled dryly. "Some people can actually do that because they realize most vampires are just, shall we say, enhanced human beings and nothing more."

"Was Adrian attacked because he tried to protect the slaves? I mean from Darnell?"

"Yes. If Lemuel hadn't been there, intending to help move them to a safer place, Adrian would have died. Instead, to save his life, Lemuel turned him."

"What... what happened to those slaves?"

"Darnell took them. I'm sure their bones are buried somewhere out there." Talbot gestured toward the window.

Ryan glanced at it then returned his attention to Talbot, glaring angrily again. "That's all well and good, and makes a terrific story. It does *not* negate the fact that Adrian lied to me from the moment I met him. If it hadn't been for Darnell"—he took a deep, shuddering breath—"I wouldn't know anything about the real Adrian. Oh, and in case he didn't tell you, Adrian pulled some lame trick after I moved here, pretending to be a ghost—I guess. Or hoping I'd think that's what was screaming like it was being tortured."

Talbot chuckled. "No I didn't know that but I suspect it's the best he could come up with. Although why he wanted you gone when he'd put up with your aunt and his own son's family is beyond me."

"Because he's an ass," Ryan spat out.

"Or"—Talbot smiled knowingly—"he found you interesting. Consider *that*, Ryan. If he did from the first then he was in a bind. He's a vampire and—although not by blood—he's your great-grandfather. Hardly a combination he could tell you about. Right?"

"I... guess."

"Did you... *do* you find him interesting?"

"Very," Ryan admitted reluctantly. "That's why it hurts so much to find out he wasn't truthful with me. We were beginning to be attracted to each other I think. I know I was. And then to find out the way I did exactly who and what he is... Damn it, Talbot, if he really does like me why couldn't he have...? Well, been honest with me."

"What part of what I just said didn't you understand," Talbot replied curtly.

"I understand, I just don't..." Ryan buried his face in his hands. "I could have accepted it. At least I hope I could have." He looked up, barely smiling. "The vampire part anyway. The whole grandfather thing is..." He shuddered.

"For the love of all that's holy, Ryan, he's not related to you by *blood*. Get that through your thick skull."

Ryan nodded. "Not that it makes the least bit of difference at this point what he is. He's gone. He's out of my life. He obviously doesn't think I can handle it all and he walked away without giving me a chance."

"Ryan," Talbot said, kneeling in front of him, "be honest with yourself. Would you have given *him* a chance? If it had been Adrian, not Darnell, who had told you what would you have done?"

"I don't know," Ryan whispered. "I honestly do *not* know. I was only beginning to understand that my feelings for him were more than just friendship. Oh I had some interesting dreams, but beyond that..." He sighed.

"You weren't about to offer to let him stay here on a permanent basis."

"Probably not. Not yet. And then Darnell showed up before I could really come to a decision one way or another."

"Unfortunate on several levels."

"No shit." Ryan looked sadly at Talbot. "What am I going to do now?"

"Hope. Hope he comes back because he cares for you. Hope if he does that you can accept him for what he is, a man and nothing more. Because, Ryan, that *is* what he is. He may not be quite average, but then a lot of people aren't. He may not be quite human, in the general definition of the word, but he feels, he hurts, he laughs, he probably cries although he might not admit to that. In other words, he's not that much different than you except for the fact he's been around a bit longer, and has"—Talbot chuckled—"strange dietary requirements."

"Do you know," Ryan asked hesitantly, "does he hunt for... victims... the way Darnell does."

"Nope. Lemuel told me that both of them are, as he called it, baggers. They have sources for bagged blood."

"That's a relief."

"I'm sure it is. And it holds true for most vampires these days."

"Like you? I mean, I'm presuming you're one too."

"You presume wrong."

"Oh? Then what are you because I'm very certain you're not human like me."

"I'm a dhampir and a werewolf."

Leaning back on his hands, Ryan studied Talbot in shocked silence for a moment. "That's possible?"

Talbot grinned. "I'm living proof. My mother was a human/werewolf hybrid. She fell in love with my father who was a vampire. Because of her human side and the fact when a human mates with a vampire their offspring is a dhampir, I sort of got some of everything."

"Wow. I bet you're pretty unique then."

"To the best of my knowledge I'm one of a kind although there is a rumor of another one who was created a part of an experiment gone wrong. If it's true I've never met him."

"I think I'll stick with being purely human. Much less complicated."

Talbot laughed. "Can't blame you for that."

"Thank you." Ryan paused before saying earnestly, "Thank you for making me talk to you, or at least listen to you."

"You're welcome. I think in The End you did a fair share of talking too. Hopefully, things will work out for you in time."

"If he ever comes back."

"Somehow"—Talbot smiled knowingly—"I don't think he's gone too far away. And on that note, I should pick up my toys and leave."

"You never set up a security system for me."

With a wide grin, Talbot replied, "Not so surprising since I have no clue how to do that." And then he vanished.

"Figures," Ryan muttered.

Chapter Nine

Ryan managed to sleep after Talbot left. Exhaustion, both physical and mental, contributed to that and he didn't wake up until mid-morning. He might not have even then if it wasn't for the fact that Constable was standing on his chest, kneading it while meowing piteously.

Groggily, Ryan muttered, "I have to teach you how to use the can opener." All he got in return was Constable moving to the edge of the bed to sit and look at him as if to say, "Well?"

When he got up, he realized he was still wearing the sweatpants he'd gone to bed in. *Just what I don't need. A reminder of what happened last night. Of what I've lost. Not that I ever really had it. Him.*

"Yeah, I'm coming," he said when Constable went to the bedroom door then looked back at him. They went down to the kitchen where Ryan made short work of opening a can of cat food, spooning half of it into the cat's bowl. After filling and turning on the coffeemaker he went back upstairs to shower and get ready to face the day.

Half an hour later he was at the computer, opening the file for his most recent book. He knew he had to go over it again, editing and revising it one more time before sending off to his beta reader. Knowing and doing however turned out to be two different things. His mind kept going back to his talk last night with Talbot, as well as everything that preceded it.

One thing Talbot had said kept coming back to Ryan—'I don't think he's gone too far away'.

What if he was trying to give me a clue without coming right out and saying it? After all, Talbot's a dhampir and from what I read about them somewhere they can sense the presence of a vampire. If he could feel Adrian's presence close by…

"That's it! He's still here in the house. But where? Think, damn it. The house was a station for the Underground Railroad. Adrian said as much and he was the one who built it. Where would he have put a secret room? How would it be accessed?"

He remembered Talbot saying that Darnell attacked Adrian and the slaves just as he was getting ready to transfer them to Lemuel's care. To Ryan that seemed to say the entrance to the room was somewhere on the exterior of the house. *More logical than walking them through the house to the back door.*

Springing to his feet, he went outside, with Constable following at his heels. Logically, he decided, the entrance would be at the back of the house where it would have been less visible to passers-by. Twenty minutes later he gave up in disgust, telling the cat, "If it was here it's been so long since it was used that time and nature have concealed it too well to be found."

He decided to check the cottage, on the off chance Adrian had gone to ground there. When he got inside, he moved the two broken-down chairs that sat on top of what looked like a trapdoor. As he did so he thought he had to be on the wrong track because the thick layer of dust hadn't been disturbed. *But then he's a vampire. They can mist into places.* He was surprised to find that the idea that Adrian *was* one didn't bother him nearly as much now as it had last night. He still wasn't happy about the idea, but as Talbot had pointed out very succinctly, Adrian was still a man with all the human traits he'd had before his turning.

A good man, I think, then and now. No, I know he is. He only lied to me because... well what else could he do under the circumstances. Maybe given more time together, once he realized our feelings for each other were real, he would have told me. After all it was just yesterday that we kissed. Damn. It feels like a hundred years ago but... He smiled, recalling the kiss.

"Then Lemuel showed up and put an end to that." When Constable cocked his head, Ryan said, "Just thinking out loud."

He found a couple of old rags and used them to dust the top of the trapdoor. On one edge there was a small iron ring. It took a lot of tugging but finally the door opened with a loud creaking of ancient, un-oiled hinges. There was a ladder, which Ryan used to descend cautiously, worrying that at any second one of the wooden rungs might snap under his weight. *Then, a hundred years from now, someone would find my desiccated bones.*

The room under the cottage was small, maybe ten feet by twelve, with shelves lining three walls. Along the fourth he saw bits of straw that looked as if mice were using them for nesting. *Just what you'd expect for a cold-storage room. Still, it would be a good place to hide slaves in a pinch. Maybe, back then, there was a lot of straw and they hid under it, or behind it.* Possible he supposed although he couldn't fathom why anyone would have straw in a storage room. *Unless, maybe, they had ice down here to keep things cold and the straw kept it from melting too fast. Hell if I know. Guess research is in order. Or…* He sighed. *Or if I can find him, I'll ask.*

With that thought, and since it was obvious Adrian wasn't hiding out under the cottage, Ryan returned to the house. He realized he was hungry, which didn't surprise him much since the last time he'd eaten was at dinner the previous night and it was now late afternoon. He wasn't in the mood for cooking though, so he made soup and a sandwich then sat down at the kitchen table to eat. He was just lifting the first spoonful of soup to his mouth when Constable patted his leg. Startled, Ryan managed to spill the soup down his sweatshirt.

"My last clean one," he grumbled, glaring at the cat. "Guess what I'm doing after supper. Laundry. And it's all your fault."

Constable just patted his leg again before looking at his empty food bowl. With a roll of his eyes, Ryan filled it and they both settled in to eat their meals.

* * * *

"I hate laundry, I hate laundry," Ryan muttered as he lugged the hamper down to the basement and put half its contents into the washing machine. While he was doing that, he noticed Constable was exploring the basement. The cat disappeared from view and soon Ryan heard him scratching on something. Then he meowed loudly.

"Now what?" Ryan stepped out of the laundry room, saw Constable at a closed door and shook his head. "Do you think mice are in there? There hadn't better be. It's just another old pantry. See." He opened the door and switched on the dim overhead light.

Constable darted in, coming to a sharp stop at the far end of a set of shelves. "*Meeeowmeeow. Meeeow.*"

"I swear." Ryan went to see what had caught his attention. "Holy shit. That wasn't here the last time I looked." 'That' was a door. It took him a moment to realize the shelves that must have hidden it from sight had been moved. "This has to lead to the hidden room. And more to the point, for some reason Adrian must have shown it to Talbot last night." He tried the handle. It twisted but the door didn't open. *And twenty-to-one wherever the key is I'll never find it. Still…*

He hurried upstairs to his computer and began searching to see if there was a way to make his own lockpick. *Got it!* He found a site with a demo of how to do that using just standard large paperclips. After getting several from one of the desk drawers, and a pair of needle-nose pliers he kept in the kitchen, he set to work. Then he studied how to use them.

"Now for the big test," he said when he got back to the door in the storage room.

It took a while, and several muttered curse words, but finally he felt the lock give and he was able to open the door.

Chapter Ten

Adrian had been awake for only a few minutes when he heard something at the bottom of the stairs leading to the exit from his room.

Thinking it must be Talbot—because he knew that as a dhampir the man could tell he was still here in the house—he hurriedly put on a pair of jeans and a T-shirt. By then the vague sounds had transformed into footsteps slowly coming closer to the top of the stairs.

"Talbot," he called out, "I know you can move faster than that."

"I'm not him."

Adrian's emotions soared momentarily when he heard Ryan's voice. Just as quickly they dropped and he almost misted away, not wanting to face him. But he didn't.

I might as well get this over with. Then—he cringed at the thought—*I really will move on. Move out. Find somewhere new to stay where I'll never have to see him again and he won't have to see me.*

Ryan came into view at the top of the stairs. His gaze locked on Adrian just briefly before he looked around. "Nice digs, if a bit small," he said, a tiny grin lifting his lips.

"I don't require much room."

"Of course not. I'm sure you spend most of your waking hours creeping around the rest of the house, playing ghost now and then."

"I've… been known to."

"Do you mind if I sit?" Ryan asked, nodding toward one of a pair of fairly comfortable looking carved chairs at one side of the room.

"Please be my guest."

Ryan stepped around the marble-topped coffee table and

settled in one of the chairs. When Adrian remained standing, Ryan said, "This would be easier if you sat too."

"Easier how?" Adrian asked, not budging an inch. "To tell me what a lying bastard I am? You can do that without my moving."

"All right. You're a lying bastard. Now that we've cleared the air about that, I understand why. I mean why you lied. You could hardly have walked up to me and said, 'Allow me to introduce myself. I'm Adrian, I live in a hidden room in your house, and I'm a vampire'."

Adrian managed a small smile. "That would have sent you running for sure. Or had you calling the nearest sanatorium to have them send men with straitjackets."

"Exactly. Okay, so yeah, last night I was a bit pissed."

"A bit?" Adrian cocked an eyebrow.

"Well maybe more than a bit. At least until Talbot explained a few facts of life to me."

"So now you're not angry," Adrian asked cautiously.

"I'm… debating it. I know that from your standpoint this will sound crazy, but I wish you'd trusted me enough to think I'd have been able to handle it. Maybe not in one large chunk of information but a hint here, a word there, until I finally asked what the hell you were trying to tell me."

Adrian finally moved to sit in the other chair. "At which point you think you could have dealt with my answer?"

"It would have been easier than having Darnell lay it all out for me in words of one syllable. Of course at first I didn't believe him even though he managed to prove to me *he* was a vampire." Ryan glanced at the healing cut on his arm then back at Adrian. "Do your nails turn into claws when you fight?"

"Yes. And I have fangs."

"And if you bit me when we had sex…" Ryan instantly turned a bright shade of red. "I read that somewhere. That if you did... Well, you know."

"Is that a possibility?" Adrian asked, feeling hope spring up.

"That someday we might make it into the same bed, at the same time, and not just to sleep? Maybe. First we have to come to some sort of agreement about things. About us. If there is an 'us'."

Very softly Adrian replied, "I'd like there to be."

"I think I would too." Ryan leaned toward Adrian, his look intense as he scanned Adrian's face.

Adrian wasn't about to take the chance he'd move away. Cupping one hand at the nape of Ryan's neck, he closed the distance between them and kissed him.

"It seems to me we've been in this position before," an amused voice said.

Adrian ignored his uncle and deepened the kiss once he was certain it was what Ryan wanted. Apparently it was because Ryan ignored Lemuel as well. For long moments they continued the kiss and then Ryan pulled away, panting. "You might not have to," he said, tapping Adrian's nose, "but for me breathing is a must, not an option."

Adrian laughed. "I'll remember that for next time." After dropping another, very swift kiss on Ryan's lips he finally turned to look at Lemuel. "To what do I owe this visit?"

"I wanted to see how you were handling things. Last night you weren't at all." Lemuel chuckled. "I'd say that's changed."

"We're working on it?" Adrian said, his gaze now locked on Ryan.

"That pretty well says it all," Ryan agreed. "It's not going to happen in an instant."

"Good things rarely do," Adrian replied softly. "But when they finally fall into place the wait becomes worth it."

"Then I'll leave you to it." Lemuel clapped a hand on Adrian's shoulder. "Do not be a stranger."

Adrian snorted softly. "Says the man that I see once in a blue moon if that often."

"You know where I live," Lemuel pointed out.

"When you're not traveling."

Lemuel nodded. "There is that." And then he misted and vanished.

"That is truly weird," Ryan said, shuddering.

Adrian took his hand, holding it firmly. "You'll find out that a lot of what we can do is weird, in the grand scheme of things. Do you think you can handle it?"

"For damned sure I'm going to try—with your help."

"I'll be here."

"Here like here?" Ryan pointed down, "Or here like in the house and… well you know."

"If you have no objections, I'll go back to the room I've used since we first met." He felt almost hesitant to ask that, even though this was his house. *I guess I've finally gotten it through my head that my house is his home now.*

"None at all. I think Constable would be upset if you didn't." Ryan managed to say that with a straight face although Adrian saw he was fighting hard not to laugh.

"Well I can't upset him, now can I?"

"Nope. He turns into a real tiger when he's pissed."

"Ah, so he's a shapeshifter?"

"Damned well better not…" At that point Ryan broke down, laughing hard. "One super… natural in my… life is… enough," he sputtered.

* * * *

Once Adrian returned to the bedroom he'd chosen, it

didn't take long for him and Ryan to settle back into the routine they'd established before Darnell had shown up. Of course now he wasn't paying rent for it. He was a housemate with all that implied.

Early one evening a week after the 'talk' as Ryan thought of it now, he was in the kitchen fixing supper when Adrian joined him. Knowing Adrian could eat, although he rarely did, Ryan asked, "Would you like some?"

Adrian chuckled. "That's a pretty suggestive question but taking it the way you meant it, no thanks."

Ryan grinned, moving into Adrian's personal space. "Maybe I meant it both ways? I'm willing to offer a kiss in lieu of supper if you're interested."

"Very tempting."

"But no taker?"

Adrian answered that by cupping Ryan's face and kissing him. It was something they'd done more than once but this time it seemed as if Adrian's heart wasn't in it. As if he was doing it because it was what Ryan wanted.

Stepping away, Ryan studied Adrian. He looked pale. Much paler than usual. "What's wrong? Are you sick?"

Adrian smiled wryly. "Vampires don't get sick. I am however hungry so if you'll excuse my asking, would you give me a ride into town?"

"Of course!" Ryan turned to shut off the stove only to have Adrian stop him.

"Eat first. I'm not going to starve to death in the next few minutes."

Resisting the chance to make a bad joke about Adrian's already being dead, Ryan dished up his meal and sat down. As he ate he kept sending worried looks at Adrian.

"I'm fine. Honest," Adrian told him at one point.

Ryan nodded. Then he had an idea. "Would it be

possible for you to have your own supply here at the house?"

"Perhaps. I'll ask Emily, Doctor Beals, about that. She might be able to arrange it."

* * * *

"I don't see why not," Emily said an hour later. "I can't have it shipped directly to you, Adrian. That would cause more than a few questions. But I can bring a supply out to the house as long as you have a safe storage place for the bags."

"By that you mean somewhere other than the refrigerator?" Ryan asked.

"Oh that would work, but I suspect if you had company they might wonder why you were storing blood," she replied with a laugh.

"Very true. Not that we have visitors. Well not…" Ryan hesitated.

"I think," Adrian filled in, "he's trying to be polite and say human ones."

"Yeah, that. Still we should get a second fridge and put it in the basement maybe?"

"That would work," Adrian agreed.

"Excellent," Emily said. "Now for the more pressing problem." She got a bag of blood, handing it to Adrian.

Ryan watched with fascination, and no small amount of relief, when Adrian let his fangs drop then pierced the bag and drank. Adrian's color, as much of it as he ever had, returned almost immediately. It got even better when he drained a second bag.

Then something occurred to Ryan. Something he should have thought of earlier. "You waited much longer than usual, didn't you?" he asked Adrian with some severity.

"Not all that much longer."

"Why? Were you afraid of what I'd think? For the love of God, Adrian, I know what you are now. Don't ever try to hide, well anything from me about what you need. Understand?"

"Yes." Adrian smiled and hugged him. "I won't from now on. I promise."

Chapter Eleven

The next morning while Adrian slept, Ryan called the small appliance store in Kennett Square to be certain they carried refrigerators. They did, so he made the trip into town, picked out a small one and asked that it be delivered. They said they could have it at the house later that afternoon. From there he went to a national office supply store on the highway out of town to buy a wastebasket and biohazard liners for it. Feeling a sense of accomplishment he returned home.

He had finally sent his book off to his beta reader so the first thing he did was check his email to see if she'd responded and, more to the point read and commented on it. She had so he downloaded the marked-up file and set to work.

He didn't realize how late it had gotten until he heard the doorbell. It was the delivery men from the appliance store. When he told them where he wanted them to put the refrigerator they didn't even bat an eye although one of the men did ask if he was planning on taking up canning.

Ryan chuckled. "Nope. Definitely not my thing. It's more for emergency food storage since I hear winter around here can get hairy at times."

"Boy howdy." The man went on to tell him about one particularly bad storm two years ago.

"That I did *not* need to know," Ryan said with a laugh when the man finished. "So I wasn't being too much of a pessimist in buying this?"

"Not even. You're actually smarter than a lot of people in town."

Now if he only knew the real reason. Ryan chuckled to himself as he showed the men out then went back to his computer to complete his editing so he could send the book to his publisher.

* * * *

"Are you planning on spending all night on that?" Adrian asked sometime later, resting one hand on Ryan's shoulder.

Ryan glanced at the time and sighed. "Give me half an hour and I should be finished."

"Okay. I'll go feed Constable. He was looking at me as if I was his second choice for supper."

Ryan snorted out a laugh. "He does that every time his meal is late by his standards. You should know that by now. Oh, by the way, I got the fridge and it's set up in the basement."

"Thank you! How much?"

"Don't worry about it."

"Ryan," Adrian said sternly. "You're not exactly rich whereas I have more money than I know what to do with. I will pay for it and, since we're on the subject, I'll chip in at least half for all the expenses. Understand?"

"Yes." Ryan grinned wickedly. "Just how rich are you anyway?"

"Let's just say I've had nothing to spend my money on other than blood and occasionally some new clothes, so the rest has been earning interest for the last century and a half."

"Whoa. That would be"—he frowned—"a sizable amount. Okay. Now I feel like a bit of a sponger."

"You're not! Get that idea out of your head right now. We're housemates. It's only right I pay my fair share. So deal." Adrian kissed him quickly. "Now there's a cat that needs dinner."

An impatient "*MeeeOW*" from the doorway accented Adrian's word so he left to take care of the problem.

I'm not *going to put myself in a position where I feel like he's supporting me. I* will *pay my fair share. Especially if this book is a good as I think it is and sells well.* Then Ryan chuckled. *Okay, maybe he can deal with the property taxes if he volunteers. After all, he did build the house and owned the land. A lot of land. Not that I'm complaining about that. It makes my…* our *house… ours with nobody watching what we're doing from their windows. Much nicer than an eight-foot privacy fence.*

With that thought, he got back to what he'd been doing and true to his word he finished in half an hour, attached the file to an email to his publisher, and with a great deal of relief hit 'Send'.

* * * *

"You look happy," Adrian commented when Ryan came into the kitchen.

"The book is wending its way to my publisher. Time to celebrate."

"And that entails what?"

Ryan laughed. "No clue. Usually I go out for a beer."

"Then let's."

"You're sure?"

"Well I'll stick to wine," Adrian admitted. "I never have understood why anyone would drink that nasty, bitter brew."

"It's not *that* bad," Ryan said with a grin. "Okay, give me a minute to get changed into something less… casual." He looked down at his well-worn but comfortable sweatshirt. "Something that doesn't have holes in the elbows."

When he took off, Adrian was tempted to follow and see if the celebration couldn't be done at home—in bed. *Too soon*, he decided. *We may be headed in that direction, but he's still not ready. I don't think.*

* * * *

Upstairs, Ryan was having somewhat the same debate. *I*

could just suggest we stay here. I've got beer in the fridge and wine. We could relax, and then… maybe… He looked at his bed, wondering—since it seemed antique—if it was the one Adrian had used when he was still alive.

That would be weird, having sex in the same one where my grandfather was probably conceived. That of course brought up another problem. One he'd tried to push to the back of his mind. Adrian was his great-grandfather.

Of course we're not related by blood. And for damned sure he doesn't look like he's related to me or that he's really my ancestor. When it comes down to it though, when the time is right, will I be able to get past that?

"Don't be an idiot," he admonished himself as he pulled off his sweatshirt, tossing it in the general direction of the hamper in one corner of the room. "It hasn't bothered me when we've kissed. And those definitely were not chaste kisses on the cheek. So why would I care if we take it further?"

Going to the closet, he took out a shirt, checked to be certain it was decent and put it on. *He's just a man. Nothing more. Well, something more but still just a wonderful man who I'm very, very attracted to. I have to remember that because it's all that really counts.* He nodded sharply. *It is* all *that counts.*

Chapter Twelve

"You don't know *how* to drive," Ryan protested a few hours later as he leaned against the car. He wasn't drunk, but he definitely wasn't sober either. Something Adrian had pointed out wryly as they left the bar.

"I've watched you. I can figure it out."

"What if the cops…?"

Adrian chuckled. "They'll probably give me a medal for not letting you drive."

"Or a ticket for not having a license."

"Either way, *I* am driving so in you get." Adrian opened the passenger-side door for Ryan.

"You need the keys."

"I have them." Adrian dangled them in front of Ryan's face. "How do you think I opened the door?"

"Oh. Yeah."

Once Ryan was inside, Adrian went around the car, slid into the driver's seat and turned the key in the ignition. *At least it's not a stick shift. Not sure I could deal with a clutch.* He glanced over at Ryan, smiling confidently. "See, I got it running."

"Big deal. A kid could do that. Let's see you get out of the lot without sideswiping any cars."

Adrian did, pulling out onto the street to Ryan's grumbled, "Okay, so you can steer it too. Just remember to stay under the speed limit but not by too much."

"Yes, oh great and wise one."

Not too surprisingly, since the road home was not a major one, they made it to the house without running into any cops. When they got out of the car Ryan actually complimented Adrian on his driving skills.

"Which are better than your walking ones at the

moment," Adrian replied with a laugh when Ryan staggered a bit. Putting his arm around Ryan's waist, he helped him negotiate the stairs to the porch. Then, unlocking the door, he led him inside. "Bed time, young man."

Ryan started toward the sofa, muttering, "Yes, daddy."

Adrian winced even though he was fairly certain Ryan didn't mean that the way it sounded. "Not down here," he told him.

"But the stairs are too long," Ryan protested.

"Not a problem. Hang on." Adrian picked him up, almost tossed him over his shoulder and decided that might not be the best idea under the circumstances and held him in his arms instead.

Ryan wrapped one arm around Adrian's neck, resting his head on Adrian's shoulder. "Can you do this every night?"

Snorting softly, Adrian said, "Not unless you're too drunk to make it on your own."

"Not drunk. Just sleepy and happy now."

"Followed by grumpy, dopey, and bashful in the morning?"

"What?"

"The seven dwarves. Just kidding you." By then they were upstairs and in Ryan's bedroom.

Adrian sat him down on the edge of the bed, suggesting he at least remove his shoes. Ryan did, by dint of toeing them off. When he started to fall back on the bed, Adrian stopped him so he could unbutton his shirt for him. Ryan let it slide off his shoulders and Adrian grabbed it before it ended up under him as Ryan curled up on the bed.

"Okay, I'll see you… well tomorrow evening since I doubt you'll wake up before I go to bed," Adrian said, leaning down to kiss Ryan's forehead.

"Don't go," Ryan pleaded. "Stay with me. Please. Just…

hold me until I go to sleep?"

Against his better judgment, Adrian agreed. When he took off his shirt and shoes he heard Ryan hiss in a breath.

"For an old guy you're in real good shape," Ryan whispered as he stared at Adrian. "I mean… for a guy who's older than me. Umm, for a…"

"Stop there," Adrian said, trying to smile. "I get what you're saying." He sat down on the side of the bed, ruffling Ryan's hair. "Now go to sleep."

"Uh-uh. Not until you're holding me." When Adrian didn't move, Ryan sighed. "I didn't mean that the way it came out you know. I wasn't thinking. I already decided that you're just a man and nothing more." He eased up on one elbow. "A man I'm very attracted to and the fact we're not really related doesn't play into that at all. Because we aren't. Related I mean. So you're just a wonderful"—he yawned—"man. And I'm tired and sorta not drunk but"—he yawned again—"not totally sober yet and I should shut up and you should get in here." He patted the bed, yawning. "I promise not to assault you. Tonight."

Adrian shook his head, chuckling. "But tomorrow?"

"Definitely a possibility? I mean if you're willing."

Adrian settled down beside him, pulling Ryan against his chest. "Willing is an understatement. But for right now, you'd better get some sleep."

"Going to," Ryan murmured before pressing his lips to Adrian's. "Because I want to be wide awake when…"

Adrian smiled, realizing Ryan had fallen asleep mid-sentence. "And I want you to be," he said softly. "I most definitely want you to be."

* * * *

The next day seemed to creep by as far as Ryan was

concerned. He hadn't been surprised when he'd awakened that morning to find Adrian wasn't there beside him. Disappointed, definitely, but he understood why.

Tonight though… He's going to find me in his bed, or at least his bedroom, when he wakes up.

Of course the very idea of that had Ryan on pins-and-needles with anticipation and worry.

What if he kicks me out? What if he's not in the mood? I have to figure out what I did with the lube. Do I even have any still? Should I really get into bed with him before he wakes up or just be there in the room? If I'm there what should I wear? Nothing? Jeans? Good Lord you'd think this was my first time ever. Well it will be—with him. If *anything actually happens. If he really meant what he said last night. Maybe he was just…* No, *he's not like that.*

The only that kept him from going off the deep end was Constable. The cat insisted on going outside and then wouldn't budge until Ryan joined him. From there it was a stroll around the grounds with the cat checking out everything as if he'd never been there before. That happened just before lunch and then again soon afterwards. When they came back in the second time, Ryan got on the computer to check mail and his social pages. Glancing at the time when he was finished, he realized it would still be at least an hour until Adrian woke up, so he killed the time with many rousing games of solitaire.

Finally, trepidation and excitement racing through him, he shut down the computer and went upstairs, still undecided what to wear—or not wear.

* * * *

"Are you just going to stand there staring?" Adrian asked, cocking one eye open.

"Maybe?" Ryan looked a bit abashed, as if he'd been

caught doing something he shouldn't.

Adrian sat up, letting the sheet slide down to his hips. He almost laughed. Ryan looked so nervous. He also looked very sexy in low-slung jeans and nothing else.

"Come. I won't bite." He beckoned Ryan closer. "Although if I remember correctly you seemed interested in finding out what would happen if I did."

Blushing, Ryan came closer. Almost within arms' reach. Adrian slid forward to take his hands, losing the sheet in the process.

"You sleep"—Ryan gulped—"naked."

"I do. Don't you?" Adrian asked in amusement as he tugged Ryan close enough to rest his hands on his hips. "Or do you sleep in these." Casually he flipped open the button at the waistband of Ryan's jeans.

"No. Sweatpants," Ryan managed to get out, his gaze flicking between Adrian's face and his half-swollen cock.

Ratcheting down the zipper, Adrian watched as the jeans slid off Ryan's narrow hips and down to the floor. He was totally nude now, which didn't surprise Adrian in the least. If you're going to seduce someone, the less worn the better and he had the feeling that was why Ryan was here. To try to seduce him. *Probably only a sense of decorum made him wear pants to come into my bedroom.*

Ryan licked his lips, stepping out of the fallen jeans. "May I?" he asked, looking at the bed.

"Good Lord yes!"

Ryan sat carefully, murmuring almost under his breath, "I was afraid, Adrian."

"Of me?" Adrian gently drew him closer. He wanted nothing more than to ravish the younger man but instinct told him Ryan needed to talk first. To work out what he was feeling and how to act on those emotions.

"No," Ryan replied shyly. "Afraid you'd send me away."

"If I was ever tempted to, and there was a time when I would have, that is long past. I would never…"

"I meant now. Tonight."

"I know. But I meant, I mean—ever. Well unless you decide differently. If you don't want me in your life…"

"I do!"

"Please let me finish." Adrian smiled, placing a finger over Ryan's lips. "Tonight will be the first time for the two of us and I pray it won't be the last. But, if you ever change your mind I'll understand. A day from now, a week, a year… If you tire of me then you'll be free to go and I won't stop you." He pressed a kiss to Ryan's lips. "Or I'll try to convince you otherwise, but only with words and then it will be up to you."

Ryan looked at him, nodding slowly. "I think I get what you're saying. Being what you are, you could control me the way Darnell did. But you won't." He returned the kiss with one of his own. "You're too honorable. You won't do that to make me stay and you won't do it to make me leave."

"Never," Adrian agreed adamantly.

"The same goes for you. If you get tired of me just tell me and I'll go."

"I doubt that will ever happen."

"But it could," Ryan replied seriously. "We're only human."

Even though the conversation was important, as they seemed to be setting up parameters for the future, Adrian couldn't help but say, "When it comes to human, speak for yourself. Others would disagree that I am."

Ryan grinned. "Well others aren't me. You're human. You're devilishly handsome to my way of thinking, and damned sexy. So sexy that I don't think I can keep my hands to myself any longer."

"Did I ask you to?" Adrian retorted, grinning back.

"Well now that you mention it…" Ryan pushed Adrian onto his back and looked down at him, tracing his forefinger along the lines of Adrian's muscular chest before diving in for a long, deep kiss.

From there things took their natural course. Ryan had even remembered the lube, although he had to stop what they were doing to dig it out of the pocket of his jeans. Adrian found that amusingly frustrating although he refrained from saying so.

When Ryan panicked seconds later because he'd forgotten condoms, Adrian sighed. "Vampire here. We don't need them."

"Oh? Oh! Yeah, the whole…"

Adrian kissed him to shut him up and they got back down to the business at hand. Ryan's only complaint when they finished—"Quite gloriously" in his words—was that Adrian hadn't fed from him when they came. "Now I'll never know whether that story is the truth or not."

Adrian wrapped him in a tight embrace, murmuring, "Do you think this was the only time we'll make love?"

"I sure hope not because it was—you were spectacular."

"I could say the same about you so we *will* do it again—often I hope—and you now have something to look forward to."

"Adrian," Ryan said fervently, "even if you never do the feeding thing I'll always, always, look forward to our making love. But"—he looked wistful—"I hope you do."

"Perhaps next time," Adrian replied, kissing his forehead.

"That would be in, umm, twenty minutes?"

"All right, I'll revise that. Perhaps tomorrow night, if I think you're up for it. And do not"—he grinned at his lover—"turn what I just said into a bad joke."

"Would I do that?"

"Probably. Definitely. Now before we go for round two I think you should eat supper. I don't want you fading in the stretch because you're starving."

"Kill joy," Ryan grumbled. But, after sharing a very passionate kiss with Adrian he got up. When Adrian remained where he was, watching Ryan, the young man said, "Well are you coming?" Then he laughed. "And no bad jokes from you about *that.*"

"Never even crossed my mind."

"Ri-ight."

Adrian joined him, with neither of the bothering to get dressed. When Ryan opened the bedroom door they found a very irate looking Constable sitting just outside.

"Get used to it, cat," Ryan said, picking him up. "At times there are things more important than feeding you. This was one of them and it will"—he glanced at Adrian—"happen often."

"Indeed it will," Adrian agreed heartily as the trio made their way down to the kitchen. "Very often."

Epilogue

Ryan took two bags of blood from the basement refrigerator, handing one to Adrian. Then they both let their fangs drop and drank.

It had been two years now since Adrian had turned Ryan. Five years since they had first met. Five wonderful years as far as Ryan was concerned and he knew Adrian felt the same.

After they both drained second bags, Adrian opened the cooler sitting on the table next to the fridge and they filled it with the remaining blood bags. Adrian took it upstairs while Ryan went to get the cat-carrier.

"Next stop, New Orleans," Ryan said when he came into the living room, setting the carrier on the floor.

Constable looked at it with disgust.

"Well we could leave you here for the next three months," Adrian told him. "But you don't know how to use the can opener."

As if he understood what Adrian was implying, Constable stalked into the carrier and Ryan closed the door.

"Are we forgetting anything?" Ryan asked.

Adrian snorted, glancing at the bags sitting by the front door. "If we are, I don't know what. We'd better get moving though. You know how Lemuel's pilot is. Flight plan filed, flight plan followed to the minute, come hell or high water."

Ryan went to get the car, a new small SUV that had replaced his battered Taurus when it had finally give up the ghost. Between them they managed to get everything, including Constable, into it and took off for the airport.

Five hours later they were pulling their rental car into the garage behind their winter home in the French Quarter. They carried their bags across the small courtyard with its bubbling fountain into the modern kitchen that had granite countertops and stainless steel appliances. As soon as the door was closed behind them, Ryan let Constable out of the carrier, dug the cat dishes and a can of food out of one cupboard and filled one bowl with food, the other with water. Meanwhile Adrian stored the blood bags in a small refrigerator hidden under the dining island in the middle of the room.

They carried their luggage through the living room—with its hardwood floor, beige walls and brick fireplace—up the stairs to the master bedroom.

"Unpack now?" Ryan asked, eyeing the king-sized bed at the far side of the room from the walk-in closet and oak dresser. "Or light the fire and unwind."

Adrian chuckled. "By unwind you mean light a fire of a different kind."

Ryan answered that statement by closing the distance between them, wrapping his arms around his lover and kissing him passionately. It didn't take long for them to strip and make heated love, falling asleep just as the sky behind the dark curtains began to lighten the city.

* * * *

The two lovers spent the next evening settling into their house and shopping for necessities, like wine, more cat food, and food. The food wasn't for them. They had made a few friends soon after buying the house and occasionally invited them over for drinks and barbeque when they were in town.

Then they headed to one of the clubs on Bourbon.

"I was wondering when I'd see you two again," a familiar voice from the past said seconds after Adrian and Ryan had found seats at the bar. "It's been a long time."

"What the hell!" Adrian turned to look at Talbot. "What

are you doing down here? As if I couldn't guess."

Talbot chuckled. "You'd guess right. I've been hired to find someone rather like Darnell." He studied Ryan, cocking an eyebrow. "So you came to the dark side."

Ryan grinned. "It took a bit of convincing but Adrian won me over. On all fronts."

Adrian hugged him before telling the bartender who appeared in front of them that they'd have wine. "Something for you?" he asked Talbot.

Talbot held up his empty beer bottle and Adrian ordered another one for him then suggested they find a table. As soon as their drinks were delivered and paid for, they did.

"Still living where you were before?" Talbot asked once they were settled.

"Nine months of the year. We spend winter down here," Adrian replied.

"Snow free," Ryan added. "After the last big snowstorm up there three years ago, Adrian—well we—decided we'd had it. So, here we are."

"Can't blame you for that," Talbot said. "Although I don't mind snow." He chuckled. "Good thing I don't, considering where I live when I'm not off on a job."

"Let's see," Ryan looked at him pensively before saying very quietly, "Half wolf so probably somewhere where you can run free when you want to. Maybe in the mountains?"

"You're good. Yep. I have a home outside of Silver Plume. Before you ask, it's a small town about fifty miles west of Denver."

Ryan shivered. "Six *months* of snow."

"It's not that bad. Okay, close."

"I'll stay here and at our place, thanks. Maybe visit you in… July?"

"Feel free to. I'm rather fond of you."

"Oh really?" Adrian said with a trace of rancor in his voice.

Talbot grinned. "Not that way. Damn. I like both of you. I consider you friends, if distant ones."

"That I can deal with," Adrian replied, relaxing again.

"Doesn't get out much, does he?" Talbot whispered to Ryan. "Otherwise he'd get that men can look at you with interest but that you'll always be faithful to him."

"Always," Ryan said softly, his gaze locked on Adrian as he leaned close enough to kiss him. "Until The End of time."

* * * *

Talbot watched them, a wistful look on his face.

Adrian broke the kiss, turning to Talbot. "Your time will come."

"Promise?" Talbot asked.

"Yep. I have the gift of foresight. Not." He smiled. "But yeah, someday you'll meet the right person and it'll be all over but the shouting."

"Time will tell. Anyway…"

They continued talking, Talbot enjoying their catching up on their lives since they'd last been together. Finally, well after two, Adrian and Ryan returned home when Talbot told them he needed to get on with doing what he was best at—"Finding a rogue vampire who is on the loose in the city."

Talbot watched his friends disappear around the corner onto St. Lewis St. *Maybe someday. Maybe I'll find a love as enduring as they have. Until then…* He continued on, his senses open for any sign of his prey.

The End

Talbot and the ENFORCERS

Edward Kendrick

Blurbs

Talbot, a loner—and lonely—hybrid dhampir/werewolf, is asked to help the Enforcers find a turncoat in their midst. Reluctantly agreeing, he meets werewolf Ulrik and things become… interesting, when the team is sent to New Orleans to stop a rogue and catch a traitor.

Talbot is a hybrid werewolf/dhampir. The only one of his kind, he thinks. A loner, he hires out to eliminate rogue vampires. When Antton, a head Enforcer, asks for his help to find a turncoat within the group, Talbot reluctantly agrees. The turncoat uses rogues to trap and kill Enforcers, sometimes finishing the job himself when necessary.

Talbot meets the team he'll be working with to go after a rogue werewolf that Antton is certain is being used by the turncoat. The other men on the team are Dante, a vampire, and Ulrik, a werewolf. When Talbot saves Ulrik from a vampire, they realize that Ulrik's home has been compromised, so Ulrik stays with Talbot until the team leaves for New Orleans to try to complete their mission. Although Talbot is attracted to Ulrik, he resists his feelings, believing that it is one-sided at best.

Will Talbot find out that he's right, or will Ulrik reciprocate? And will it matter if the turncoat manages to kill them both before they can stop him?

Dedication

For Shy, who puts up with my 'Now where should I go from here?' moaning.

Trademarks Acknowledgement

The author acknowledges the Trademarked status and Trademark owners of the following wordmarks mentioned in this work of fiction:

Thunderbird: E & J Winery Corporation
Chateau Lafite Rothschild: Les Domaines Barons de Rothschild (Lafite)
AA: Alcoholics Anonymous World Services, Inc.
PayPal: PayPal, Inc.
Realtor: National Association of Realtors Corporation

Chapter One

"Talbot? Like the guy in that werewolf movie?" The man took a sip of his beer, looking warily at Talbot.

Talbot resisted sighing. "That was Larry Talbot. I'm Talbot Randel. Trust me. I'm not a werewolf nor am I afraid of wolfbane and I don't howl at a full moon." *Mostly true, excluding the werewolf part. At that, it's only half of what I am.* No way would he tell that bit of information to the man sitting next to him at the bar, anymore than he'd tell him he was also half dhampir. *No sense scaring him into next week—or having his friends call for the men with straightjackets when he tried to convince them he'd met a 'night creature'.*

"Too bad. I always thought werewolves, at least the lady ones, were pretty sexy when they weren't out looking for their next meal."

"Somehow, someone wanting to turn me into dinner wouldn't be sexy, no matter what," Talbot said, playing along. All the while, he kept his senses open for the rogue vampire he was after.

Rumor had it the rogue was known to hang out at this bar, in one of the seedier sections of New Orleans, looking for victims. He also trolled along Bourbon Street on occasion—again according to rumors. That's why Talbot had been on Bourbon and had run into Adrian and Ryan, who he hadn't seen in close to five years. They had spent an enjoyable hour together before his friends headed back to their home and Talbot had continued on north, past Rampart, to Aunt Blue's Joint.

The man bending Talbot's ear was well into his forties, with at least two days' worth of scrubby beard and the air, and smell, of a dedicated drinker—beery, boozy, and slightly rancid. So Talbot wondered exactly what the man's definition of sexy involved. *Big boobs, eight-inch heels, and less clothes than the average stripper, probably.*

Turning away from the man, Talbot scanned the bar's patrons. There wasn't one of them who could put up even half a fight if the rogue attacked them. *He's got no class. I mean… come on. If you're going to be a killer, at least do it in style. Pick on someone worth the time and energy.*

The only reason he'd been hired for the job was the fact that the rogue was the creation of an older vampire, who would lose face if anyone discovered he'd lost control of his Child. "The sooner you find him and stop him, the happier I'll be," the vampire had said. In this case, he meant he'd pay Talbot twice his going rate for the execution.

"If I have to hang around here much longer," he muttered under his breath, "I'll triple my fee."

He wouldn't really do that. Despite the prevailing belief within the vampire community that a dhampir would kill any vampire he came across, that wasn't true—at least not for Talbot. He figured it was because he was a hybrid. His werewolf and vampire parts seemed to have come to some sort of agreement, thanks to mediation by his human side. Therefore, while he had no love for most vampires, he also didn't think the only good one was a dead one.

Look at Lemuel and Adrian. They were good people before they were turned. Why would that change afterwards? The same with Ryan and a few others I've made friends with. Live and let live, unless they don't follow the rules.

He stiffened when he became aware of the presence of a vampire who had just entered the bar. Then he relaxed, although he didn't let down his guard. The male didn't come close to the description of the rogue. The vampire—unaware that Talbot was a dhampir since he was shielding—found an empty stool at the far end of the bar and ordered a glass of wine. From the look on his face a moment later when he tasted it, it was closer to Thunderbird than Chateau Lafite Rothschild.

And why would he be surprised unless he's new in town and doesn't realize he's well away from the good parts of the city?

Talbot took another sip of his beer, his gaze gliding over two more new arrivals. Then, a moment later, his target entered. He fit in well, his clothing working class, his walk more of a slouch, as if he'd just gotten off a job. He looked dead tired and ready to end the night with a couple of drinks, like many of the other men there.

The target, Christian by name, stopped at the bar to order a drink then made his way to a vacant table along the wall beside the rear exit. He leaned his chair back on two legs, holding the bottle and watching. He spotted the other vampire but after a momentary glance, he ignored him. Finally he homed in on a middle-aged man who was staggering toward the back door. As soon as the man left, Christian was on his feet, following him. Talbot waited for the count of twenty to give Christian a chance to approach his intended victim then went after them.

Christian was so intent on what he was doing, pulling the surprised and very drunk man between two overfilled dumpsters, that he was unaware they had company.

By the time he reached them, Talbot had pulled out his sword. Until he needed to use it, it was invisible in an equally invisible sheath slung across his back. "You know," he said, his lips turned up in a sneer, "you shouldn't play with your food. Especially if it's pickled human."

Christian barely got out, "Who the hell…" when his head and body parted ways and instantly turned to dust.

The drunk looked on in disbelief, muttering, "I think I'll stick to water for a while. The booze is getting to me," and staggered off.

"I'm better than AA at times like this," Talbot commented with a laugh while sheathing the sword. Then he sauntered down the alley to the street and from there to where he'd parked his car.

* * * *

"Ah, home sweet home." Talbot closed the front door behind him then headed upstairs to the loft. After tossing his bags on the bed in the master bedroom, he went into the bathroom to shower.

He loved his house, nestled on three acres of forest land well north of Silver Plume in the Colorado Rockies. Two stories high, the downstairs contained a large living room with a stone fireplace, a small dining area, and a very modern kitchen. The second floor loft held his bedroom, a guest room, and the study. Each room up there opened onto the exterior balcony that circled the cedar-sided home.

After finishing his shower and dressing in a pair of well-worn jeans and a turtleneck, he unpacked and went down to the kitchen to fix something to eat.

"Ham and cheese, peanut butter and jelly?" He scoffed at the latter and ended up with roast beef topped with lettuce and tomatoes.

When the thick sandwich was made, he put on a warm jacket, since the temperature was just above freezing at the moment. With his food and a beer in hand, he went out onto the covered back porch, dusted snow off the table, sat, and ate.

"Well hello there," he whispered, smiling when a deer ventured out of the trees to stand and stare at him. *Now if I was in my wolf form…* He chuckled. Even if he had been, the deer would have had nothing to fear. He never hunted the animals that populated the area and had posted signs in several places around the edges of his property that warned 'No hunting allowed. Trespassers will be shot on sight'. He wished that was true for the whole area but he knew that would never happen.

By the time he finished eating it was dusk, with long shadows from the trees inching their way across the snowy yard. He took the plate and empty bottle back to the kitchen, returned to the porch, and with a thought he shifted. His fur was raven black, like his hair in his human form. The only variation from that was the slightly gray coloring on his muzzle and chest.

For the next hour he traversed the forest, racing through the pine trees and up the rocky snow-covered slopes, pausing to drink from the small lake on his property, half a mile from his home. Eventually, feeling at one again with his animal half, he returned home, shifted, and went inside. Getting a book from the shelves that lined one wall of the living room, he settled down to read until it was time to head to bed.

* * * *

It snowed hard overnight, so the first thing Talbot needed to do after breakfast was clear the driveway. He smiled as he did, remembering Ryan telling him that's why he and Adrian spent the winter months of the year in New Orleans. "Snow free," Ryan had said enthusiastically, much to Talbot's amusement.

When he returned to the house—thankful that he'd had the common sense to buy a decent snowblower a couple of years ago—he went up to the study take care of email in his two accounts.

He opened the account for what he laughingly called his business. A 'business' that he didn't advertise—obviously. The email address was known by only a select few vampires who acted as intermediaries between him and their community. The only reason Mordecai—the sire of the rogue in New Orleans—had been able to contact him directly was because he *was* one of the select few. There was no mail but he did send an email to Mordecai, telling him that he'd completed the job and Christian was now truly dead. Not more than ten minutes later, while checking his regular email, he heard from PayPal that a sizable amount of money had been sent to him, and he immediately transferred it to his bank. After a final return to his business email to send one thanking Mordecai for paying promptly, he closed down his computer

Looks like everyone's behaving, thank goodness. I could use some downtime.

The job in New Orleans had been the third one in the last month, taking him from one city to another, spread across the country.

He spent the rest of the day doing some cleaning and laundry then settled down to watch a movie. After dinner, he took another run in his wolf-form, came back, and went to bed, with a good book to read until he fell asleep.

The next two days followed pretty much the same routine—dealing with email, reading or watching a movie, a fast shopping trip to Silver Plume one morning to restock his pantry, and long runs.

By then the weekend had arrived. Talbot decided to head down to Denver for the evening to eat a good meal he didn't have to cook and to visit one of the clubs he sometimes frequented.

Chapter Two

"Well, look who finally decided to show his face again."

Talbot grinned at Carl, the bartender, replying, "I do… on occasion." Taking a seat at the bar, he ordered a beer then said when Carl asked, "I had sales trips that I swear took me over half the country—New York, Chicago, Tampa." He chuckled. "I should have stayed in Florida where it's warm."

"Naw. You know you love snow, ice, sleet, wearing ten layers of clothes."

"Uh-huh. Not." Talbot took a drink of the beer Carl handed him. "So, anything new happen while I was gone?"

"Humm. The place next door closed and someone bought the building. The rumor is it's going to be another used book store—or was it antiques? Hell if I remember."

Talbot laughed. "I suppose technically some used books could be considered antiques."

They continued bantering when Carl wasn't serving other customers. When he was, Talbot took the time to watch the men at the tables or on the dance floor. If he'd been looking for company, there were several options, but he wasn't. Being a loner, he rarely did. *A loner because of what I am.* He smiled wryly. *Still, I don't suppose I'd change that, even if I did have the choice. Not after almost seven hundred years.*

Talbot tensed at the scent of a werewolf, his gaze immediately going to the front door of the club. A tall, dark-haired, bearded man entered. For a moment he paused, his gaze moving from customer to customer as if he was searching for someone. Then it landed on Talbot and the man strode toward the bar.

"Any idea who that is?" Talbot asked Carl.

"Nope. Never saw him before."

"Perhaps because I've never been in here before," the man said, obviously having overheard them. That he had didn't surprise Talbot, given that werewolves have extremely sensitive hearing. The man took the vacant stool next to Talbot and ordered a beer. After it arrived and Carl had moved away, the man said, "Allow me to introduce myself. I am Antton Ochoa."

Talbot smiled dryly. "And why should I care? I'm here to relax and enjoy the scenery. Nothing more."

Antton chuckled. "I'm not trying to pick you up. At least not in the way you think." He glanced around before returning his attention to Talbot. "You and I have, shall we say, common interests."

"Do we now? Given that you're in a gay bar, I'd say that was obvious."

"Not that sort of interest. You are known in certain circles as someone who makes it his business to handle problems of a unique nature."

Talbot frowned deeply. "If that was the truth, why would you care?"

"I'm..." Antton paused before saying, "If you're willing, I'd like to take this conversation somewhere more private."

"And if I'm not?"

Antton shrugged. "You will miss out on an opportunity to join a rather unique group of like-minded individuals."

"I work alone. If you had done your homework, you'd know that."

"I do, and there is something to be said for that, I'll agree. There is also something to be said for having allies when the need arises."

Talbot tapped his fingers together. If he was reading Antton correctly, the man was not trying to lure him into a trap of some sort. *If I'm not... what do I have to lose by listening to what he has to say? Other than my life, of course, if I'm wrong. In for a penny, in for a pound?*

"Lead the way."

Antton stood, put money on the bar for his drink then headed to door with Talbot right behind him. When they were outside, Antton suggested they walk as they talked. After opening his senses to be certain there was nothing around of the supernatural type that he should be worried about, Talbot agreed.

They turned onto a side street at the next corner, leaving the crowded main street behind.

"Now," Talbot said tautly, "tell me who told you about me?"

"Lemuel."

"I'll have his head on a platter," Talbot muttered.

"Something you're quite capable of doing," Antton replied with a grin. "Don't worry. He doesn't brandish your name around. He and I are friends of a sort. I ran into him about a week ago and he told me about a favor you did for him and his nephew… five years ago?"

Talbot nodded. "That's about right. I'll have to have a word or two with him. He knows better than to reveal my existence to just anyone."

"I'm not just anyone," Antton replied a bit tartly. "I work for an organization bent on eliminating rogues. Not the run-of-the-mill ones who are young and unwilling to obey their sires or alphas, but the older, more powerful ones—or insane ones of any age."

"I've dealt with my fair share of those, as far as vampires go."

"So I've learned." Antton stopped walking, glanced around then suggested they go into the small park just ahead of them. They did, dusting the snow off one of the benches before sitting.

"Tell me more about this organization," Talbot said. He wasn't the least bit interested in doing what he thought Antton was implying—joining it. But he did want to know more details.

"It's run by a council comprised of two vampires and two werewolves, all of them very powerful in their own rights. Under them are men like me who are in charge of territories. Mine comprises the southwestern quarter of the country. While I have some men who work almost exclusively with me, when I need them I can—and do—call in other Enforcers."

"That's what you call yourselves?"

"Yes. Most Enforcers are, for lack of a better description, freelance. They may generally work in a specific territory, but they go where they're needed."

"Interesting. Why haven't I heard of them before now?"

"For the same reason very few people outside of your immediate circle know about you. We don't want humans to find out Enforcers exist."

"Only humans?"

Antton smiled dryly. "All right. We work better if no one knows about us—human or otherwise. Some supernaturals do find out. Unfortunately, that seems to happen when we are trying to end their rogue existence. The ones we go after are old enough, insane enough, and wily enough that they sometimes realize they're being hunted by Enforcers. Or..." Antton frowned. "Our existence is betrayed to them."

"Meaning the occasional turncoat within the Enforcer group."

"Not occasional. It has happened three times since I've been with them."

"How long has that been?"

"For approximately five hundred of my six hundred years."

Talbot cocked his head, looking at him. "I'm impressed."

"Don't be. It's unusual, but not impossible, for a werewolf to live much longer than I have."

"So I've been told, but still…"

Antton chuckled. "I'm still younger than you, from what Lemuel told me."

"Good genes on my part."

"More like your dhampir and werewolf halves acting together." Antton tapped his chin thoughtfully. "I wonder…"

"Umm?"

"We have a young man working for us who is like you. I was just wondering if he'll still be around in seven hundred years."

Talbot looked at him in surprise. "I've heard rumors that there was another dhampir/werewolf hybrid. However…"

"You didn't believe it?" Antton chucked. "Unsurprising. It's a virtual impossibility, although I guess you're proof that it can happen. So is Brand, although he was… made, for lack of a better word, not born that way."

"Do tell."

Antton did. When he finished, Talbot shook his head. "It's a damned good thing you dealt with his creator before he tried doing that again."

"I agree. I consider us lucky to have found Brand and saved him. He's been an asset to the Enforcers, now that he's learning how to handle his werewolf side more effectively."

"If you have him, why do you think you need me?"

"Good Lord, Talbot, that's like saying if I have one well-trained guard dog, why would I need another? The more we have working to protect the world from the rogues, the better."

"Good point. However, I've never worked as part of a team. I'm not all that certain that I could. I've been a loner for too long."

"Would it hurt to try? We need you, especially now."

"Why now?"

"I told you, there have been three turncoats in the organization. Two were many years ago and they were eliminated. The third one is…" He scowled. "Someone who is—or has—worked for me or two of the other head Enforcers."

"Has worked for you… as in someone you, or the other two, brought in for a specific job?"

"Yes. We've narrowed it down to five possibilities, but they're only that—possibilities. Beyond that, I'm at a loss."

"So read the suspects or have someone you trust do that."

"Don't you think we've tried? Damn it. Whoever it is, their mind is locked down tighter than…"

"Fort Knox? To keep it clean."

Antton chuckled. "That works. I did have something a bit more ribald in mind. Anyway, back to what I was saying. We could use you."

Drumming his fingers on the bench, Talbot replied, "Let me think about it. How can I get in touch with you?"

Antton took a card from his wallet, handing it to Talbot.

"Ochoa Protection Services? Are you kidding?"

"We needed a front, and what better one than a security company?"

"True." Talbot stood, pocketing the card as he did. "I'll let you know one way or the other what I decide."

"Please do—and soon. We've already lost one good man because of the turncoat and had a rogue go in the wind because he was notified of our plans for him."

* * * *

Antton arrived home to find he had a visitor. An unexpected but welcome one.

"To what do I owe this honor?" Antton asked.

"I'm bored?" Ulrik chuckled.

"Why don't I believe that?"

"Because you know it's not the truth." Ulrik paced to the window in the living room that looked out over the back of Antton's property. After staring out at the mountains for a long moment, he said, "Émilien's dead."

"When?" Antton asked in shock. "How? Why haven't I been notified?"

"It happened in France, less than twenty-four hours ago. Fabrice sent me to tell you, as he's too busy trying to figure out what went wrong. Or more to the point, who the bastard is who sold us out."

"You were there?"

"Yes. We—Émilien and I—had just found the rogue we were after when it happened."

"Malthe. Yes. I know about that. He was headed to Lyon last I heard."

"That's what our intelligence showed." Ulrik spun around, saying angrily, "It was a set-up, Antton. We got to his hideout on an island in Lac des Eaux Bleues and walked into a trap. We did manage to kill Malthe, but at the cost of Émilien's life." Ulrik scrubbed his hand angrily through his relatively short, dark blond hair. "I barely made it out, and wouldn't have if I wasn't a werewolf. Émilien took to the air, but someone shot him. A silver-tipped arrow to the heart."

"I presume you didn't see who it was."

"If I had," Ulrik snarled, "he would be dead now. Damn it, Antton. We have to find out who's turned on us. This was a top-secret mission—or it was supposed to be—and yet Malthe knew we were coming."

Antton bowed his head for a moment. Then, straightening, he said, "Let me get with the Council to find out just how many of us knew you'd been sent to take out Malthe. Once I know..." He blew out a harsh breath. "You know we've been aware for some time that there's a turncoat in the organization. Perhaps now we can at least narrow it down more than we've been able to so far."

"Do it soon, before we lose more good men. And when you do, I want to be involved in stopping him."

For the first time since they'd begun talking, Antton smiled. A brief one, but nonetheless a smile. "I expected you to say that, being you. You'll be one of them."

"Who else will you bring in?" Ulrik began pacing. "We need a combination of vampires and werewolves, but they have to be ones we trust implicitly. If only Brand was a bit older and more attuned to his werewolf side... He would be perfect."

"Interesting you should say that."

Ulrik looked at him aghast. "Surely you're not thinking of using him. Whoever we're up against must be old and wily—and very evil. How he's been able to hide his wickedness from us is..." He shook his head.

"A good question. No, I won't use Brand. However there is another like him, only born, not made."

"Are you serious?"

Antton nodded. "Very much so. Do you know Lemuel?"

"Yes, and if you try to tell me it's him, I'd call you crazy."

"No. He's a pure vampire. However he told me about a friend of his. This man is indeed a dhampir/werewolf hybrid. He's also very much of a loner. Few know of him and those who do keep it to themselves. From what Lemuel told me, this man goes after rogue vampires—for pay. He's... well, I suppose you could call him a hit man of sorts. A few, very select vampires know of his existence and they act as liaisons between him and anyone who wants a rogue eliminated."

"Interesting. Are you thinking of contacting him?"

"I already have, and I told him we could use his help. He said he'd think about it."

"Hardly an enthusiastic response," Ulrik said.

"No." Antton smiled with wry amusement. "But better than 'No way in Hell'."

Ulrik nodded briefly in agreement. "There is that."

Chapter Three

"I should do this why?" Talbot muttered that, or words to that effect, on and off as he returned home after his talk with Antton.

I work on my own. Always have. And I'm damned good at it. Why am I even considering taking him up on his proposition? But apparently I am because I didn't outright tell him no.

As he drove the final half mile, his house came into view, standing out starkly against the snow-covered trees surrounding it when the headlights lit the area.

I don't live here because I'm looking for lots of company. He chuckled wryly as he parked the car and got out. *This is the life I like. But still…*

Going inside, he shed his outerwear, went upstairs to his study, booted up his computer, and went online. The first thing he did, although he was certain it was an exercise in futility, was run a search on Enforcers. He got lots of hits, but none related to Antton's group. Then he checked out Ochoa Protection Services. *It is legitimate and apparently all inclusive when it comes to what they offer—everything from bodyguards to setting up business and home security.* The only thing the site lacked was photos, other than one of the building housing the company. That hardly surprised him. In fact, he'd have been leery of them if it had. In that line of business you don't let the world know who works for you or who your 'satisfied' clients are.

Knowing it would be useless to dig deeper to find out something about the Enforcers—despite the fact that he had some very covert sources for information—Talbot sent an encrypted email to Lemuel. He knew it would probably be a while before he got a reply, so he got ready for bed then settled down to continue reading the book he'd started earlier that day.

An hour later, he heard the ding that said he had mail.

Going back to his study, he opened the email from Lemuel. After apologizing, somewhat tongue-in-cheek, for having told Antton about Talbot, Lemuel went on to verify that Antton was exactly what he purported to be. "I have known him for over three hundred years and in that time I've had reason to become involved with his group—only for a specific mission, not as a member. They know what they're doing. If they are interested in you—and I take it from what you said that they are—I would seriously consider Antton's offer, if I were you."

But you're not me. On the other hand, I do trust your instincts—and my own.

Talbot sent a short reply thanking Lemuel for his input, shut down the computer, and went back to his bedroom. Going to the window, he looked out over his property and the forest behind it. *If I decide to join them, there's nothing to say I can't continue what I normally do; hire out to find rogues and otherwise continue living here. I'm sure working for the Enforcers is not a twenty-four/seven job, except when there's an assignment. So what the hell. I'll give him a provisional yes and take it from there.*

* * * *

Talbot called Ochoa Protection early the next morning, asking to speak with Mr. Ochoa. He was told the man wasn't available at the moment and left the receptionist his number, asking him to call back. Less than five minutes later, Antton did and they set up a meeting at Antton's home for early that evening.

When he arrived there, Talbot studied the large house set on over an acre of land—he guessed—in the foothills on the outskirts of the city. "Impressive," he murmured, while he parked in the driveway. As he got out of the car, the front door opened. Antton stood there and once Talbot joined him, escorted him to the living room. The furnishings were more modern than Talbot expected, but looked comfortable. There were two bay windows, one overlooking the front yard, the other giving a wide view of the mountains behind the house.

A man—or rather a werewolf, Talbot discerned—stood in front of the fieldstone fireplace. Leading Talbot to the man, Antton introduced him as Ulrik Jansson.

"Swedish?" Talbot asked, after Antton introduced him to Ulrik.

"Born and bred," Ulrik replied, eyeing Talbot. "Interesting name, given what you are."

"So help me if you make any cracks about that damned movie and Larry Talbot…" Talbot grumbled.

Ulrik laughed. "Now would I do that?"

"Hell if I know, since we just met." Talbot studied the blond, blue-eyed man. "I presume you're… more than a friend of Antton's."

Ulrik shrugged. "That depends on how you mean that. Since Antton's straight, we're not lovers or some such, if that's what you're asking."

Talbot snorted. "I wasn't. I was just being circumspect, although the fact that you're in the room tells me you probably are part of Antton's organization. And I don't mean his protection company."

"Actually, he's part of both," Antton said. "Any Enforcer who works with me on a more or less full-time basis is also an employee of my company. On paper at least."

"Do you live in Denver?" Talbot asked Ulrik.

"I have a condo here, as well as a home outside of Östersund. That's in Sweden."

"I figured that out from the name."

"Smart man."

"I have my moments," Talbot replied before crossing to one of the low-backed armchairs and sitting.

Antton took a seat at one end of the sofa, while Ulrik sat at the other end.

"Now that we're comfortable," Antton said, "have you considered my offer, Talbot?"

"I have, and provisionally, I'll accept it."

"Just what does that mean?"

"At this point, that I live my life the way I have been and when you need my help, you'll get it as long as I'm not off on a job of my own."

Antton nodded. "Do you have any jobs on your horizon?"

"Nope."

"Therefore, you can start with us today."

Talbot spread his hands. "I don't see why not. What do you need?"

"Help with what we discussed last night."

Talbot glanced at Ulrik. "I take it he knows what's going on and you trust him."

Ulrik bristled momentarily then laughed softly and relaxed. "A legitimate question. I was almost a victim of whoever's betraying us. One of the other Enforcers was murdered while we were taking out a rogue. Not by the rogue, although he knew we were coming for him and was prepared."

"Your companion was killed by one of this rogue's friends?"

Ulrik blew out a breath. "Possible, of course. However, if that was the case, why didn't he step in to help Malthe instead of waiting until he was dead?"

"True. So either he's the person you"—Talbot glanced at Antton—"are looking for, or he was sent by him. Meaning, chances are he was hoping this Malthe would be able to deal with you and the other Enforcer. When you killed Malthe, this person did what he was being paid for—tried to take out both of you. How did you manage to escape, Ulrik?"

"The same way you probably would have. I teleported out. Émilien is—was—a vampire. He started to fly away and was taken down by a silver-headed arrow."

"You stuck around to check that out?" Talbot asked in disbelief.

"I heard him scream just as I took off, so I flashed back and, since he disintegrated the moment it hit his heart, it wasn't hard to figure it out."

"This happened out of doors?"

"Yes," Ulrik replied. "Malthe had a hideout on one of the small islands in Lac des Eaux Bleues. We didn't sense anyone there except him. Whoever killed Émilien was exceptionally well shielded, even from Émilien, who was close to two thousand years old."

"Then you have no idea if the killer was vampire or werewolf."

"No."

"That, Talbot, is why we need your assistance," Antton said.

"Set me up as bait and see what happens?" Talbot replied dryly.

"Not exactly. I don't want anyone except the three of us—and one more Enforcer who will be arriving soon—to know that you even exist. Well, exist in terms of being connected to us. My plan, with the approval of the head Enforcer in the south-eastern region, is that I'll be sending in two men to deal with a rogue running rampant in New Orleans who—"

"Hang on. I just came back from there," Talbot broke in. "I didn't hear anything about him—or her, I suppose."

"Not surprising. You go after vampires. This one is a werewolf—a male who has been alive for over two hundred years. He's only recently turned rogue, for no discernable reason."

"All right. That explains why I didn't know about him. Is he a native of New Orleans?"

"No. He was born near Bay Sirius in what was then Attakapas County, before it became St Martin's Parish in 1807—five years before Louisiana became a state."

"The bayou."

"Actually, Talbot, it's technically a swamp," Ulrik told him. "No clue what the difference is."

"Be that as it may," Antton continued, "he migrated to Lac des Allemands in the late eighteen hundreds and from there to New Orleans."

"Does he have a name?"

"Yes. Sorry. Remy Savoy."

"Cajun?"

Antton nodded. "Although you wouldn't know it to talk to him. He's managed to lose any traces of it in his speech."

"You've met him?" Talbot asked in surprise.

"I have. About fifty years ago. Long before he became a rogue. He was a good man with no aspirations other than taking care of his pack. I wish I knew what happened since then for him to go rogue."

"So he's an alpha. That will make it twice as hard to stop him. What does he look like?"

"He's about six foot tall with tan skin and long, dark brown, almost black, hair. Brown eyes. When I knew him, he had a mustache that curved down beside his lips. Obviously that could be gone at this point. He has a very straight, almost thin, nose. There's one thing that will tell you if you've found the right man. He has a scar here." Antton ran his finger from just below his cheekbone to the corner of his lip.

"From a battle with another—" Talbot stiffened suddenly and reached over his shoulder. "Tell me the person you're expecting is a vampire. Otherwise someone is going to lose their head."

"Put away your sword, if you please. I am indeed expected." The speaker materialized by the door to the dining room. "Dante, at your service, providing you don't decapitate me before I can be." He was of average height with long, auburn hair that reached past his shoulder blades, even though it was tied back.

Talbot studied Dante as he took a seat in another of the armchairs. "You're Old."

Dante chuckled. "I prefer to think of myself as well-seasoned, but yes, I'm over one thousand, so in the vernacular, I'm Old." In turn, he studied Talbot. "Since you knew I was here despite my shielding and misting in, I presume you're a dhampir. But there's more to you." Suddenly his eyes widened in shock and he turned to Antton. "I thought Brand was sui generis."

"As did we all until Lemuel told me about Talbot. Dante, this is Talbot Randel, a dhampir/werewolf hybrid. Born, not created."

"Interesting." Dante returned his piercing gaze to Talbot. "How old?"

"Verging on seven hundred."

"Good Lord."

Talbot laughed. "No, good genes."

"I'd say so."

"Now that we're all here," Antton said, bringing everyone's attention back to him, "We have to come up with a plan not only to stop Remy Savoy but to draw out the turncoat in the process."

"Since I've never gone after a werewolf, what will we be

facing?" Talbot smiled slightly. "I know how I'd react if I was cornered in my werewolf form—with fangs, claws and every ounce of power I possessed. Or, being more practical, I'd just teleport away and live to fight another day."

"Therein lies the problem. He might just do that, unless we incite him to the point that he would rather take us out than flee," Ulrik said.

"My thought," Antton replied, "is that the turncoat might push him into fighting back. Correct me if I'm wrong, Ulrik, but Malthe did that when you and Émilien found him."

"He did," Ulrik agreed. "He must have known he had backup, so to speak, because he fought as if he expected help to arrive. It's what made him… well, not easy to kill, but easier, if that makes sense."

"It does. Based on what happened with him—and in other cases where one of our own was slain *after* taking out a rogue, instead of by the rogue—I think the turncoat is, pardon the phrasing, killing two birds with one stone. If the Enforcers eliminate a rogue instead of the rogue killing them, then they're murdered in a surprise assault afterward."

"You have no idea if the turncoat does that himself?" Talbot asked.

"Unfortunately, no," Antton replied. "If we did, then we'd know who he was."

"Not when his victims are dead," Talbot pointed out. "How often are two or more Enforcers sent after one rogue?"

"Almost always. It's how we work, because we go after only the most powerful rogues."

"I never asked," Talbot said. "How long has this been going on?"

"We became aware of what was happening approximately six months ago. Since then, we've lost ten Enforcers. All good men who shouldn't have died."

"And in every case it was obvious that the rogue they were after knew they were coming?"

"Yes."

"Is it normal that only one of the team members is killed?"

"That depends," Antton replied. "In two cases the rogue, having been forewarned, was able to set up a trap and eliminate both of our men."

"How do you know this if both men died?"

"We know the abilities of the people we send in. In both cases, there was no way the rogue should have been able to trap them unless he knew in advance they were coming for him."

"Doesn't any smart rogue know he's being hunted? God only knows, most of the ones I eliminate are on their guard, unless I catch them in the middle of feeding." Talbot smiled dryly. "Something I wait for, if at all possible. I don't have a death wish."

"Of course they know," Dante said sourly. "That makes it all the harder to stop them. But, from what Antton's told me, in these cases it was a well set-up and executed trap."

"It was in my case," Ulrik agreed. "We were led to believe that Malthe had been wounded by another werewolf who found him attacking a human. Supposedly he was badly hurt and had gone to ground on a small, uninhabited island. We got there, obviously very carefully since even wounded, Malthe would have been a force to be reckoned with. Believe me when I say he was in the peak of good health."

"No one checked to see if the information you had was the truth?"

Antton replied tightly, "It supposedly came through channels from a reliable source. I contacted the source as soon as Ulrik told me what had happened. He had no idea what I was talking about."

"You're certain he was telling the truth?"

"I am, and I'm backed up by Fabrice, the head Enforcer in France, who set up the operation. He read the man and he's not lying."

Talbot nodded slowly. "You said you… meaning, I suspect, this council you told me about as well as you personally, have narrowed down who the turncoat is to five possibilities."

"Yes," Antton replied.

"How do you intend on setting it up so you can find out which one it is? I'm presuming our going after Remy Savoy is at the heart of your plan. Wait." Talbot paused as something occurred to him. "I have another question first. You said there were only two cases where both Enforcers were killed, and it was by the rogue they were after. That means there were six times when one of the Enforcers, Ulrik being a case in point, managed to escape. Do you think the turncoat planned it that way?"

"Meaning?" Antton asked.

"He's obviously bent on destroying the Enforcer organization. What better way than to create seeds of doubt about who can be trusted? That is, presuming people are aware of what's happening."

"They are," Antton said, his voice taut with anger. "And you're right. There have been rumblings about who might or might not be responsible—that it could be anyone from a Council member, to one of the head Enforcers like myself, to someone in the rank and file."

"That last definitely hurts us," Ulrik said, "if we're teamed with someone we don't know personally. To be honest, I watched Émilien very carefully at first and I know he was doing the same with me. It made it hard to work together as a team until it came down to the actual fight. Then… well…" He spread his hands.

"You knew he was trying to kill the rogue, just as you were," Talbot said quietly.

"Exactly. If he'd been the turncoat, he'd have stepped back and let me die trying to destroy Malthe."

Talbot turned to Antton. "Has there ever been a situation where that seemed to happen?"

"How can I answer that? The team kills the rogue then someone kills one of them. If the survivor is telling the truth—and believe me we do everything possible to make certain he is—then a third party came out of the woodwork to murder his partner, always from a distance."

"Which is what happened in my case," Ulrik pointed out. He shook his head, saying sourly, "I'd be hard pressed to prove I wasn't Émilien's killer, I suppose, if Fabrice hadn't read me while I told him every detail of what had occurred. I passed—and here I am."

Dante said seriously, "Damned good *thing* you passed, since Antton is teaming me with you." When Ulrik lifted his middle finger, Dante laughed. "Just kidding. I'd trust you with my life—and have several times."

"As have I with you," Ulrik replied. "The same goes for Antton."

"May I ask who you suspect, Antton?" Talbot asked.

"Of course. All of them are Enforcers, although I suppose that goes without saying."

"Not necessarily," Talbot injected. "You said there were rumors that he could be one of the Council. Or he could be someone connected to an Enforcer—a husband, wife, lover. Or someone employed by the Enforcer organization."

"We have no employees, if you're thinking in terms of secretaries or what have you. We handle everything on our own and always have. The majority of the Enforcers are single. Of those who aren't, most are with another Enforcer." Antton smiled dryly. "We're not a large organization. More like a close-knit, if substantial, family. While most of us who head territories have men and women who work under us on a regular basis, Enforcers are sent where they're needed."

"That's the reason I ended up in France to help take out Malthe," Ulrik said. "Fabrice has what?" He glanced at Antton. "Ten total for the entire country?"

"Ten now," Antton replied sourly. "It was eleven until Émilien was murdered."

"True. Anyway, Talbot, he was shorthanded at the moment so I was sent in to help out. That's how it works. When we were after Fedor, the vampire who experimented on Brand, Antton brought in Dante and three others. It took all six of us to destroy Fedor and his minions. He was that evil and powerful."

"Actually, seven," Dante pointed out. "Brand was definitely a part of that."

"Indeed he was," Antton agreed. "Be that as it may, as I was saying, there are approximately four hundred Enforcers spread out around the world. Not a large number, all things considered."

"I'd say not," Talbot agreed, "considering how many rogues I've dealt with. And they were just vampires. Add in werewolves and you must have your hands full."

"Since we only deal with the worst of the worst, it's not as bad as it sounds, but it does keep us busy. That's why having your help with this is greatly appreciated."

"Not a problem," Talbot replied. He realized he meant that, much to his surprise. After listening to the three men and getting a better perspective on what was happening, he was more than willing to lend a hand. In his eyes, someone who betrayed their comrades needed to be destroyed. *Even more so than the worst of the rogues.* Leaning back, he tapped a fingernail to his lips. "For the turncoat to shield against any mental inquisition you put him through, he must be extremely powerful. He'd also have to be smart enough to figure out what you're doing and give you the replies he knows will keep you from discovering that it's him. How did you narrow it down to the five under suspicion?"

"To begin with, each of them knew which rogues were being targeted. Okay, let's start at the beginning. Four of the five have also worked almost exclusively for me, Fabrice in France, and Quentin, who is in charge of the eastern third of Canada."

"Only the three of you?"

"Yes. They are men we trust to get the job done quickly and quietly. Not"—Antton glanced at Ulrik and Dante—"that we don't expect that of every Enforcer, but these five have been with the organization for a very long time and know more about it than most Enforcers, with the exception of those of us who head territories."

"In other words, they have earned the trust you put in them."

"Precisely. They are dedicated to the cause." Antton shook his head angrily. "Or four of them are. It seems the fifth one may have had a change of heart."

"Has something happened to them that could have made one of them angry enough to want to betray the organization?"

"Perhaps. It's why four are in our sights. The head of the northeastern quarter of the States died seven months ago. Before you ask, he was a werewolf and it was a natural death from extreme old age. When that happened, the Council considered five men to take his place. Obviously, since I'm telling you this, four of the five are the ones we're looking at as the traitor. Anyway, once the perspective replacements were announced, all the territorial heads were asked to vote on them. One candidate stood out. Rhys. Still, it was a difficult decision and no one got a majority of the votes in the first round. So we tried again. On the second vote, Rhys won."

Talbot cocked an eyebrow. "Let me guess. You, Fabrice, and Quentin were the deciding votes and it wasn't a secret ballot."

"Yes. Our feeling, after we realized we had a traitor in our midst, was that it most likely is one of those four. The timing is right. If it is one of them, he might think we backstabbed him by voting for Rhys. As for the fifth suspect—Costel—he was involved with a female Enforcer that Quentin sent on a particularly dangerous assignment. The rogue caught her, raped and tortured her then killed her. Costel blamed Quentin for her death."

"Was the rogue caught?"

"No. You'll be hunting him when the three of you go New Orleans."

"I see," Talbot said, frowning. "I still don't understand why you need me though. As I said, I've never hunted a werewolf. What good will I be?"

"I don't expect you to be involved in finding him. That's Ulrik and Dante's job. The five men we're focusing on are all vampires. You'll be able to sense that they're around, waiting to take out Ulrik and Dante if Remy doesn't."

"You said you thought whoever it is might send someone else to do his dirty work."

"I did, and that's a possibility. But"—Antton's expression was grim—"given who we're going after and who I'm sending to do the job, I suspect he'll show up in person. He'd take great joy in eliminating both Ulrik and Dante, as they are two of the best Enforcers we have."

"Maybe not the best, but we do give it our all," Ulrik said.

"And I trust both of you," Anton replied with a smile. "A definite plus in this case."

"When do we get started?" Talbot asked, deciding to cut

to the chase.

"I'm sending you down tomorrow evening," Antton told him.

"Why not tonight?"

"It's late and by the time you'd get there, it will be morning. Dante can deal with some sunlight, but..."

"Right. I forgot."

"That I'm a vampire?" Dante asked with amusement.

"Actually, yes." Talbot chuckled. "Guess I've gotten to the point that I think of you as just a person, if that makes sense."

"It does—and I'm glad. If we're going to be working together, I'd rather not be worrying that you might forget yourself and decide the only good vamp is a dead one."

"Actually," Talbot replied seriously, "it's been well over six hundred years since I thought that. I put it down to my vampire side coming to terms with my werewolf half, with the part of me that's human arbitrating. While I'll admit I have no great love for vampires, I do realize there are more good ones than bad." He turned to grin at Ulrik. "The same for werewolves."

"Big of you," Ulrik replied with a laugh.

"All right, gentlemen. If there's nothing else you want to discuss, I suggest you get some rest and prepare yourselves. Dante, as always, you're welcome to stay here. The same goes for both of you," Antton said, gesturing to Ulrik and Talbot.

"I'll pass," Talbot replied. "I need to go home and pack."

"The same for me," Ulrik said. "What time tomorrow?"

"Be here at six, please," Antton told them.

As soon as they were outside, since the only car in the driveway was his, Talbot asked Ulrik, "Do you want a lift back to the city?"

After a brief pause, Ulrik replied, "Sure. I could teleport, but it'll give us a chance to get to know each other a bit better."

"Not a bad idea, since we'll be working together." Talbot unlocked the car and as soon as they were both inside, he turned it on and drove down the long driveway to the street.

"Where to?" Talbot asked.

"You know the Baker District?"

"Like the back of my hand. It's my stomping ground when I'm down here."

"I thought… I was under the impression you lived in the city."

Talbot shook his head. "I have a home outside of Silver Plume."

"That seems a bit out of the way."

"Probably no more than your home in… Östersund, if I remember rightly."

"True, and you did," Ulrik replied.

"How did you get hooked up with the Enforcers?" Talbot asked, keeping an eye on the early morning traffic that, while not heavy yet, was picking up.

"My father was one. I just seemed to migrate to them when I was old enough. I have certain skills—above and beyond being a decent fighter—that interested them. I am an expert at going undercover. To wit…"

Talbot took a quick glance at him. Ulrik's body language, his bearing, everything about him except the clothes he wore, projected the idea that he was at least fifty, and somewhat shopworn. "Nice trick," Talbot said, returning his attention to his driving.

"Or I can go the other direction." When Talbot looked at him again, he appeared to be ten years younger than his ostensible age of thirty-five. His hair, which a moment ago had been scraggly, hanging around his face, was now slicked back. He was sitting straight, and he wore a T-shirt, which Talbot presumed had been under the shirt he'd had on at Antton's house. His jacket, which had worked well for the older man persona, now hung over the back of the seat. In just the T, Talbot could see Ulrik was well built. Not overly muscular but decidedly toned.

"You definitely have a useful talent."

Ulrik chuckled. "It's gotten me out of trouble more than once, and helped us find rogues."

"I can see that. But why don't they sense that there's a werewolf in the area?"

"My shielding is primo."

"Primo?" Talbot snorted in amusement. "Been hanging on the streets a bit too long?"

Ulrik shrugged. "There are times when I'm doing the homeless thing. You'd be surprised how often people don't see me when that happens, because they'd rather push the homeless aside than admit there's a problem and address it."

"Yeah. They think people living on the streets do it by choice. It's never a choice. It's the only alternative most of them have to escape what drove them from their homes in the first place, be it abuse, foreclosure, loss of jobs…" Talbot shook his head. "I've seen it, when I've been out hunting."

"Do you do anything about it?" Ulrik asked.

"Much to my discredit, no I don't, other than to give spare change or maybe a burger from the closest fast-food place."

"That's better than most people do." Ulrik leaned back, turning his head to look out the side window. "We live in a hellish world, Talbot, and it's not all caused by the kind of creatures you and I hunt."

"Indeed we do." Talbot made the turn off of Sixth onto Broadway. "Unfortunately, it's illegal to take out the people in charge of how this city—or this country… hell, this world—is run."

Ulrik turned to look at him. "One can dream though," he said dryly. Then he pointed. "Turn right here."

Talbot did and at Ulrik's instructions, pulled up in front of a tall red brick building.

Ulrik got out of the car, then asked before closing the door, "Want to come up for coffee before your drive into the hills?"

Talbot considered that for a moment then shrugged. "Why not?"

Chuckling, Ulrik said, "Enthusiasm at its most hidden."

"Yeah, sorry. I'm tired."

"Then maybe another time."

"Probably a good idea." Talbot waited for him to shut the door then watched as Ulrik headed through the small courtyard to the entryway of his building. Suddenly Talbot sensed the presence of a vampire. An Old one. It was apparent from his casual demeanor that Ulrik had no idea it was there. Talbot was instantly out of the car, his sword in hand. *"Get down,"* he ordered Ulrik, mind to mind. Without waiting to see if Ulrik had heard him, using his inhuman speed, he was beside Ulrik in the blink of an eye, shoving him to the ground. Then he turned to face the vampire, who was invisible to anyone but him. Talbot knew the vampire's intentions were not friendly from the fact his fangs were out and his nails were long claws.

Kill or capture? He decided the latter was not an option. As old as the vampire was, he undoubtedly had the power of flight and he could definitely mist away. It was apparent the vampire was momentarily stunned by the sudden turn of events, trying to figure out what had just happened. Talbot didn't give him time to recover. With one swift swing of his sword, he decapitated the creature.

"What the hell?" Ulrik spat out, getting to his feet.

"Didn't you hear me tell you to get down?"

"Yeah, but you didn't give me a chance to before you took matters into your own hands," Ulrik muttered. "Why?"

Talbot pointed to the small pile of ash on the pavement. "Vampire, and not a friendly one."

"Fuck. This doesn't bode well."

"No shit."

"What did he look like?" Ulrik asked as he dusted off his hands and took out his keys to unlock the lobby door.

"Five nine, five ten, shoulder-length brown hair, dark eyes." Talbot shrugged. "Your average Old vampire. Nothing special that I picked up on in the brief moments before I killed him." He followed Ulrik into the lobby, saying, "Get whatever you're planning to take with you to New Orleans. You're coming home with me."

Ulrik arched his eyebrows. "Oh really? I'm quite capable of taking care of myself."

"Yeah, so I saw. You'd be dead, or at the very least badly wounded, if I hadn't been here and seen him. He was shielded and playing for keeps." Talbot cocked his head in question. "How many people know you live here? People that count, that is?"

"Ones who know what I am?" Ulrik frowned. "Other than Antton, of course, maybe a handful of Enforcers, all of whom I count as friends."

"Yeah? Well I'd say either one of them let your address slip out or we were followed when we left Antton's place."

"I didn't see anyone," Ulrik said.

"Neither did I. And I didn't sense the vampire until the last minute. To my way of thinking, that means you've been compromised. So…"

"Pack up and come with you." Ulrik smiled—barely. "Guess you get that coffee after all while I do."

They took the elevator up to the tenth floor then walked down to Ulrik's unit.

"Not bad," Talbot said once they were inside. "Spacious."

The early morning light came in through a bank of windows along one wall, glinting off the highly polished hardwood floors. Talbot took a seat at one end of a long leather sofa, watching as Ulrik went into the open kitchen to start up the coffee maker.

"I'll be out in a minute. Cups are in the cupboard above the sink," Ulrik said before disappearing down a short hallway that led, Talbot presumed, to his bedroom.

It took longer than a minute for Ulrik to return. By the time he did, Talbot had a cup of coffee that he was sipping as he gazed out the living room windows at the panoramic view of the mountains off in the distance.

"Are we driving?" Ulrik asked, putting his bag on the floor beside the kitchen counter so he could pour some coffee into a large mug.

Talbot turned to look at him, shaking his head. "Probably better if we just teleport. Is there somewhere I can safely leave the car?"

"In the garage under the building. I have two spots. They come with the unit. Give me your keys and I'll move it there. The less anyone sees of you around here the better, all things considered."

Talbot handed him the keys and Ulrik left, returning a few minutes later saying, "That's taken care of, so let's hit it." He picked up his bag after returning Talbot's keys, Talbot gripped his shoulder, and seconds later they were in the middle of Talbot's living room.

Chapter Four

"Good morning—or to be more accurate, good afternoon," Talbot said when Ulrik came downstairs just after four pm.

"Almost evening. I didn't expect to sleep that long." Ulrik sat in one of the armchairs, taking out his phone. "I should have called Antton this morning when we got here to tell him what happened."

"He knows. I emailed him the details before I went to bed. He was not happy."

"I'm sure. I'm not too pleased either. I liked my condo and now I'll have to find a new one."

Talbot chuckled. "That's all that bothers you about what happened? That you'll have to go house hunting now?"

"Of course not," Ulrik replied with some asperity. "I want to know who let it out where I live—and why they did."

"So does Antton. He's also worried your house in Östersund might have been compromised."

"Unlikely. He and the head of the Scandinavian territory are the only two people who know exactly where it is. All anyone else—and it's only a few people—knows is that I have a home somewhere in the country, but that's it."

"Good. Are you hungry? I can throw something together if you are. Antton isn't expecting us for"—Talbot checked the time—"another hour or so."

"Starving, actually. The last time I ate was—hell, lunch yesterday at Antton's."

"Steak okay?"

"I'm a werewolf. What do you think?"

Talbot chuckled, going into the kitchen. Ulrik got up and went to lean on the doorjamb, watching him as he set to work fixing supper. *He's like a well-oiled machine. Every movement counts. He's graceful about it too. I wonder if he's like that... Down boy,* he chastised, realizing where his thoughts were headed. *This is not the time or the place... Okay, maybe the place but definitely not the time. Still...* He studied Talbot, admiring his slender, muscular body, accented by a pair of tight, black jeans and a dark blue turtleneck. *The shirt should be red to accent his black hair. And since when have I become a fashion maven?* He chuckled softly.

"Do I want to know what you find amusing?" Talbot asked, glancing at Ulrik.

"Probably not. Do you want some help?"

"Sure. There's fixings for salad in the fridge."

With a nod, Ulrik set to work and soon they were seated at the table, eating quickly and silently. Ulrik did note, with a bit of amusement, that both their steaks were very rare, reminding him of a comment Dante had told him that Mag, Brand's boyfriend, had made soon after he'd met several of the Enforcers. "Raw meat for everyone," Mag had said, to the amusement of everyone else in the room at the time.

As soon as they finished eating, Talbot put the dishes in the washer, turned it on, and said, "Ready to go?"

"Yep. Let me get my bag." He did, Talbot got his, and with a thought, they vanished, landing at Antton's living room together a brief instant later.

* * * *

Antton looked up from his laptop when Talbot and Ulrik appeared. "Anything else happen after the attack?" he asked.

"Nope. But then no one knows where I live," Talbot told him. "And in my case, I mean *no* one."

"Not possible," Dante said, moving away from the

fireplace to sit across from Antton on the sofa.

"Possible. The house is not in my name. For some strange reason"—Talbot smiled wickedly—"the people who live in the area think it belongs to the government. Especially since there are signs posted around the edges of the property warning that no hunting is allowed and trespassers will be shot on sight. Interestingly enough, at the bottom of the signs is a logo that looks very much like a government seal, which cements the 'threat'."

"I doubt that would keep out someone hunting for *you*," Dante replied.

"Anyone, or anything, getting within twenty feet of the house triggers the security system."

"And if it's a werewolf," Dante said, "who can teleport in? Or a vampire who can mist?"

"A werewolf would have to be able to see the interior first, which isn't possible since the windows are one-way glass. As for vampires, even in mist form they'd trigger the system if they tried coming in under a door or down the chimney," Talbot told him. "It's that sensitive. But that's all moot. No one, but no one, knows the house belongs to me. Well"—Talbot nodded toward Ulrik—"except him, now."

"I'm the first visitor you've had?" Ulrik asked in surprise.

"Unless you count the wild animals that live in the area, and they never get inside."

"Dante," Antton said mildly, "his place is more protected than here, from the sound of it." He glanced at Talbot. "I like the idea of one-way glass. I might implement that once this is over."

"Do. It's worth it." Talbot finally sat, asking, "When do we leave?"

"I have a plane waiting at a private airfield for you," Antton replied.

"If I may make a suggestion. I know New Orleans well at this point. It would be easier and faster just to teleport in."

"Do you have a specific—and safe—spot in mind?" Ulrik asked.

"No. I thought I'd dump us in the middle of Jackson Square," Talbot retorted with a straight face. "Of course I have a specific place in mind. Saint Louis Cemetery number one."

"Ghoulies and ghosties and long-leggedy beasties and things that go bump in the night," Dante muttered.

The others laughed, Ulrik saying, "It suits us. Don't you think?"

"Speak for yourself. I'm neither a ghostie nor a long-leggedy beastie. A ghoulie…" Dante shrugged. "I suppose some would think so."

"Children," Antton grumbled. "Might I suggest you get moving?"

"Good idea." Talbot sent a mental visual to Ulrik of their landing spot, they gathered up their bags, and with Talbot gripping Dante's arm, they vanished.

* * * *

"You are *so* kidding," Dante said when he saw where they'd landed. "You not only dump us in a cemetery, but right beside Marie Laveau's tomb? Talbot, you're evil."

"*Moi*?" Talbot chuckled.

Dante just shook his head, asking, "Now where to?"

"A quaint little motel I stayed at last time I was here. It's not much to look at on the exterior, but…"

A short walk later and they were outside the motel. From the look on Dante's face, it was obvious he considered the motel less than quaint and closer to a dive. By mutual agreement, Dante and Ulrik waited in the shadows of the building across the street while Talbot went inside.

"Mister Lednar. A pleasure to see you again," the desk clerk said. "The room you used last time is available, if you'd like it."

Since the room in question was at the back of the building, facing the parking lot, and Talbot knew that all the rooms were the same size, he said that would be fine. Taking out a credit card for 'Albert Lednar', he paid for a week's stay, got the key to the room, and walked down the hallway from the front desk to the elevator.

"Room 212," Talbot told Ulrik via mind speak as soon as he'd entered the room, giving Ulrik an image of it. Seconds later Ulrik and Dante appeared.

"Better than I expected. Not!" Dante said when Ulrik let go of his arm. "At least there are two beds." He tossed his bag on one of them while Ulrik put his down next to Talbot's on the miniscule desk along one wall.

"And three men," Ulrik pointed out. "Do we toss for who gets to share?"

"Later," Talbot replied. "Right now we need to start looking for Remy Savoy. According to the intelligence Antton gave us, he seems to favor this area of the city." He took the map Antton had given them from his bag, spreading it out on one of the beds. "We're here." He tapped the map. "The area where he hunts encompasses this." He drew a finger around the area in question.

"A third of the damned city, more or less," Ulrik said.

"You thought otherwise?" Talbot asked with a wry grin.

Ulrik shrugged. "Now to figure out how Dante and I can patrol it."

"Well, if we're right about the turncoat letting him know we're here and looking, Remy should reveal his whereabouts," Dante said. "At least that's the premise."

"And I'll be with the two of you while you're out there, as per the plan," Talbot said. "Not that anyone will know it, of course."

"As long as you're well shielded. A werewolf could sense your presence if you're not."

"I know that, Dante. As I said before when we first discussed this, I've never gone after one. That doesn't mean I'm stupid. I'm sure Ulrik can find me, even if I'm half a mile away, just by my scent."

"I can," Ulrik agreed. "You can probably do the same with me."

"Of course."

"So while we're out there, the two of you will know if Remy's anywhere close by," Dante said.

"No. We'll know if there are any werewolves in the area," Ulrik replied. "As we don't know Remy's specific scent, we won't know if it's him until we get close enough to see him."

"All this talking is getting us nowhere. We need to be out on the streets," Talbot pointed out, adjusting the sheath holding his sword. Of course, since they were both invisible, the others didn't know what he was doing.

"Got an itch?" Ulrik asked.

"Yeah, to get moving and stop both Remy and the turncoat." Talbot drew his sword, making it visible to Ulrik and Dante.

Dante whistled, backing away. "That's a weapon of mass destruction."

"It's just your everyday bastard sword. Okay, admittedly its blade is silver, but…" Talbot smiled wickedly as he re-sheathed it.

"It'll do the job once we find our targets," Ulrik said. "So let's hit it and see if you can put it to good use."

* * * *

"We've seen parts of the city I bet no self-respecting tourist would set foot in," Dante grumbled several hours later.

On the roof directly above them, Talbot chuckled. *"You might be surprised. Tourists love the idea that there just might be vampires, and so go looking for them."*

"Idiots, all," Ulrik responded, garnering a dry grin from Dante—and from Talbot, although Ulrik couldn't see it. "At least we got to visit more cemeteries," he added aloud with a derisive snort.

"Lucky us. Where to now?" Dante asked.

"At this point I'd say back to the motel and try again tomorrow night. If there were any werewolves roaming around, they kept well away from us."

"Not so for vampires, but they were all benign," Talbot added, before dropping down from the roof to join them. "Fly or walk?"

"No way I'm flying us back, even if I could," Dante told him. "And technically..."

"Yeah, yeah, teleporting is not flying. Got it," Ulrik said with a bit of asperity. "For damned sure I'm not walking. My feet are killing me."

"Poor man," Talbot said with feigned sympathy, putting his arm around Ulrik's shoulders.

"I'll 'poor man' you," Ulrik growled, but he didn't move away.

"Dante..." Talbot held out his hand, Dante gripped it, and instantly they were back in the motel room.

"Do we want to call down for a rollaway bed?" Dante asked.

"Just where the hell would it fit?" Talbot replied. "And how would I explain needing it."

"Good point. Have fun sharing that one, because this one is mine," Dante said, moving his bag and pulling back the covers. He took out his kit and a pair of sweat pants from his bag, headed to the bathroom, and closed the door behind him.

"Guess we get this one." Talbot sat down on one edge to take off his shoes.

Ulrik chuckled. "We could always tell him to do his bat imitation and hang from the ceiling like a good little vampire."

"I heard that," Dante called out. "It ain't happening."

"Didn't figure." Ulrik stripped off his T-shirt and toed off his shoes.

Talbot watched him with more interest than he knew he should have, given the circumstances. *But damn, he's built and…* He blew out a breath. *Sexy.*

Ulrik caught him looking and cocked his head. "Going to sit there and drool?"

"I wasn't."

"Okay, in reality you weren't but…" He came to stand in front of Talbot and tapped his temple. "Up here you were."

"Mindreading?" Talbot asked with a small smile.

"Projecting, because if the situation was reversed I would have been, so take off that shirt so I can."

Talbot nodded toward the bathroom door. "Now is not…"

"He's showering, so loosen up and strip."

"Damn, Ulrik."

"Well not totally."

Talbot shook his head and pulled off his turtleneck.

"Nice," Ulrik said with admiration. "Exactly what I expected."

"Hot and sweaty?" Talbot replied, since he was. Even at night, New Orleans wasn't exactly cool and he hadn't changed from what he'd been wearing before they left Denver.

"Very hot," Ulrik murmured, stepping closer.

"Keep this up…" Talbot said, his voice suddenly hoarse with unexpected desire.

"And you'll be giving me a show I'm not certain I want to see," Dante said, coming into the room. "Will you two cool it? Please."

Ulrik backed away, saying sourly, "Talk about having a bucket of water thrown over us."

"Well," Dante smirked, "you're both canines—or part canine. Isn't that what you're supposed to do to them when things get hot and heavy?"

"Go to bed before I stake you," Ulrik growled.

Talbot took a deep breath to calm down then laughed. "You two make quite a pair."

"We've known each other long enough we can joke around and not take it too personally," Dante told him as he crawled into bed.

"Says him," Ulrik said, taking a shaving kit and a pair of cut-offs from his bag and heading into the bathroom.

"He likes you," Dante said, his hands behind his head as he looked at Talbot.

"I like him too," Talbot admitted. "That doesn't mean anything is going to happen, because I'm not looking."

"Neither is he, to hear him tell it. However things can change when you meet the right person."

"Have you?" Talbot asked.

"Yes. She's a beautiful woman—and a vampire. Someday, with luck, we'll make it permanent."

"For your sake, I hope so. Everyone deserves someone to care about forever."

"That, Talbot, includes you and Ulrik."

"We'll see what happens, if anything." Talbot thought back to Adrian's words, the last time he'd seen him. 'Someday you'll meet the right person, and then it'll be all over but the shouting,' and how desperately he had hoped that was the truth. *Maybe he's right. Time will tell, I guess.*

Chapter Five

Talbot awoke, groggy and drenched in sweat. "Who turned off the damned AC?" he grumbled, trying to get up to rectify the situation. That's when he discovered something was restraining him. Not in a bad way, he figured, once he realized the 'restraints' were an arm and a leg—Ulrik's arm and leg, to be precise.

Great, just great. Now what do I do? His libido kicked into high gear so he tried, unsuccessfully, to move away.

"Going somewhere?" Ulrik asked, laugher tingeing his words.

"Yeah. To turn on the AC."

"It's on."

"Like hell!" Talbot managed to turn over and look at Ulrik. Then across him to Dante's empty bed. "Where's our friendly vampire?"

"He went looking for supper. At least that was his excuse." Ulrik moved his arm, but not in a way that gave Talbot the freedom, or the desire, to move.

"What are you doing?" Talbot barely whispered when Ulrik wrapped his hand around Talbot's now throbbing cock.

"What we both want, I think. I hope," Ulrik replied softly.

Talbot swallowed hard. "It is. But…"

"Will you hush and just go with it. This is not a declaration of love. Just one of interest in exploring the possibilities."

"Well, hell. In that case…" Talbot reached between them to find Ulrik's hard cock, teasing one finger over the leaking slit. "I am definitely interested."

"I noticed," Ulrik replied, groaning low when Talbot slid

his hand down to cup Ulrik's balls, rolling them between his fingers.

"You're sure he's going to be gone for a while?"

"Who?" Ulrik asked, his thoughts obviously on something other than Dante.

"Never mind." Talbot pressed his free hand against Ulrik's shoulder, urging him to lay back. When the werewolf did, Talbot slipped down between his legs so that he could lave his tongue the length of Ulrik's cock before taking it into his mouth.

"Fuck," Ulrik groaned, tangling his hands in Talbot's hair.

"Not yet. First..." Talbot sucked hard, pulling Ulrik's cock farther in, the taste of the werewolf's pre-cum exciting him more than he was already.

"There won't be a 'yet' if you keep that up."

Chuckling as he deep-throated him, Talbot wrapped his fingers around the base of Ulrik's cock. *"I think there will be."*

"Bastard," Ulrik muttered, moaning deeply.

"Moi?"

"Tu."

Talbot released Ulrik's cock after one more hard swallow, but still gripped the base as he looked up at him. "Now comes the important question."

"Both," Ulrik replied before Talbot could finish asking. His gaze went down to Talbot's thick member, and he licked his lips. "But first..."

"You can restrain yourself?"

"Restraint is my middle name," Ulrik replied with a grin. The second Talbot let go, Ulrik flipped him over and began licking each of Talbot's nipples.

"Damn," Talbot whispered, as bolts of fire seemed to go straight to his already too hard cock.

Ulrik nipped each one lightly then proceeded down,

finally taking Talbot's cock into his mouth. *"How much can you take of this?"*

Talbot groaned deeply. *"Not… much… if you want me to fuck… you."*

"In that case…" Ulrik continued sucking for a moment more then sat back on his heels. "And who decided you'd be the fucker?"

Talbot grinned. "Me?"

Ulrik laughed. "Bossy man. But next time…"

"We'll toss for it. Hell, I don't suppose…"

"Lube? Yep." Ulrik got off the bed to open his bag, returning quickly to toss Talbot a tube.

"You come prepared."

Grinning, Ulrik said, "Never leave home without it." Then he sobered. "Not true. It's been a long time since I've needed it. I guess I just… hoped?"

"Me too," Talbot admitted quietly, squeezing some onto his fingers. By the time he was finished, Ulrik was on his hands and knees. Gently, given what Ulrik had said, Talbot pushed one finger in, murmuring, "Relax."

"Trying to," Ulrik replied, followed by, "Gods… there…"

Talbot stroked Ulrik's gland, feeling him tremble as he moaned with need for more. Carefully, after inserting a second finger, Talbot stretched him. Then he pulled his fingers out, chuckling at Ulrik's deep groan of frustration.

"Soon," Talbot murmured as he lubed his cock then pressed it to Ulrik's entrance. "If I hurt you…"

"I can deal," Ulrik told him. "Just… Damn it, Talbot, fuck me."

"Now who's bossy?" Talbot bent to kiss the nape of Ulrik's neck before pushing the head of his cock into Ulrik's tight channel. "Relax," he whispered, unsure if he meant Ulrik or himself. At the moment, all he wanted was to be balls deep into the werewolf, screwing him into oblivion.

"I won't break, damn it!"

"Didn't think you would." Slowly Talbot moved deeper, savoring the pleasure he was receiving, hoping he was giving as much to his lover. Talbot figured he was when Ulrik thrust back to take him fully in.

"Now, move…" Ulrik muttered. "I'm not doing all the work."

Talbot snorted, even as he pulled almost out and then slammed into him. "Wouldn't want you to."

"More. Faster," Ulrik ordered, adding, "please," with a deep, needy moan.

So Talbot gave what he—what both of them—wanted. As excited as the two of them were, it didn't take long before he felt Ulrik tighten around him. Almost in unison they came and Talbot cried out in ecstasy as his orgasm consumed him.

They collapsed, Talbot sprawled over Ulrik's back, their shuddering slowly abating. Reluctantly, totally drained, he pulled out and rolled off onto his side to look at Ulrik. "We should do this again," he murmured before tentatively kissing him.

Ulrik wrapped his arms around Talbot, returning the kiss with unfeigned interest. "Indeed we should. Often," he agreed when they broke apart.

"Now I really need…"

"A shower?"

"Big time."

"I'd suggest we share it but…"

"Our friendly vampire would probably return before we're finished."

"Yep. So go." Ulrik kissed him again.

"Going." Talbot smiled happily, returning the kiss.

"I meant now," Ulrik suggested as the kiss deepened. *"Or*

Dante might walk in on something he'd wish he hadn't."

Talbot pulled away, laughing as he got off the bed. "Good point." As he went into the bathroom, he realized he was the happiest he'd been in a long time. He cautioned himself that fucking all too often did not mean more than just that, in the grand scheme of things. *But who knows? It could be the start of something more, I hope. I like him. Maybe more than I should, but I do.*

Chapter Six

"Might I suggest," Dante said, walking into the motel room, "that now you two have taken care of your more pressing needs, we get out there and find Remy—or let him find us."

Talbot nodded, pulling on a black turtleneck. Ulrik was already dressed in jeans and a yellow T-shirt that said 'It's Always Humid in New Orleans'.

Dante tapped Ulrik's chest, saying, "You're not really going out in that, are you?"

Grinning, Ulrik took out another one from a bag sitting by the side of the desk. Apparently, somewhere along the line in the last twenty-four hours, he'd managed to sneak out and go shopping. "Want me to wear this?" It was gray, with a crawfish in red and the words 'Don't Eat the Straight Ones' emblazoned on it in black.

Talbot doubled over laughing and even Dante smiled, shaking his head. "I guess the yellow one will catch Remy's eye, even in the dark, if he's around to see it," Dante admitted.

"Only one way to find out. If we're correct, by now he definitely knows we're in town. Well, Talbot excepted. He'd better not know about him," Ulrik said.

"True," Talbot agreed while adjusting his sword and sheath. "We ready?"

"Let's do it," Ulrik replied. "Where do we want to start?"

"Here," Talbot said, pointing to the map that now sat spread out on the desk. "It's the southern edge of his hunting grounds, but since we had no luck in the main area, we might want to give it a shot."

"Not too far from the motel." Ulrik cocked an eyebrow at Talbot. "Is that why you chose this place?"

"Nope. Dumb luck."

"Dumb is right," Dante muttered. "If you know the area though, Talbot, I suggest we start a few blocks east. No sense bringing him right to our doorstep if he is in the district."

Talbot nodded and after a moment's thought, he remembered a rundown auto repair shop half a mile away, in the direction they'd be heading. As usual, he gave Ulrik the image, gripped Dante's shoulder, and instantly they were behind the shop. Ulrik swore under his breath when he landed on a pile of tires beside the wall.

"Hell, don't blame me," Talbot said. "They weren't there the last time I came by."

With no damage done, except to his ego, Ulrik started toward the alley. Dante followed while Talbot made quick work of getting up to the roof of the nearest building. He wasn't too happy with the occasional peaked roofs he had to cross. However, there was nothing he could do but cope and be glad when he was back on flat ones.

They had traveled seven blocks when suddenly Ulrik came to a stop, pressing deep into a building's back doorway. Dante instantly followed suit before vanishing from sight.

"Something?" Talbot asked, shielding his thoughts so that only Ulrik could hear them as he flattened himself on the roof to peer over the edge. He knew, or at least he hoped, that Ulrik had the same ability to channel his thoughts to only those he wanted.

Apparently Ulrik picked up on Talbot's concern because he replied, *"I can and so can Dante,"* before he nodded, holding a finger to his nose then pointing to a doorway two buildings down.

"Werewolf, I presume."

"Yes. His scent is strong. Almost too strong. Like he laid it down on purpose."

"Does he think we're idiots?" Talbot asked dryly.

"I doubt it. More like he's got extreme confidence in his abilities,

which would be unsurprising considering how long he's lived. If the turncoat is playing into that by telling Remy he'll help him capture us before we can destroy him, then the scent is probably the prelude to a trap."

"If it's his and not some other werewolf's."

Ulrik nodded and for a moment, Talbot thought it was in agreement. Then he heard Dante say as he appeared beside Ulrik, *"It's Remy. Scar and all. He's not alone. I couldn't see who else is there with him, but I sensed the presence of a vampire."*

"Given that the five possibilities for the traitor are all vampires, we can figure the one you sensed is our man."

"I'd say that's logical, but not a given."

"Only one way to find out," Ulrik said. *"What's the layout, Dante?"*

"The door leads to a storage room. I'm guessing the place designs and silk-screens T-shirts from the markings on the boxes. At one side of the room are stairs leading down to a basement."

"In New Orleans?" Ulrik said in surprise.

"There are some, though most places have what are called 'raised basements'. And I am not going to explain that at the moment," Talbot replied.

"As I was saying," Dante continued, *"the basement is there and broken into four rooms, going by the doors I saw from the bottom of the stairs. I wasn't about to go any further, because if I could sense the vampire, chances are he knew I was there as well."*

"But he was in the basement?" Ulrik said.

"Yes."

"I can go in and deal with him. He won't know I'm there until it's too late," Talbot suggested.

"But Remy might if he smells your werewolf scent," Ulrik replied. *"It would be better if Dante and I enter first. My scent should cover yours, Talbot, when you come in."*

Talbot nodded. *"All right."*

"Give us five minutes head start," Ulrik said.

Remaining where he was, Talbot watched as Ulrik and Dante slipped silently down the alley. He had no intention of waiting five minutes. He knew full well that it could take only seconds for a trap to be sprung that would end with both his friends maimed, imprisoned, or dead.

Shielding physically and mentally, he followed a few yards behind Ulrik and Dante. He was unsurprised to see Ulrik shift to his sleek, powerful dark blond wolf form. Dante misted, but Talbot knew exactly where he was as he and Ulrik slipped into the building. Keeping his distance, Talbot entered as well, just in time to see them go down the stairs to the basement.

"The lady or the tiger?" Talbot heard Ulrik's wry question to Dante and smiled momentarily as he opened his senses to locate the enemy vampire. Since he was shielded to hide his presence, Talbot couldn't reply but he knew the answer. The 'tiger', meaning Remy, was in the room behind the second door from the left. The vampire, and Talbot realized immediately he was Old and powerful, was in the room beside Remy's.

Ulrik, nose to the ground, was obviously following Remy's scent to where he was waiting. Dante continued on to the room holding the vampire, misting under the door.

Torn for a moment, wanting to be with Ulrik when he faced Remy but knowing that killing the vampire traitor was more important, Talbot watched as Ulrik shifted momentarily to open the door before going back to his wolf form as he sprang into the room.

By then, Talbot was holding his sword at the ready. He strode to the vampire's room, easing the door open just enough to peer inside. Dante was back to his human form, his hands held out in front of him. Talbot inched the door open until he could see the turncoat. The vampire was of medium height with long brown hair and red eyes. The sneer on his lips spoke to how little he thought of Dante, as did his words when he said,

"Do you really think you can take me on? *Me?* I have been around for twice the time you have."

Fire fanned out from Dante's hands, only to meet empty air as the older vampire moved with incredible speed, coming up behind Dante. Dante howled in pain when a wound opened on his shoulder, blood spewing. Still, he turned to face his attacker, letting loose with another stream of flames.

The turncoat went invisible as he moved across the room, avoiding the fire while using his Killing Gift to tear a wound into Dante's thigh. Dante fell, and the vampire watched with glee. That was all Talbot needed, for the vampire to be still. He was beside him, his sword arcing toward his throat, and seconds later the vampire's head rolled across the floor before turning to dust, just as his body had.

Talbot started to kneel beside Dante, who was too pale by half from loss of blood, only to be told in no uncertain terms that he was to go help Ulrik. "I'm… healing… already," were the last words Talbot heard as he dashed from the room.

Slamming open the door to the room next door, Talbot came upon a scene straight out of a horror movie. Blood was spattered across the floor and walls as two werewolves fought for domination. Ulrik's blond fur was covered with gore, but so was the fur of the dark brown wolf he was fighting.

Talbot was loath to interfere, knowing if he tried to strike Remy, he might well hit Ulrik instead.

Suddenly Ulrik was pinned to the floor, his neck exposed to Remy for a killing bite.

"No!" Talbot shouted, striding toward them with his sword raised.

Remy paused, obviously startled by the intrusion. *"Why should I let him live? He would kill me if he could."*

"True," Talbot agreed. "But killing him is doing just what the turncoat wanted."

Remy kept his front paws on Ulrik's chest and shoulder but didn't bite—yet. Instead he tilted his head in question. *"The turncoat?"*

"The vampire in the next room. Or, perhaps I should say the ex-vampire. He's dust now."

Remy shook his head in seeming disbelief. *"He was my friend. It was because of him I…"*

"Went rogue?" Talbot asked tightly.

"I'm not a rogue! I only deal with those he says need it."

"Good Lord," Ulrik said, pain lacing his voice. Then he added, so softly as to be barely understood, *"Antton will be… glad to know… that. I think."*

"He thought…?"

"That you went rogue? Yes," Talbot replied.

Remy backed away from Ulrik. *"I… What have I done?"* His words were filled with agony.

"You've been the pawn of someone who was truly evil," Dante said from the doorway. "At least, if we're to believe you."

"Then I deserve to die," Remy said, his gaze now locked on Talbot's sword.

Talbot shook his head. "Not by my hand." He sheathed the sword then went to kneel beside Ulrik. "We need to get him—get both of them—to the clinic." He stroked Ulrik's bloodstained head, murmuring, "And you'd better not die before I get you there."

"I'll… try not to."

"Dante, do you know where the closest clinic is that your people use?" Dante sent him an image. "Thanks. I'll be back for you momentarily." Talbot motioned for Remy to move closer. When the werewolf did, albeit cautiously, Talbot took Ulrik in his arms. "Give me your forepaw, Remy." Remy did and seconds later, the trio was in the front room of the clinic.

Two doctors appeared immediately, one telling Talbot

that Dante had warned them he was coming with two wounded men. "He didn't bother to mention they were in their wolf forms but that's fine. They'll heal faster that way, with our help." Even as he said that, more medics arrived to take Ulrik and Remy in hand.

"I'll be back," Talbot told Ulrik softly.

And he was, moments later, with Dante, who protested that he didn't need tending to. "Maybe a couple of pints of blood is all," he told the doctor when the man didn't seem to believe him. The doctor led him away, leaving Talbot alone in the room.

Another doctor came in almost immediately, asking if Talbot needed anything.

"To know how Ulrik is doing and see him, if possible," Talbot said.

Before the doctor could reply, Antton appeared in the room and immediately asked the same question about Ulrik.

"Taking everything into account, your friend is doing well. We'll keep him here, and sleeping, until he's fully healed. The same for the other werewolf."

"Remy?" Antton asked, apparently surprised. "All Dante told me was that Ulrik had been injured and the turncoat was dead."

"Very dead," Dante said, joining them. "Thanks to Talbot. That bastard had gained the Killing Gift since I last saw him."

"Ah." Antton sighed. "Then I know who he was. I was rather hoping it wouldn't be Gian. He was a good man—once. Of course, I was hoping it wouldn't be any of the candidates that Rhys beat out for the office, but…" He spread his hands. "We knew the chances were good it was one of them."

"I agree. Gian was a decent man and a damned good Enforcer. That was a long time ago, however, when I was teamed with him." Dante shook his head. "Seven hundred years, in point of fact."

"Did Remy have any excuses for why he turned rogue," Antton asked Talbot and Dante.

"Apparently," Talbot replied, "he didn't. According to him, he was only helping Gian take out—I think his words were—'those who needed it'."

"They were," Dante confirmed. "I do wonder how Gian was able to convince him of that, especially since Gian was a vampire."

"Something I'll have to ask Remy when I talk to him." Antton turned to the doctor. "When will I be able to do that?"

"My guess would be not for several hours at the least. He was as badly wounded as Ulrik."

"Then I suggest the three of us go find somewhere with decent food," Antton said to Talbot and Dante. "If we hang around here, we'll only worry and be in the way."

"Talbot especially," Dante said with a knowing grin.

"Oh?" Antton shot a look at the dhampir.

"Well, you see…" Talbot muttered, feeling like a specimen beneath a microscope under Antton's piercing gaze. He went on to explain in a little detail as possible as they left the clinic, heading toward the Quarter in search of somewhere to eat.

Chapter Seven

Shifting from his wolf form, Ulrik wondered as he did where he was. Then he remembered and slowly moved to check that everything was working the way it should be.

"You're awake. Finally."

Ulrik turned his head to see Talbot sitting beside the bed. "Not certain I want to be," he grumbled. His wounds were, to a greater extent, healed. But he still felt as if he'd done ten rounds with a crazed mixed martial arts champion.

"You look like hell," Talbot told him.

"Thanks. Not. You, on the other hand, look like you came through everything unscathed."

"The advantage of being what I am. By the way, it's a damned good thing I didn't wait five minutes like you ordered. We'd be down one pissy vampire." When Ulrik asked, Talbot told him what had happened with Gian.

"Gian, huh? I thought he was better than that."

Talbot quirked an eyebrow quizzically. "Good enough to avoid my beheading him?"

"No. I meant I thought he was a decent man, for a vampire."

"Just what's wrong with vampires? I'm part one," Talbot pointed out.

"You're part everything," Ulrik retorted with a ghost of a grin. "Human, vampire, werewolf. For all I know, there's some cat in the mix too—and bird, and…"

"I'd better call the doctor. I think you're delirious," Talbot grumbled, resting his hand on Ulrik's shoulder.

"Nope. Just happy to have survived and to see you."

"Really? I mean… the seeing me part."

"Do you doubt it?" Ulrik asked softly.

"I…" Talbot shrugged. "I'm not willing to jump to conclusions just because we spent part of yesterday in bed together. It could have been a one-time thing."

"Do you really believe that? After all, I did say we should do it often, if I remember rightly."

"True. But…"

"Look," Ulrik said, gripping Talbot's hand, "as I also said, I'm not about to declare undying love or anything of that sort, but—"

"You want to explore the possibilities," Talbot broke in. "Said in the heat of the moment."

"And that makes it less real?"

"Well… maybe not." Talbot chewed his lip, a gesture Ulrik found strangely appealing.

"For someone who's been in this world almost as long as I have, you're awfully unsure of yourself in some areas," Ulrik told him.

"Like believing that someone could want me for *more* than a one-night stand? Trust me. I've found out that's not true more than once. I'm not easy," he added hastily. "I'm just not…" He shook his head.

"Give yourself some credit, Talbot. You're sexy and very interesting on many levels." Ulrik tried not to smile at the look of disbelief on Talbot's face. "You have a lot to offer the right man."

"Like my expertise at killing vamps? Yeah, I have that. Otherwise…" Talbot took a deep breath. "I suppose this sounds inane, but I watch friends who've found their other half and felt happy for them, but I've never seen it happening for me."

"Maybe now is the time to consider it might be possible, if you're willing to take the chance."

"Don't commit yourself unless you mean it," Talbot replied testily, but Ulrik saw the faint look of hope in the dhampir's expression.

"I do mean it," Ulrik told him. "The question is, are you willing to take the *chance* that I do."

* * * *

Talbot bowed his head, staring down at the floor. "Perhaps," he barely whispered, uncertain if that was the correct answer. *Should I have said emphatically yes? I want to, but can I accept that he really is interested in me? It's too soon. He doesn't… Thrown together the way we were, we barely know each other. Hell, am I really interested in him?* He sighed softly. *Stupid question because I know the answer. Yes, I am.*

"What are you thinking?" Ulrik asked, putting his fingers under Talbot's jaw to make him look up.

"Debating."

"What?"

"How little we know of each other and yet we still seem… to mesh?"

"That's not a debate. It's a fact. Does it worry you?"

"To be honest, it scares the hell out of me," Talbot admitted with a rueful smile. "It makes me wonder about myself. Am I… needy enough that I'm seeing what I want to and not what might be the reality? Being good in bed together does not mean that on a daily basis we would be."

"I'll say it one more time. We won't know until we try. Right?"

"Right."

"Come here," Ulrik said, cupping his hand at the nape of Talbot's neck. When Talbot leaned forward, Ulrik kissed him. "To seal the promise."

"That we'll try?"

Ulrik nodded, smiling. "And succeed, if I have anything

to say about it."

Talbot grinned. "Do I have a say in it too?"

"Well, duh, to quote a much overused teen phrase." Ulrik kissed him again and this time Talbot returned it quite enthusiastically. "Now," Ulrik said when they parted, "would you please do me a favor and go see if you can find a doctor. I want out of here."

"You bet!" Talbot replied, jumping to his feet. *I feel like a giddy teen. Stupid I know, but I do.* As he left the room he glanced back at Ulrik. *With good reason—I hope.*

Chapter Eight

Ulrik and Remy were released from the hospital, Remy moving from there into Antton's custody. Then, after the team picked up their bags at the motel, everyone went back to Antton's home.

First, Antton debriefed Talbot, Ulrik, and Dante. Then the four of them sat down with Remy. If asked, which he wasn't, Talbot would have admitted he was surprised that Remy hadn't teleported away and gone back into hiding. He found out why when Antton asked Remy what amounted to that same question.

Remy sat straight, looking at the men, replying, "I have done nothing wrong. Or perhaps I should say that I did, but I was under the impression I was doing what needed to be done. Gian was"—he shook his head angrily—"very convincing. He told me what he was—an Enforcer. Of course I knew about them. About you." He looked at the men. "Then he asked for my help. Naturally I agreed. Who wouldn't?"

"That 'help' included torturing and raping…"

Before Antton could finish, Remy said in shock, "I never… I wouldn't do that! Yes, I killed. I've already admitted to that. But that was it, and I swear I believed that the ones I killed deserved it. Gian would point me at them, telling me they were humans who knew of our existence and planned to reveal it to the world. Some, he claimed, were people who were blackmailing either a vampire or a werewolf, in exchange for not letting anyone know what they really were. Twice, they were supernaturals that he claimed had betrayed us."

"How could you fall for that?" Dante asked him.

"I had no reason not to." He looked hard at Dante. "If it had been you, would you have questioned him?"

Dante considered his query and then admitted,

"Probably not. After all, he was a fine Enforcer until he decided he wanted what he couldn't have—to be the head of the northeastern territory of the States."

"Did he use other werewolves the way he did me?"

"Unfortunately, he did," Antton replied. "We lost several good men because of him."

"The way you almost lost those two," Remy said, nodding at Ulrik and Dante, "if he"—his gaze went to Talbot—"hadn't been there too. What are you? When you appeared, I sensed werewolf, but you're more."

"I'm a little bit of a lot of things. Werewolf, human, vampire."

"That's—"

"If you say impossible…" Talbot grumbled. But he smiled as he did. "I'm a hybrid—werewolf and dhampir, to be exact."

Remy shook his head. "Impossible."

"What did I tell you?"

"Sorry." Remy studied Talbot. "Are you an Enforcer too?"

"No. I was just helping out because they needed what I am."

"The dhampir half."

"All of me actually," Talbot replied, chuckling. "I don't split into pieces."

Remy actually smiled at Talbot's joke. Then he turned to Antton. "What's going to happen to me?"

"You could go back to doing what you were before Gian got his claws into you."

"So you believe me?"

"Let's just say that to this point, I'm firmly convinced you've been telling the truth."

There was a moment's silence then Remy spat out,

"You've been reading me!"

"If you were in my position, wouldn't you?"

"Yes. I suppose so. It is an invasion of privacy, however."

"I'm sorry, but it's a necessary one. You were a good man when I last met you. I needed to be certain that was still the case. I'll admit I was shocked when I heard you'd turned rogue. It wasn't, I'd thought, something you would do—especially when I learned about the rape and torture of Costel's woman."

"Gian set me up well," Remy said in disgust. "I wonder who was really responsible for that."

"If I had to guess," Antton said, "it was Gian himself. He needed us to think you were total scum, so that we'd come looking for you when the time was right."

"I'm beginning to wish I'd made Gian's death more painful," Talbot muttered.

"If you hadn't killed him fast, he might have used his considerable powers to take you out," Dante told him. "The Killing Gift is nothing to screw around with, as I found out. I suppose I should be glad he decided to toy with me before using it full force."

"Indeed," Antton said. "Now, to get back to the question you asked before we got sidetracked. You could return to your regular life, Remy, if that's what you want. Or, provisional on the Council approving it, you could join us as an Enforcer."

"You can't be serious. After what I did?"

Antton smiled, slightly. "What you did, you did well. Not that that's a recommendation, but you do have abilities we could use."

"From rogue to Enforcer. That's a bit of a jump," Dante said.

Ulrik smiled dryly. "He is a good fighter. I had the wounds to prove it, and I'm no slouch in that department."

"Not to brag," Remy said, "but I'm also good at going undercover. It wasn't until Gian set up his final plan that I got caught." He shot a look at Talbot. "And if you hadn't been there, that wouldn't have happened."

"Which brings me to another thing," Antton said. "Talbot, do you still want to work with us when we need you?"

"I have no problem with that."

"Would you consider joining us instead?" Ulrik asked, locking his gaze on Talbot's face.

Talbot looked back at him, a small grin quirking up his lips. "I could be persuaded to, I suspect."

"I think that could be arranged."

They continued to look at each other, oblivious of the other men in the room, until Antton coughed loudly, saying, "Unless anyone has anything else to add to the business at hand, I suggest we adjourn. I need to call a council member to suggest Remy join us. I'm sure the rest of you have things to do as well. Remy, do you want to stay here until I get an answer?"

"Yes, thank you. In reality, I have nothing much at home that needs my attention at the moment. My son is the Alpha of our pack, with my approval." Remy smiled ruefully. "I had planned on retiring to New Orleans and living out my life in peace. Then Gian appeared and—well, you know how that went."

"Then you are welcome to remain here as long as you wish. If the Council approves you, I'll help you find a home here in the city, or you can return to New Orleans and be at my beck and call the way Ulrik and Dante are."

Ulrik snorted. "Meaning you'll never get a moment's peace, so you might as well do as I did and get a place of your own here."

"Speaking of which," Talbot said, "are you going to keep it, now that we know Gian was responsible for that vampire finding you?"

"Good question."

"We don't know for certain he was," Antton pointed out, glancing at Remy.

"Don't ask me. I just did what he told me to. He didn't take me into his confidence beyond that."

"Then I guess I'm going house hunting," Ulrik grumbled.

"Don't worry, we'll find you something," Talbot told him.

Dante grinned wickedly. "Until then, you can bunk with Talbot."

Ulrik and Talbot both flipped him off, but Talbot nodded nonetheless. "I have an extra bedroom. You can use it if you want."

"I want," Ulrik replied succinctly.

Chapter Nine

Thus, an hour later, Talbot was unpacking his bag in his bedroom while Ulrik did the same with his in the guest room. They would have been there earlier, but Antton had offered everyone a late supper, and they'd accepted.

As soon as he was finished and had changed into a comfortable set of sweats, Talbot went to the study. Booting up the computer, he checked his email to see if there were any jobs pending that needed his attention. At the moment there weren't, much to his relief. He wanted some downtime to just relax. *And see if there really is something going on between me and Ulrik besides good sex.* He realized the 'good sex' was based on only one afternoon, under somewhat stressful circumstances.

"You busy?" Ulrik asked from the doorway.

"Nope. Just thinking about going for a run if you're interested."

"Definitely. This is perfect weather for it."

"In umpteen feet of snow? Oh, right, you're used to it."

"It's my Swedish blood. There can't ever be too much snow."

"You, Ulrik, are weird."

Leaning against the doorframe, Ulrik said, "You prefer the New Orleans heat?"

"Well… I don't think I could stand it twelve months out of the year, but it was a nice change."

"If you say so. I'll stick with Colorado where we get all the seasons."

"Truth be told, so will I." Talbot turned the computer off and stood. When he got to the doorway, Ulrik remained where he was, effectively preventing Talbot from leaving the room. Talbot cocked his head in question and, suddenly, found himself wrapped in a firm embrace, followed immediately by a hard, probing kiss that brought his libido to full alert.

"I thought you wanted to run," Talbot said when he could speak again.

"I do. I just figured we should get warmed up first."

"Warm? Hell, I think we're beyond that and into a raging inferno," Talbot retorted, pressing his hand against the very obvious bulge in Ulrik's jeans.

"And that's a problem why?"

"For no reason I can think of. Maybe we should—"

Ulrik smirked. "Run to cool down?"

"I was thinking more along the lines of adjourning to my bedroom to take care of your more than obvious—problem." Again, he palmed Ulrik's erection, wishing the jeans weren't in his way.

"Problem?" Ulrik arched one blond eyebrow before steering Talbot toward the suggested destination. "I call it evidence of how much I want you."

At least physically, you do. But on a truly personal level?

As if reading Talbot's thoughts, Ulrik said, "And I meant that in every way possible. Not just your body, but all of you." He paused until they were beside Talbot's bed then embraced him again. "Believe that," he said softly before kissing Talbot.

It was, at first, a slow meshing of lips. That soon changed as their physical needs took over. The kiss became heated, broken only as they stripped off shirts, then shoes and pants. Ulrik tumbled them onto the bed when they were naked. Resting on his elbows he looked down at Talbot.

"You do believe me, don't you? That I want more than just your body?"

"I'm beginning to," Talbot replied.

"You're a hard man to convince, Mr. Randel," Ulrik grumbled, before kissing him again. He started with Talbot's lips then inched his way down—his chin, the hollow of Talbot's throat, each nipple—finally reaching his destination. He laved his tongue slow over Talbot's balls then up from there to his leaking slit, swiping his tongue over it, eliciting a needy groan from his lover.

Talbot almost came on the spot when Ulrik took his cock into his mouth. Only Ulrik's fingers wrapped tightly around the base kept that from happening.

"I could do this for hours," Ulrik said, as he tormented Talbot's throbbing member.

"How does the threat of death sound, if you try to?" Talbot growled between moans.

Ulrik chuckled, sending more waves of pleasure through Talbot. *"I think I'll pass on that."*

Finally, Ulrik pulled back but didn't release his fingers' grip. Looking up at Talbot, he asked, "Have you ever been fucked?"

Talbot nodded. "Not often but… yeah. So if you want to."

"I would love to," Ulrik told him, sliding up to kiss him. "But only if you're really willing."

Talbot glanced down at Ulrik's cock, trying not to wince at the size of it. "I am. For you. With you. If that makes sense." When Ulrik kissed him again, passionately, and then sat back on his heels, Talbot started to turn over.

"No," Ulrik said, placing his hands on Talbot's shoulders to still him. "Stay as you are and lift your legs. Please?"

Surprised, Talbot did. No one had ever asked him to do that before.

Looking hopeful, Ulrik opened the nightstand drawer. "Whew," he murmured as he took out the lube, squeezing a large dollop onto his fingers. Locking his gaze on Talbot's face, he pushed one finger through the tight ring of muscle.

Talbot winced at the brief pain, then gasped when Ulrik found his gland and began to stroke it. Intense pleasure flooded him to the point that he was barely aware when a second finger entered to stretch him.

"I think you're ready," Ulrik finally said, removing his fingers. After generously lubing his cock, he pressed it to Talbot's entrance. "I will stop if I think I'm hurting you," he warned.

"Don't you dare," Talbot told him. "I'm not a baby you have to coddle."

Ulrik laughed, although he was intently watching Talbot's face as he pushed the thick head of his cock into Talbot.

Talbot tried not to react to the burst of pain. Unsuccessfully he realized, when Ulrik instantly stopped. "I'm okay," Talbot managed to get out through clenched teeth.

Instead of continuing, Ulrik bent forward to kiss him gently, murmuring, "Relax," against Talbot's lips.

Taking a deep breath, Talbot did his best to follow Ulrik's order as the werewolf pushed further into him. When the head of Ulrik's cock brushed over Talbot's gland, a wave of ecstasy removed any thought of the slowly abating pain. "More," Talbot whispered, his gaze locked on what he could see of Ulrik's hard member. It was extremely erotic to watch as his lover thrust in, pulled out slightly then drove in deeper.

"Are you all right?" Ulrik asked, hope and concern in his words.

"Better than…" Talbot managed to gasp as the pleasure mounted.

With one hand now wrapped around Talbot's cock, Ulrik began to ride him harder and faster, his own elation from what he was doing showing in his expression. Talbot loved that, seeing his lover was getting as much as he was giving.

Each thrust, each stroke of Ulrik's hand on Talbot's

throbbing cock, brought Talbot closer to fulfillment.

"I can't… I'm going to…" Talbot moaned, wanting to wait for Ulrik, even as his balls tightened as a prelude to release.

"Come for me," Ulrik whispered, giving Talbot's cock one more pump.

Talbot did, his orgasm shattering him. He was barely aware when, moments later, Ulrik cried out his own release before collapsing on Talbot's chest.

"Damn, that was… intense," Talbot proclaimed when he could talk again.

Leaning on one elbow, Ulrik looked at him with a crooked grin. "That's one way to describe it. I'd go more for fantastic, amazing—"

His words were cut off when Talbot pulled him back to give him a wholehearted kiss of agreement that was returned in kind.

"So," Ulrik said as he finally rolled off Talbot, pulling out as he did, "we should try it again sometime?"

Trying to remain very serious, Talbot replied, "I suppose so."

"We don't have to," Ulrik said worriedly. "I know you're usually a—"

Once again Talbot stopped him with a kiss. *"I am whatever you want me to be."*

"My crazy dhampir lover?"

"Crazy?" Talbot broke the kiss to look at him.

"Okay, scratch the crazy. My dhampir lover, in bed and out of it."

Talbot smiled widely. "I think… Yes."

Chapter Ten

"Good gods," Ulrik muttered. "This is not what it was cracked up to be on the website.

Talbot had to agree as they walked through yet another condominium, while the Realtor waited in what had been purported to be the 'large, airy' living room. "Pictures can be deceiving," he pointed out.

"No shit. A hamster might survive here. Maybe."

Laughing, Talbot asked, low enough so the Realtor wouldn't hear him, "If you know any hamster shifters, send them her way."

"Somehow, I doubt there are such things," Ulrik replied just as the Realtor joined them.

"So what do you think?" she asked.

"I think I'll pass. Again. I need room. Lots of room. So far everything I've seen…" He shrugged.

"There is one place," she said hesitantly. When he looked at her in question, she told him, "It's a townhouse, not a condo. And, well, it belonged to a very, umm, eccentric man.

"How eccentric?"

She bit her lip. "He's been accused of five murders. The police found one body buried in the basement."

"I think that goes beyond eccentric and into macabre," Talbot said. "Is he in prison now?"

She sighed. "No. He disappeared before they could arrest him. According to the police, from the condition of the bodies he apparently was under the delusion he was a vampire. There were bite marks on the throats and they were drained of blood."

Ulrik shot Talbot a look. When Talbot barely nodded, Ulrik told the Realtor, "I'd like to see the place." He chuckled at her shocked look. "Well, you did suggest it," he pointed out. "And I'm a big mystery fan. It could be interesting. One question though… Why is it for sale?"

"He vanished over eight years ago. His brother had him declared legally dead once the seven year time limit had passed, and put the townhome up for sale. To be honest, once a buyer finds out the history of the place, they decide they're not interested."

"I'm not terribly surprised. All right, let's go take a look at it."

Twenty minutes later, as the townhouse was across town, the Realtor pulled up in front of it. From the exterior it didn't look particularly impressive, Ulrik thought, with its small covered porch and flagstone walls. When they got inside, his opinion changed. The living room was spacious with double doors that opened onto a fenced-in patio. The kitchen was off to the side of a nicely sized dining area and had all the necessary amenities. There were two bedrooms on the second floor, each with its own bathroom and large, walk-in closets.

"Now for the basement," Talbot said, sotto voce, when they returned to the kitchen. Beside the back door, there were steps leading down. When they got to the bottom, they found one large room containing cabinets and a washer and dryer. Off to the side was a door leading to a smaller, unfinished room with a dirt floor.

"The scene of the crime—or crimes?" Ulrik wondered aloud.

"Since she said the body was buried, I'd presume so," Talbot agreed.

"Any sign he's still hanging around?"

Talbot opened his senses then shook his head. "That doesn't mean he doesn't come back from time to time, of course, if he really is a vampire and not just a deluded fool."

"And if he is a vampire, is he on the Council's rogue list? He should be, if the cops have tagged him for five killings." Ulrik frowned. "Maybe I'm wrong, but he could be young and out of control, and perhaps the brother isn't aware that he's been turned."

"You need to talk to Antton," Talbot said as they headed back to the ground floor.

They found the Realtor in the living room. She looked hopefully at Ulrik, although it was apparent she thought he would want to move on to look at other places.

Instead, Ulrik told her, "I'm interested. We"—he nodded to Talbot—"need to talk to a friend first, but barring any complications, I'll be in touch with you tomorrow to start the process."

"You just made her one very happy woman."

"Hey, even if it is the site of at least one killing, I like the place—big enough, airy, private."

"And in the city."

"That too." Ulrik caught a flash of disappointment in Talbot's expression. His immediate thought was that Talbot had been hoping he wouldn't find a place he liked—meaning he'd continue living at Talbot's house. If that was true…

"Let's go see Antton then we have to talk," Ulrik said quietly as they followed the Realtor back to her car.

As soon as the Realtor dropped them back where Talbot had parked the car—in the lot by her office—the two men drove over to Antton's house. They found Antton in his office and told him about the possible vampire rogue.

"I haven't heard anything about this man, if he really is a vampire and not just another crazy who thinks he's one," Antton told them. "I take it there wasn't any indication at the house that he was hanging around there."

"Nope," Talbot told him. "Although, since they did find

one body buried there, I suspect if he's got brain one, he's moved on. I'm surprised these killings didn't make the news. They love weirdos like this."

"The police may well have blacked out the information to keep the public from panicking. The Realtor said the murders happened over seven years ago?"

"Yes," Ulrik replied.

"Then the chances are great he's moved on to some other city. I'll let the Council know what we're thinking and get in touch with an acquaintance who works with ViCAP to have him run a search for similar killings. I don't suppose you asked her what his name was."

"Sorry," Ulrik said, "but if you look up the sales history on the townhouse, you can probably find out." He told Antton the address and within minutes, using the computer, Antton found what he wanted. "Jonathan Holtz. I'll get on it and let you know what I find out. If he really is a rogue, we'll set someone to finding and stopping him."

Ulrik nodded. "Please do. Right now though, we're going to go find something to eat. All this house hunting has me half starving to death."

"We are?" Talbot asked. "I mean… we are."

Antton chuckled, thanking them for giving him the information and walked them to the door.

"Twenty-to-one he'll be back on the computer before we get to the car," Ulrik said.

"Probably," Talbot agreed.

* * * *

"There," Ulrik said, pointing to a parking spot that had just opened up half a block from the restaurant.

Talbot pulled into it, wondering again as he did what it

was Ulrik wanted to talk about and why he still hadn't. There had been plenty of time while they'd been driving to and from Antton's house. *Was he afraid I'd lose control of the car and drive off the road?* He smiled wryly at that.

It wasn't until they were seated cattycorner from each other at a small table in the restaurant, their meals ordered and coffee in front of them that Ulrik finally broached the subject.

"I want to ask you something," he said with quiet intensity. "And I'd like an honest answer, not what you think I might want to hear."

That set Talbot's nerves jangling as he replied, "I'd never lie to you, so ask away."

"When I told the Realtor I was interested in the house, you seemed disappointed. Was that because you thought it really isn't the right place for me?"

"If you like it, it's the right place," Talbot said. That was the truth, as far as it went.

"That didn't answer the question."

Taking a deep breath, Talbot told him, "Okay, total honesty. I was hoping nothing you found would strike a chord with you. Or more to the point, I really like having you at my house, and it's large enough for both of us if you'd consider moving in on a permanent basis."

"Why didn't you say so before now?"

"You seemed intent on finding a new home to replace your condo. Speaking of which, you have to get everything out of there at some point, you know—something I'm sure you considered when you were looking today."

"Like would what I own fit into one of them? Yes, I was." Ulrik took Talbot's hand in his. "Most of the furniture I own is just stuff I bought because I needed it. There are no special memories attached, even though I've lived there for quite a while. The really personal mementos are at my house in

Östersund. So, if you're wondering how the furniture I own would fit into your place when we combine households, don't worry about it."

It took Talbot a moment to comprehend what Ulrik had just said. Then his heart leapt, even though he tried to keep his elation from showing. "We don't really know each other that well, which was another reason I was hesitant to broach the idea."

"True." Ulrik smiled, squeezing Talbot's hand. "But can you think of a better way for that to happen than living together?"

"We could, umm… date for a while. But that means you'd have to rent a place in the meantime, or chance living at your condo when we don't know if Gian sent that vampire or if someone else is after you."

"Dating is highly overrated, and when it comes down to it, if there is someone else after me, they'd never find me at your house. Right?"

Talbot nodded. "Then you really are willing to—well, as you put it—merge households?"

"Talbot, I can't think of anything I'd rather do than that. We're compatible, we like each other, we… Damn, this is beginning to sound like we're trying to hook up on one of those matchmaking sites." He made air quotes. "'I like cats and pasta and midnight walks'."

"I'm more of a dog person," Talbot said, laughing.

Ulrik grinned. "We'll compromise on a parrot?"

"Only if you clean the cage."

"I can handle that." Ulrik smiled then, asking, "When can I move in?"

"I'd say after we eat, but it's pretty late. So tomorrow morning, maybe?"

"Let's plan on closer to noon, since I intend to spend the

night making love to you to celebrate, and we should get some sleep afterward."

Talbot looked intently at him for a moment, then taking a deep breath he said, "This is really going to happen, isn't it?"

"As far as I'm concerned, it's a done deal. I want to be in your life. I want you in mine."

"So do I," Talbot replied quietly as he leaned toward Ulrik. Ulrik met him halfway and they kissed, only breaking apart when the waiter let them know he was there with their meals.

"I'm not sure I'm still hungry," Talbot said, looking at what he'd ordered.

Ulrik pointed to Talbot's plate, saying, "You will eat every bite because, my dear man, you will need the energy when we get home and—"

"Make love all night."

"And then sleep until noon and move what I'll be bringing to your place."

"Our place, I think," Talbot replied with a contented smile.

"That sounds good to me." Ulrik gave him a quick kiss. "Very good indeed."

Chapter Eleven

Three months later:

"Be careful. He's killed more humans than we can count. Just set him up. I'll do the rest."

Ulrik nodded as he stumbled down the alley. He looked for all the world like an inebriated homeless man—the sort of person that the vampire, Jonathan Holtz, seemed to be targeting these days. They had been at this for the last three days, moving hourly from alley to alley in hopes of running into Holtz before he killed again.

With the help of his contact in ViCAP, Antton had found out that the serial killer—who had left one body buried at a house Ulrik had considered buying—had been moving around the country since he had left Denver eight years ago. Because he was a vampire, not a human, the FBI had been unable to do more than track his attacks. Holtz rarely stayed in one place for more than a month, killing and draining his victims in such a way that law enforcement considered him to be a deranged vampire wannabe.

Then Antton had received a report from the Council that Holtz might be in Cheyenne. Since the city was within Antton's territory, he had sent Talbot and Ulrik to deal with him.

From his perch on a rooftop above the alley, Talbot watched as Ulrik collapsed beside a dumpster. There were a few other homeless people scattered up and down the length of the alley, but Ulrik made certain he was the most prominent among them.

"Now we wait and hope," Ulrik said.

"Isn't that what we do too often?" Talbot replied, somewhat sourly.

"Getting tired of all this already?"

"No. Not really. I guess it's not different than what I used to do; only now they're bigger and badder."

There was a smirk in Ulrik's voice when he replied, *"And when it's over, we can go home and celebrate in our own inimitable fashion."* He sent Talbot an image of what he meant.

Talbot laughed silently, telling him, *"Stop that! I can't concentrate."*

Ulrik did, and they went back to why they were there in the first place. Ten minutes later Talbot said, *"Vampire to your left, just entering the alley. He looks fairly much like the pictures we have of Holtz, but he's dressed like a street kid, shaggy hair and all."*

"I don't see him," Ulrik replied in frustration.

"Because the kid can fly," Talbot said when he saw their target soar a few feet up to the slanted roof above one of the alley doorways.

"Yeah, now I see him. Hang on."

Ulrik pushed erect, placing one hand on the wall, as if to keep from falling again. Holtz froze, eyeing Ulrik in speculation. Seconds later he was in front of Ulrik, hissing angrily. "A werewolf? In my territory? Not happening," Holtz said, as his fingers turned to claws and his fangs appeared.

Ulrik gripped his arms, pushing him away. By then, Talbot was there and with one swift movement, the silver blade of his sword decapitated the vampire.

"Holy shit!"

Talbot swung around to see a man in tattered clothes staring at him in horror from a doorway a few feet away. Talbot met his gaze and wiped away the memory of what he had witnessed, replacing it with the idea that the man had just awoken from a nightmare.

"Nice work," Ulrik said, slinging his arm around Talbot's shoulders after the dhampir had sheathed his sword, making it and the sheath invisible again. "Now report to Antton and head home?"

"Now home, and I'll email Antton," Talbot agreed and they were instantly in the study of their house deep in the Rockies. As he typed up and sent their report, Talbot said, "Someday soon you're going to take me to your home in Sweden."

Ulrik nodded, and in the blink of an eye, they were standing in the living room of Ulrik's house.

"Homey," Talbot commented, following his lover's lead and removing his boots while taking in the knotty pine walls and the hardwood floor that had hand-woven rugs scattered over it. As he set his shoes next to Ulrik's by the front door, he noted the brown leather sofa sat along one wall, and through an arch he could see the dining/kitchen area with a blue bench under one window. He liked the white table with matching blue chairs that sat in front of it. They reminded him of his childhood. A cast iron stove sat on a brick ledge at the edge of the kitchen, and, much to Talbot's relief, there was a relatively modern refrigerator, as well as a microwave oven.

Ulrik lit the stove, saying that it was the main source of heat. Given that it was still early spring and much farther north than their shared house, Talbot was glad for the warmth that began pouring out minutes later. He hadn't realized how chilly he was until then.

Stairs behind the dining area led to the second floor. There was one large bedroom, the wooden-framed bed huddling under the slant of the roof. A second, smaller room had been turned into an office, with a surprising modern computer and all the needed peripherals.

"I even have a real bathroom," Ulrik told him, swinging open a door that Talbot had thought led to a closet. The room was longer than wide, with a claw-footed tub, a toilet, and a sink with a white cupboard above it.

"Now that you've seen the basics, I think I'll change into something a little less ragged and dirty."

Talbot looked him over with amusement. "I think the homeless look suits you. Sort of macho filthy."

"I accept the macho," Ulrik replied with a smirk. "The filth I'd rather pass on, thanks." He disappeared into his bedroom, returning a couple of minutes later with a towel wrapped around his waist. "I'm going to shower. You're welcome to join me. In fact I insist on it. Water is at a premium this far from town."

Talbot had no problem with that and soon they were washing—and playing—until the water tapered off to a cold dribble.

"Now," Ulrik said as they toweled off, "I'm going to take you on a tour of the area, so we won't bother to get dressed." He led the way to the small back porch and they both shifted. As always, Talbot was impressed by Ulrik's deep blond fur that so closely matched his hair. But then, Talbot's black fur matched his own raven hair.

For a while, they loped through thick stands of trees and Talbot felt as if he hadn't left home. Then, after crossing a road, they were suddenly facing an icy blue lake that seemed to stretch on forever.

"If it weren't so cold," Ulrik said, *"we could swim. I do it often in the summer, once the sun's gone down so that no one will see me."*

"Then we'll have to come back again in a couple of months, because I love swimming in either form."

"Deal," Ulrik replied, giving the wolf version of a toothy smile. *"For now, however, let's get back to the house. I'm sleepy and hungry and horny, though not necessarily in that order."*

For the next two days, they spent their time relaxing and enjoying each other's company. Then real life intervened and they returned home.

One thing they had discovered however, during their brief hiatus. As Talbot put it, and Ulrik heartily agreed, "No matter where we are, or what we're doing, as long as we're together, life is good."

The End

About the Author

Born and bred Cleveland, I earned a degree in technical theater, later switched to costuming, and headed to NYC. Finally seeing the futility of trying to become rich and famous in the Big Apple, I joined VISTA (Volunteers in Service to America), ending up in Chicago for three years. Then it was on to Denver where I put down roots and worked as a costume designer until just recently.

I began writing a few years ago after joining an on-line fanfic group. Two friends and I then started a group for writers where they may post any story they wish no matter the genre or content. Since then, for the last three years, I've been writing for publication. Most, but not all, of my work is m/m, either mildly erotic or purely 'romantic', and more often than not it involves a mystery or action/adventure.

Blog:
http://edwardkendrick.blogspot.com/

Facebook:
https://www.facebook.com/edward.kendrick.5

Google+
https://plus.google.com/u/0/115527711406227698357/about

Email:
edward_kendrick_001@yahoo.com
AuthorEKendrick@aol.com

Titles by Edward Kendrick

Available from **Fireborn Publishing**:

Sui Generis
The Housemate
Talbot and the Enforcers

Available from **Wilde City Press**

The Actor and the Thief
Majors' Folly
L'histoire de Francois-Vampire
The Vampire's Angel

Available from **JMS Books**

Sins of the Fathers
Hell, Look at Me
Wrong Side of the Law

Available from **Totally Bound**

Yin and Yang
The Hit Man Cometh

Available from **Dreamspinner Press**

You Belong to Me

Made in the USA
Columbia, SC
12 January 2018